FOR THE CALL OF A FRIEND

by

SUSAN NYSWONGER MCCRACKEN

Third in a series:
For the Love of a Friend
For the Gift of A Friend

Copyright © 1997 Susan McCracken
All rights reserved. Written permission must be secured from the publisher to use or reproduce any part of this book, except for brief quotations in critical reviews or articles.

Printed in the United States of America
Published by Friends United Press
101 Quaker Hill Drive
Richmond, IN 47374

Library of Congress Cataloging-in-Publication Data
McCracken, Susan, 1950-
For the Call of a Friend / Susan Nyswonger McCracken.
    p. cm.
"Third in a series: For the Love of a Friend, For the Gift of a Friend"--T.p.
    ISBN 0-944350-41-0
1. Quakers--Iowa--History--19th century--Fiction. I. Title.
PS3563.C352485F56   1997
813'.54--dc21   97-18695
                                                      CIP

Cover design: Kathy Kline Miller

*This book is dedicated to my good friend,
Kathleen O'Donnell Brown,
who helps me remember that we women
can be anything God calls us to be!*

CONTENTS

1.	From the Mouths of Children Summer 1879	1
2.	First Yearly Meeting Revisited	11
3.	A Miracle from the Past	25
4.	Weighty Matters	35
5.	Trials on Every Hand	45
6.	Conflict & Resolutions	55
7.	New Roads	65
8.	The Four R's	75
9.	Extended Family	87
10.	Fire and Ice	97
11.	Snow Fest	109
12.	The Best Laid Plans...	119
13.	The Change	129
14.	Meeting Light	140
15.	Evangelistic Meeting	151
16.	Holiness	161
17.	New Birth	171
18.	Upholding One Another	183
19.	Where There's a Will	193
20.	A Light at the End of the Tunnel	203
21.	A Powerful Witness	215
22.	A Higher Calling	225
23.	Future Choices	235
24.	The Answer	249
25.	Honor Thy Father & Thy Mother	259
26.	By Any Means Available to Man	269
27.	Overcoming Obstacles	281
28.	Through the Open Door	293
29.	New Trails to Travel	303

CHAPTER 1

FROM THE MOUTHS OF CHILDREN... SUMMER, 1879

The blistering July sun beat relentlessly on the backs of David and Julia as they worked to rid their family garden of weeds. Sweat made trails in the dust that now covered their faces and grim determination was all that kept them going.

"I HATE working in this awful garden!" Julia exclaimed when she could no longer bear the monotonous, back-breaking work.

"Thee had best not let mother hear thee speak that way," came David's quiet reply.

"I am old enough to have my own opinions, David Jones, and I would like to remind YOU that I did not ask to be a slave, and I do not wish to be treated like one. I might as well have black skin the way Mother demands I do her work!"

Ignoring her use of 'you' instead of the preferred plain language 'thee' that Friends spoke, the anger in David's voice betrayed his calm appearance.

"Julia, thee has no idea what it would be like to be a Negro. Thee has heard the horrible tales Uncle Daniel and Aunt Abigail have shared. Thee knows the slaves they helped escape had been tortured, and beaten, and chased by blood-thirsty dogs. Thee also knows children our age and even younger were sold to other slave owners and forever separated from their families. For thee to compare thyself to a Negro slave is simply cruel and thoughtless. Our parents have given us everything we could possibly need, including love and hope for a bright future. I think thee is a spoiled little girl who should grow up!" As he turned back to the monotonous task of weeding the garden, the fierce attack of the hoe to the soil spoke almost as loudly as his words.

"My, my...that was such a fine, fine speech, Master David! You should consider becoming a traveling evangelist with such a talent for words!" Julia was careful to conceal the laughter she felt. She knew she had managed to rile David, and that in itself was no small task!

"And that is another thing, Julia. Thee knows Friends do not use the formal "you" when speaking to one another, nor do we address someone as "Master" or "Mistress." Thee knows we treat all humans as equals." Annoyance was clearly evident as David once again returned to his hoeing.

"You are too consumed by the small things, David, whereas I look beyond to nobler ideals."

"The only ideals thee is interested in are books and boys, and arguing with anyone in authority!" David laughed, clearly having resigned himself to tolerate his sister.

"You know so little about me!" Julia spoke with a dramatic sweep of her hand. "You only know of farm work and Meeting. What a dull life you live!" As if dismissing David, Julia picked up her hoe and headed for the tall, two story home just up the hill from the garden. "I have done enough slave work for one day," she called back haughtily, her shoulders tall and proud. Pausing to wipe the sweat and grime from his red face and lean against the smooth, warm handle of the hoe, David once again looked at the sister who could exasperate him so. The fiery red hair, now tangled and blown from their morning of labor, was directly related to Julia's fiery disposition, of that David was convinced. Julia was fifteen, but had many of the emotions of an adult. She was fiercely independent, yet could be more fun than anyone he knew in Salem. He was certain their parents worried about her, yet like him, felt pride in the way she approached everything in life: with great zeal and determination. Except for gardening, David thought with a laugh. Julia had hated working with soil and seeds and weeds since she had been old enough to do her share. He thought it a tribute to their mother that she always insisted Julia do her part, never letting her choose housework instead. Yes, Julia was a handful, but she was a free spirit and he loved her.

Picking up the hoe, David headed for the house, looking forward to a cool glass of the lemonade he had seen his mother preparing that morning. Knowing the garden would never be completely free of weeds, he decided to work at it again later in the evening when the sun could no longer beat relentlessly against his body.

As he approached the house, he could hear the raised voices of Rebecca, his mother, and Julia. Here we go again he thought. His mother and Julia seemed to be in constant disagreement these days, and he wondered the cause of their latest confrontation.

"I will NOT go to Yearly Meeting with you this ninth month," Julia exclaimed.

"With Thee, Julia! Thee knows we do not use that kind of language in this home. And thee WILL go to Yearly Meeting, Julia, of that there is no question. We have attended the annual sessions of Iowa Yearly Meeting of Friends since the first gathering in '63, and we will continue to attend as a family. David wants to go and he is almost 18 years old! Thee will be able to see Friends thee has not seen since we met together last year. Surely thee can look forward to that!"

"Seeing my friends would make the long trip bearable if it were not for the never ending business sessions. It is damp and cold in those rooms—especially the women's side of the building, not to mention the hours and hours of waiting in the silence. Besides, what do I care about the women's missionary work or the Indian missions or the problems with Bear Creek Meeting? I could accomplish so much more here in Salem!" Her voice took on a pleading tone as she entreated her mother to try and see the whole idea of Yearly Meeting through her eyes.

Rebecca, however, was used to the theatrics of Julia. No amount of pleading would ever cause her to change her mind. She knew Julia would never fully understand the deep feelings she felt toward Yearly Meeting, feelings of joy and hope for the future of Friends in Iowa. She also realized Julia had little appreciation for the peculiar beliefs of Friends and the history that made them what they were today. That did not mean Rebecca would allow Julia to make decisions as major as whether or not to attend Yearly Meeting, however. She could only hope that some day Julia would have a change of heart where her faith was concerned. What faith she had, anyway.

"THEE leaves me no choice but to go to my room!" Julia announced, sensing the subject of Yearly Meeting was closed. Although the words were harsh, the look in her slate-gray eyes spoke of resignation. "Call me when thee needs me to help with supper," she spoke when reaching the stairs leading up to her room. No sense getting Mother too angry just now. She still thought there might be a way to persuade Mother to let her miss Yearly Meeting, but she would have to be on her best behavior for now.

Shutting the door to her room, Julia once again felt a peace sweep over her. This was the place she felt most at home, the place she could think whatever thoughts she wished, and read whatever books she could find. Sometimes she selected volumes from her father's library-medical journals and diagnostic themes, even occasionally thumbing through the monthly *Friends Review* her father seemed to enjoy so much. Today, however, she was looking for something more entertaining, something to take her mind off Yearly Meeting. Scanning the volumes on her shelves, nothing seemed to meet her needs. Throwing herself on her large, but plain framed bed, Julia thought again about the prospects of Yearly Meeting. Spring Creek was such a dull place, and Oskaloosa was not much better! Though many friends would camp on the Yearly Meeting grounds, Julia and her family would stay at the hotel in Oskaloosa, then take the horse drawn shuttle to the Yearly Meeting House four miles away. Hours of long, boring business sessions filled with the monotony of dull, droning voices. This would be followed by even longer hours of sitting in the silence, waiting for someone to feel led to speak. Though she would never dare express the thought to anyone else, but she was convinced some of the women who spoke in meeting just liked to hear their own voices and ideas! There were few young people her age who attended all the sessions, and the thought of spending a week with Hannah Johnson, the daughter of her mother's best friend, was not at all appealing. Hannah was a dull girl whose only interest was in finding some man willing to marry her! Fortunately, Julia had four weeks left to come up with a plan for staying home in Salem while her family went to Oskaloosa.

"Julia, someone is here to see thee!" Rebecca's voice interrupted Julia's daydreaming.

Jumping from her bed, Julia quickly smoothed her skirt and tried to run her fingers through the long, tightly coiled mess of curls cascading down her shoulders. Ugh! I hate my hair! Why could I not have had straight hair like David? I am cursed with the Jones's hair, the Jones's gray eyes, and the Jones's tall body. David got the Wilson traits from mother: dark skin, deep brown eyes, and dark straight hair. It was so unfair...he was a boy! What did he care about the way he looked?

"Julia!" came Rebecca's exasperated voice.

"I am coming!" Julia returned, just as exasperated. Whoever it was could certainly wait a few minutes, she thought, leaving her room and slowly descending the stairs to the kitchen.

"Julia, I do wish thee would be more prompt!" Rebecca admonished quietly. "Thy friends deserve to be received in a timely fashion."

"Hello, Julia. Thee looks lovely today."

"Thank thee, Thomas. You look...you look...HOT!" Julia tried to keep her tone of voice serious, but Thomas was sweating profusely from his ride over, and she couldn't help but laugh at the look of sheer adoration on his thirteen year old face.

"THEE, Julia!" Rebecca reminded her rebellious daughter once again.

"Yes, I have been a disrespectful child, Thomas. THEE should not want to spend time with such a naughty person as I," Julia teased.

"I...I...think thee is a fine person, Julia," Thomas replied.

Once again Julia looked at this poor, forlorn looking boy. Thomas Johnson was Hannah's younger brother, and Julia knew he had a crush on her. He was nice enough, she supposed, but he was such a...a....boy! His favorite thing to do was go swimming in the river near his cabin, and he always looked so disheveled when he came to visit.

"Why are you here?" Julia found herself asking, in spite of her resolution to be nice.

"Julia, I think thee could offer Thomas a glass of lemonade," David interrupted. He had been working on a wood project in the corner of the room, and could no longer ignore his sister's rude behavior.

Turning to look at David, Thomas gave him a look of gratitude. David felt sorry for Thomas. Their young neighbor obviously thought anything Julia did was perfect, and he never sensed her less than kind treatment.

"I am sorry, Thomas," Julia retreated. "Would thee like a glass of lemonade?"

"That would be very nice," Thomas replied politely.

As Julia went to pour the sweetened lemon drink, David reworded the question Julia had asked earlier.

"Did thee need something today, Thomas?"

"I am sorry, I never answered Julia when she asked. Father asked me to inquire as to whether thee could help with the hay crop tomorrow, David. That is assuming it does not rain."

"So thee did not come to see me after all," Julia teased as she set the glass of pale liquid before Thomas.

Turning a shade of red slightly darker than Julia's hair, Thomas shook his head shyly. "I...I...I am sorry if thee thought I had other intentions," he stammered. "I had thought I would inquire as to thy health as I did not see thee at Quarterly Meeting in Richland."

"Thomas, Quarterly Meeting was weeks ago!" Julia burst out laughing. "I could have been dead and buried by now!"

Now more embarrassed than ever, Thomas rose to leave. "Well, then I am glad thee is feeling well," he said rather stiffly. "David, may we count on thy help with the hay tomorrow?"

"Of course. Tell thy Father I shall arrive at the tenth hour. That should give the dew time to evaporate."

Just then Rebecca returned from the cool cellar where she had been taking baskets of apples to be stored for the coming winter. "Thomas, please tell thy mother I shall travel with David tomorrow and we can visit while the men work with the hay. We have not had a chance to see each other recently."

"I will, Mrs. Jones. And I thank thee, David. And it was nice to see thee again, Julia," he said as he pushed open the heavy door.

"It was my pleasure, Thomas," Julia returned, managing to hide the smile on her lips but not the twinkle in her eye.

"Julia," David began after Thomas was well on his way, "I do not think it is pleasing to our Lord when thee ridicules another of His children, especially one who thinks so highly of thee."

"Oh, be reasonable, David. He is just a child and I was just having a bit of fun. Thomas knows I am not serious!"

"David is right, Julia," Rebecca agreed. "If thee cannot speak kindly to our good friends, thee should refrain from speaking."

"I did not ask for Thomas to visit, and I do not feel I have wronged him. If he feels that I have spoken unkindly, perhaps he will not visit here in the near future!"

"Julia!" was all Rebecca could think to say. She would have liked to have found a willow branch and used it on this impudent child. What kept her from further action was the image that suddenly entered her mind. An image of herself as a fifteen year old when she had first traveled by covered wagon from Indiana to Iowa. She was reminded of Joshua and the way she had sometimes treated him. That was different, she reminded herself, as it was JOSHUA who had done all the teasing, not herself. And didn't she have the right to treat him in a manner fitting his disgusting behavior? Sinking into the closest chair, she began to laugh at herself! She laughed so hard the tears were coursing down her cheeks when David and Julia came running to see if something terrible had happened to their mother.

"I am sorry," Rebecca finally managed after getting the bout of laughter under control. She then told them how she had been so disturbed by Julia's behavior with Thomas, and then remembered her treatment of Joshua. The children knew Joshua had been their mother's first husband, and that he had died of a tumor several years after their marriage. They had not known, however, that the relationship had had such a rocky beginning!

"Just because thee eventually married this boy thee could hardly stand," Julia retorted, "is no reason to believe the same will happen with Thomas and me! Thee knows I am not interested in any boys. Just the thought of marrying Thomas makes me laugh!"

"Just be certain thee closes no doors, Julia, before thee knows what lies on the other side," Rebecca said gently.

"Thee need not worry about ME, Mother. I will know when—and if—I ever meet a man I wish to spend the rest of my life with! Would I not be lacking in honesty if I allowed Thomas to believe I were interested in him when nothing could be further from the truth?!"

Rebecca remained silent, but her prayers that day and for many to come would be that this willful young woman, this beautiful creature God had given to her and Charles, would know the will of God for her life. She also prayed that God would give her patience in dealing with this child, and that in her concern for her daughter she would not neglect David, who seemed to do everything right. Motherhood was certainly more complicated than she could ever have imagined in those years when she had so desperately wanted a child with Joshua, but it was also one of the most rewarding experiences one could ever have. Most of the time!

CHAPTER 2

FIRST YEARLY MEETING REVISITED

As the first rays of the morning sun formed patterns on Julia's plain quilt, she sleepily managed to pull the pillow over her head with a vow to sleep later than the usual 6 A.M.. While every other member of her family managed to rise with a cheerful spirit and desire to get right to work, Julia despised the early morning. She heard her father's voice downstairs in the kitchen, realizing he would soon be leaving for his office. She knew the community of Salem depended on her father's knowledge of medicine, and she had a suspicion he would rather rise a bit later if it were not for the need of a good doctor. She also thought of her mother's training to work with her father. He had told her many times of the way Rebecca had stood up to him when he thought she was trying to practice medicine with no training. Not only had he changed his opinion of her, but eventually she came to Salem to train with him. Though she had never received any formal medical education, the community of East Grove had depended on her for many of their less serious medical problems.

That had all taken place while she was married to Joshua, of course. Rebecca had told Julia of her past when she was old enough to understand, and though her mother rarely spoke of Joshua, Julia knew there was a part of her that would always belong to him. Not that she doubted her mother's love for her father. They seemed to be a perfect match. Both serious, both dedicated to the Meeting, and both contributing to the community. But although Julia respected her parents, she could not help but feel impatient with their lifestyle. She dreamed of a life of excitement; of a career in a big city like Chicago. She thought of the travelers that sometimes passed through her father's office. Some of the tales they told! Streets paved with brick! (The thought of no more mud was itself pure pleasure!) Theaters where men and women performed to the applause of huge audiences! Restaurants where exquisite dishes were served to men in tuxedos and women wearing long flowing gowns of all the colors of the rainbow!

Once, when she had gone with her father to meet several Friends coming from the East on the train, she had caught a glimpse of the beautiful clothing now being worn by women in the cities. She remembered the shame she had felt as she stood in her plain black dress and bonnet, feeling certain the women looking out the train window were gazing at her in pity.

Julia had heard her mother on more than one occasion explain the view of Friends on clothing. She knew Rebecca felt the plain clothing they wore was a Quaker badge, announcing to the world their desire to be a people set apart. She also knew her mother believed it was a shield to protect them from the evil influences of the world. Evil influences! How could a pretty dress ever be thought of as evil? Had not God created beauty?

There were many ideas of the Religious Society of Friends with which Julia did not agree. The thought often crossed her mind that if the founder, George Fox, had been living in 1879 rather than two hundred years earlier he might have had a change of heart! This was America, after all, not England!

Julia slowly opened her eyes, knowing her active mind had ended any hope of extra sleep. She took in the plain bedding and curtains that lacked imagination and joy. She was sure she would even be happy to rise at 6 A.M. if bright yellow curtains with flowers or stripes were the first things her eyes saw each day.

No sense wishing for the unattainable! And no sense lying in bed another minute. Rising quickly, Julia dressed and washed in the bowl by her bed. At least Mother allowed her to have a pitcher and bowl of her own!

"Julia, it is nice to see thee looking so bright and cheery this morning!" Rebecca greeted her only daughter as she entered the warm kitchen.

"I would feel even more cheerful if I had a colorful dress and bonnet," she said wistfully, more to herself than to her mother.

"Oh Julia! Could we please not have this discussion again?! Thee knows the beliefs of the Meeting."

"And why does thee think the Meeting is always right? Is not the 'Meeting' simply the members who attend? And if the members who attend are mere humans, could they not be mistaken about some of their ideas?"

Julia had not meant to get into an argument with her mother this morning. In fact, she had vowed to begin the day in a pleasant way. But her mother could be so trying at times! She wished she understood how Mother could accept the decisions of the Salem Friends Meeting without even asking why!

Julia was surprised to see a smile form at the corners of Rebecca's mouth. Was she laughing at her? She had never known her mother to treat her children with anything but respect.

Seeing the hurt look on Julia's face, Rebecca spoke quickly and calmly to reassure her daughter. "Thee is not alone in thy thinking, Julia. There are many Friends who have similar questions. There was a time when I, too, felt God would surely love beautifully colored clothing if He created the lovely butterfly and the brilliant sunset. However, as I became an adult and asked for the confirmation of the Inner Light I began to appreciate more fully the position Friends have taken."

"Thee can have thy own opinions, Mother, but I hope thee will not be upset if I have slightly different ideas!" Julia spoke, trying to hide the annoyance she felt.

"Just try to weigh carefully the opposing views, my independent one!" Rebecca finished, carefully wrapping an arm around Julia's shoulder and gently squeezing.

Rising to finish preparing a lunch for Charles, Rebecca turned to propose the idea that had first formed in her mind the previous day—an idea she knew Julia would probably not want to hear.

"Julia, I think it would be nice for thee to have a break from thy garden work."

Julia quickly looked up from her breakfast, a suspicious look crossing her face.

"Thee knows I am planning to travel to the Johnsons with David this morning, and I am certain Hannah would be happy if thee were to visit as well. Thee has neglected thy friendship lately, and good friends are not easy to find!"

"Mother," Julia began, as though speaking to a small child so as to make sure she understood exactly what each word meant, "I have no real desire to visit Hannah today. Hannah and I have very little in common. She is older than I and has different concerns. We just..."

"Older, indeed!" Rebecca interrupted, deciding it was time to be a bit firmer. "Hannah Johnson is one year older than thee. She is a fine young woman, and I know she would be happy to see thee. And if it is Thomas thee is worried about, I am certain he will be in the hay field the entire time we are there."

"I am not worried about that boy!" Julia replied with disgust. "I simply do not have anything to say when I am with Hannah."

"Then it is time thee learned how to create stimulating conversation," Rebecca said firmly, leaving little room for disagreement.

Julia lowered her eyes and finished the last corner of bread she had been nibbling on for several minutes.

"David will bring the buggy to the house at half past nine. Please be ready to travel."

Julia slowly rose and cleared the dishes she had used. "Would thee like for me to sweep the floor?" she asked stiffly.

"That would be nice," Rebecca replied simply, not willing to have further disagreements with her daughter.

Hannah seemed truly happy to see Julia. Her smile was genuine when she saw the unexpected guest proceeding up the dirt lane, though her shyness did not allow her to show any more emotion than that. "I am glad thee came with thy mother and brother," she said simply. Julia noticed her glance across the yard to where David was unhitching the horse.

"It is nice to see you again," Julia returned, deliberately using 'you' rather than 'thee.' Although Hannah looked a bit startled at the bold act of defiance, she remained quiet. Rebecca looked uncomfortable, but Betty, her best friend, moved quickly to ease the strain of the moment.

"Tell me about Charles," she said, linking Rebecca's arm with her own and walking toward the cabin.

"Charles is the same as always...working too many hours, but trying to spend as much time with us as his practice will allow. He is wonderful, of course," she added with a grin which was followed by the squeeze of Betty's hand. "And how is Luke? Apart from trying to get the hay harvested, of course!"

"Luke, that handsome man you once had a crush on?!" Betty teased.

Rebecca laughed at the remark, glad she had long ago forgiven Betty for falling in love with the man she thought she might have a future with.

"Yes, that Luke. Does he regret buying the Reynold's place to provide an opportunity for Jeremiah to farm?"

"Luke would never say he regretted anything he had done for his children. And perhaps regret is not what he feels. But there are times, like today when he has to work in the fields rather than stay in the carpentry shop, that I am certain he wonders if he has done the right thing. He knows Jeremiah could never manage everything alone, though, so he is willing to do what he must to help get the work done."

"And what about James and his family? Has thee heard from them recently?"

"James and the children were well the last we heard. It has been hard for him since he lost his dear wife Sarah to dysentery, but he seems to do as well as possible. Did I tell thee he has a new job? He is working for the Excelsior Coal Mine west of Oskaloosa."

"Does that frighten thee," Rebecca couldn't help but ask, "to have him working in the mines?" She had heard stories from Friends at Yearly Meeting about the terrible working conditions in some of the underground shafts.

"I certainly worried when he first told us. But the salary is very generous, and he feels the hard work helps take his mind off Sarah. There is an elderly widow who lives next door to them in Oskaloosa who cares for the children while James is at work. For that I am grateful. I learned a long time ago to trust in the Lord for the things I have no control over. I know He will take care of James and his family."

"And what about Ruth?" Rebecca asked fondly, having assisted Betty in the delivery of her first daughter.

At the mention of Ruth's name, Betty nearly beamed. "Thee knows Ruth and John have moved closer to Bear Creek, but thee does not know they are expecting a child after the first of the year."

"That is wonderful news, Betty," Rebecca said warmly, happy for this young woman who had held such a special place in her heart. "Does this mean thee will not be able to see her at Yearly Meeting?"

"I am not certain considering recent happenings in their Meeting."

"What does thee mean? Is there a problem?"

"I am not free to discuss it at this time, but I am really concerned for the spirit of unity at this year's annual sessions."

They had reached the cabin, the log walls having been smoothed by the years of wind and rain and snow. The structure had seen three additions to accommodate the Johnson's five children, though now several rooms were used for storage since only Hannah and Thomas remained at home.

"Why not sit in the shade?" Hannah asked, she and Julia having been silent during the catch up time of their mothers.

"What a good idea!" Betty agreed, motioning to the benches Luke had crafted for sitting outside when the cabin became unbearably hot.

Sometimes Rebecca was almost embarrassed when she thought of their new home in Salem. Even though she and Charles had been careful to avoid extravagance, it was still far superior to the simple log structure of their friends. As if reading her mind, a look of anticipation came upon Betty's face.

"All right, tell me what is causing that look on thy face!" Rebecca exclaimed.

"Luke is going to begin working on a new home for us next month!"

"That is wonderful! Where will thee build it?"

"Just over the south hill, near the place where the river curves toward East Grove. That way we can still be close to the farm and carpentry shop, and Jeremiah and Rachel can have the cabin."

Rebecca was quick to pick up on the second bit of news. "Jeremiah and Rachel are getting married? When did this happen?"

"He has been seeing her for over a year now," Hannah quietly joined in. "He thinks she is the most perfect woman on earth!" she said with a laugh, though Julia sensed a note of longing in her voice.

"Just be glad thee is not falling for some sappy man," Julia quickly returned. "I mean, thee has time to go to a university, or travel, or just spend time doing the things thee has always wanted to do!"

A strange look crossed Hannah's face, as though she did not quite know what to make of this strange comment from the strange girl who sat beside her sipping tea.

"I am not very good with books," she said after pausing for a time. "I can really think of nothing I would rather do than be married and raise a family."

Julia's face spoke more than words could have expressed. Contempt was more than evident to the women listening to the conversation.

"Will thy family be attending Yearly Meeting?" Rebecca asked quickly, trying to relieve the embarrassment she knew Hannah and Betty must be feeling. She also wanted to know more about the Bear Creek problem Betty had alluded to earlier.

"Yes, thee knows Yearly Meeting has always been a priority for our family. We have never missed a session, just as thy family has attended every year. I always enjoy the time of sharing with Friends, though I must admit I get a bit weary during some of the business meetings."

Julia looked triumphantly at her mother, but knew this was not the time to say "I told thee so."

"I will never forget that first meeting," Betty continued, as her mind raced back through the years. "Though I am always blessed by Yearly Meeting, there will never be another to compare with that first one!" She looked at Rebecca as she finished.

Sensing a story she had never heard, Hannah quickly spoke up. "What happened to make it so special? Did thee have a great moving of the Holy Spirit? Was there some difficult situation?"

"No, nothing like that," Betty laughed. "Does thee think the girls are ready for the story of our first Yearly Meeting?" she asked, looking at Rebecca.

Though a bit reluctant, Rebecca slowly nodded her consent. "Just tell the important parts," she implored.

"No, tell us ALL the parts," Julia spoke up, her interest piqued at the thought of something mysterious happening at the first yearly meeting. "Where should we begin?" Betty asked, glancing at Rebecca for guidance.

"We might as well tell them the entire story, then maybe they will understand why Yearly Meeting is so important to both our families," Rebecca said slowly.

"Yes, we must. Now, let me see," Betty began, not wanting to leave anything out. "It all began when a committee was organized to study the possibility of establishing a Yearly Meeting in Iowa back in '58. There were four Quarterly Meetings at the time: Salem, Pleasant Plain, Red Cedar and Western Plain," Betty began.

"Western Plain is now Bangor Quarter," Rebecca reminded her.

"I do not want to seem ungrateful, Mother," Julia interrupted, "but I do not believe either Hannah nor I wish to hear all the history behind Yearly Meeting. Could we please just skip to the interesting parts?" Julia finished, never one to show a great deal of patience.

"Julia," her mother quickly reprimanded, "thee should have an interest in the history of the movement of Friends in Iowa. Please continue, Betty."

Julia looked quickly to Hannah for support. The look on Hannah's face, however, was one of anticipation, not boredom. Realizing she was not going to hear anything exciting for a time, Julia slipped off her bonnet and began to use it to brush the flies that seemed to be feasting on her skin.

"Indiana Yearly Meeting had to give their approval since the Iowa meetings were all under the Indiana body. Of course Indiana was very supportive of our wish to have our own Yearly Meeting," Betty continued, "as it was difficult for them to send members to support and supervise the meetings here."

"But what did thee DO all day?" Julia interrupted. "Was it not the same long, dull meetings that we must endure every year?"

"Some of us find them to be quite interesting!" Betty said with a laugh. "But I suppose you young ones might find some of our business to be a bit slow."

Turning to Hannah, Julia said under her breath, "Slow does not begin to describe Friends' business meetings!"

When Hannah had no response, Julia was certain it was because she was afraid to speak up to her mother. Sighing, she turned back to the women.

"I found the first sessions to be extremely exciting," Rebecca continued the story, picking up where Betty left off. "Epistles were read from Yearly Meetings in London, Dublin, New England, New York, Baltimore, Indiana and Western. It was so inspiring to hear the words of encouragement from such far away places."

"Oh yes!" Betty agreed. "And there was the important task of selecting members for the various committees that were to meet that week. These committees would be the framework for the tasks Friends hoped to accomplish in Iowa. Rebecca was asked to be a member of the Book and Track Committee, her knowledge of books making her a wonderful addition. Unfortunately, she did not feel she could serve at that time."

"Why did thee not serve, Mother?" asked Julia, puzzled.

Rebecca shifted on the wooden bench, obviously uncomfortable with the question.

"She had a good reason," Betty replied quickly. "I was fortunate to be asked to serve on the General Committee on Education. Our job was to confer with the various representatives from all the Meetings and record the number of First Day Schools, pupils, teachers, libraries, volumes, and other such items dealing with education."

"Sounds like a lot of work to me," Julia said skeptically. "Did thee have no time for visiting, or looking at the various shops in Oskaloosa?"

This time it was Rebecca who answered. "The times for visiting were some of the most wonderful moments of Yearly Meeting. Most of us were camping on the grounds at Spring Creek, the ninth month being a perfect time to convene with the heat of summer behind and the evenings cool enough for a fire. There were numerous campfires blazing every night. Not only did the flickering flames offer warmth and light, but also a warmth of spirit among the Friends who shared their lives with one another. Not only their lives, but their hopes and triumphs, as well as their tragedies."

"THEE camped, Mother?" Julia asked incredulously. "In a tent?"

"Actually, I slept in the Johnson's wagon with Betty. Hannah was a baby, and she slept between us while David and the other children slept with Luke in the tent. It was actually rather pleasant in the wagon as Betty and I had a chance to visit with each other—sometimes until late in the night!"

"I cannot imagine how sleeping in a hard wagon could be much fun!"

"Julia!" Rebecca began, "The wagon was filled with soft straw and lined with quilts. It was almost like being in a cocoon!"

"But wait..." Hannah spoke for the first time. "If I were a baby at that time, and Julia is a year younger than I, was she there too?"

Rebecca's face began to show just the slightest blush of pink as she turned to answer Hannah's probing question. "I was expecting Julia at the time. She was not due to arrive until the twelfth month, so I did not feel uncomfortable traveling to Spring Creek, nor even sleeping in the wagon."

"Where was Father?" Julia suddenly wondered.

Again, Rebecca seemed uncomfortable with the question. "Thee knows our family has always attended Yearly Meeting together, Julia. The first one was a bit different, however. Charles was only able to attend the sessions for two days before he felt a strange urging to return to Salem. I was very upset at the notion he would even entertain the thought of leaving me in my condition, especially on what seemed like a whim. But he felt so strongly that he took our horse and carriage and traveled immediately back home."

"That does not seem like Father," Julia said disbelievingly. "I cannot imagine he would leave a pregnant wife and travel seventy-five miles on the basis of some *feeling* he had!"

"As fate would have it, there *was* an emergency in Salem!" Rebecca said, the anger over Julia's insolence beginning to show in her voice. "Just as Charles arrived at his office, two young children were brought to him. They had been trying to cross a swollen stream on a fallen tree when first one boy, and then his brother slipped into the swirling, foamy water. Their father had eventually been able to pull them to safety, but not before they both ingested a great deal of water. Fortunately, Charles was able to revive them."

"It was not fate, Rebecca," Betty gently chided, "but the prompting of the Inner Light. Charles saved two lives because he was obedient to the Holy Spirit."

Julia was beginning to understand why her mother had been reluctant to talk about that first Meeting. "That seems so strange!" she could not help but add. "Father seems so...so...STABLE! I can not imagine him leaving his family in Spring Creek, especially a pregnant wife!"

"Thee does not know thy father as well as thee thinks thee does!" Rebecca said quietly. "He is a very complicated man."

"That is quite a story!" Hannah exclaimed. "No wonder thee has not told us of the happenings. Thee must have been very proud of Charles, Rebecca," she said, looking at her mother's friend with growing admiration.

"Well, the story is just getting to the interesting part," Betty laughed. "Wait until thee hears what happened toward the end of the Meeting!"

Having been somewhat shocked at the previous revelation regarding her father, Julia was not certain she wanted to hear any more tales from the past! Her sense of the dramatic, however, kept her mind from wandering while the women began the final chapter of their first Yearly Meeting!

CHAPTER 3

A MIRACLE FROM THE PAST

"There is one thing that puzzles me," Julia said, rising from the hard bench where she and Hannah had been sitting, listening to their mothers for nearly an hour. She paused, unsure how to word the question that was on her mind. "I still do not understand why thee did not serve on the Yearly Meeting Book and Tract Committee, Mother. Thee loves books, and thee has handed hundreds of tracts to persons coming to the office to seek Father's help. I would have thought thee would have been anxious to serve with that group."

"There was a good reason, Julia," Betty assured her. "Rebecca, thee had best reassure thy daughter that she does not have a lazy mother!"

"The reason I did not serve when asked," Rebecca said slowly, "was due to the fact that I began to experience a bit of discomfort nearly as soon as we arrived at Spring Creek. I did not want to begin a work I could not finish."

"What kind of discomfort?" Julia asked suspiciously.

"The first pains of birth," Rebecca answered simply.

Even the outspoken Julia was disturbed by this revelation.

Sensing Julia's confusion, Betty spoke to ease the tension. "Thy mother did not tell any of us she was not feeling well, especially when Charles was sensing the call to return to Salem. She was quite good at concealing her pain. Not even Charles recognized her discomfort."

"I was determined not to spoil the week for our two families," Rebecca said simply. "The feelings of unity and oneness of purpose were strong; so strong, in fact, that I felt any disruption would quench the Spirit."

"The birth pains must have stopped rather soon after they began," Julia said stubbornly, "since I was not born until the second week of the twelfth month!" She laughed at her powers of reasoning, but the nervous sound betrayed her calm appearance.

Determined to get to the heart of the experience, Rebecca quickly filled her in on the events that had transpired nearly sixteen years earlier. "It was the most trying time of my life," she said, taking a deep breath before continuing, "even harder than Joshua's death. I was so frightened that I would lose this child I wanted more than anything. Though God had already blessed us with David, I wanted another child to complete our family. I was no longer a young woman, and I feared if I lost this child it might be my last opportunity. I suppose one could say I did not handle the crisis well."

"The discomfort began to increase soon after Charles left, and I am afraid I became nearly hysterical. Everyone was in committee sessions when the worst pain arrived. I pleaded with God to spare my child, to allow it to stay in the womb until the proper time."

"As I was lying in the wagon, my moaning must have been much louder than I realized. In just a few minutes someone was calling from outside the wagon, asking if I needed help. One of the women had brought her restless child back to the campsite and had heard my cries. When I tried to reassure her all would be well, she saw the agony on my face and left immediately."

Rebecca paused, a slight smile crossing her face. "I was certain I had frightened her so badly she would never return!"

"Not only did she return," Betty interrupted, "but she brought every woman representative at Yearly Meeting with her! When this Friend came rushing into our meetings saying she thought a woman was in labor at the camp site, I knew it had to be Rebecca. Realizing she must be in danger, I explained that it was not yet time for the child to be born. They all agreed immediately that a prayer meeting at the campgrounds was a bit more urgent than committee work!"

"When the women got to the wagon," Rebecca continued, "I was a sorry sight! Wailing, I believe, would describe the sounds coming from my pain-wracked body. I was certain I was going to lose my baby, but I tried to calm down and listen to the prayers that were being offered by those wonderful Friends. One by one each woman took her place by my side, laying her hand on the small child within me as she offered prayers for the labor to cease."

Turning to Julia, Rebecca clasped her hands. "Because of the prayers of these women, Julia, you are here today to listen to this story. A miracle occurred in that wagon nearly sixteen years ago. And the miracle is you!"

For once in her life Julia was at a loss for words. Hannah was the first to respond. "What a wonderful story! To witness a miracle in thy own life! But I do not understand why thee has never told us before! It seems like such a moving experience for the first Yearly Meeting!"

"I am the one responsible for keeping the story untold," Rebecca answered. "I felt so foolish trying to keep the pain to myself. If I had told Betty how I was feeling that morning, perhaps no one else would have had to know. It all seemed so embarrassing afterwards. If I had just kept quiet, the pains would have stopped and the entire Yearly Meeting would have been spared."

"But Rebecca," Betty said gently, "then we would not have been witnesses to a miracle!"

"And I would not have to be reminded of that day by nearly every Friend at nearly every Yearly Meeting! I just find it somewhat humiliating," Rebecca returned.

"I find the whole story rather disgusting," Julia spoke sharply. "To be the subject of Yearly Meeting gossip for the past fifteen years...how will I ever face my friends again?"

"Julia," Betty answered, "There has never been any 'gossip' as thee puts it regarding thy attempted early arrival. The only talk has been of the miracle that took place that day. And think about it for a moment. If thy friends were going to tease thee about the event, they surely would have already done so by now!"

"I suppose," Julia spoke with reservation, "but I would rather not discuss it again, if thee does not mind!"

"I think our discussion is over for the morning," Betty said, looking across to the hay fields. "It looks as though the men will coming for the noon meal shortly." Rising and turning toward the cabin, she added, "I can manage if thee would rather stay in the shade where it is a bit cooler."

"I would be glad to assist thee. You girls may stay and visit while we prepare the food." Rebecca said, giving Julia a look that said this would be a good time to practice making conversation with Hannah.

As soon as the women left, Hannah looked admiringly at Julia. "That was the most amazing story about Yearly Meeting."

"That is easy for you to say—you were not the subject being discussed!"

"But a miracle took place! Thee is here because a miracle saved thy life!" Hannah said, unable to believe Julia did not understand the significance of what had happened.

"I do not believe in miracles, Hannah. I believe I am here because the ninth month was not my time to arrive. Nothing more, nothing less. If you wish to believe in such happenings, that is up to you! I am too intelligent for such beliefs."

Hannah was at a loss for words, her mouth hanging open. She had never heard any one speak the way Julia had just spoken. While she was shocked that Julia would admit her feelings of disbelief, she was just the tiniest bit awed over a girl who would say such a thing.

"Hello, Julia," came a familiar voice from across the lane.

Julia turned to see Thomas arriving from the field. What was it Mother had said? Something about Thomas helping with the hay all day? Some chance of that! Obviously Mother had failed to consider the fact that Thomas would have to come in for the noon meal.

"Hello Thomas. Nice to see you again." Although Thomas seemed a bit shocked at Julia's language, he had no intention of making her angry. As he tried to think of something to say, he noticed Julia looking toward his older brother as he walked up the well-worn path to the cabin.

"Hello, Jeremiah!" she called, just a bit too happily, Thomas thought.

Not only did she call to Jeremiah, but she rose from the bench and started walking toward him. "How is the hay crop? Does thee think it will provide enough forage for the cattle this winter?"

Taken aback by this forward young woman, Jeremiah answered politely. "The crop would have been better if the leaf hoppers had not gotten to the leaves before we did! Hopefully the later crop will be better. The three crops we have this season should be enough to supply rations for our few cows this winter."

Not really caring to listen to the answer, Julia continued to think of how she might use Jeremiah to help Thomas see there was no chance she would ever be interested in him.

"Julia?" Jeremiah repeated for the second time.

Realizing she had been deep in thought, she quickly apologized. "I am so sorry, Jeremiah. What did thee say?"

"I asked if thee had a garden this year."

"Of course, doesn't everyone?!!" Realizing how that must have sounded, she quickly amended her reply. "I mean, everyone depends on raising a fine garden, and I believe mine will supply many of our winter needs."

Julia continued to entertain Jeremiah with tales of garden work, just slightly exaggerating the amount of time she spent with the hoe. Jeremiah seemed rather amused at this female who had suddenly attached herself to him. Deciding it was time to end their discourse, he turned toward her.

"It was nice to visit with thee, Julia. Now if thee will excuse me, I wish to wash before we break bread."

"Julia," Hannah spoke when Julia had returned to where she had been sitting prior to her conversation with Jeremiah, "did thee know Jeremiah is engaged to be married when the new home for Mother and Father is completed?"

"Yes."

"And does thee know he is 28 years old?"

"Well, I knew he was getting up there. Why has he never married before?"

"I have never asked, but I suppose he never met the woman God planned for him," Hannah replied.

"Do you believe that idea?" Julia turned to ask the older girl. "That God plans a special man for you?"

"Yes, of course. Thee believes that as well, does thee not?"

"If God plans a special man for each woman—or a special woman for each man—what happens if one never meets their chosen one? Or what if one decides they do not wish to ever marry? Or what if one partner dies...like Joshua? Does that mean my mother should never have married my father because Joshua was her chosen mate?"

Hannah looked truly confused. "Thee asks such hard questions, Julia! I suppose if one's spouse dies, perhaps God would have another person prepared."

"Did you know my father was married to someone before my mother?" Julia asked.

"He was? In Salem?"

"No, he was a doctor in Chicago before moving here. He loved his first wife more than anything in the world."

"Then what happened?"

"She died giving birth while my father was off trying to help some other woman who had already had her baby." There was a bit of anger in her voice. "His wife's name was Julia. When I was born Mother agreed to let him name me after her. Now that I know about the problem Mother had at Yearly Meeting, I understand why he wanted to name me after his first wife. I am sure he would have felt terrible if something had also happened to his second wife because he was off treating some unrelated patient of his!"

"I am sorry thee feels that God does not provide thy life's mate for thee. In the case of thy mother and father, it seems to me God provided an opportunity for them to meet and develop a love for one another after the loss of their first partners."

"I believe things happen by chance, Hannah. I believe God created this world, but I think he lets us make our own choices here. If I ever meet some man I decide I want to spend the rest of my life with, I will certainly not wait for a miracle to make it happen!"

Once again Hannah was at a loss for words. Fortunately, Betty called the girls to come and join them in breaking bread.

After the meal the men rested for a bit in the shade. Thomas did not seek Julia out again, for which she was grateful. She did not mean to be rude to him, but he was such a child. Perhaps he had finally gotten the message that there was no future for the two of them.

The men finished loading the crop by mid-afternoon, so Julia did not have to work at thinking of good conversation for Hannah. Hannah seemed to be quiet most of the time, no doubt still trying to understand the meaning of Julia's earlier words. Her closing remarks let Julia know she had given her friend much to think about.

"I will be praying for thee, Julia. I hope thee finds the man God has for thee, just as Jeremiah and Rachel have found each other."

Julia laughed, understanding the not so subtle message Hannah was giving her. "You need not worry, Hannah. I have no desire to make your brother my choice for a future mate. Neither of your brothers, for that matter!"

Hannah's face blushed, though she managed to say farewell before quickly turning to walk toward the cabin.

"What was that about?" Rebecca asked after she had said good-bye to Betty and they were on their way down the lane.

"I was just letting Hannah know I would not be pursuing her brothers, that is all."

"What does thee mean...'pursuing' her brothers?"

"It is a long story, Mother. I am tired, and I would rather not discuss it."

"Thee did not upset Hannah, did thee? I thought thee was going to try and work on being a good conversationalist."

"I was a perfect conversationalist. We spoke of her family and of church. We even spoke of God and His plans for us."

Rebecca breathed a sigh of relief. She was anxious for Julia to have friends, and she could think of none better than quiet Hannah. Betty had been such a wonderful friend to her when she was Julia's age, and she had so hoped their daughters would continue the tradition.

Looking fondly at Julia, she began to tell her again of the time she and Betty were teaching in a one room cabin and got stranded in a snow storm. Julia listened politely, having heard the story numerous times before. She knew her mother wished for her and Hannah to have a similar friendship, but as far as she was concerned it was probably never going to happen. She and Hannah had nothing in common except their mothers' friendship. She could not imagine sharing her deepest secrets with Hannah! Besides, she had her own friends in Salem. And in the fall she would be going to the academy in Pleasant Plain. There would be many girls to choose as friends there, and she was more than anxious to meet someone who knew more of the world than Hannah Johnson!

CHAPTER 4

WEIGHTY MATTERS

"Rebecca, there is a letter for thee from Anna!" Charles called as he came through the door of their white clapboard home early in the ninth month, having finished his work early for a change. Charles was proud of the home he and Rebecca had planned together, though he realized his pride was not in keeping with Friends' testimonies of simplicity and humility. He felt no guilt over his thoughts, however, believing their home was simple compared to many he had seen in Chicago. What else would they have built? A log cabin hardly seemed prudent when sawmill lumber was available. Log homes were drafty and hard to heat, not to mention dirty and insect infested. It only seemed logical to use the superior materials that had been available.

Charles thought of the changes in his life since he had made the decision to become a member of the Salem Friends Meeting some twenty years earlier. He had learned to use the plain language of Friends—the 'thee' and 'thou' Julia complained of so much; he had accepted the plain clothing as well, though that had meant very little change due to his practice of wearing black and white as a physician; and he had wholeheartedly supported the peace testimony of Friends, having been strongly opposed to the war between the states. Many times Friends had brought sick or injured Negroes to Charles late at night for treatment. But though he respected this religious group he had joined, he shared many of the sentiments of his daughter: Friends were human, and one always needed the confirmation of the Inner Light before accepting the beliefs of others.

It was distressing to Charles when he heard of Friends disagreeing with one another to the point of separation. A number of years earlier conservatives in their own Salem Meeting had chosen to pull out and begin their own group for worship. Even though Charles thought their belief that Friends had strayed from the original teachings of George Fox might have merit, it made him sad to think that reasonable humans worshiping the same God could not seek to find a common ground.

These thoughts were on his mind more and more often as the time for Yearly Meeting rapidly approached. He did not have a good feeling about what was going to happen with the Bear Creek Meeting. He had never enjoyed conflict—as some men he knew—and he almost wished he could stay home and let the others disagree without him. As a representative from Salem Friends, however, he knew it was his responsibility to attend and speak for his meeting.

"Rebecca!" Charles called again, laying the letter he had been holding in his hand on the table. That is strange, he thought, I know David and Julia are helping the Hocketts harvest apples this afternoon, but Rebecca said she would be here all day. She must have gone visiting. Taking off his good clothes and changing into everyday attire, Charles began to worry about Rebecca. It was not like her to leave without at least writing a note.

Perhaps she was in the garden. Walking down the hill to Julia's least favorite place of labor, Charles broke into a run as he saw the still form of his wife lying next to where she had been digging in the potato patch. Immediately Charles's mind flashed back to the day he had returned home to find his first wife's body in nearly the same position as Rebecca's now lay. His precious Julia had died trying to give birth to their child. Died because he had left her alone to try and help some other man's wife.

"No!" he sobbed. "Please, God, no! Thee would not take another love from my life!"

Reaching Rebecca, a gasp of relief escaped his lips. Her pulse was strong and her breathing even.

"Rebecca," he gently spoke her name, almost in reverence as he gathered her in his arms. "My precious Rebecca," he whispered. "What has happened to thee?"

She lay still for what seemed like an eternity before finally stirring. "Charles? What has happened? Why is thee here?"

Looking around she realized she was still in the garden, her neat pile of potatoes resting where she had been stacking them. How long ago was that? Noting the sun in the western sky, she guessed a great deal of time had passed since she had dug her last potato.

"I have no idea what happened," she murmured, mostly to herself.

"Thee will be fine," Charles reassured her. "Thee must have fainted in the hot sun."

"The sun was very mild today, actually," she mused. "I must be coming down with something. I feel a bit nauseous when I raise my head."

"Probably the malady that has been making its rounds in the area," Charles agreed as he picked her up and began the trek back up the hill. "I will...give thee...a thorough exam...when we get...inside. Whew! Thee is heavier than I remembered!" Charles grinned as he struggled to carry Rebecca into their house and lay her on their bed. She was such an important part of his life! She had to be all right!

"Maybe if thee had carried me once or twice since our wedding night thee might have remembered what it felt like!" she retorted, feeling much better now that she was in bed.

After Charles's examination, he sat at the kitchen mulling over the results. Rebecca's gentle snore could be heard from where he sat. Was it possible? Could Rebecca possibly be carrying another child? She was forty-seven years old, yet he knew of a number of women who had given birth at a much older age than that!

He thought again of the exam he had given her. There was an unmistakable bulge in the lower abdomen. Add that to the fainting spell and nausea and the picture was fairly clear.

A baby. Why would God decide to bless them with another child at this stage of their lives? David and Julia would be on their own in a few years and he had been looking forward to the peace and quiet of life with Rebecca. A baby. Nighttime crying and feeding, diaper changing, worrying about illnesses. A toddler. Moving through the house with reckless abandonment, nothing safe from the exploring little hands. Then there was the fact that he would most likely have grandchildren and a teenager at the same time! That was enough to frighten anyone!

The more he thought about it, however, the lighter his spirit became. He had always wanted a large family, and didn't a baby bring joy and laughter to any home?! He must tell Rebecca! She would be so pleased!

No, she needed her rest. He'd tell her later.

What would David and Julia say? Would they be jealous of a new sibling that would undoubtedly change their well-established routine? One thing he was sure of: he and Rebecca would wait to tell their children they were going to have a new brother or sister as there was always the possibility of miscarriage in older women. Suddenly he found himself praying for God to keep this baby alive and well until its appointed time. He remembered the fright they had had with Julia. He still cringed to think of how he would have felt if Rebecca had actually lost their baby while he had been back home in Salem.

He had to tell Rebecca. He could not contain his excitement a minute longer.

Rebecca, however, did not receive the news with nearly as much enthusiasm as her husband.

"Thee must be joking, Charles. I am too old to bear children. I have been experiencing the change of life for some months now."

"Yes, but thee knows that as long as thy body produces even one egg thee still has the opportunity to conceive."

"I do not wish to sound ungrateful, Charles, but I was really looking forward to being alone with thee after David and Julia left home. David was born only a year after our marriage vows, and I never felt like we had the opportunity to enjoy one another."

"I felt exactly as thee," Charles assured her, "but just think of the joy we will experience with the first word, the first step, the first recognition of the Light of God within. This may be just what we need to keep from becoming old and grouchy!"

"Speak for thyself, my dear husband. I will never be grouchy even if I live to be one hundred!"

"I will remember that the next time I forget to bring thee something from the general store!" Charles laughed.

"A baby!" Rebecca said, almost reverently. Remembering how she had longed for just such news twenty years ago, she smiled. How we change, she thought. We want something so badly, and then when we get just what we pray for, we no longer want it.

"Oh, I almost forgot," Charles exclaimed, rising from the edge of the bed. "Thee had a letter from Anna today. I'll get it for thee."

"Oh good!" Rebecca exclaimed as she read the letter. "I invited Anna and Levi and the twins to camp with us and the Johnsons at Yearly Meeting. Anna says they are going to try to camp, though they might return home early if the boys become too much of a burden. Help me up, Charles. It is time I started gathering our equipment for camping."

When she tried to sit up, Rebecca realized she was still a bit dizzy.

"I think Yearly Meeting preparations can wait until tomorrow," he said, gently helping her lie back down. As Charles started to leave, he paused at the door as if wanting to say more, but not sure how to put it into words.

"Just say it, Charles!" Rebecca admonished. "I do not know why thee is sometimes reluctant to share thy thoughts with me. Thee knows thee can say whatever is on thy mind."

"Well, it is about David and Julia. I think it would be wise to wait until we are certain about the baby...there was the problem with Julia, and, well, I just thought it would be better not to mention it to them just yet."

"I agree," Rebecca said nodding. "David will most likely be pleased, but Julia will be another story!" Little did she know how Julia would react to the news!

Yearly Meeting was always held the first full week of the ninth month. Julia was still not pleased with having to attend, but at least it would be a break from work! She had been busy the entire eighth month helping various Friends and neighbors in Salem. It seemed that whenever a patient would mention some task they had no idea how they would get done because of whatever it was that ailed them, Charles would quickly volunteer the services of his children. Julia had picked apples, dug carrots and potatoes, scrubbed walls, read to little children, and washed dishes. Yearly Meeting might be dull, but it would be better than working one's fingers to the bone!

The plans for Yearly Meeting had been finalized a few days before the sessions were scheduled to begin. Julia and her family would drive their rig to Pleasant Plain and spend the night with her mother's brother Levi and his family. They would then travel to Oskaloosa together. Julia was looking forward to seeing her twin cousins again. They had been learning to walk the last time she saw them, and now they were almost three years old and probably talking!

Julia's mind was in a whirl during the entire trip to Pleasant Plain. She had been amazed at how quickly she and her mother had gathered the items they would need for camping. Rebecca had agreed to bring the utensils for cooking over the campfire, as well as the dishes and silver for their group's use. The Johnsons would bring the tents and bedding. Since this was Anna's first camping experience, the older women assured her they would have plenty of supplies for everyone, and if she had garden produce that would make good soups and stews, that could be her contribution.

Julia thought back over the past few days. There was something about her mother's behavior that was different, but she wasn't sure what it was. It was almost as if she were calmer, more relaxed. It must be Yearly Meeting, she thought. Mother always did say Yearly Meeting was a great source of inspiration.

As they approached Levi's cabin, Julia's thoughts were quickly interrupted by the sight of her young cousins. Bounding out of the cabin, they ran to the edge of the split-rail fence and waited impatiently for their relatives to arrive.

"Juwea! Juwea!" they both called in unison, their chubby little bodies bouncing up and down in anticipation.

Julia had to smile. It was obvious they had just learned to talk and had been practicing saying her name.

"Greetings, Andrew and Timothy!" Julia called, amazed at how the two had grown! Both boys ran to her as she climbed down from the rig, each reaching for her to take him. Bending down, Julia put her arms around their waists, squeezing gently.

"Is dee gowing to wiv wif us?" one of them asked. Since Julia did not know which name went with which boy, she decided her first order of business would be learning to tell them apart.

"Yes, in just a few weeks I will be living with thee and going to school with thy father. But first we have to go to Yearly Meeting!"

"Will dee tell us tories?" the one with lighter hair asked.

Julia had to pause and think about the question before answering. "Oh...will I tell thee stories? Of course. That is what cousins do. We tell stories to each other!"

Just then Levi and his wife Anna reached the buggy. After a round of hugs and warm greetings, talk turned to the upcoming event.

"I heard someone say Yearly Meeting was at Oskaloosa this year," Anna spoke up. "Have they moved the sight from Spring Creek?"

"No," Charles answered, "The last time I took the train to Oskaloosa for supplies, there was mention that Spring Creek was now a part of the larger city. Oskaloosa is growing quite rapidly now that the railroad passes through. I am anxious for Rebecca and Julia to see all the businesses that have sprung up in the past year," he finished, the excitement evident in his voice. Julia had a notion her father had never quite gotten over leaving the big city of Chicago for the backwoods of Iowa.

"The railroad has certainly made a difference in our town!" Levi said enthusiastically. "Main Street is constantly growing, new businesses starting every day."

When the evening meal was finished and a time of Bible reading and prayer completed, everyone retired for the night. They were planning to leave for Oskaloosa early the next day and wanted to be rested for their trip. There was a sense of excitement and anticipation in the air. Even the twins had a hard time settling down.

Both families were on the road well before dawn, David offering to ride with Levi and Anna to help with the twins. The day was perfect, just cool enough for comfortable travel. The trip was uneventful, except for the occasional stops to let the boys run off a bit of their excess energy. Even Charles, normally calm and reserved, was telling amusing stories from his days in medical school. Julia was surprised to realize her father had never talked much about that chapter of his life.

As they pulled into the camp grounds late in the afternoon, Julia was once again amazed at the sheer numbers of Friends gathered together. Tents were being erected and fires built for as far as she could see. It had been five years since they had stayed at the camp grounds, her father preferring the hotel in downtown Oskaloosa. She was quite certain her mother must have used all her powers of persuasion to convince her father to return to the camp grounds.

They soon found the Johnsons and set up camp in the spaces that had been reserved for them. Julia wondered how much pleading it would take to get Hannah to sneak out with her some night later in the week. Julia knew it was a tradition for the teens at Yearly Meeting to meet late at night, but she had been too young to try it when they had camped five years ago. This year she was determined to see just what these late nights were all about.

The Johnsons were glad to see both families, and Betty made sure everyone felt welcome and comfortable.

As they sat around the campfire later that evening, the conversation was serious.

"My heart is so heavy," Betty began, looking at the faces of her friends around the circle. "Luke, tell them what thee heard today."

Luke had been silent up to this point, obviously bothered by the news of the day. "It is the Bear Creek Meeting. The conservatives have decided to split from the evangelicals, but they have both sent representatives and reports to Yearly Meeting! Joel Bean is a fine clerk, but he is going to need a great discerning of the Spirit to handle this delicate matter!"

Julia admired Hannah's father, though it was hard for her to understand why this seemed to be such a major problem for him. Perhaps she wasn't spiritual enough to discern these things! I will have to listen carefully during the business meeting tomorrow, she thought. Then perhaps I will know just who the conservatives and evangelicals are. Julia turned to look at Hannah who had been sitting to her left.

No Hannah. That is strange, she thought. Hannah had been so happy to see her, and had hardly left her side since returning to the camp site. She must have been tired and decided to turn in early, Julia thought, realizing for the first time just how tired she herself was.

"If thee will all excuse me," she said, "I believe I will retire. Hannah must have really been tired to have beaten me to bed!"

Julia didn't quite understand the meaning of the look that passed between Betty and her mother, but she was too tired to try and figure it out. Besides, she wanted to be ready for the events of the next day. There were sure to be some sharp words over the Bear Creek issue, and she didn't want to fall asleep in the middle of the what promised to be an exciting business session!

CHAPTER 5

TRIALS ON EVERY HAND

Julia woke early to the noises of the campground: the crackling of revived fires, pots and pans clanking as preparations were made for the first meal of the day, and the muted voices of Friends quietly preparing themselves for the conflict they were certain would unfold during the meeting.

Rising on one elbow and looking across the inside of the quiet tent, Julia noticed the women were already gone, probably preparing the meal for their group.

Hannah was still sleeping, no doubt tired after her late night! Julia had been shocked when she had gone into the tent the night before and found Hannah's bedding neat and untouched. Julia had no idea where the girl had been, but it looked as though Hannah had turned the tables on her. Here she thought she'd be begging Hannah to sneak out when Hannah had not needed a bit of encouragement!

The twins were still sleeping as well. They had had two late nights in a row and were now catching up. It had been great fun watching their antics around the campfire: dancing, making shadows on the tents and talking to anyone who would give them the time of day. Julia smiled thinking of the fun they would have when she was actually living with them.

"Juwea?" Timothy asked sleepily.

"Yes, Timothy?" Julia whispered, hoping not to wake Andrew. She had discovered Timothy was the towhead and that's how she now told them apart—T for towhead and Timothy!

"Juwea, I hafta go to da outhouse."

"All right, buddy, I'm coming! Don't wet your bedding!" she admonished. The thought of wet sheets and quilts in the small tent was not pleasant!

As soon as the group was finished with their morning grooming and breakfast, everyone pitched in to tidy the campsite, making sure the fire was extinguished. It would be several hours before anyone returned to the campgrounds, so it was important to see that there were no sparks that might be picked up by the wind.

Anna had found a group of young mothers who were planning to share in the task of caring for all the small children. They were happy to have another woman to join their group and take a turn watching the youngsters. Anna would watch them on the fifth day.

The women's meeting house was a study in contrast when Julia, her mother, Betty, Hannah and Anna arrived. Several members sat toward the front with heads bowed, obviously seeking guidance for the day's business. Most of these women wore the conservative dress of Friends. In the rear of the room was another group, these women visiting quietly with one another, some in the traditional garb, some in more modern clothing. Both groups appeared to be in a serious mood.

Julia, Rebecca and Anna chose to sit in the middle of the room, Betty and Hannah directly behind them. Julia was certain she could feel a spark of excitement in the air, and her senses were alert. She glanced across the room to see if there were any young women her age present. She recognized a few from her own Quarterly Meeting, as well as two girls that she had seen camping a few tents down from theirs. She wondered if any of these would be at the late night gathering—if in fact there was such a thing.

As was common in the women's meeting—and Julia supposed the men's as well, though she'd never bothered to ask anyone—the session began with a time of centering down. Centering down was supposed to help one focus on the Inner Light of God in order to be sensitive to the leading of the Spirit. Julia found this to be an extremely difficult task, her mind constantly wandering.

After what seemed like a millennium, a short, rather round woman stood before the now still group. Julia presumed she was the Presiding Clerk, the woman who would lead the business meeting. The woman called the meeting to order and the Recording Clerk read the roll call of representatives' names. Betty and Anna were both representatives from their respective meetings and answered 'present' when their names were called. There was a tense moment when a woman rose at the finish of the roll call and gave her name as representative from Bear Creek. The Recording Clerk looked confused, having already called the name of the representative from that meeting. The Presiding Clerk, obviously having considered this possibility ahead of time, asked the Recording Clerk to enter both names as present.

The roll call was followed by epistles...letters sent from other yearly meetings. Most of them offered encouragement and best wishes for a good session. Julia thought this bit of business was about as exciting as working in the garden and found, her patience rapidly growing thin.

Reports from each meeting's activities during the past year were normally read after the epistles. Julia thought it strange that the presiding clerk told them she had decided to wait and have the reports read at another time.

As there were a number of Friends visiting from other states, the next order of business was to introduce these women. Most of them thought it their duty to rise and give greetings from their home meetings. Julia felt annoyed that they were taking so much time when there were more exciting issues to claim their attention.

Appointment to the various committees was the final business for the morning. Julia was too young to serve, so she let her mind wander as the clerk's voice droned on and on.

Tonight was the night. She would persuade Hannah to go with her to see what the other young people were doing. At least she hoped there would be some young people doing something somewhere! She was nearly sixteen, and even though Hannah was a year older, Julia knew she was as ready for a little time away from parents as her meek friend! That Hannah! What had she been doing the night before? What went on down by the river, which was where she had heard the gathering usually occurred? Would any of the young women sitting in this room be there? Julia felt the excitement beginning to build at the prospect of their late evening escapade.

The appointments finally made, the clerk announced they would close the morning session with another time of silence. Once again Julia tried to center down, but just about the time she thought she was succeeding, her mind wandered back to her plans for the evening. She was suddenly brought back to the present when a woman rose in the back of the room.

"Many of you have heard of the dissension occurring at Bear Creek. I believe it is important for you to know the reasons for our concern." Julia was dying to turn around and see who was doing the talking, but as the woman was almost directly behind her, she would have to be content with listening.

"Many of you were blessed by the evangelistic services conducted by Stacy Bevan and John Bond on their way to Kansas nearly ten years ago," she began. "We at Bear Creek were privileged to hear the mighty Word of God as spoken through these two messengers. Some of you surely experienced what many of us felt as they ministered...a spirit of joy and great excitement." The woman paused and several minutes passed before she continued.

"Yes there was singing. But my sisters in the Lord, it was singing unto our Savior and Redeemer. If you had been there, you would have felt the anointing of the Holy Spirit as we sang not unto ourselves but unto the Lord.

"And yes, there was a call for sinners to rise and move to the facing bench to repent of their sins and seek the filling of the Holy Spirit. It is important for you women to know that this was not just an emotional experience for many present that night! A number of families were added to our membership in the days and weeks that followed. Many of these converts remain in our meeting yet today.

"Now I ask you as holy women before God...does this sound like the work of Satan to you? Must we hold so tightly to our past that we cannot accept any other way for God to move than in the silence? I personally gain much from our times of silent worship. But I must tell thee...the moving of the Spirit on my life during those evangelistic meetings is something I will never forget.

"So I am asking each representative here to carefully consider your response to anyone who says those of us in Bear Creek who are seeking the Spirit in ways other than the silence are in error."

The woman quietly sat down and there was absolute silence. Julia had never been in meeting when it had been as still as it was at that moment!

Julia thought about the woman's words. She had only been to one evangelistic meeting, the one in West Branch that she had gone to with Aunt Abigal and Uncle David. She had thought nothing of it at the time, both Daniel and Abigail had seemed to enjoy the service. I was only six at the time, she thought, but now I wonder what they had really thought of the meeting!

Just when Julia thought the clerk was going to close the time of worship, another woman rose, also from the back of the room. As soon as she heard the voice, Julia knew it was Ruth, Hannah's sister.

"I have been feeling a restraint," she began, "as though bands of iron were holding me to the bench. But as I sought the Inner Light, I knew I must speak. I beseech thee to hear not my words, but the words of the Spirit.

"I, too, am a member of the Bear Creek Friends Meeting. I was not present at the previously mentioned evangelistic meetings, having only recently married and moved to the community. I have, however, participated in several similar services and I must tell you my heart is heavy. I would never be one to cling to the past, but neither am I quick to accept alternatives to what I know is true and meaningful worship.

"I am concerned when Friends gathering for worship spend more time singing together than waiting for the moving of the Spirit. How many of you can be sincere and sing in the spirit when song after song is sung? I for one find my mind wandering no matter how hard I try to think of the words that pass my lips.

"I am also grieved when I hear Friends say one must go before the Meeting and kneel to confess her sins before she can be saved. Who of you has read any of the writings of Fox where he suggests such a requirement for salvation? George Fox, our founder and example, was the very one who said the rituals of the church were meaningless before God. Only the Light of God from within can convict a soul, and only through inward repentance can a person know and experience the Spirit of God.

"Oh my dear Friends," she continued, her strong voice quavering, "I have no desire to cause dissension among us. I simply ask that you consider your heritage and that any new idea be held before the Light until all members are free and unified. Although I am the representative from the 'Bear Creek Conservatives' as we are now being called by some, I love my dear neighbor and Friend Jane who spoke as the representative of the 'evangelicals.' It is my prayer that we can hold together and reach a consensus on this matter without judging one another, or going our separate ways."

There was an eerie quietness in the room as Ruth took her seat. Julia was so impressed by Ruth's speech that she wanted to stand and shout 'Amen!' It was certainly easy to recognize this woman was Betty's daughter. Betty was the one who hated dissension, always being the peacemaker of their group. Julia thought she understood both of the speaker's positions, though she was not certain who was correct. Perhaps each woman spoke truth as she understood it.

The clerk rose and stood before the group of women. "I am going to call a special meeting of the representatives to meet at the second hour in order to decide which of the Bear Creek representatives to acknowledge, and which report to receive. All whose whose hearts are free may be dismissed."

No wonder the reports had been postponed! Julia was secretly delighted about the called meeting for the afternoon. While any Friend was free to attend the business sessions, special called meetings were only for representatives. As Julia was not a representative, she would have some much anticipated time to herself. Maybe she would see if Hannah wanted to take the bus into Oskaloosa and see what new shops were there. The ride over would give her a chance to talk with Hannah about their late night activities—at least she hoped there would be some activity!

Julia lay in the tent that night, struggling to keep her anger under control. Why would Hannah do this to her? Why would she refuse to even consider sneaking out with her? And why would she choose to spend the afternoon with her sister when the stores of Oskaloosa had been calling them?!

When the women had returned to the campsite after the morning's business session, Hannah and her mother had informed the others they were going to eat the noon meal with Ruth. Ruth had shocked them both when she stood in Meeting, especially when she said she was a representative of the conservative group at Bear Creek. Luke and Betty had been certain their daughter would not want to attend the sessions this year after the problems at Bear Creek. What a surprise!

"When will thee be back?" Julia had asked Hannah, finding it difficult to keep the disgust from her voice. She had had such great plans for the two of them!

"Probably sometime later. Ruth will not go to the called meeting until the other representatives decide which woman from Bear Creek to recognize, so I will most likely stay and talk to her. We have not had a chance to visit since she was married last year."

Great! They get the gift of a free afternoon and Hannah decides to spend it with her sister! Could she not hear the call of hat shops? Could she not smell the leather of fine boots waiting to be slipped on her feet? Could she not see herself trying on the latest fashions? No, Hannah probably could not, Julia thought disgustedly. But she could!

"Perhaps the two of us could take the carriage into town," Rebecca said. Rebecca had been thinking of the new clothes she would have to make in the coming months as the little one within her grew. Her hand went instinctively to her abdomen, though it was impossible to feel any bulge beneath the gathers of her skirt. Would it be a boy or a girl? Would it look like her, or Charles, or David or Julia? The involuntary smile produced by her thoughts evoked a response in Julia.

"All right, Mother," she finally relented, seeing how happy her mother seemed to be at the prospect.

"What?" Rebecca looked up, quickly returning to the present.

"I will go with thee into Oskaloosa."

"Good. We'll leave as soon as the noon dishes are finished."

And they had done just that. It had not been anything like Julia had fantasized. No shoe shops, no hat shops, and certainly no dress shops. All her mother had wanted to do was look at yard goods. She said she needed to purchase material to make some more dresses for Julia before she went to the academy. Which made no sense to Julia. Her mother had been sewing for her all summer to get ready for the coming school year. She could not think of a reason to have any more dresses that looked just like the others she already owned.

When Julia and her mother had returned to the campsite, Hannah and Anna had been preparing the evening meal with the help of Timothy and Andrew. The boys had been given the task of washing the carrots and potatoes for the stew, although they seemed to be getting more water on themselves than on the vegetables!

"Hannah," Julia had said when the others were out of earshot. "could I speak with thee for a moment when thee finishes thy work?"

"Certainly, Julia. I will soon have these vegetables cut and then I will have some time while the stew simmers."

Hannah had probably thought she wanted to know what Ruth had said about Bear Creek. Actually, Julia did not really care all that much about the problems in a meeting half a state away. The only thing on her mind right then was late night!

"I am sorry," Hannah had replied when Julia told her of her plans. "I just cannot go with thee tonight."

"Why?" Julia had asked incredulously. "I know you were out last night. Do you think just because you are seventeen and I am sixteen that you are old enough and I am not? I thought you were my friend!"

The hurt look on Hannah's face was quickly replaced by a steel resolve. "I am thy friend, I just cannot go with thee."

"But why not? Thee hasn't given me a reason."

"I really am sorry, Julia. I like thee a lot. But there are reasons I cannot share with thee now. Please try to understand. Thee will have lots of opportunities to go out in a year or two." Hannah had then turned and gone into the tent, obviously anxious to get away from her pestering friend.

I'll show you, Hannah Johnson, Julia thought as she lay waiting for the adults to retire and go to sleep. I knew I should never have depended on you to be a friend. That will be the last time I ever try to include you in any of my plans. You think I am not old enough to be out at night. Well, if you can go out, so can I. I do not have to go with you.

Just imagining the look that would be on Hannah's face when she saw Julia arrive at the gathering would be worth the risk of being caught by her parents.

Young people, here I come! she thought. Yearly Meeting need never be dull and routine again!

CHAPTER 6

CONFLICT AND RESOLUTIONS

Julia was certain the adults were going to sit and talk all night. The longer she waited for them to retire, the more animated their conversation became. Just when she thought the circle of friends was going to break up, Joel Bean came. Oh great! she thought, now they'll *never* quit talking!

As the adults discussed the dissension of the day, their voices grew louder and louder, carrying through the walls of the tent so that no matter how hard she tried, Julia could not help but hear the discussion.

"I'll never forget my teaching days at Salem," Joel was saying. "It seems it was only yesterday my students were trying to pull their little pranks. The boys all thought I was a real city slicker, being from the East and all. I just wish you could have seen the looks on their faces when I calmly picked up the snake they had hidden in my desk drawer and carried it outside! That was one disappointed group of students!"

"And even though I have been to the Sandwich Islands and across the great Atlantic since that time," he continued, "I have never loved any place more than Iowa. Of course, this Bear Creek matter has been a heavy burden for me, and as Presiding Clerk of the men's meeting I feel a responsibility to both the conservatives and evangelicals."

"What happened in the men's meeting?" Julia heard Betty ask. It spoke well for the Religious Society of Friends, Julia thought, that a woman could sit in a circle of men and have a part in the conversation.

"It was not pleasant," Luke answered. "Betty, I wish thee could have seen the looks on the faces of Friends when two different men stood and said they were Bear Creek's representative. You could have heard a pin drop!"

"It was the same in the women's meeting," Rebecca confirmed. "Though I thought Jane handled the matter quite well."

"What did she do?" it was Charles's turn to ask a question.

"She simply asked the recording clerk to enter both names in the minutes and then called a special meeting for the representatives to meet and decide which member to acknowledge," Rebecca answered.

"I wish our meeting had gone as smoothly," Joel lamented. "I was afraid we were going to dissolve into a shouting match before we were finished! Both sides are so certain they have the leading of the Holy Spirit. Now I ask you as dear Friends whom I consider to be as wise as any I have met...can the Spirit be divided? Jesus told the Pharisees that *Every kingdom divided against itself is brought to desolation; and every city or house divided against itself shall not stand.*" He paused, then continued. "Friends, please listen to my thoughts and judge them with the Light that is within thee. When I am honest with myself, I know my views are more in line with the conservative group. I do feel we as Friends have strayed from our calling to be a separate people, a peculiar people, if you wish. It is not that I believe there is inherent danger in evangelistic meetings, or group singing, or even prayer meetings. But here is where I need your confirmation. Does it not seem reasonable that Friends might get caught up in the emotion of the moment, rather than yearning for the deep things of Christ? Help me, please, if you see my thinking is flawed."

Again there was silence. Julia wanted more than anything to peek through the opening of the tent and see the expressions on the faces of those she knew so well. But she remained motionless, waiting for a vocal response.

It was Luke who finally spoke. "It would seem to me, Joel, that thee has given a great amount of prayer to the problem, and that thy position is in direct response to the Inner Light. But even though we may agree with the conservatives, I do not see how we can uphold their decision to pull out of their meeting."

"Thee is one hundred percent correct there, my Friend," Joel agreed. "Only by holding together can we ultimately come to the right decisions. And that is what I feel I must say to the representatives tomorrow: that in spite of our differences, we have a common heritage and it is in our best interests to work together on this matter."

"I will certainly support thee," Julia heard her father say.

"As will all of us," Luke confirmed.

"I know Betty, Anna and I will convey the same message to the women's meeting," Rebecca added.

"Good. I feel much more at peace than when I came," Joel responded warmly. "I knew I could count on my friends from the Pleasant Plain Quarter!"

Julia could hear the rustling of skirts as the circle of friends stood. "Could we have a time of prayer together?" Betty asked. "And could we unite our hands as well as our hearts?"

There must have been a silent agreement, for the next thing Julia heard was a single sentence from each member present. She found herself closing her eyes and praying with them. She also found herself overcome by a strange feeling...as if she had been present in a holy meeting. Somehow thoughts of sneaking out had completely left her mind as she continued to ponder the words of the adults. It was for only a few moments, however, as the next thing she knew it was morning.

The men's and women's business sessions the following day were both similar: the representatives had decided to accept the reports of those who had remained in the meeting, that mainly being the evangelicals, or orthodox as some were calling them. Both Joel and Jane, as presiding clerks, gave impassioned pleas to their respective bodies. Each expressed sympathy for the two groups, saying they would never disown any gathering of Friends. Unfortunately, their speeches did little to ease the pain of the conservatives. Julia heard more than one tearful conversation over the matter. The rest of the business meetings were as usual: dull reports and dull committee findings. The services for worship were not much better, the tension and hurt feelings preventing most from experiencing true worship.

As the Yearly Meeting sessions began to draw to a close, Julia's thoughts once again turned to late night. If she did not take a bit of a risk, she would have to wait a whole year before finding out just exactly what Hannah had been doing every night! She knew David had been going somewhere as well, and her curiosity threatened to consume her.

On the last night of camping everyone was weary, the emotions of the week seemed to drain them all. There was no sitting around the campfire, no visiting with other Friends. As soon as the sun had set, each family had retired to the tents—the women in one, the men in the other.

As Julia lay there, it seemed that she must have been destined to have her chance at late night. The tent was soon filled with the slow, even breathing of those asleep, and Julia quietly began to make her escape. She had just gotten to the tent opening when her mother sat and began to speak.

"Is there a problem, Joshua? Thee knows the cattle are taken care of for the night."

What in the world did she mean by that? Julia was baffled. Then it occurred to her that perhaps her mother was talking in her sleep! She had heard her father tease her mother on several occasions about the things she said in her sleep.

When Rebecca continued to stare at her, Julia decided talking back might be her best strategy.

"Everything is fine Rebecca, thee may go back to sleep now." Julia said firmly, hoping her mother would not wake up and wonder what in the world she was doing.

Julia let out a sigh of relief when Rebecca lay back down, realizing she had been holding her breath while waiting for her mother's response.

The rest of the escape was easy. The fire had nearly died out so its glow did not expose her. Julia walked carefully down the makeshift road the wagons and carriages had carved between the rows of tents that week, keeping out of sight as much as possible. She had no idea what she would say if she were stopped and questioned as to her purpose in walking away from the campgrounds alone.

She had asked several of the young women she had met at the campgrounds for directions to the river earlier that day. Curiously enough, several of the girls had wondered why she wanted to know. She had decided this could mean only one thing: they wanted to keep their plans secret.

They had, however, told her how to get to the river, and now she was nearly there. Up ahead she could see what looked like the burning embers of a small campfire. Not really knowing what to expect, Julia slowed her walk and tried to proceed as quietly as possible. She could hear muffled voices, obviously trying to be quiet. Soon she began to feel like a spy, creeping slowly through the brush on either side of a well-worn path.

Julia was nearly to the opening when she recognized one of the voices. No doubt about it: David. As she crept closer, she could begin to decipher his words.

"I have never felt this way before, Hannah. I have wanted to tell thee this for so many weeks now."

Never felt this way about what? Julia wondered. And why had he waited weeks to tell her something? Their two families had been together on a number of occasions the past month.

Silence. What was Hannah thinking? What was going on? Where were all the other young Friends?

"I suppose I should just say what is on my mind," David continued.

Julia's heart began to pound. Suddenly she realized the seriousness of this conversation she was overhearing.

"I think thee is a wonderful girl, Hannah, and these past few evenings have been the best times of my life. If thee has any similar feelings, would thee mind if I asked thy parents for permission to court thee?"

Julia held her breath, waiting for Hannah to answer. How could her brother do this? Hannah Johnson? Plain Hannah? Not very bright Hannah? David was handsome and well thought of in their meeting and in the Quarterly Meeting as well. He would go to medical school some day and be a pillar in some community. Was there not some beautiful woman just waiting for such a wonderful mate? Someone *other* than Hannah?

"I hope thee knows how much I think of thee," Hannah was saying. She sounded hesitant. Perhaps she was going to turn down his offer.

"I would like to wait until my eighteenth birthday, if thee does not think that is too long."

Another period of silence. Maybe David would tell her to find someone else!

"I would wait a year—even two—if thee asked," he said. "I just want to spend time with thee, and if thee thinks it is appropriate to wait until thy birthday, I will wait."

"It will only be a few months," Hannah added affectionately. "It will be the happiest day of my life!"

Silence once again. Or almost silence. Julia was certain she could hear what had to be the sound of a kiss, though she dared not look for fear of being caught. As quietly as she could, Julia crept back up the path, then on the road, and finally to the tent. Whether or not there was a late night gathering of Young Friends somewhere else, she had no idea. But after the shock of her unintentional discovery, any chances of having a good time were gone.

What had happened to David's common sense? she asked herself as she lay on her bedding, still fully clothed. But maybe it was not too late. Perhaps she could persuade David to look elsewhere for a mate. She was certain there would be some attractive young women at the Academy. If she could introduce David to a girl who would sweep him off his feet, and do it before, Hannah turned eighteen, maybe she could save him from a life of boredom. She would make it her first project when she got to the academy.

Julia realized she would have to be extremely careful when approaching David about a girlfriend. She had no intention of letting him know she had been spying on him and Hannah!

Hannah! Now there was another problem. How could she face this girl she was supposed to be friends with? No wonder Hannah had not wanted to sneak out with her that first time she had asked. She already had plans! And their parents...they had to have known what was going on! Julia remembered the look that had passed between her mother and Betty when she thought Hannah had gone to bed early that first night. What a fool she had been! Julia, she thought to herself, you should have put the pieces of this puzzle together a long time ago!

This would be the last time she was caught off guard, Julia vowed! The very last! As she stumbled past the meeting house on the way back to the camp grounds, Julia was surprised to see the lights burning in both the men's and women's sides. Perhaps prayer was what she needed right now. Trying to manage her life on her own had gotten her no where!

As Julia quietly entered the women's door, she was surprised to see a number of women kneeling in prayer, both those of the conservative and evangelical persuasions. Julia quickly dropped near the closest bench and closed her eyes. The problems of the two yearly meeting factions were not her concern on this night; her life, even her future were at stake. Why should she be so upset with Hannah and David? If they were happy with each other, why should it matter to her? Was it because she herself had no interest in finding a marriage partner? What was wrong with her? Every other girl her age could hardly speak of anything but which boy would make the best husband. Was she, Julia Jones, so different from everyone else? She wanted to be like the rest...didn't she? No, she thought fiercely, I do not want to be like everyone else. I want to *do* something with my life...I want to make a difference! Mother had made a difference...she had assisted her father in his medical practice. But I can not stand the sight of blood! she thought with a shiver. Surely God has another way to use me.

As Julia began to pray, she found herself pouring her heart out to God, asking Him to use her in a special way. Though she had not realized it, her prayers had become audible and soon there were several women kneeling beside her, feeling compassion for the distraught girl they knew only by sight. When Julia knew no more words to pray, the voice of Ruth Johnson began to offer a prayer.

"Our dear loving Father," she began, "bless this precious child of yours who desires to commit herself to your service. Show her what you would have her to do...where you would have her to go...what you would have her to be. Anoint her with your Holy Spirit that she might know your leading in her life. Give her peace, Lord, and comfort, and may we, her friends, support her on whatever path you may choose to lead her. In Jesus name, Amen." Several other 'Amens' could be heard as the women silently rose and returned to their benches.

Julia did indeed feel a peace in her soul, and a knowledge that God had been with her that night in a special way. How He would use her she did not know, but she knew she would be open to His leading and would do her best to follow Him. Julia returned to the campsite with much on her mind and heart, and with a feeling of peace that not even David and Hannah could dispel.

There was a touch of sadness in the air as the families packed their belongings to return home on the last day of sessions. In years past Julia remembered the last day as a time of rejoicing over the moving of the Spirit during the sessions. Although there had been times of spiritual blessings this year, the splitting of the Bear Creek Meeting had hung like a shroud over their worship services.

When the good-byes had been said and promises made to write and pray for one another, families climbed into their wagons. As the various groups organized to travel, a messenger arrived at the campgrounds spreading the word that something was about to happen at the Meeting House. Friends scurried like ants to the site, each wondering if an agreement between the dissenting groups had at last been reached.

When Julia and her parents hurried to where the crowd had gathered, they quickly noticed everyone looking to the top floor of the Meeting House. Julia could see the shadow of a figure through one of the windows, though nothing else.

Suddenly a man thrust his upper body through the window and began to shout. "All ye who are Friends of George Fox...all ye who believe the Religious Society of Friends has strayed from the straight and narrow way...all ye who would like to remain true to our calling are asked to gather at the city hall, room two for the organization of a *new* yearly meeting. Let Iowa Yearly Meeting of Friends become like every other modern religious group—men and women who have compromised to meet the demands of worldly Christians. We who have the courage to hold to the original testimonies of George Fox will unite and continue to be a beacon to a dying world.

"Come, dear Friends, be a part of the new Yearly Meeting. We will be gathering within the hour and all are encouraged to join."

As quickly as he had appeared, the messenger disappeared, obviously anxious to get to city hall. The crowd was stunned, silence being its first reaction. Quietly members began to talk to one another, some deciding to at least go to city hall and see what this new Yearly Meeting was going to stand for. Some, like the Joneses, Wilsons and Johnsons, returned to the campgrounds, agreeing unanimously to stay with the original body.

A statement of their position on faith and practice was prepared by this new group who would from that day forward be known as the Iowa Yearly Meeting of (Conservative) Friends.

CHAPTER 7

NEW ROADS

With the trauma of Yearly Meeting behind her, Julia began preparing for her departure to the Pleasant Plain Friends Academy. It was her hope that while attending the academy she would somehow discover what God had planned for her life. Her family, particularly her father, seemed unaware of her commitment to God, however, and were constantly giving her advice on how she should conduct herself while at school.

"Thee must be certain never to walk the streets alone, especially at night," her father admonished one evening as they finished their family time of devotions and were discussing appropriate behavior for a fifteen-soon-to-be-sixteen-year-old girl.

"Does thee remember I will be living with Levi and Anna and the twins?" Julia reminded him, her tone of voice conveying her disgust. "As their cabin is a mere mile from the city, I do not believe there will be many opportunities for parading down the streets of Pleasant Plain!"

"Thy temperament is also a concern to me, Julia," Charles said solemnly. "Thee does not show proper respect to thy mother, nor thy elders. I certainly hope thee remembers thy uncle and aunt have been gracious in offering thee a place to reside while thee continues thy schooling. I will be most disappointed if thy tongue is unleashed on these fine relatives."

"I am sorry thee feels my tongue is a problem," Julie said contritely. She knew she had been a bit bold with her father and it would be best if she not cause unnecessary trouble before leaving. "I will do my best to be a kind, considerate and mild-mannered niece while I am living in Levi's home."

Not fooled by his daughter's supposed apology, Charles continued his fatherly advice. "And another concern...I do not want thee to be alone with any of the boys at the academy. Thee is only fifteen and too young for such interests."

"Almost sixteen," Julia couldn't help but interject. She wanted to ask her mother just how old *she* had been when Joshua had taken an interest in her, but she was certain it would not be wise to bring up the past. She knew Joshua and her mother had come from Indiana with their families in the wagon train, and that Rebecca had been exactly fifteen at that time. She would remain silent for now. Once she was in Pleasant Plain it would be rather impossible for her parents to know exactly what she would be doing!

"I have no interest in boys, Father," Julia replied emphatically. "There is also the fact that I shall have to spend a great deal of time with my studies. It would be a terrible embarrassment to thee if I were to fail any of my classes!"

Rebecca found it difficult to contain the laughter she felt bubble within her at the thought of Julia failing in school. Julia had always had the highest marks in her class, and in fact it was this stellar performance that finally convinced her parents to let her continue her studies at the academy.

"I shall be quite surprised if thee manages to fail a class," Rebecca finally said, amusement coloring her voice. "Thy father and I will expect only the highest marks from thee."

"That is the problem!" Julia burst out, forgetting her intention to refrain from upsetting her parents. "*You* think I should be perfect! Everything I do must be the best so as not to spoil your reputation as good parents!"

Ignoring her accusation, Charles was remarkably calm in his reply. "I doubt thy teachers will accept the use of "you" and "your" in their classes. I suggest thee amend thy ways before thee finds thyself sitting in the office of the principal!"

"Father, I do not mean to be disrespectful, but I believe Friends would be wise to abandon this archaic tradition! I realize George Fox had a good reason for not wishing to address the various classes of people in different ways. But this is a new country...there is no royalty here, no class system. *We Friends* seem to be the ones putting ourselves above the farmers and storekeepers in Salem with our "thees" and "thous!"

Charles and Rebecca both sat in silence, their eyes communicating their thoughts. Only a few weeks earlier the two of them had a very similar conversation! It was difficult to reprimand their own child for having the same thoughts. David finally broke the silence.

"Julia, thee is certainly free to form thy own thoughts under the revelation of the Inner Light. Thee must remember, however, that Friends have always tried to be unified in their beliefs so as to be effective witnesses to the lost. If thee wishes to address the issue of language, perhaps thee could seek the proper channels at Yearly Meeting next year."

Julia could not miss the look of admiration in the eyes of both their parents. David was always the reasonable one, always knowing what to say and do to make their parents proud. Why couldn't they just once look at her with such pleasure, Julia wondered? She always managed to say the wrong thing at the wrong time.

"David has a fine point," Charles was quick to agree. "In the mean time, I suggest thee try to remember to use thee and thou while attending the Friends Academy."

"Yes, Father," Julia said stiffly. "If *thee* would please excuse me, I have more packing to do." Rising quickly, Julia was just able to get to her room and shut the door before the tears began. Throwing herself across her neatly made bed, Julia gave way to the sobs which soon shook her thin body. Tears for the feelings of inadequacy, tears for the family she would soon be leaving, tears for a brother who had failed to share his feelings for Hannah with her, and tears of remorse.

Would she ever be pleasing to God? She knew she was too bold in her speech, but what if she was right and the Meeting was wrong? What if she did get sent to the principal's office? What if Levi and his wife became so upset with her they refused to let her remain in their home? Finally the questions faded and sleep overtook her tense body. Her mind, however, continued to be active, as dreams of the academy and principals with long wooden sticks prevented an escape from her anxieties.

Excitement replaced anxiety as Julia prepared to depart for Pleasant Plain. Each member of her family seemed to go out of their way to make her final days as pleasant as possible. Hannah and Betty came the morning Julia was to leave, having risen well ahead of the sun in order to arrive before her departure.

"Thee is so fortunate to be going to the academy!" Hannah exclaimed as soon as she found Julia packing the final items in her trunk.

Looking at Hannah, Julia struggled to control her emotions. Here was a girl who pretended to be such a good friend, yet kept her feelings for David a secret. Julia could not decide whether to just boldly ask Hannah about her intentions, or pretend everything was the same between them. Although Hannah was a bit dim-witted, she was probably smart enough to wonder how Julia could know about David. No, she could not bring up the subject without risking exposure, so her best plan would probably be to encourage Hannah to talk and see if she would divulge any information.

"If thee wants to attend the academy," Julia tried to make her voice sound natural, "thee should ask thy parents to allow thee to attend. I suppose there *might* be other options for a girl, however, like marriage," Julia said, hoping she had not said too much.

The look on Hannah's face would be hard for Julia to forget. It was one of sorrow and hopelessness, longing and resignation. "I am too young for marriage, Julia. I would give anything to be able to attend school with thee. Unfortunately, my Father spent all the money he had saved over the years to purchase the farm for Jeremiah. There is also a problem with my marks. School is not as easy for me as it is for thee. I wish I had the ability to understand the number problems thee can do. Or memorize...thee can recite a passage after a few minutes study whereas it takes me several days to successfully commit the words to memory."

"I believe a woman can do whatever she sets her mind to," Julia answered firmly. "If you believe you can do well, you can! You—I mean thee—should just decide to remember the words and thee will!"

Hannah only shook her head. How many times had she tried to do just that? Her mind would simply not cooperate. But how could she make Julia understand? Julia was so blessed, though Hannah doubted she realized just what a gift she had been given. Even though there was the possibility of marriage some day—maybe even with David—right now the only thing she really wanted to do was go to the academy

"Will thee write?" Hannah asked, anxious to change the subject.

"Oh Hannah, I would rather not promise thee." Seeing Hannah's fallen face, she quickly added, "But I will try. Just give me a bit of time to get settled into the routine of my new school and then perhaps I will find a way to write."

Hannah was a nice enough person, Julia had finally decided, but she felt smothered by her—as well as betrayed. Hannah tried too hard to be her friend, especially when she had secrets she wasn't willing to share.

"There," Julia said, placing the final items in the old trunk and fastening the latches. Her father had brought the trunk with him from Chicago, and she loved the scent of the rough wood and leather straps. "I am going to see if Father is ready to leave," she said, her packing finally finished.

Hannah followed Julia down the stairs to the kitchen where the adults and David were sitting. It was obvious from the abrupt break in the conversation that Julia had been the subject of their discussion.

"Ready?" Charles asked quietly.

"Yes, everything is packed. I would like to have taken more of my books, but the trunk is nearly overflowing as it is"

"Levi has quite a nice library in his home," Rebecca reminded her. "I am certain he will allow thee to read his volumes." "We will certainly miss thee!" Betty said warmly, rising to give Julia a hug. "Please remember to pray for us at East Grove when you pray for your Salem Meeting." "I will, Betty," Julia said, almost shyly. She really did like her mother's friend, and would miss not seeing her.

"I know Hannah will miss thee too," Betty added, noticing her daughter's silence. "She really admires thee. I am so glad the two of thee are becoming good friends—just like your mothers!"

"I will miss Hannah too," Julia said, though her reasons for missing this simple girl were of a different nature.

"Maybe David can keep me informed of your schooling since thee may be too busy to write," Hannah spoke up. "That is, if he would not mind." She turned to look at him, her dark eyes saying words Julia didn't want to see. "I would be happy to tell thee of the tales of Julia," he said in a teasing tone, looking fondly at his impulsive sister.

"Well, if thee is ready," Charles said, rising from the table, "we had best be on our way. It will take us most of the day to travel to Levi's, and I would rather not be gone any longer than need be."

Before long the carriage was loaded and they were on their way to Pleasant Plain. David would remain in Salem, working in his father's office. He had been helping his father for as long as he could remember, though only one or two days a week. Everyone in the family knew Charles wanted his son to go to Chicago for formal medical training, but David did not feel he was ready. It was the only area of discord between father and son. David realized he would eventually have to take that step if he wanted to make medicine his life's work, but for now he was content to do the small jobs—mostly stitching wounds and setting broken bones.

There was another reason for his reluctance to leave Salem...Hannah. Though he had never shared his feelings with the members of his family, the times they had been able to steal away at Yearly Meeting had been wonderful. He thought Hannah was the kindest, gentlest girl he had ever known. She was also pretty. She was so tiny, her nearly black eyes and hair making her look like a princess.

The Jones family had been invited to the Johnson home to help Hannah celebrate her eighteenth birthday. But even though David knew he had Hannah's permission to ask her father to come courting, he was hesitant. Charles was constantly reminding him of his need for further education on a regular basis now. How could he ask permission to court a woman when he himself might be gone within a few weeks or months to medical school?

And then there was Julia. As much as he hated to admit it, he was afraid of what her reaction might be if she knew he was interested in her friend. Although that was part of the problem. David sensed they were not really friends at all! Now that Julia would be away for a while, perhaps he would summon his courage and explain his dilemma to Hannah. How could a person decide between two futures, one with the woman of his every waking thought, and one with the career of his dreams? He knew one thing that would help—prayer. He would spend as much time praying as possible in the coming days, and perhaps God would show him the solution to his problem.

The ride to Pleasant Plain for Julia and her parents was uneventful, the day being mild and the sun bright. Julia sat in the back of the carriage, her mother and father on the front seat. Not wanting to hear any more advice from her parents, Julia leaned against the hard side of the carriage cover and pretended to sleep. She was almost certain her parents would not be fooled by her pose, but she hoped they would respect her wish to remain silent.

As soon as they pulled into the lane leading to Levi's home, the reality of separation hit Julia. It would be the first time she and her family had been apart for more than a day or two at a time. Her mind began to race...did she really want to do this? Did she really need more education?

Her thoughts were quickly interrupted by the sight of her three-year-old twin nephews. Bounding out of the cabin, they ran to the edge of the split-rail fence and waited impatiently for Julia's arrival, just as they had done the last time she had seen them.

As Charles pulled the carriage up to the cabin, Levi and Anna emerged from the open door, the smiles on their faces speaking more loudly than words. After a round of hugs and warm greetings, Charles and Levi carried Julia's trunk into the cabin. "Bring it this way," Levi said, motioning to the back of the room.

"I do not remember a room back here," Charles said, a puzzled look on his face. "I hope thee did not add one just to accommodate Julia!"

"I just completed it last week," Levi responded. "We knew we would need more room for our family some day, and this seemed like a good time to do the work. Thee knows I am not fond of being idle when school is not in session, and my part-time job at the paper office hardly wears me out!"

As they entered the fresh-smelling room, Charles was touched that his brother-in-law would go to this much trouble for his daughter. The addition was built of mill cut lumber rather than the rough logs that made up the rest of the cabin. There were two fair-sized windows, also ready made.

"This is quite nice, Levi. Perhaps thee should have been a carpenter!"

Levi's laughter spoke otherwise. "I hit my thumb with the hammer so many times it will probably never grow a full nail! No, carpentering is not a line of work I would enjoy. On the other hand, I love everything about teaching...especially the look on a student's face when he or she is successful!"

"To each his own," Charles said. "I enjoyed teaching Rebecca about medicine, but I am afraid I do not have the patience to teach young children!"

"Fortunately, the students at the academy are nearly all at least fourteen years of age, and their minds are sharp as tacks! I can hardly wait to hear just what difficult questions this smart niece of mine will ask!"

As Charles and Levi returned to the main living area of the cabin, the women were discussing Yearly Meeting. Rebecca and Anna were reminiscing about the times of sharing among the three families who had camped together, though neither woman cared to mention Bear Creek.

"It was a wonderful time of fellowship for me," Anna summed up her feelings. "Just the chance to have intelligent conversation with other adults meant so much!"

"What about me?" Levi interrupted, overhearing his wife's comment. "Am I not an adult? Do we not have stimulating conversations?"

"Levi Wilson, thee knows what I mean! When thee returns from thy teaching duties at school, spends time with our sons and then prepares for the next day's lessons, there is little time for 'stimulating conversation' as thee puts it! And thee knows how much I love our boys, but conversations that revolve around toys and food and naps does little to stimulate my mind!"

"I will have to work on correcting that," Levi said firmly. "I cannot have my wife's mind rotting from lack of stimulation!"

As soon as Charles and Rebecca had eaten a mid-afternoon snack, they prepared to leave. Though Julia had vowed to control her emotions, she could not prevent the tears that formed as her mother and father each held her close and said a prayer for her safety as well as success in her new surroundings.

As the carriage faded from view down the well worn path, Julia remained rooted to the ground, staring at the spot where they had said good-bye. The day had finally come. She was nearly on her own, responsible for her own decisions. Suddenly she felt free...freer than she had been in a long time. She vowed to make the best of this new opportunity. She did not know what the future held, but she was certainly going to do her best to find out!

CHAPTER 8

THE FOUR R'S

With classes beginning at the academy the day after Julia arrived, she had no time to even think about being homesick.

"Julia, we must be leaving now," came Levi's call the morning of the second day. Julia hurried to finish gathering her papers and pens. She had to admit she was a bit nervous, wondering if the courses would be too hard, wondering if anyone would want to be friends with her, wondering if she could remember to say "thee" to the instructors.

"*Julia!* " the tone of Levi's voice was less than patient. "It would not be suitable for me to be late the first day of school!"

"Coming," Julia called out, quickly running to catch up with her uncle.

"Is thee anxious about today?" Levi asked as they walked the mile to the academy.

"Just a bit," she admitted. "But I am certain when I am registered for my courses I will feel better." Unfortunately, her words expressed more confidence than she felt.

"I believe thee will enjoy the other teachers we have secured for our three courses," Levi said warmly. "I feel fortunate to have been offered a position in the three year Academic Course."

"What are the other two courses?" Julia asked, wondering in which one she would want to enroll.

Levi paused, obviously thinking about something else. "Perhaps I should tell thee a bit about the academy before thee hears about the course work.

"You see, the Pleasant Plain Academy Association of Friends is the group that secured the twenty-five dollar subscriptions from Friends throughout the area to build the school. They eventually raised over twenty-two hundred dollars to construct the two story building. Did thee see it when thy parents brought thee to our home?"

"Yes, it looked like a fine structure. There are few buildings in Salem that would compare in size," Julia answered.

"It is a fine building, to be sure," Levi continued. "But just as the committee spent many days planning and building the structure, they also spent a great deal of time visiting country schools to see which courses were being offered in the rural areas. They wanted to be certain our class offerings would not conflict with what was already being taught."

"When they finished their survey," he continued, "they established the three areas of study we now offer. Students who need help with the basic skills are enrolled in the Intermediate Course. Then there is the Grammar Course which covers subjects not commonly offered in the rural schools, such as complex math, or science courses needing a laboratory."

"If a person took either the Intermediate or Grammar Course, wouldn't they have all the schooling they might need before entering college?" Julia asked, confused as to why there would need to be a third offering.

"Yes, most of the subjects are exposed in those two courses," Levi explained patiently. "It was the committees' feeling, however, that perhaps it would be wise to have a comprehensive course which would be a three year program to prepare students for a variety of occupations. A person taking the three year course would be assured of a complete secondary education."

"Naturally, all three courses are based on the same four "R's" emphasized in all the rural schools," he continued, "Religion, Reading, 'Rritin', and 'Rithmetic. At the academy we simply master the basics and then delve deeper and branch out to other fields," he said, his description finally complete.

"Did thee serve on the committee to establish the academy?" Julia asked, beginning to enjoy this uncle she had never had a chance to get to know.

"Yes, I was asked to serve by the Pleasant Plain Monthly Meeting, and I felt it was my duty to give whatever assistance I might offer. Thee knows I have been teaching in the country schools since I was fourteen, first near East Grove and then here near Pleasant Plain."

Feeling she had had as much history as she needed for now, Julia quickly reworded her earlier question. "So, Uncle Levi, in which of the courses should I enroll?"

"That is for thee to decide, Julia. I suppose thee needs to consider how many years thee will be able to attend."

"Three, of course!" Julia answered immediately. Then adding quickly, "if thee does not find my presence to be a burden."

Levi burst out laughing, realizing this niece could certainly be charming if she chose. "I think Anna might find some chickens to be plucked, or walls to be scrubbed if thee becomes too much of a burden!"

Julia hoped she was able to conceal her reaction to Levi's suggestion. The thought of doing *anything* to a poor helpless chicken was revolting!

"If thee stays three years," Levi said, answering Julia's original question, "the Academic Course would seem like a good choice for thee." Just as Levi finished, the Pleasant Plain Friends Academy came into full view.

The sight was awesome...buggies with students who had been driven by one or both parents, students on horseback, and many students on foot. Julia had never in her life seen so many girls and boys her age! She estimated fifty or sixty students must be gathered outside the building.

Levi asked to be excused so that he might help the principal prepare for registration. Julia stood alone for a bit, taking in the scene before her. A smile found its way to her face as she thought of the good times she might have with some of these friends. But which ones would she want to get to know?

Just then two young men made their way to where Julia was standing.

"Hello!" the taller of the two spoke first. "My name is Joseph Bell, and this is my friend Jonathan White."

Julia was not certain she should speak to these two strangers, but they *were* students, which surely meant it was acceptable to at least greet them.

"I am pleased to meet thee," Julia returned, trying not to seem too anxious. Joseph was obviously the more outgoing of the two, and she would guess a bit older, probably around David's age. While he was tall, he was also a bit on the plump side, indicating he had enjoyed a plucked chicken or two in his lifetime!

Jonathan, on the other hand, was closer to her size, his light hair and fair skin indicating a Scandinavian heritage.

It was Joseph who chose to continue the conversation. "And just where might such a fine lady as yourself call home?" he asked, his expression puzzling Julia. She thought she could detect just a trace of condescension.

"I am from Salem. If thee has never traveled much, perhaps thee has never heard of our fine city." She would give this young man a taste of his own medicine.

Jonathan burst into laughter at Julia's response. His eyes were twinkling as he enjoyed the quick thinking of this girl with the fiery red hair.

Not to be outdone Joseph quickly replied, "Oh yes, Salem...is that not the little farming village near Mount Pleasant?"

"As a matter of fact," Julia retorted, "Salem was one of the first settlements in Henry County. We have a number of fine businesses, and my father and mother are the doctors of our *city*."

"Thy *mother* is a doctor, too?" Jonathan asked, admiration coloring his voice.

Now it was Julia's turn to be embarrassed by the way she had stretched the truth. "Actually, she assists my father, or at least she did before my brother and I were born. She still helps if a need arises."

"I imagine thee must be good with books," Jonathan continued, "Perhaps thee might assist me if I find I cannot adequately do the work."

Julia liked this young man. He obviously recognized an intelligent woman when he met one! "I would be most happy to study with thee if the course work becomes difficult for us. I doubt if thee will need much help, though. My Uncle Levi is a teacher here, and I know he will be sure to cover the material well," she said warmly, giving her most winsome smile.

Joseph seemed to be irritated with the direction the conversation was taking. Excusing himself, he grabbed Jonathan by the arm, dragging him to a point some distance from Julia.

"What's going on in that mind of yours, Jon? It was my idea to talk to this girl, and now you are trying to get on her good side! You know you never have trouble in school! You double-crossed me!"

"I think thee is getting excited for no reason," Jonathan spoke, quickly trying to reassure his friend there was no wrong intention on his part. "I was only trying to make conversation."

"And I find it a bit odd that a straight-A student would need to ask a girl for help!" Joseph countered.

Julia wondered what the animated conversation between the two boys was about. Joseph seemed to be upset for some reason.

She had no time to find out, however, as the principal appeared—or at least she assumed it was the principal—and began to ring the bell.

As soon as the students and parents had gathered around the stern-looking middle-aged man, he introduced himself.

"Greetings, young ladies and gentlemen. I am Chester Dorland, and I will be your principal this year. "This is my wife," Mrs. Dorland, and she will be the assistant principal. If thee will all follow me into the assembly room, we will commence with the registration."

Julia was toward the end of the line, no longer able to see the two boys with whom she had made acquaintance. It was probably just as well...she knew what her father would say if he had seen her talking to these young men.

Once inside the assembly room, Julia quickly found the table where students were registering for the Academic Program. She noticed Jonathan was also a registrant for this course, but that Joseph was in line for the Grammar Course.

"Is thee going to be here for three years?" she found herself asking Jonathan, hoping he would not think she was too bold.

"I was here last year, when the academy opened, for the three months of the spring term. I am hoping to take an extra course this year as well as next in order to finish in the spring of '79."

"What does thee plan to do then?" Julia wondered.

"I hope to go to St. Louis and study law. I have always had an interest in the legal field, and believe I could help those who find themselves in need of legal assistance yet unable to afford the fees of most attorneys. I see myself representing the poor and the oppressed for whatever they might be able to pay." Jonathan was surprised at how easy it was to talk to this girl. "I am sorry," he stopped abruptly. "I must have forgotten my manners! I never even asked thee thy name!"

"I am sorry, too," Julia laughed. "I was so anxious to keep Joseph from getting the best of me that I neglected to tell thee my name. I am Julia Jones, and I am pleased to meet thee."

"Likewise," Jonathan said. "I take it from thy speech that thee is a Friend?"

"Yes, from the Salem Meeting, though sometimes my speech would not please some of the Friends back home! And thee? Which meeting does thee attend?"

"I am from the West Branch Meeting, Springdale Quarter," he replied.

Excitement lit Julia's eyes. "Might thee be acquainted with Daniel and Abigail Wilson from Springdale?"

"Well, I have seen them at Quarterly Meeting activities, but I do not know them well."

"Abigail is my mother's sister," Julia said proudly. "Abigail and Daniel ran a station on the Underground Railroad before the War Between the States."

"As I said, I have heard of them and also of their work," Jonathan reiterated. "I know they are fine Friends."

"Why have I not seen thee at Yearly Meeting?" Julia asked, suddenly curious.

A sad look crossed this young Friend's face. "I am afraid my family was never very active in the Meeting. Mother would attend with my six younger brothers and me, but Father said he never had time. Then he was killed in an accident helping build the track for the Rock Island Railroad. Mother took on extra work to try and support our family, and there was never any money for trips to Yearly Meeting. That is one of the reasons I desperately want to be successful here at the Academy. Once I graduate from law school, I hope to be of significant help to my family."

This boy is even more serious than I realized! Julia thought, studying him once again in the light of this new revelation. "I am sorry about thy father," she said, "and I think it is admirable thee wants to help thy mother and brothers."

"What about thee?" Jonathan asked, returning from his trip to the past, "What does thee hope to do when thee finishes thy studies?"

"I have not yet had a clear leading of the Spirit," Julia said, remembering her prayer for guidance at Yearly Meeting. "I am hoping my studies will give me some direction where my future is concerned. I am definitely going to do something with my life—something other than getting married and having children!" she added emphatically thinking of Hannah. Jonathan looked somewhat stunned by this new revelation.

"I would be happy to pray for thee, if thee would like," Jonathan finally said as he quickly moved to look for his friend..

It was soon Julia's turn to register, and she had no other opportunities to meet new friends. As soon as she had signed up for her classes, she was asked to take her list and find where the rooms were located in the building. Her education at Pleasant Plain Academy would commence as soon as the registration was completed.

As there were only two floors in the school, and a good share of the first floor was the assembly hall, Julia soon found where her coming days would be spent. She slowly sat down by a window in the first room on her schedule, hoping to catch a glimpse of the businesses on Main Street.

Levi had led her across harvested fields on their morning trek to the academy, thus missing most of the town. She was anxious to see just what establishments were available for her free time pleasure.

"Is this your first year?" came a quiet voice from the seat next to Julia.

As Julia turned toward the questioner, she was shocked at what she saw. Here was a near duplicate of Hannah Johnson! If Julia had not known better, she would have been certain Hannah had taken her advice and made up her mind to come to the academy after all.

Upon closer examination, she noticed this girl was larger than Hannah, though her features and voice were very similar. Finally able to speak, Julia tried to apologize for staring.

"I am sorry, I know I was staring, but you look exactly like Hannah Johnson back in East Grove! Who are you? I mean, what is your name?"

As this Hannah duplicate started to back away, Julia realized how she must have sounded and tried again. "I really am sorry if I seem rude. I am Julia Jones, from Salem, and yes, this is my first year. Is it yours?" Julia realized she had slipped back into her "you" habit, but she was so used to using it with Hannah that she said it to this look alike without even thinking.

Smiling just a bit the girl replied, "Yes, this is my first year. My name is Suzannah Johnson, and I am Hannah's cousin. My father is Luke Johnson's brother."

No wonder there was a likeness, Julia thought. This was just what she needed...another Hannah! She needed to find a unique, beautiful, smart woman for her brother. So far all she had met was a carbon copy of what David already had! Hannah...Suzannah...even their names sounded alike!

Shifting in her seat, Julia turned away, hoping Suzannah would not want to continue the conversation.

"Are you scared?" Suzannah asked, seemingly oblivious to the fact that Julia was now looking out the window.

She certainly is more persistent than Hannah, Julia thought, turning back toward her. "No, I am not afraid. What is there to worry about? You do your studies, recite in class, take your exams and graduate. Simple."

"Well I do not believe it is quite as simple as that!" Suzannah replied, much to Julia's surprise. "I think we will have to study in all our spare time, and compete with other bright students for grades. That is why I am just a little scared about the next three years."

"My Uncle Levi says you just have to master the four "R's: Religion, Reading, 'Ritin' and 'Rithmetic and you will do well," Julia said, trying to reassure her. "Levi teaches here, but I see from my schedule that I will not have him this session."

"Is his last name Wilson?" Suzannah asked excitedly.

"Yes, do you have him?"

"Right after lunch each day...for Bible Studies."

"You will like him," Julia assured her. "He will help you if you have any problems in his class."

"Oh, I do not expect to have trouble as long as I work hard."

Julia pondered Suzannah's last sentence as the instructor entered and silence quickly swept across the room. Here was a girl that looked like Hannah, but certainly stood up for herself. Julie thought perhaps she might like to get to know this interesting young woman. She seemed like a level-headed person, yet Julia thought maybe Suzannah knew how to have a bit of fun as well.

"Did thee make some new friends today?" Levi asked as he and Julia began their trek home at the end of the day.

"Yes, I met Jonathan White from Springdale, and Suzannah Johnson who lives two miles south of town."

Levi nodded. "I know both of them, and they are fine young people. I had the privilege of teaching Jonathan last year, and he is both bright and ambitious. And I have known Suzannah since she was a baby, having been in Meeting together. Thee did a fine job choosing thy friends today," he said, smiling.

Julia thought about Levi's comment most of the way home, in spite of chatting with him about her classes and teachers. *Had she chosen her friends, or had they chosen her? If she believed in such things, she would almost think God had led them to her. Wait a minute...what was she thinking? She did believe in such things! If she had truly committed herself to God was it not possible that he was even now directing her life, leading her toward her future? Was that possible?*

One thing she knew: she had no interest in becoming friends with Joseph Bell. He might be friends with Jonathan, but she would simply make it a point to refrain from speaking with Jonathan if it meant Joseph had to be included. Life was too short to pretend to like someone you did not want to be around.

Julia found herself looking forward to the next day. The four "R's" were going to be a snap. And with God's guidance she would do well in the subject of friends as well!

CHAPTER 9

EXTENDED FAMILY

Life soon settled into a routine—too much of a routine to suit Julia. Every day was the same...rise early, help Anna get the twins up, dressed, and fed, get herself ready for school, and walk with Levi to the academy. Each day's classes were becoming routine as well, much of it review for Julia. Her birthday was the only bright spot on the horizon!

Julia had gotten to know several of the students at the academy, Suzannah being the most pleasant surprise. She was much more willing to try new things than her conservative cousin Hannah! Many of the shops in Pleasant Plain had been explored by the two girls while Julia waited for Levi to finish his after school duties each day. Occasionally Jonathan would walk the two blocks from the academy to Main Street with the Julia and Hannah, though he drew the line at the Ladies Dress Shop. He could not believe the girls would even think of asking him to go with them into that women's store!

Joseph, too, was a surprise. When Julia had declined an invitation from Jonathan to try out for the debate team because she knew Joseph was already a member, Jonathan convinced her to give his friend another chance. Although she still believed Joseph was an arrogant know-it-all, he was a good debater, and Julia rather enjoyed being on the opposing team.

Julia had learned that Joseph was a member of the Presbyterian faith, and that he lived in Washington. His favorite pastime seemed to be hunting pheasants and turkey, something Julia thought to be repulsive. Joseph talked mostly of his friends, so Julia knew little of his family. When she would ask him about his home he would quickly change the subject. Jonathan, on the other hand, was becoming a good friend. Julia loved taking walks with him and Hannah after school, though most days he rushed off to his job at Mealy's Drug Store. Julia knew he needed all the extra money he could make to pay for his room and board with the Mendenhall family. Not only did Jonathan work at the drug store, he also did much of the janitor work at the academy in order to pay his tuition. That was one of the reasons Julia was so impressed by him. Even though he was putting himself through school by holding two jobs, she had never heard him once complain!

Julia would never forget the conversation she, Jonathan and Joseph had had on the subject of tuition one morning prior to the commencing of school. Julia seldom let herself become embarrassed, but that morning she had made a complete fool of herself.

"I personally think tuition should be raised," she had begun as the three of them were discussing the fact that teachers at the academy were not being paid a regular salary. "Uncle Levi practically lives in poverty because he never knows if there will be enough money left for salaries after Mr. Dorland pays the expenses. If my father were not paying Levi for my room and board, I have no idea how he and his family would survive."

She paused, then continued. "I am convinced many of the students I have seen in this school could certainly afford to pay a bit more than sixty-five cents a week!"

"That's easy for you to say, Miss High and Mighty Doctor's Daughter!" came Joseph's angry response. "Not all of us have a rich daddy to pay our way!"

Jonathan knew the reason for Joseph's outburst, and he felt the need to help Julia understand. "I certainly have sympathy for thy uncle, Julia. He is one of the finest teachers I have studied under, and he deserves to receive a regular salary. Some of us, however, find it difficult to come up with the twenty-five cents a week that is charged for hardship cases, let alone a tuition increase."

Realizing she had unintentionally hurt Jonathan, Julia tried to make amends. "I am sorry, Jonathan. I was not being very thoughtful. Thee makes a good point, though I still believe some of us could afford to pay a bit more for the fine schooling we are receiving," she finished, looking directly at Joseph. Joseph always had fine clothes and expensive writing pens, convincing Julia his family must have some wealth.

With a look of utter disgust, Joseph abruptly turned and walked away.

"He must have gotten up on the wrong side of the bed!" Julia said lightly, her attempt at humor quickly fading when she saw the look on Jonathan's face.

"Oh Julia," he said, "I wish thee would not always feel compelled to say everything that pops into thy head! Joseph is an orphan and has been working to support himself at various odd jobs since he was twelve. Did thee know he is twenty years old? He had to work and save enough money for tuition and room and board before he could even attend here."

"I...I..." Julia stammered, for once at a loss for words. "I just assumed he was from a well-to-do family. He has nice clothing and a gold-embossed writing pen...I...I was certain he must have a lot of money."

"Joseph works hard to conceal his background, Julia," Jonathan said admiringly. "He has not had a proper family upbringing, so his occasional lack of manners is sometimes annoying. But he has a good heart, and I think thee could be a bit more patient with him." Then he added as an afterthought, "Please, Julia, never tell Joseph thee knows of his past. He would never forgive me if he knew I told thee his secret. He resents thee enough as it is!"

"I would never break thy confidence, Jonathan, please believe me!"

"All right, my fiery one," he teased her. "Let's get to class."

Even though Julia understood part of the reason for Joseph's behavior, she still thought he could use a few lessons in common courtesy!

Julia received a letter from her parents the last week of the eleventh month saying they had decided to travel to Pleasant Plain to help celebrate her birthday. Julia thought this was a bit strange...her parents had always said birthdays were important only so long as one took time to reflect on what they had done with their lives up to that point, and then consider what they would do in the future. It was also somewhat dangerous to travel very far from home this time of year when one never knew what the weather might bring. Regardless of the reasons for their visit, however, Julia was pleased at the thought of seeing her family. The two months had passed quickly, but she had missed her parents and David a great deal.

Julia debated whether or not she should make sure David had a chance to meet two of the academy girls she felt might take his mind off Hannah. One of them was Suzannah. She really liked this girl who had seemed so shy yet been so bold. She had also begun spending some time with Harriet Hutchins. Harriet was in her trigonometry class and had asked Julia if she would care to study with her once a week. Although Julia hated hanging around the academy after classes finished, she decided Harriet might be just the one to take David's mind off Hannah. Harriet was as beautiful a girl as Julia had ever met, and she seemed very sincere in her schooling.

The biggest problem was knowing what was happening back in Salem. David never wrote, and Rebecca's letters were filled with chatty news of the town and Meeting, but never anything serious. Hannah had already turned eighteen, so maybe David had made his move and it would be too late for any match-making.

Julia couldn't help but consider the possibilities, however. If David chose either Harriet or Suzannah he would have a great partner for life. The only problem was figuring out how to get David and the women together.

A last minute wedding shower for one of the teachers and his wife at the academy provided Julia with the perfect opportunity to introduce David to her friends. It was planned for the seventh day of the second week of the twelfth month; the day of her birthday. All she had to do was persuade David to accompany her to the gathering at the school.

Convincing Levi she could walk the mile home by herself the day her family was scheduled to arrive, Julia quickly dashed out the door when the teacher finally said 'dismissed.'

"Julia, wait for me!" came Jonathan's call as he saw her hurrying down the street. He caught up with her at the edge of town. "I know...thee is anxious...to be on thy way,...but I thought...I might... walk with thee today...since thy uncle is not here," he gasped, clearly out of breath.

Not slowing down a step, Julia replied, "That is thoughtful of thee, Jonathan, but I really *do* know the way! And I really *do not* believe there are any big ferocious animals waiting to jump out and devour me!"

Jonathan couldn't help but laugh at her words. One of the things he liked so much about Julia was her quick wit.

"Let me try this again," he said. "Julia, may I have the pleasure of accompanying thee to the home of thy Uncle and Aunt? I promise to be on my best behavior!"

"Oh Jonathan," she relented, still a bit annoyed, "I know thee secretly thinks thee needs to protect me, and even though I do not need a protector, I suppose thee may join me. I do want to get to Levi's as quickly as possible, though, to see if my family has arrived yet from Salem."

"Oh...I did not realize...I mean, if thy family will be there...perhaps I should accompany thee another evening," he stammered.

"Is there a problem with my family?" Julia teased, sensing Jonathan's reluctance to meet them.

"Oh, I am certain they are a fine family, but they do not know me, and perhaps they would assume something they should not assume."

"Such as?" Julia was not about to let him off the hook.

"About our relationship, I mean."

"What about our relationship, Jonathan?" While Julia did not want to encourage Jonathan to believe she might be interested in him, she could not help but tease him just a bit.

Turning several shades of red, Jonathan stopped. "Thee is teasing me, Julia. I realize that now. Nevertheless, I would not want to spoil thy reunion. I will just turn back now. Have a good visit and..."

"And what, Jonathan?"

"And...I would be happy to accompany thee to thy home any day I am not obligated to be at the drug store."

"That is certainly a relief! I shall never again be afraid I might have to walk the entire mile by myself!"

"Julia, thee is too much for words. Will I see thee at the wedding shower tomorrow night?"

"I will know more after my parents arrive. I am hoping to persuade my brother David to accompany me. There are two very nice girls I would like for him to meet."

"Julia...please tell me thee is not trying to get thy brother paired with some fine woman from our school!" The disbelief was evident in his voice.

"And why not, may I ask?" Julia shot back.

"Julia, a man likes to be in control of his destiny! The last thing he needs is a female interfering!"

"And sometimes it takes a female to help a man realize just exactly what his future might be," Julia answered hotly, disturbed by the sound of superiority in Jonathan's voice. "I happen to view this situation as an opportunity to provide suitable candidates from which my brother might select a future mate," she finished. "I see nothing sinful in such activities!"

Realizing there was nothing he could say to dissuade this complex young woman, Jonathan gave up trying to change her mind. "I will see thee at the shower, then," he called, quickly turning on his heel and starting back toward Pleasant Plain.

Julia walked quickly up the lane to her new home, still disturbed by Jonathan's comments. Her heart began to beat faster when she recognized her father's rig at the hitching post.

David was the first to spot his sister, quickly running down the lane toward her. Throwing his arms around her small waist, he picked her up and spun her around and around.

"Hey big brother! Put me down!" Julia laughed, clearly pleased with his greeting.

"I have missed thee, My Little Fireball. And I can not wait to hear about school." Julia smiled at the familiar nickname. David had been calling her that for as long as she could remember.

"I have missed you—I mean thee, too!" Julia replied. "And I think thee is going to enjoy what I have planned for thee while thee is here!" Might as well take the direct approach, Julia thought. A slight flush appeared to color David's cheeks, though it was hard to tell in the dusk. "Why are we standing here in the cold?" she asked, realizing David seemed uncomfortable with the discussion for some reason. "And where are Mother and Father?"

"Playing with their nephews, no doubt, " David laughed. "I said I would watch for thee if they wanted to see Andrew and Timothy."

Julia wished she didn't feel the pang of jealousy that stabbed at her heart. Of course her parents would want to see Rebecca's nephews...but at the expense of their own daughter?

"Anna, I am home," Julia called as she and David opened the heavy door to the cabin. If her parents were going to choose their nephews over her, she would simply ignore them.

Rebecca was instantly on her feet, her face beaming. "Julia," she cried. "I have missed thee so much!"

"I have only been away six weeks!" Julia tried to sound cool, but she really was glad to see her mother. Charles was soon standing beside her as well, and he quickly gave her shoulders a squeeze. "It is good to see thee, Julia. Has thee been helping thy aunt and uncle with the work here? Have thy studies been going well? Thee hasn't been associating with the boys, has thee?"

"I imagine Julia has had a hard day at school, Charles," Rebecca said gently, "I am certain she will answer all our questions in good time. We have two days to catch up on the past two months."

Julia looked closely at her mother. It was not like Rebecca to speak on her daughter's behalf. What was causing this change in behavior?

There was something else about Rebecca that was different. But what? She looked like she'd gained weight...had she been eating because of her loneliness?

"There are many fine shops in Pleasant Plain!" Julia burst out, hoping to squelch the new thought that had suddenly crossed her mind.

"Has thee been spending thy time in the stores rather than keeping up with thy studies?" Charles asked immediately.

"Oh no, Father. I have been prompt with all my assignments."

"Levi?" Charles turned to his brother-in-law who had just entered the cabin and was hanging his wraps on a peg by the door. "Has my daughter been doing as she says?"

"Yes, Charles," Levi said with a smile, "Julia is doing well. Although she is not in any of my classes, her teachers keep me posted on her progress."

It was Julia's turn to be surprised. She had no idea her uncle had been spying on her! She would have to have a word with him when they returned to the academy!

When the evening meal was finished and a time of Bible reading and prayer completed, everyone retired for the night. Charles, Rebecca, and David were tired from their journey and they all agreed they would enjoy themselves more the next day if they got some much needed sleep.

As Julia lay on the floor, having given her bed to her parents, the image of her mother would not go away. No matter how she tried, she could not put it out of her mind. Could it be possible? No. Perhaps she was imagining things. Her mother was forty-eight years old. Too old for...she couldn't even say the word. And if Rebecca was...in that way...why had she not told her only daughter before now? She would be sixteen tomorrow. Sixteen years old. She had waited a long time to reach this age. Too long to let her day be spoiled by the prospects of a new...brother or sister? No, it couldn't be true. She *must* be imagining things. Perhaps her mother had indeed been eating more than her body needed. That was it! Her mother must have missed her so much that she turned to food for comfort and the result was a bulging stomach. That had to be the explanation. It was a pretty low bulge for a stomach, Julia had to admit.

Tomorrow. She would confront her mother tomorrow and she would have the answer to the riddle.

CHAPTER 10

FIRE AND ICE

When the rooster crowed to signal the arrival of a new day, Julia felt as though she had not slept even an hour. Her mind had gone back and forth between her suspicions regarding her mother and her plans for David. There had also been the hard floor...Julia had slept on the ground every night at Yearly Meeting and adjusted very well. There was just something about the unyielding wood of the cabin floor that made it nearly impossible for her body to get comfortable.

She could hear the adults in the kitchen, obviously having risen earlier. Her parents must have been extremely quiet when they rose or else she had finally fallen into a deep sleep about the time they were rising!

As Julia dressed she renewed her vow to discover what was going on with her mother. She also knew she had to persuade David to accompany her to the shower that night.

And this is my birthday! Julia thought, smiling at the prospect. Perhaps God thought more of celebrating birthdays than Friends believed! Would He not be pleased with his creation—even to the point of doing a little celebrating Himself? Of course, that would mean every day would be a celebration for God! It was a rather nice thought!

As Julia entered the kitchen she was surprised to find that everyone—even the twins was sitting around the rough-hewn table. "Did thee finally get some rest?" her mother asked. "Thee tossed and turned so much in the night I was certain thee was having trouble with the floor. I am sorry we took thy bed!"

"I was fine, Mother, really," Julia insisted. "What time is it?"

"It is half past the ninth hour," Anna said with a smile. "Thy mother thought we should wake thee at the regular time, but I persuaded her to let thee catch up a bit on thy sleep. Thee has worked hard helping me with the boys each morning, and I thought thee deserved to rest."

"But I thought I heard the rooster crow..." Julia looked confused.

Levi laughed. "Our poor rooster gets a bit confused. This morning the clouds were thick and it wasn't until the sun poked through that poor Isaac announced the day's arrival. I keep telling Anna we would get better use of the old bird by making chicken and dumplings, but she seems somewhat attached to the creature."

"Isaac was a wedding present from the Hocketts, Levi." Anna retorted. "I would no more think of sacrificing him than Abraham did the real Isaac!"

Julia shuddered at the thought. She had witnessed the slaughtering of several chickens by her hatchet-wielding aunt, and it always pained her to think of ending life in such a cruel way.

"We hope thy birthday is a pleasant one," Rebecca said with a smile, interrupting Julia's thoughts. "I know Friends believe one's birthday should not be formally celebrated, but I believe we can rejoice in the birth of one of our children without becoming like the heathen!"

"We are indeed happy to have shared these past sixteen years with thee, Julia," her father added. "Every father rejoices when he learns a part of himself and the woman he loves will soon arrive to bless their lives."

Charles looked quickly at Rebecca, and she nodded slightly. Julia's quick eye saw the look and instinctively knew what was to come.

"In fact," Charles continued, "Rebecca and I find ourselves in a similar situation even as we speak."

David, Levi and Anna all looked puzzled, though Julia knew exactly what her father was saying. So it was true. There was to be an addition to their family.

"We are expecting a child the first week of the fifth month," Rebecca said quietly.

For a moment no one spoke, the news obviously surprising everyone but Julia.

"Congratulations!" Levi finally spoke. "I imagine it was a bit of a surprise after all these years...I mean...Julia being sixteen now and all!"

Charles and Rebecca both laughed. "Yes, it was a surprise," Rebecca admitted, "but a pleasant one, once we became accustomed to the idea!"

"David?" Charles looked at his son. "Does the thought of a new brother or sister appeal to thee, or would thee rather not say?!"

"I...l had no idea! I will be going to school soon, so I suppose a child would be welcome company to thee both," he concluded, looking neither exuberant or distressed.

"Julia?" her father asked. "Does thee feel the same as thy brother?"

"I do not believe my feelings really matter," she said, trying to keep the anger from her voice. "If thee will excuse me, I promised Suzannah I would meet her in Pleasant Plain to purchase a gift for the shower this evening."

"But thee has not eaten yet," Anna started to protest.

"I have no hunger this morning. Please, may I just be excused?"

"Of course," Levi answered, sensing Charles and Rebecca's news had upset his niece more than she was willing to admit.

Julia rose without looking at either of her parents. "David," she turned and spoke to her brother. "If thee has no other plans for the morning, I would appreciate thy company."

"Certainly, that is, if Uncle Levi has nothing planned for me to do this morning," he said, turning to look at Levi.

"No, go ahead. Thee may take my horse and carriage if thee would like. The days are becoming quite cool, and if thee will be gone for a time it might be wise to have a ride home waiting for thee."

"Just take my carriage," Charles spoke. "It is already at the hitching post where I left it yesterday. Thee will have to bridle the horse in the barn, but I suppose thee knows that."

Charles looked at the two young adults before him. David, so like himself and nearly an adult; Julia, so like he imagined Rebecca at that age, though without the sharp tongue. A new baby was nearly like beginning their family anew. Was he certain he could manage the rearing of another child? He supposed he had no choice! He did hope Julia would have a more favorable reaction when she had a chance to consider the news.

"Why would they want to have a child at this age?" Julia asked David as soon as they were on their way to Pleasant Plain.

"I rather suppose it was not actually planned," David said dryly.

"Then they should have planned how not to have a child!" she said angrily.

"I think it might be good for them to have another child since we will both be away soon."

"And that is another thing, David Jones. Why has thee not written me of thy plans? I had no idea thee had made arrangements to go to school. What about Hannah?"

A look of incredulity crossed David's face. "What does thee mean?"

I've done it now, Julia thought to herself. I've thought about Hannah and David for so long I forgot I wasn't supposed to know about their mutual fondness for one another.

"I am sorry, David," she answered, deciding honesty was perhaps the best route to take. "I know thee has an interest in Hannah—as more than a friend. Please do not ask how I know, just believe me when I say the discovery was unintentional."

"I thought thee might know something, but Hannah insisted thee had no idea," he admitted. "Hannah and I have decided it would be wise for me to get my formal medical education finished before we made any sort of commitment to one another."

"What made thee decide to go to medical school? As I recall, every time Father mentioned thy going to school, thee was very opposed to the notion!"

"It was Hannah," David said shyly, smiling. "She helped me see the error of my thinking. She said if I did not make the commitment now I might never be able to do the one thing I really desire—helping other people."

"When will thee enroll?" Julia asked, suddenly feeling as if her entire world was coming apart.

"Father and I went to Chicago two weeks ago to the school he attended—The Chicago School of Medicine. After taking hours of tests to determine my suitability, they agreed to accept me for the winter term. I would never have qualified if it were not for the hours I have spent working with Father. I leave next week for Chicago."

"Next week?!" Julia shouted, causing the horse to shy.

"Yes, their winter quarter began this first week, but they allowed me to begin a week late so I could finish my business in Salem. And so I could say good-bye to thee as well."

So that was why they had come for a visit! It had nothing to do with her birthday! Their mission had been to break the news of the addition to the family, as well as to tell her of David's move to Chicago.

"How long will thee be gone?" Julia finally choked, visibly upset by her discovery.

"It will take nearly three years to complete all my training, but there will be opportunities to return to Salem for visits. We will have to try and arrange our trips home for the same times or we will never see one another!"

Julia was not sure what to think. David sounded as if he and Hannah were committed to one another, in spite of David's plans to go to medical school. Should she still try and introduce him to Suzannah and Harriet? Would he resent her for interfering in his life? Not if she were careful, she decided. What harm could there be in seeing that David met two friends of hers? Absolutely none as far as she was concerned. David might think he and Hannah were perfect together, but how could he know when all he'd ever done was talk to her at Yearly Meeting and kiss her one time? No, it might not be too late, and it certainly could not hurt anything. David will just think they are friends of mine, she decided firmly.

"Who did you say we were meeting today?" David asked as they entered main street.

"I must confess I invented the story of meeting someone as an excuse to get out of the cabin. I was so upset about the news of the baby that all I wanted to do was get away from our parents. I know I should not have misled them, and I really do need to get a gift for Mr. Coffin and his wife."

"Julia," David said in a resigned tone of voice. "I wish thee could learn to speak the truth in all things in the manner of Friends, though I do understand thy need to leave the cabin. I was glad to get out as well. Just between me and thee, I was a bit undone by the news myself!"

As they drove down the street, Julia pointed out the various businesses; the Broadway Hotel, the Church of the United Brethren in Christ, H. Jones Grocery Store, O'Donnell's Millinery,

Mealey's Drug, Hackney's Boot and Shoe Store, Kendall's Grocery and Dr. Thomas Mealey's office. Dr. Mealey had officially retired the previous year, but everyone knew he would treat anyone who came to him with a need.

"Where would thee like to shop?" David asked, turning the rig around at the end of the street.

"Let's try Kendall's first," Julia answered, "they have a variety of nice things for the home. I thought I might look for a lamp. One can never have enough light in a dark cabin—especially in the winter when the days grow shorter and shorter."

"Kendall's it is," David replied as he pulled the sweaty horse up to the hitching post.

Kendall's indeed had a number of lamps, some of them rather ornate, though Julia chose a simple lantern which would look nice on the mantel. Julia and David spent most of the morning wandering through the stores in Pleasant Plain, laughing at some of the items available, wishing they could afford the beautiful set of china, even though they knew it would not be considered simple enough for Friends. Although they tried to laugh and enjoy each other's company, there was an underlying tension in each of their voices. Julia sensed David's apprehension about going to Chicago to study, as David sensed her unhappiness over the baby.

Julia wanted to ask David about accompanying her to the shower that evening, though she found it difficult to find the courage to ask him in his present state of mind. Finally, as they were approaching the Wilson cabin, Julia just blurted out her question.

"David, would thee go to the shower with me this evening? I know thee does not know any of the students or teachers, but I would be happy to introduce thee, and I know thee would like them. I especially want thee to meet Jonathan White. He is a rather special friend."

Julia knew the mention of a "special friend" would probably be enough to pique David's interest, though she was sorry to use

Jonathan in such a way. If it got David to attend, and thus meet Suzannah and Harriet in the process, it would be worth it.

"Who is this Jonathan White? I mean, where is he from? Is he a suitable young man? And Julia, thee is only sixteen—and just barely at that!"

Laughing out loud, Julia replied, "I wish thee could hear thyself, David Jones. Thee sounds just like Father!"

"I am sorry if thee feels I am interfering in thy business. But thee must know how much I care about what happens to thee. Just the thought of some big oaf taking advantage of my little sister makes my blood boil!"

"Thee had best be careful, I would not want thy blood to boil over! The only way thee will know anything about Jonathan White is to attend the shower with me."

"Thee leaves me no choice, though I suspect thee planned this all along. What time does it begin?"

"At the seventh hour. I can not wait for thee to meet..." catching herself just in time, Julia finished, "some of the girls and boys, too, of course."

"Julia..." David began, looking over at this sometimes devious sister of his. "Thee wouldn't be planning any special meeting would thee?"

"I am surprised at thy suspicions, David. Just come with me and enjoy our last evening together for who knows how long!"

There were a number of rigs already outside the school when Julia and David arrived that evening. Julia could feel the excitement rising, mainly at the prospect of introducing David to Suzannah and Harriet. Surely one of them would make a favorable impression on her brother.

David was surprised at how many of those present seemed to be friends with his sister. He hoped he would be able to make friends as easily in Chicago. He wasn't as outgoing as his sister, and meeting people was one of the hardest things for him to do.

"David," he heard Julia say, bringing him back to the gathering. "I would like for thee to meet my good friend Suzannah Johnson, Hannah's cousin."

"Hello, Suzannah," David said warmly. "Hannah has spoken of thee a number of times. She said the two of you might have been twins, and I can see she was correct! I am glad to make thy acquaintance."

"Hannah has told me about thee as well," she said warmly. Hannah is a lucky woman to find someone she can share her hopes and dreams with."

Julia was speechless. Suzannah knew about Hannah and David? She had never said a word to her. Didn't she know David was her brother? Of course she did. Julia had mentioned him on a number of occasions. Well, she could forget about Suzannah winning David's heart. That only left Harriet. The only problem was that Harriet had not arrived and it was almost time to begin. As they were making their way to an unoccupied bench near the bride and groom, Jonathan suddenly appeared at Julia's side.

"Hello, Julia. I am glad thee was able to attend. Is this thy brother?"

"Oh, excuse me. Jonathan White, this is my brother, David. He agreed to chaperone me this evening in case I encountered any ferocious animals on the way." Julia's eyes were twinkling, and Jonathan thought he would never be able to keep a straight face, though he somehow managed.

"I am pleased to meet thee," Jonathan replied, "Julia has mentioned thee on a number of occasions."

"Has she now?!" David looked from the young man to his sister. "And I hope everything she had to say was favorable?"

"Very much so. From what Julia said I had imagined thee to be as near perfection as one could hope to be in this life!"

"I am afraid I do have a few flaws!" David laughed. "And I am pleased to meet thee as well. Julia has spoken of thee often!"

David! Julia thought, I have barely mentioned Jonathan's name. Why would you seek to embarrass me this way? Then in a flash of insight, it suddenly occurred to her that David might be doing the very thing she had set out to do—find her a suitable mate! She suddenly began to laugh, the sound carrying throughout the assembly hall. Fortunately for David and Jonathan the shower was ready to begin.

After many words of advice had been offered to the newlyweds, the gifts were opened and thanks expressed to by the happy couple. A time of refreshment followed, which gave Julia a chance to find Harriet.

Grabbing David by the hand, Julia headed straight to where she had seen Harriet talking to the married couple. As soon as Harriet turned to leave, Julia was at her side.

"Harriet, I would like for thee to meet my brother David. David, this is Harriet."

"I am pleased to meet all of Julia's friends," David said, emphasizing the all.

Julia noticed Harriet studying David as if trying to see if he measured up to her standards. Suddenly Harriet slipped her hand through David's arm. "I would greatly appreciate thee accompanying me to get a glass of grape juice."

David looked at Julia as if to say, 'Now what do I do?' Turning back to the woman on his arm, he forced a smile and said, "Certainly."

"My, my, my!" Jonathan said, approaching Julia. "I see Harriet has latched onto thy brother. Maybe she will be successful this time."

"What...what do you mean by that?" Julia was too shocked by his words to remember to use 'thee.'

"Why, everyone knows the only reason Harriet came to the academy was to find a husband! She has tried to get nearly every boy here to take an interest in her!"

"Even thee?" Julia couldn't help but ask.

"Of course! Does thee not think I would be one of the first Harriet would choose to pursue?" he said teasingly.

Julia, however, was not in a teasing mood. "Why would Harriet think David might be interested in her?" As the words came out of her mouth, she realized the irony in what she had just said. Only a few minutes earlier she had been anxious to have her brother meet this girl. But that was before she knew the truth about Harriet...before she realized the girl had no moral scruples!

Deciding they had stayed long enough, Julia quickly sought to rescue David. Reaching his side, she grabbed his arm and said, "We must be on our way now!"

"Oh, so soon? David and I were just getting to know one another!" Harriet said, looking coquettishly at her new friend.

"My sister is right. We promised our parents we would be back at the cabin early. It was nice to meet thee, Harriet."

"It was my pleasure!" Harriet said, her eyes glowing, the mile-wide smile speaking her feelings. "When will thee be this way again, David?"

"Oh, not for some time, I am afraid. I will be traveling to Chicago from here to attend school."

"Then please give me thy address and I will write thee!" Harriet said.

"I have no idea what it will be. Why not wait and see if our paths cross again some time in the future."

Turning to Julia, he quickly put his hand on her back and guided her to the door .

"Was I ever happy to be free of that girl!" David confessed as soon as they were out the door. "She attached herself tighter than a leech and refused to let go. I even told her I was committed to another woman, but it seemed to make no difference!"

"She is definitely not your type!" Julia said emphatically, wondering how she could have been so wrong about Harriet.

"And just what is my type?"

"Well, I guess that is for thee to decide," Julia finally admitted, realizing how miserably she had failed at matchmaking.

"I am glad to hear thee say that. Will thee promise to make no more attempts to find me a suitable mate?" he asked teasingly.

"I...I...what makes thee think I would do such a thing?"

"Just admit it, Julia. Thee thought thee would introduce me to some nice girls at the academy and I would be swept away by their kindness and beauty. I know thee is not fond of Hannah, but it is my hope that over time thee will grow to love her as I do."

"And by the way," he continued when Julia had no response, "I really liked Jonathan. He seems like a responsible young man."

"I am so glad thee approves," she said sarcastically. "But just for the record, unlike the Harriets of this world, I am not interested in any man. I do not believe a woman must spend her life looking for someone else to make her happy. I believe God has something special planned for my life and I intend to find out just what it is!"

David turned to look at Julia with bewilderment. "I will never understand thee, Julia Jones! Thee devotes an entire evening to finding a suitable mate for me, but declares thee does not need a husband! I think thee just wants to get a reaction from me!"

Julia laughed, knowing she had gotten the best of her brother again. Seeing the scowl on his face, however, she knew she must make amends. "I am sorry, David. I suppose thee has a point. I should let thee take care of finding thy own wife. If Hannah is the one for thee, then I shall accept thy decision. I am quite serious, however, about God's call in my life." She then proceeded to tell him about her prayer at yearly meeting and how she just knew God was planning something special for her life.

David was speechless, though admiration shone in his eyes. He might never understand this younger sister of his, but life was never dull when she was around! He hadn't realized just how much he had missed her since she had been gone. And now he was going to Chicago. Their family life would never be the same again, he thought sadly, but perhaps it was time they each went their separate ways, wherever God was leading them.

CHAPTER 11

Snow Fest

The first snow of the season arrived just before Christmas. Since Julia's parents had made the trip to Pleasant Plain earlier in the twelfth month for her birthday, they had already been agreed they would not be meeting for Christmas. Since there would be no holiday gathering, Julia decided the first snow deserved to be celebrated, though she wasn't certain just what she and her friends should do.

Christmas was on a First Day, which meant school would be dismissed for one week commencing two days before the celebrated birth of Christ. On the first day of the week before their break, Julia quickly sought out Jonathan to see if they might plan something special for the time school would not be in session.

"I will be working most of the days," Jonathan replied hesitantly when Julia approached him during the noon break. "I am promised at the drug store every day but one, and I must see that the academy is maintained during the time no one is present. What did thee have in mind?"

"Nothing for certain," she answered, "I just thought it might be nice for a group of us to get together and do something with the snow!"

"What can a person do with snow?" Jonathan teased. "There is hardly enough to drive a sleigh on right now!"

"Then thee is not interested in any plan I may develop?" Julia asked, just a bit perturbed at Jonathan's lack of enthusiasm for her idea.

"I did not say that, Julia. Thee knows I am willing to try anything once—unless it involves thy brother and some girl thee is trying to arrange for him to meet!"

"Thee will never let me forget that, will thee?" Julia asked disgustedly. "I told thee I had been wrong. What more does thee want? Should I get down on my knees and seek thy forgiveness?!"

"That might be nice!" Jonathan retorted, ducking to avoid the playful swing Julia took at him.

"Non-violence, my fiery one, non-violence!" Jonathan teased.

"Just answer me this," Julia persisted, "If I arrange some type of gathering for our friends, will thee join us?"

"If thee promises it will not get us into trouble with anyone!"

"Good! I will talk to Suzannah after school today and then we will stop by the store and tell thee of our plans."

Julia hurried off to her first afternoon class, her head buzzing with ideas. Unfortunately, her instructor seemed to feel this was the day to call on daydreaming students, and she asked Julia several probing questions with little response.

"Julia, I must say thee seems to be on another planet today! Thee usually answers any question I ask of thee. Is thee feeling well?"

With every head turned toward her, Julia felt the heat rise in her cheeks. Though she enjoyed speaking her mind, the one thing she did not enjoy was being singled out.

"I am sorry. I suppose my mind was on another planet!" she tried to sound cheerful, though it did not seem to influence the teacher.

"Then I suggest thee return to earth and get thy mind on thy studies!"

The sternness of the educator's voice convinced Julia this woman meant what she said. Try as she might, however, it was still difficult to concentrate on compounds and molecules when her mind wanted to think about snow and parties.

"Hey Julia," came Joseph's irritating voice as they filed out the front door at the end of the day. "I hear you have been daydreaming in class! You should be listening to old lady Pigeon instead of thinking about which male you might ensnare with your charms!"

Julia knew her face was the shade of a ripe tomato, but she refused to be bated by Joseph Bell! "I think thee should have a bit of respect for thy teachers, Joseph. Marian Pidgeon is a fine woman, and "old lady" is hardly a becoming term by which to address her!"

"You did not answer my question, Julia. From the talk around school, you were not there in science class today—at least your mind was absent. I would think you might have an explanation for such unladylike behavior."

Forgetting her resolve to avoid an argument, Julia gave Joseph a piece of her mind.

"First of all, for your information Joseph Bell, I have no desire to charm any member of the male species, especially not one like you! And secondly, I was thinking about what a wonderful time my friends and I are going to have when we plan for our snow fest."

"Snow fest my foot! You are not planning any such thing. Why, there is not enough snow on the ground to support the tiniest bit of activity, let alone a snow fest!"

"Just wait and see!" Julia stormed off, determined to show that smart mouthed boy just what fun he was going to miss because she was not about to invite him to any gathering she was going to plan!

Julia still wasn't certain why Joseph irritated her so. She remembered listening to her mother and Betty talk about their trip to Iowa by covered wagon when they were teens. Betty kept telling stories about the things Joshua did to Rebecca to irritate her. And then they always laughed because Rebecca ended up marrying Joshua! Julia found it hard to believe a person could change her feelings that much toward someone she could hardly tolerate. She was certain beyond a doubt that she and Joseph would never even be on friendly speaking terms with one another, let alone anything more!

She hurried to catch up with Suzannah and Julia quickly retold her encounter with Joseph.

"He is such a disgusting person!" Suzannah agreed. "How anyone can be a friend to him is more than I can understand. Of course Jonathan is a saint where Joseph is concerned. Does thee not agree?" she looked at Julia with a grin on her face.

"Jonathan just refuses to see the nasty side of Joseph—the side he always seems to display when I am around!"

"But that makes Jonathan all the more special. And besides, as children of God we are to love everyone with the Light of Christ within—even Joseph Bell."

"Maybe you should become a traveling evangelist, Suzannah Johnson," Julia's voice gave evidence of the irritation she was beginning to feel. Suzannah should have been supportive of her best friend, not preaching a sermon on the subject of loving others!

Suzannah knew Julia was upset, but she also knew her friend's anger would probably leave as quickly as it came. Suzannah had grown quite fond of her red-haired friend, though she was sometimes taken back by Julia's boldness and quickness to judge others. Suzannah thought about the time she and Julia had been walking down Main Street after school, and Julia had suggested they go into the millinery shop and try on hats. Suzannah had tried to be strong in her belief that fancy hats were not pleasing to God. She also remembered Julia's persuasive argument.

"Suzannah," she had begun, with a look of seriousness. "God gave beauty to the peacock in the form of multi-colored feathers. How can it be a sin for us to wear one of those stunning feathers in a head covering? Thee knows the apostle Paul said a woman was to keep her head covered. Why is a covering made with one of God's creations not acceptable?"

Suzannah laughed as she remembered how persuasive Julia had been, and how they had indeed tried on hats and thought of the shock it would bring to the other women in Meeting if they were to exchange their gray and black scuttle bonnets for brightly plumed head coverings!

"I believe thee is the one who should become the traveling evangelist, Julia!" Suzannah said with a grin. "Thy powers of persuasion are quite remarkable!"

Suzannah noticed the strange look that crossed Julia's face when she mentioned 'traveling evangelist', but when Julia remained silent, she quickly sought to change the subject.

"So tell me about thy plans for a get together over break!" Suzannah said excitedly.

"Who told thee about my idea?" Julia asked, quickly forgetting all thoughts of the possibility of being an evangelist.

"Jonathan and I were talking before Bible class began. He said you had some crazy idea for a snow party, but he had no idea how you would get anything done with only a few inches of snow on the ground." Suzannah laughed, remembering the look on Jonathan's face when he had told her.

"So he thinks my idea is crazy, does he?" Julia's irritation with first Joseph, and then Suzannah, was now turned on Jonathan. "Maybe I will neglect to even tell him about my plans. I think I will just let him hear about the fun we had after our snow fest!"

"Oh Julia, Jonathan was just teasing. I could tell by the look in his eyes that he really admired you for trying to organize a bit of fun for the rest of us. Thee needs to quit jumping to conclusions all the time!"

"There you go again—preaching!" This time Julia's teasing tone told Suzannah her friend was no longer angry with her.

"So what are you planning?" Suzannah asked, the excitement beginning to build.

"You are going to help me, Suzannah Johnson. We are going to have the greatest time of our lives since coming to the academy. Have you ever heard of a traveling sleigh party?"

"Julia, I know thee will say I am preaching again, but I do wish thee would keep with the plain language."

"Fine! Thee! Thee! Thee! Thee! There, now I have said "thee" four times to make up for the times I said 'you.' Now, answer my question. Has thee ever heard of a traveling sleigh party?"

"No!" Hannah laughed. "I think it is something thee made up! Tell me the truth, Julia—has thee ever heard of such a thing?!"

"Well, I have had the idea for a long time, though I have never actually heard of anyone doing such a thing. But let me tell thee how it might work. First, we meet somewhere—like outside the meeting house. Then, we all climb into one sleigh and travel by moonlight to your house. At your house we have a bite to eat."

"A bite of what?"

"Whatever you have...bread, or cornmeal, just something to get us started. Now be quiet and just listen!" Julia was becoming a bit exasperated. "After we finish at your house, we go to Sarah's house. She provides us with some type of meat dish. Deer, or rabbit, or squirrel, whatever they happen to have. Then we get back in the sleigh and travel to the Mendenhalls where Jonathan is staying. He provides us with something sweet. Martha Mendenhall is a wonderful Friend, and I know she would fix something for our group.

"When we finish there, we go to Levi's cabin where we pop corn and sit around the fireplace and tell about our greatest fears and our greatest hopes. Levi and Anna and the boys can sleep in my room that night so we will have the main part of the cabin for ourselves. When we finish, Jonathan can drive everyone back to the meeting house and then they can go their separate ways."

When Suzannah had no immediate response, Julia began to worry.

"Is there a problem? Have I forgotten something?"

"Thee has given me so much to think about. The main concern I have is with our parents. I have a hard time believing all of them will allow us to travel over the countryside after dark without a chaperone!"

"Then we will have to find a way to convince the parents there will be no reason for them to worry. We will show them how responsible we are, and help them see how much fun we will have!"

"I think thee is dreaming, Julia," was Suzannah's skeptical response. "I cannot imagine my parents allowing me to do such a thing."

"Then we will tell them thee is spending the night with me."

"And thee thinks that is being honest?"

"Thee can spend the night with me! That will be the truth!"

"I still think..." Suzannah began hesitantly.

"Thee thinks too much!" Julia said earnestly. "Let's finish making the plans and then worry about how to convince the adults we are responsible young women and men."

The two girls began to make lists of what they would need to do. They agreed to invite two other girls and four of the boys, Jonathan being the first on their list, for a total of eight young people. All of them except for Julia and Jonathan lived within a few miles of Pleasant Plain, so they would not be away for the break. One name that was not on the list was Joseph Bell. Julia had expected Jonathan to insist they include his friend in their plans, but to her surprise he had not mentioned his name.

Julia found Sarah the next day and told her of their plans, including the stop at her cabin. Sarah's enthusiasm more than made up for Suzannah's hesitancy.

"That sounds like the most wonderful time!" Sarah said, her eyes shining. "I know my mother and father will agree to a stop at our home. Mother was just saying the other day how she hoped I was making new friends at the academy!"

Julia looked at Sarah in this new light. Until now Julia had considered her a plain girl (even plainer than the Friends she was used to!) with very little personality. After her misjudgment of Harriet, Julia had vowed to stick with Suzannah and avoid trying to get to know any of the other academy girls. Perhaps she should have given Sarah a bit more consideration.

Jonathan helped them plan the date, his work allowing him to be free the sixth day of the week of Christmas. By having the day free he could help the girls with the sleigh plans. He had also volunteered to pick up two of the young people who lived near Mendenhalls so they would not have to leave a horse and sleigh at the meeting house for the evening.

The biggest surprise of all had been their parents. There had been no objections when they learned it would be a big group, and that Jonathan White was one of the planners. Jonathan seemed to have a reputation among Friends for being a mature and responsible young person. The fact that parents would be at each stop also seemed to ease everyone's minds.

The day the academy dismissed for break, all the friends who were invited to the get-together met in front of Mealey's Drug for final instructions.

"Does everyone know the plan?" Julia asked, wanting to be certain nothing went wrong.

"Perhaps thee should tell us the times and places again since this is the first time we have all been together." Peter Groves spoke up. "That way if someone is late they will know where they can catch up with the rest of us."

"Good idea, Peter," Jonathan said. He then proceeded to go over the gathering time and place for meeting as well as the time they would arrive at each cabin. "Does anyone else need a ride?" was his final question.

When no one answered, Suzannah looked from person to person and asked the question that had bothered her from the beginning. "Do all of thy parents know and approve of the plans?" While no one spoke, heads nodded in consent.

"Good," Suzannah replied, "because we do not want any of you to have to disobey your parents in order to join us. We want the time to be happy and free from worry!"

The young men and women stood around for a bit longer, though the damp chill in the air led some of them to believe another snow might be on the way.

"What will happen if we have a snow storm sixth day?" Sarah wanted to know.

"Unless there is a terrible blizzard, we will keep our plans as we now have them," Julia vowed, in spite of the concerned looks on some of the faces. "A little snow in the air will make the night perfect!" she said forcefully.

"I am surely glad thee did not invite Joseph Bell," Sarah said to Julia and Suzannah as they walked together after the group broke up.

"Sarah," Julia said with a laugh, "thee does not know me very well if thee thinks I would even consider asking Joseph Bell to join us!"

"Good!" Sarah said, relief evident in her voice. "I know we are to love everyone, but Joseph is just plain rude sometimes! He called Marian Pidgeon a 'fat cow' to her back one day!"

"Perhaps he is having a hard time recognizing the Light of Christ within himself," Suzannah said slowly, obviously having thought about this troubled young man at some point in time.

"I do not think the Light is anywhere to be found in that boy," Julia said with disdain. It was just like Suzannah to stick up for him. Suzannah could be a lot of fun, but she never liked for anyone to speak poorly of another student.

"Let's not talk about Joseph!" Julia blurted before Suzannah had a chance to scold her for her statement. "Tell me what food thee is having at thy house, Sarah."

When the girls finally split up to go their separate ways, each knew what the other was serving, what they would wear, how they would wear their hair, and what the seating arrangement would be in the sleigh. Julia did not really care who she sat by, but she had tried to arrange the other girls next to boys she thought would make good conversation with one another. Of course if there were no more snow, they would have to use the wagon. It would not be much of a snow fest, and it would not be nearly so pretty as the scene she envisioned with the moonlight reflecting off the frosty white snow cover into the eyes of those in the sleigh.

Julia became excited just thinking about it! It had to snow before sixth day...it just had to!

CHAPTER 12

THE BEST LAID PLANS...

The morning of Julia's great day dawned bright and clear, a perfect sign of a perfect evening. The heavy snow that had fallen the day before left a layer of white fluff just right for sleigh travel. Julia had worked the two previous days on their cabin, scrubbing floors, wiping walls, and preparing her room for Levi's family to spend the night so she and her friends could have the main area of the cabin. Julia was going to do everything in her power to insure a successful evening.

As the time drew near for Levi to take her to the meeting house to join the others, Julia began to experience a nervousness she was unaccustomed to feeling. She had always worked hard to be in control of every situation, but this gala affair was larger than anything she had tried before...what if something went wrong? No, she told herself, she would only think in positive terms. Everything had been planned to the tiniest detail, and nothing was going to spoil their good time.

As Levi pulled the horse and sleigh into the drive of the meeting house that evening, Julia immediately sensed something was amiss. Where she had expected to hear laughter and gaiety there was only quiet talking. Perhaps everyone was feeling a bit shy, never having been in such a social situation as this with their peers.

Several of Julia's friends came to greet her from behind the sleigh Jonathan had secured for the evening. Through the dim light of the setting sun, Julia's heart began to beat faster as she saw the strange look in Suzannah's eyes.

Quickly jumping down and motioning Levi to go on back home, Julia welcomed her friends. "Greetings! What a glorious night! The stars are perfect, the snow is perfect, and we are going to have a wonderful time!"

Suzannah's mouth was drawn into a tight line, her bottom lip quivering. Julia knew her fears were confirmed: something had gone terribly wrong, but she had no idea what it might be.

"What is it, Suzannah? Is someone not able to come? Because there is no problem if everyone can not be here. We do not need eight people to have a good time!"

"No," Suzannah said slowly, "everyone we invited is here."

"Then why the long face? Thee is going to spoil the evening!"

"I think thee should know..." her friend began, only to be interrupted by an all too familiar voice.

"Well, well, well...if it isn't little Miss Party Planner herself!" came Joseph's taunting greeting.

"Joseph Bell! What are you doing here?!" Turning quickly to find Jonathan, Julia repeated her question. "Jonathan, why is Joseph here?"

"Thought ya could get rid of me by not invitin' me, didn't ya?" Joseph said bitterly, a slight slur to his words. "Well, I decided to come without an official invitation from you! So whadaya think a that?"

"I think you can turn your horse around and go back to Washington this very minute!" Julia was not going to be intimidated by this loud oaf who threatened to ruin their evening.

"Julia," Jonathan quickly moved between his two friends. "It is dark, and it is hard traveling over the fresh snow with a horse—especially all the way to Washington. And besides, I do not think Joseph should travel alone this evening."

"What do you mean by that?" Julia was growing more suspicious by the moment. Just then Joseph pulled out a corked jug from under the sleigh.

"He thinks I've had a bit too much of this fine corn whiskey, Miss Julia. But I assured him I brought plenty for everyone! What's a little party wifout somthin' to get the blood circulatin'?!"

Julia's face was ashen as she gazed at the brown clay jug Joseph was waving in front of everyone. Each of the guests seemed to be frozen to their places in the snow, totally shocked by Joseph's behavior.

"Joseph," Jonathan began, "why not leave the jug here and then thee can join us in our evening's plans."

"See, Julia, Jonathan thinks it's just fine for me to come to your little party," Joseph took a step toward her. "Too bad you ain't as good a friend!"

"Jonathan," Julia said tightly, "May I please speak with you for a moment—alone!" She grabbed his hand and quickly led him to the other side of the meeting house. "Jonathan, how could you do this to me? How could you have told Joseph about our plans? Just so he could ruin it for us? He is nearly drunk, or hadn't you noticed? I will not have a drunken slanderer at my party!"

"I am sorry, Julia," Jonathan began. "Thee will never know how sorry I really am! I had no intention of inviting Joseph to the party...it just sort of slipped out!"

"You...you...you actually invited him to my party?! How could you have done such a thing?!" As her anger began to build, Julia didn't care if the others could hear her loud accusations. "I thought we were friends, Jonathan White, but I can see I was badly mistaken!" Julia was so angry she could hardly speak. "It just proves you can not trust anyone, especially a male!"

"I know I should have asked thee first," Jonathan continued, ignoring Julia's accusations, "but Joseph was going to be by himself again this break, and he seemed so lonely that I guess I just asked him to join us before I thought about it. I really felt sorry for him. Please try and understand the reason for my actions."

"So what is thee going to do about him now?" Julia asked hotly. "He has had too much to drink, and I do not want him going with us. It is getting late, and the parents will wonder where we are."

"I will take Joseph back to the Mendenhalls and get him some hot tea. Peter can drive the sleigh for the group, and perhaps by the time the rest of you arrive at the Mendenhalls, Joseph will be in better shape and we can join you for the rest of the stops."

"Why do you think you have to take this immature person anywhere?" Julia asked incredulously. "He can travel back to his boarding home if you do not think he can go to Washington. A good long sleep is what he really needs!"

"I will not embarrass Joseph by making him face the family he lives with during the school sessions in such a condition. They think he is in Washington, and they would be quite disappointed in his behavior. I owe it to him to do what I can to help him through this tough time."

"You do not owe him anything!" Julia protested.

"I know thee does not agree, but I can see now that this is the only way. The rest of you can have a good time, and I will take care of Joseph. If I get him in better condition, we could at least join thee at thy uncle's cabin."

"If you can not come alone, I do not want you to come at all!" Julia knew the tears were close, but she was not going to let Joseph Bell spoil her plans."

"All right," Jonathan said quietly, "I am sorry thee feels this way, but I hope thee has a successful party in spite of this small complication."

Julia quickly turned on her heel and strode back to the others. "In the sleigh, everyone!" she said firmly, determined not to let Joseph ruin the rest of the evening. "Peter, will you please take the reigns of the sleigh, and we will head to Sarah's before her parents think we have had an accident!" She tried to keep her voice calm and bright, but the others knew her confrontation with Jonathan had been less than pleasant.

As they climbed into the sleigh, everyone tried to be cheerful and carry on as planned, though there was a cloud of disappointment that seemed to hang heavily over them all. Julia was certain the evening was ruined.

Sarah's parents were quite happy to see the sleigh, fearing something had happened when the group had not arrived on schedule. Her mother had prepared a toasted bread with seasoned butter which was wonderful, though Julia's appetite had completely disappeared and she could only manage to eat a small bit. Sarah's mother chatted happily with the group, obviously excited to see Sarah included in the circle of friends around the fireplace. Maybe it was only her imagination, but Julia was surprised to notice the group seemed determined to carry on as if nothing had happened! Didn't anyone feel the same disappointment and anger with Joseph that she felt?

Cutting their time short in order to return to their schedule, the group thanked Sarah's parents and returned to the sleigh.

"That was lots of fun!" James commented to Julia as she sat beside him on the front bench of the sleigh. When Julia failed to reply, he continued. "I know thee feels badly about what Joseph tried to do, but we can still have a good time. Everything is planned, Julia, and it is not the same when you just sit and refuse to join in."

"Then perhaps you should just drop me off at Levi's before the next stop!" Julia said hotly, not enjoying the criticism James seemed to think she needed.

"Julia, we want thee to be with us! We need thee to use thy special talents for keeping the conversation challenging and fun!"

"Challenging? What does that mean?"

James was glad the moon had gone behind a cloud so Julia could not see the embarrassment on his face. She could be so much fun, but he didn't know how to tell her why he felt that way!

"Thee always teases everyone, and helps them laugh at themselves," James finally said, hoping Julia could understand what he meant.

"I am sorry if I am disappointing you!" Julia said angrily. "But you will just have to excuse me if I have other things on my mind this evening!"

Julia tried to snap out of her doldrums as they traveled from place to place, but it was especially difficult at the Mendenhalls. Mrs. Mendenhall pulled Julia aside when she saw her looking for Jonathan and Joseph.

"Jonathan thought it would be best if he took Joseph to the barn while the guests were here. He was so sorry Joseph tried to ruin the party, and he thought if you young people did not see Joseph, perhaps the evening would be more successful."

"That was quite noble of him," Julia said bitterly. "Would thee please tell Jonathan when we leave that we are having a splendid time?!" Julia knew she should not take her anger out on this fine woman, but she was tired of everyone trying to protect Jonathan.

When the party finally reached Levi and Anna's cabin, Julia realized how relieved she was that the evening would soon be over. She would no longer have to pretend to be having such a good time.

The group visited quietly in front of the welcome fire, though no one seemed eager to speak of serious matters. When the popcorn was gone Julia rose to put things away—signaling to the others that the party was over.

As Peter prepared to take the friends home, it was obvious by their farewells that everyone knew how disappointed Julia was with the evening's activities.

"I thank thee for the snow fest," Sarah said. "I know thee would have liked for it to have turned out differently, but we had a good time in spite of Joseph. I hope thee gives him a piece of thy mind when he is sober!"

"She is right, Julia," Suzannah added. "I know I had fun, and the others did too. Thee went to a lot of work, and I just wish I could have done something about Joseph!"

"You are all good friends," Julia told them as they climbed into the sleigh to return to the meeting house. "I will not forget the way you tried to cheer me this evening after Joseph's attempt to ruin our plans!"

Julia stood outside looking at the crystal clear sky filled with the myriad of stars in the milky way long after the sleigh was out of sight. In all the beauty of the heavens, where was God? The night had been perfect for her plans, yet one person had spoiled it all. Julia felt no Light of God within her, only the anger and disappointment of the ruined evening.

The person she was most disappointed in was not Joseph, however, but Jonathan. He had let her down and she would not forget it for a long time! It was still hard for her to believe he had chosen to help Joseph rather than stay and go with her and their friends. Were there no young men of integrity in this world?

When Julia finally returned to the cabin, she sat at the kitchen table for a long time, unable to get her mind off the events of the evening. She knew the story of what had happened would be spread throughout the academy and she would be the laughing stalk of the student body. But what could she have done differently? That was the question Julia kept asking herself over and over again. And the answer was always the same: nothing. There was nothing she could have done to avoid the problems of the evening, because it had been Jonathan who had betrayed them all by inviting Joseph to join them.

"Julia," Julia's head jerked up as Anna's quiet voice broke her thoughts. "How was the snow fest? I thought perhaps thy friends would want to stay here a bit longer than they did."

"Oh, Aunt Anna, it was the most awful night of my entire life!" Julia was soon crying, the tensions of the evening spilling with the tears she had kept under control until that moment.

Anna quickly moved to kneel at Julia's side, taking the sobbing girl in her arms. "It will be all right, my precious one, it will be all right." Anna kept her arms around her distraught niece until she felt her calming. "Now, tell me what happened so we can soothe thy troubled soul," Anna said softly.

First in halting phrases, then angry sentences Julia told Anna of the events of the evening, and of her disappointment in Jonathan.

"I can certainly understand thy hurt, dear one," Anna said with compassion. "It is truly unfortunate that Joseph came to thy party under the influence of hard liquor. To me, however, it is even a greater shame that this young man has fallen victim to the evils of strong drink."

"I do not even care about Joseph," Julia spat out. "It was no surprise to me that he came to spoil my plans, nor that he was nearly drunk. He has never been a trustworthy individual!"

"I know thee has never cared for this boy," Anna said quietly, "but I think thee can certainly understand his behavior in light of his terrible childhood."

"How does thee know about Joseph?" Julia asked, surprised that her aunt would know about this despised classmate.

"I am good friends with his boarding family, Julia, I thought thee knew that."

"I have never wanted to know a thing about Joseph Bell!" Julia practically spat out the words.

"And perhaps that is a bit of the problem thee has in accepting this boy and his struggles," Anna replied. "I know he has said some unkind things to thee, and his actions tonight were quite hurtful, but perhaps he does not know any other way to get thy attention!"

"Why would he want my attention?" Julia asked, her eyes widening in surprise.

"Perhaps he wishes thee would occasionally show him just a bit of interest. Perhaps he has never been taught the proper way to converse with a young woman, especially one he might secretly like."

Julia was silent for some time, her mind in a whirl over these new revelations.

"I suppose thee might have a point," Julia said with conviction, "but surely Joseph knows by now that I have no interest in any boy, and certainly not in him! I have never given him any reason to think otherwise."

"Would thee do one thing for me?" Anna asked, rising to return to bed.

"What?" Julia asked suspiciously.

"Would thee make Joseph a matter of prayer? Would thee ask God to reveal his perfect will for thee where Joseph is concerned? Perhaps asking for a bit of compassion for this young man might be just what both of thee needs!" Anna's smile took a bit of the sting from her words.

"Thee is right, Anna, I know I need more compassion. But whenever I spend any time at all with Joseph, anger is the only emotion I seem to feel!"

"I know," Anna said simply, giving Julia a final hug.

Sleep was far away as Julia lay on the unfamiliar bed and thought about everything her aunt had said. She knew she would make this a matter of prayer, knowing her attitude toward Joseph had been anything but Christ-like. Joseph Bell was a troubled young man, of that she was convinced. Though it would take a miracle to change his heart, Julia knew there was only One who could make miracles happen, and with God, all things were possible!

CHAPTER 13

THE CHANGE

Much to Julia's relief, when classes resumed on second day after the Christmas holiday no one mentioned Joseph's appearance at her Snow Fest. As Julia and Suzannah met after classes finished to walk to Kendall's Grocery, they wasted no time comparing notes on the day's conversations.

"Did anyone mention our party?" Julia asked cautiously, knowing students might say something to her friend rather than directly to her.

"Only one person," Suzannah said hesitantly.

"Let me guess," Julia said with scorn. "Could it have been Joseph?"

"Well, he did not actually talk about the party, but he did ask if he could speak with us after school." Suzannah looked quickly at her friend, hoping she would not be too upset.

"And you told him to find someone else to annoy, right?" Julia asked confidently.

"Uh..no..." Suzannah paused, then rushed to explain herself. "He seemed so nice today—like he might be sorry for what he did to you. I did not think it would hurt to at least hear what he had to say."

"Then *you* may speak with that drunkard and I will pick up the flour Aunt Anna asked me to get," Julia said emphatically.

"Julia," Joseph called out as Julia began to walk quickly toward Main Street, Suzannah hurrying to catch up. Pretending she hadn't heard, Julia whispered to Suzannah to keep walking and not acknowledge Joseph's call.

Realizing what was happening, Joseph began to sprint toward the two girls. "Julia, Suzannah, please...wait for me." When the girls didn't stop, Joseph reached for Julia's arm.

"Take your filthy hand off my arm!" Julia spat, turning to stare in disgust at her pursuer.

"I'm sorry," Joseph said softly, the first time Julia had ever heard him use that tone of voice.

"What do you want?" Julia asked coldly. "State your business and be on your way."

"Julia..." Suzannah began

"I can handle this, Suzannah!" Julia interrupted. "Go ahead, Joseph. Tell me how I should have invited you to my Snow Fest and then you would not have tried to spoil it for everyone. Tell me how you never would have brought that disgusting jug of whiskey to my Christian gathering if I had just included you in the group. Go ahead. Blame me for everything!"

"I know what I did was wrong, Julia," Joseph said quietly. "Jonathan helped me understand the reasons for my actions, and he helped me find the Light of Christ within myself. I have become a new person, Julia. I know you probably won't believe me, but I really am sorry for bringing the whiskey to the party. I guess I just wanted everyone to like me as much as they like Jonathan."

Julia looked more carefully at the young man who had just given a testimony to the Light of God within. Was he sincere? Or was this just another of his plots to win her favor?

"When did this happen?" Suzannah asked, admiration clearly evident in the look she gave Joseph.

"When I could hear all of you singing and having a good time as the sleigh approached the Mendenhalls, I sort of went crazy. I refused to go with Jonathan to the barn, and I was determined to finish wrecking your happy time." Joseph looked rather sheepish as he continued. "I expected Jonathan to wrestle me to the ground, tie me up and drag me to the barn. But do you know what he did instead?"

"What?" Suzannah asked quietly.

"He put his arms around me and began to pray for me. Can you imagine that? I was being such a trial to him, and he was asking God to forgive me! And then a strange thing happened...I began to lose the anger and hurt I had been feeling, and I asked Jonathan to forgive me for ruining the evening for him. He just grinned and said I needed to ask God for forgiveness, not him, and that I, too, could have the leading of the Inner Light."

"And then thee experienced the peace of God, right?" Suzannah asked.

"That is exactly what happened!" Joseph said happily. "I realize now how much my past has affected me, and how much I envied all of you who had mothers and fathers to care about you, and families to give you a sense of belonging. I am afraid my behavior has been a reflection of the deeply embedded hurt of my past, but I hope to make up for it in the future."

"That is wonderful!" Suzannah said warmly. Then realizing Julia had not said a single word since Joseph had begun, Suzannah turned to her friend. "Julia, is this not the most wonderful news?"

The look on Julia's face was anything but happy. "That is a nice story," she said icily, turning to Joseph. "You will have to forgive me if I have trouble believing the sudden change in your behavior!"

Julia could see the anger beginning to build in Joseph and was secretly congratulating herself for proving Joseph had not changed at all. "I hope some day you will see fit to forgive my actions, Julia," Joseph said under control. "I am certain only time will prove thy suspicions wrong."

So he won this encounter, Julia thought as she turned abruptly and continued on toward her original destination. We shall see how long it is before his sharp tongue proves my point!

Realizing Suzannah had not followed her, Julia stopped and turned to see what had happened to her companion. Much to her surprise she saw Suzannah still conversing with Joseph, laughter evident in both their faces. What could they be laughing about? Surely Suzannah would not tell this drunkard about the party he had tried to ruin. Were they laughing at her? No, Suzannah would never do that, even though Joseph would take great pleasure in humiliating her. I'll just go on by myself, she thought, resuming her walk. If the two of them were going to laugh at her, they deserved each other!

When Suzannah finally found Julia at Kendall's store, she was surprised at her response. "Why would thee think we would laugh at thee, Julia? Thee knows I would never do such a thing! Thee is my best friend in the whole world, and I would rather chop off my head than laugh at thee!!"

With such a ridiculous picture forming in her mind, that of Suzannah chopping off her head, Julia burst into laughter, quickly followed by Suzannah. "So tell me," Julia said when they both calmed down, "what exactly were the two of you laughing about?"

"If thee had stayed for just one moment instead of rushing off, thee would have known!" Suzannah was not about to tell her secret until she had properly punished Julia for walking off and leaving her.

"Then do not tell me!" Julia said, more than just a bit exasperated.

"All right, I will tell thee," Suzannah said with a laugh. "Joseph was telling me what happened after he and Jonathan had prayed together in the barn."

"I suppose Joseph saw a vision from God telling him to become a missionary to the Indians, or a traveling evangelist, or some other ridiculous notion!" Julia was rapidly growing tired of hearing of the miraculous change in Joseph Bell!

"No, nothing like that," Suzannah said rather matter-of-factly. "It is nothing serious at all. Did thee not see us doubled over with laughter? It hardly seems reasonable that we would be laughing over a call of God on Joseph's life!"

"Oh, all right. Just tell me what was so funny!" Julia implored.

"Well," Suzannah began, already a smile lighting her face. "It seems the jug of corn whiskey Joseph had brought to the party was nearly full, and after his conversion the two boys had to decide what to do with it. They did not want the Mendenhalls to know about that part of Joseph's little plan, knowing they themselves would never touch any kind of liquor, let alone allow it in their cabin. So Joseph and Jonathan decided to pour the whiskey over the fence between the barn and cabin."

"I do not understand how that could have caused the laughter I heard you two sharing just now!" Julia said skeptically.

"That wasn't the funny part! When they all got up the next morning they heard the strangest sound coming from out near the area where they had poured the whiskey. When they went out to see the source of the peculiar noise, they found the rooster trying in vain to crow and sit on the fence at the same time!"

"I still do not understand. Was there something wrong with the rooster? It hardly seems funny to me to be laughing about a sick bird!"

"The rooster was not sick, Julia, the rooster was drunk! It seems that when the boys poured the whiskey over the fence, a little of it fell into the hog trough. The rooster, finding the corn flavor appealing, helped himself until he became intoxicated. Mrs. Mendenhall thought she should butcher the poor bird and have chicken and dumplings for dinner. Fortunately for the rooster, the boys persuaded her to wait until the next day to see if he recovered!"

"That poor creature!" Julia exclaimed. "That was a cruel thing to do!"

"Julia," Suzannah was becoming a bit annoyed. "It was just an unfortunate accident. The boys did not purposely get the rooster intoxicated! And anyway, the creature I feel most sorry for is Joseph. I never thought about what it must have been like for him to be an orphan. Can thee imagine no mother or father to give thee advise and counsel? I think Joseph has done quite well in spite of never having a family or home."

"He had a home, it was just different from ours." Julia was not willing to give in to Suzannah where Joseph was concerned.

"Thee knows what I mean. I do not know why thee finds Joseph so difficult to like. I think he has the potential to be a fine citizen some day! And I intend to see that he is included in our activities from now on!"

"Is thee finished preaching, Suzannah?" Though Julia's words were lightly spoken, Suzannah knew she was being reprimanded, however gently.

"I have to be home in fifteen minutes, Julia. I just noticed how late it has become. I will see thee tomorrow, and Julia..." she paused, as if not quite certain how to phrase her request. "Would thee at least *try* to be nice to Joseph? I know he would really like that."

"Farewell, Suzannah. I refuse to make any promises except that I will see thee tomorrow," Julia said, turning to leave the grocery store with her purchase. She was not about to promise to be *nice* to Joseph. Suzannah would probably treat Joseph with such loving kindness that no one else would have to say a word!

Julia turned back to see if Suzannah had left and was surprised to see her friend walking with her head bowed. Probably praying, Julia thought disgustedly. What was happening to her friends— at least the ones she thought were her friends? Jonathan had betrayed her, Joseph had ruined her Snow Fest, and now Suzannah was siding with Joseph against her. She would just have to find some new friends! That would show all of them they could not treat her this way without consequence.

As Julia walked slowly down the frozen street, she glanced longingly at the hats in the millinery window. She was particularly fond of a small green felt hat, one she was sure would go nicely with her hair. She could see the store's owner through the window, and decided it certainly could not hurt to at least try 'her' hat on. Perhaps she would become a member of the Methodist faith some day and be in need of several hats. One never knew what the future held!

Having convinced herself that the reasons for her actions were well-founded, Julia cautiously opened the heavy door and walked into the gaily colored store. She knew her mouth dropped open, and she hoped the gasp she gave was not audible. Before her was an array of items unlike anything she had ever seen before. A wooden display case covered an entire wall and in it was every imaginable color and size of ribbon as well as feathers, lace, and dried flowers in an assortment of open trays.

"May I help you?" the owner asked, a smile playing at the corners of her mouth. She knew from the young lady's dress that she was a Quaker, and she also knew few Quakers would ever feel free to enter her establishment. This girl was obviously a bold one, having the courage to enter the store rather than just stand and gaze through the window as most on them did.

"I am sorry..." Julia began, obviously having been startled by the owner. "I was just wondering..." searching frantically for a reason why she had come in, Julia blurted the first thing that came into her mind. "Would you happen to need any extra help-after school, or on seventh day?"

Now why had she done that?! Levi would never allow her to work in the millinery, of all places! Not to mention her father! Just the thought of her father hearing she was employed at the millinery sent a chill down her spine. He would more than likely respond with a two hour lecture on the evils of fancy dress—not to mention accessories!

"Well," the woman said slowly, obviously taken back by Julia's question. "I do admire thy hair. Occasionally I have a customer with auburn hair who wishes me to design a hat for her. It would be nice to have a model such as yourself to experiment with various colors and accessories for the head covering. It is always easier to have a model than to try the various ideas on one's own head. Yes, I do believe I could use you occasionally. It would certainly not be every night, or even every Saturday. But if you were available on certain evenings, I could schedule those ladies who would like your services when you would be here."

"Yes...well..." now what was she to do? Julia looked carefully at the door and thought about bolting out as quickly as she had decided to come in. But then she thought about it. Why should she not have part-time employment if she so desired? She was certainly old enough, and this store owner must believe she could do the work or she would not have offered her the job.

But could she keep this between herself and the woman who stood waiting patiently for her answer? What would she say to Levi when she needed to come in to model on a seventh day? She knew she could find an excuse to return home after school on her own, especially when the days became warmer once again. But the seventh days might pose a difficult problem.

"Would you like a bit of time to think about it?" the owner finally asked. My name is Kathleen O'Donnell, and I own the store. I am sure you will want to discuss this more fully with your parents, and then give me your decision." The smile on this lovely woman's face told Julia she knew she had not consulted any adults before boldly asking for a job.

It took courage for a Quaker girl to even enter her store, not to mention inquire about employment. Yes, Kathleen thought, she really liked this red-haired beauty who stood before her, and she looked forward to teaching her about the millinery business— for she was certain Julia's answer would be 'yes.'

"Yes, a bit of time would be nice," Julia finally stammered, certain she would probably never set foot in the store again!

"May I have your name, please?" Kathleen asked patiently.

"Uh...uh..." what should she do? What if this woman knew Levi or Anna? What if Kathleen told her aunt and uncle about her inquiry about a job? On the other hand, if she did not give her name, this woman with the fine clothing would know for certain there was a problem.

"Julia, Julia Jones" she said simply, deciding truth would probably be the best approach.

"Might you be related to Mr. Jones who owns the grocery at the end of Main?" Kathleen asked curiously.

"No," Julia answered, relieved that this woman had no idea who she belonged to. "My father is a doctor in Salem and my mother is at home." Expecting a baby, she wanted to say, but somehow felt embarrassed at the revelation.

"Fine, Julia. I will look forward to hearing from you. Perhaps you will let me know by the end of the week? I do have one customer who would be delighted to have you model a new design for her as soon as possible."

"Kathleen....would you do me one more good deed?" Julia asked, unsure whether or not making another request was wise, but feeling the need to keep this matter between the two of them.

"If I can," the woman said with a gentle smile.

"Could thee—I mean you—not mention this to anyone? I mean, if anyone should ask about my being here, that is?"

"It will be our secret, Julia, but please get your parents' permission before beginning to work for me."

"Yes, well, I will try. But with my parents living in Salem, I might have difficulty reaching them."

"In that case, perhaps your boarding family could give the consent."

"Yes, but my boarding family might not approve of my working here, though I will certainly try to gain their permission." Julia knew she would do no such thing, but it did not seem like such a falsehood since she would never be entering this establishment again.

"Let me know what transpires," Kathleen said brightly.

"I will," Julia called, quickly opening and closing the door as she made her escape.

Now what had she done? Levi would never approve, in fact he would be terribly disappointed to learn she had even considered such employment. Anna might understand, but she would never side with her niece against her husband.

Her parents would *never* approve, of that she was absolutely certain. Rebecca was totally involved in preparing for her new child, sewing and knitting numerous items for the anticipated baby. Charles would be both angry and disappointed, certain to lecture her and possibly even refuse to let her continue her education! David might be on her side, but he was in Chicago and of no help whatsoever.

It was settled. There would be no job. She would simply tell Kathleen she had not received permission and did not want to go against her aunt and uncle's wishes. And yet...her mind kept returning to the inside of that wonderful store, her fingers longing to let the ribbons run through them, to touch the fine lace and delicate flowers. And once more what seemed like reasonable arguments surfaced: why should women not be clothed as well as the birds of the air? And if the apostle Paul said women should keep their heads covered, surely that was what he meant. Who were Friends to disagree with the great apostle?

Julia was glad she had told Levi she would walk home alone, feeling the need for some fresh air and exercise.

The arguments for and against working in the millinery swirled about in Julia's mind. Her head was still spinning as she walked through the cabin's front door, barely greeting the others and immediately seeking the comforts of her room.

After several minutes Anna's soft knock seemed to break through the turmoil in Julia's mind.

"Come in," Julia said, not moving from the bed where she had collapsed in a heap.

"Is thee ill?" Anna came quickly to the bedside, her hand upon Julia's forehead in one swift motion.

"No, no, I am fine," Julia responded, realizing she would have to somehow make her actions support her words. "I suppose I am a bit tired after my walk home. The snow was deeper than I thought, and I had a difficult time staying in the sleigh tracks."

"Then I would suggest thee join us for the evening meal and retire early." Anna rose to leave, then turned once again to the still body. "Thee knows thee can talk to me about any difficulties that might come thy way."

"I thank thee, Aunt Anna. I know thee is a good listener, especially after the problems Joseph caused last week. I know thee is always ready to help if I have a problem. And I thank thee."

Still not convinced there was nothing bothering her niece, Anna left knowing Julia would talk to her only after exhausting all other possibilities on her own.

Julia roused herself and splashed a bit of water on her face from the pitcher in her room. She would be cheerful and give her second family no reason to believe there was any problem in her life. And for all purposes there *was* no problem, just a dilemma. She would think about her decision at night after she retired, and forget about it during the day.

Having thus made her resolution, she quickly went to join the others. She would find in the days to come, however, that the decision would be impossible to package and keep tucked away until the end of the day when she was alone with her thoughts. In fact, it followed her day and night until she finally knew what she had to do.

CHAPTER 14

MEETING LIGHT

Wishing the day were over, Julia quickly looked out the window as she sat in religion class on second day. Noting the falling snow, her spirits began to lift as the possibility of an early dismissal crossed her mind. It had never happened in this session, but she had heard other students tell of the principal ringing the bell early to allow students time to return to their places of residence before the snow began to drift. Yes, an early dismissal was just what she needed.

Julia's thoughts quickly wandered to her after school mission...giving Kathleen O'Donnell her answer about working in the millinery. It had been a difficult decision, but once Julia had made up her mind she refused to question the rightness or wrongness of it. Getting out of school early would give her an excuse to leave the building before Suzannah or Jonathan or obnoxious Joseph had a chance to engage her in conversation.

Glancing once more out the streaked window where snow flakes had melted on the glass and trickled down in rivulets, Julia saw with disappointment that the snow was now falling in gigantic flakes, a signal that the precipitation would soon end—along with hopes of an early dismissal.

"Julia, would thee please recite the twenty-third Psalm for the class?"

Julia's head snapped up so fast her neck hurt. "I am sorry....I suppose I was not listening. Would you—I mean thee—kindly repeat the question?" Julia knew she was blushing, and was irritated that she had allowed herself to fall into the same misfortune as the last time her mind wandered during class.

"I did not ask a question, Julia, I asked thee to repeat the twenty-third Psalm. Is that too much to ask of a student in my religion class?"

"No, I would be happy to recite for thee." Standing and looking straight ahead at the chalk board, Julia quickly recited the familiar passage. It was one she had learned many years earlier as she had sat on her mother's lap and listened to Bible stories and learned scripture verses.

"That was quite a fine job, Julia," the professor responded when she was finished. "Now suppose you tell the class what is in YOUR 'Valley of the Shadow of Death.'"

Looking puzzled, Julia's mind raced to find the hidden meaning in this man's words. What 'Valley of the Shadow of Death' could he possibly be referring to? Should she ask for clarification, or take a chance and hope she answered the question in a manner suitable to the instructor?

"I am sorry, Mr. Hoskins," Julia finally admitted. "I was not listening to the discussion and do not know how to respond to your question."

Julia quickly sat down, determined she would *never* be caught in this situation again as long as she were a student. As her fellow classmates fought to contain their laughter, the professor quickly quieted the class.

"Now, class, you see the importance of listening. Julia is not the only one who has difficulty keeping her mind on her lessons;

she just happens to be the one I called on today. Because so many of you seem preoccupied with the weather, I think it would be best if I assigned a bit of extra homework to help all of you keep your minds crisp. Tomorrow you will have the first ten Psalms memorized to perfection. Are there any questions?"

The students knew groaning or complaining would only increase their workload, so silence followed the announced homework. Julia felt as though every eye in the class were focused on her, and she realized she would never hear the end of this from her classmates.

As the bell rang for dismissal, Julia quickly exited the room, relieved that her desk was near the door. If she thought her trials were over for the day, however, she was sadly mistaken. Suzannah was anxiously waiting for her when she entered the dining area.

"Whatever happened in religion class today?" she quickly asked. "Everyone is talking about the terrible assignment they have because thee had problems with a question. That does not really sound like thee, Julia."

"I was not the only person not listening," Julia said defensively. "Mr. Hoskins said there were several students not paying attention and that is why he gave the extra homework. And it is not a terrible assignment! You know the Psalms are short. Ten Psalms is like two or three chapters in one of the gospels, and we have certainly had that much to learn in one night."

"Well, all I know is that everyone that was in religion class was really upset with thee when they came into biology. I doubt if they are going to look at it quite the way thee is," Suzannah said doubtfully.

"Suzannah, may we please speak of something else, for goodness sake. We have not seen each other for three days. Surely we can think of some topic of conversation more pleasant than this!"

Suzannah seemed to be relieved to move on to the happenings of the two days the girls had been apart, telling Julia amusing tales of her younger siblings and their first attempts at making snow balls. Julia thought about sharing her job prospect and the difficult time she had had making a decision, but for some reason she just *knew* Suzannah would not understand.

"So," Suzannah asked as they walked from the auditorium when the dinner break was over, "will thee be able to shop at Kendalls with me after school? Mother sent a list of items for me to pick up for her."

"I am sorry," Julia said slowly, trying to think of how to keep Suzannah from becoming suspicious of her plan to go to O'Donnell's Millinery. "I have...a...other commitments after school."

Totally misinterpreting her words, Suzannah said teasingly, "Oh, meeting Jonathan, is thee?!"

"No, I am not meeting that traitor," Julia said, her voice laced with irritation. "I have other business to attend to."

"Like what?"

Suzannah could certainly be persistent!

"Something personal." As soon as the words were out of Julia's mouth she regretted them.

By this time the two girls were at the door of Suzannah's next class, and she turned and walked into the room without so much as a farewell. Suzannah would just have to be angry, Julia thought. She simply could not tell her friend about the millinery...how would she ever explain even being in the store, not to mention asking for a job?!

Breathing a sigh of relief when none of her friends were in sight at the close of the school day, Julia quickly hurried to Main Street. As she approached the millinery, she glanced in all directions to make certain no one would see her enter the store. Seeing that the street was vacant, she quickly entered the establishment that had given her so much pleasure just a few days earlier.

"Julia!" Kathleen exclaimed as Julia quietly closed the door and moved to the side of the store where a passerby would be unable to see her through the window. "I had not expected to see you until the end of the week! I hope this is a good sign that you have decided to come and work for me!"

Glancing once again at the wonderful sights in the display case, Julia knew she had made the right decision. "Yes, Kathleen, I would like to model for you. But I can only promise one night a week, and an occasional seventh—I mean Saturday. My school work takes up a great deal of time and my Uncle Levi does not want me to get behind in my assignments."

"I am quite certain that will be sufficient time, Julia. I am also glad you got your uncle's permission. It is important that adults be consulted when young people make important decisions such as this."

Julia looked at the floor, suddenly ashamed that she had implied her uncle's consent. Assuming Julia to be somewhat ill at ease, Kathleen quickly sought to make her new employee feel at home. Taking her arm, she began a tour of the store, showing Julia the various materials used in hat making and explaining the steps she went through in making a new creation for a customer. As soon as Julia felt enough time had passed, she told Kathleen she was expected at her uncle's and that she must be going.

"I have a patron coming Thursday, Julia. Would you be free to stop by after school and model for her?" Kathleen asked, sensing a sudden tenseness in her young assistant.

"Yes, that would be fine," Julia said quickly, anxious to be on her way, hoping there was no reason she could not come that day.

"Perhaps we can make you a hat, too," Kathleen added. "It can be a bonus for working here."

"That would be nice," Julia answered, thrilled at the thought of helping design her own hat, even though she knew there would be no place for her to wear such finery. She would have to be creative to even find a place to hide such an article from her aunt and uncle.

As Julia quickly exited the store, she was startled when she ran head on into a man who looked nearly as shocked as she.

"Julia!" Jonathan exclaimed. "I am sorry—did I harm thee?"

"No," Julia tried to laugh, but her word simply came out in a squeak.

"I thought thee left right after school," Jonathan said, puzzled. Then glancing at the store from which Julia had come rushing out, he asked the obvious question. "What is thee doing at the millinery?"

Deciding there was no story she could invent to fool Jonathan, she simply told him the truth. "I am working here part time." Taking the initiative, Julia looked Jonathan boldly in the eye, daring him to challenge her decision.

"I do not understand. What does thee mean by 'working'?"

"What do you think I mean?" Julia asked crossly. "I work here. Work. I model hats that Kathleen is making for her customers." Again she looked squarely at Jonathan.

"But Julia, thee knows how Friends feel about frivolity. Surely thee does not believe fancy head decorations are acceptable to God!"

"And I suppose thee speaks for God?" Julia angrily challenged.

Jonathan was slow to answer, carefully weighing his words. "I would never be so bold as to say I speak for God. I do believe, however, that He makes known his will for us through the Scriptures and the Light within."

"And what would thee say if I told thee I had the confirmation of the Light within before accepting this job?" Julia asked boldly.

"Then I would say thee had best find the source of thy Light," Jonathan said simply, turning to leave.

"And just what is that supposed to mean?" Julia said, grabbing Jonathan's arm to prevent his departure.

"I am sorry, Julia, but I must be on my way to the Mendenhalls. They will be expecting me." When Julia continued to grasp his arm, he gently removed her hand and strode briskly down the quickly darkening street.

Realizing she herself would have a great deal of explaining to do if she were any later, Julia quickly turned to the west and began the trek to Levi's. The more she thought about Jonathan's words, the angrier she became. How dare he think he spoke for God?! And how dare he suggest the Light within came from some source other than God himself? Jonathan was becoming just a bit too full of himself! 'Self-righteous' was the term which immediately came to her mind. She would have to do a little Bible study on her own and find some verses which warned of the consequences of thinking too highly of oneself! Jonathan White wasn't the only one who could preach from the Word of God!

Julia was looking forward to worship the next First Day, anxious to seek the Spirit in the quiet. Though she usually found her mind wandering during the long periods of silence, today she was hoping for some revelation that would put Jonathan in his place.

As Julia arrived in the sleigh with Levi's family, the Mendenhalls were approaching from the east, making it impossible for Julia to ignore Jonathan as he leaped from the sleigh.

"Greetings, Julia," he called cheerfully, acting as though their encounter in front of the millinery had never happened.

"Greetings, Jonathan. And farewell." Julia quickly turned toward the door to the women's side of the meeting house, determined to avoid any further words with this righteous 'boy' she had once thought a friend.

"Thee was a bit brief with thy friend Jonathan," Anna chided, catching up with her niece a few steps before they entered the plain wooden structure.

"I had my reasons," Julia said simply, glad they were at the door where all conversation would cease.

The women in the room were sitting on the straight benches, most with heads bowed in preparation for worship. Julia felt a pang of guilt as she looked at the rows of plain bonnets on most of the heads present. She herself was wearing a black bonnet, determined to keep up the appearances of a Friend dedicated to the principles of George Fox and other early Friends leaders. It was only in her heart where she felt the rebellion against the traditional clothing.

As she sat in the silence, Julia once again remembered her prayer of commitment at Yearly Meeting. Why had she not felt the leading of the Spirit since that day? She had thought that attending the academy would help her find God's calling for her life. Instead she had encountered boys like Joseph and trials like the snow fest disaster. Julia listened as a number of women rose to share at the prompting of the Spirit, though none spoke directly to her need. Just when Julia thought the elders would rise from the facing bench to announce the end of worship, Martha Mendenhall, one of the most respected members of the Meeting, slowly rose to speak.

"I am concerned," she began, "for the welfare of our young members. The Spirit has revealed to me this morning that there are women among us in this very meeting who are being led astray; women who desire the things of the world more than the things of God. I would beseech each of thee to petition the Lord on behalf of these young women, that they would once again return to paths of righteousness and seek forgiveness for their sins."

Martha sat down, and Julia felt a tension in the room that had not been present before. Had Martha been speaking directly to her through the Spirit? She knew Friends believed one could receive a message from the Holy Spirit through another person. But why should she think the message was just for her? There were three or four other young women present, including Suzannah and Harriet. Harriet! She was probably the one for whom the message was intended! After her disgusting display that night at the wedding shower, surely God would want to send a message to her! She knew of several young men who had been taken by this young creature's charms; surely that would warrant a reprimand from the Holy Spirit.

Julia considered the message Martha had spoken in meeting most of the way home. Her main concern was discovering which young woman had not been giving God her first love. It certainly could not have been herself, she decided quickly. She had not missed a single worship since arriving in tenth month, and outside of an occasional lapse from the plain language, she had followed the customs and beliefs of Friends to the best of her ability. Her work at the millinery was certainly not a love, since she had only worked one afternoon, and then for only an hour at the most.

Feeling quite satisfied with herself, Julia began to chat with the twins, laughing quietly as they told of watching a mouse play during worship in the men's room. Once again Julia felt blessed to be staying with relatives during her boarding term rather than with a strange family. She had really enjoyed getting to know her cousins and helping them learn the English language. They loved hearing the stories she invented for them as she tucked them into bed each night.

The rest of the Sabbath passed quietly, each member of the family resting or reading a book of some sort during the afternoon. In the evening the family gathered around the table for the nightly Bible reading and prayer time. When Levi had finished reading the fifteenth chapter of John, Julia volunteered to close with prayer. Levi looked at her strangely, as if totally unprepared for her offer. "Well, thee knows we usually wait for the Spirit, Julia. If thee does indeed feel God's leading, I am certain we would all be blessed by thy words."

Julia sheepishly bowed her head, realizing she had failed to even consider the leading of the Spirit. In fact, now that she thought of it, she had not really even felt the Presence of the Spirit during worship that morning. She had been so busy trying to figure out which young person might be sinning that she had failed to enter into worship herself! Quickly bowing her head,

Julia asked for forgiveness, then tried to listen for a message from the Holy Spirit. When thoughts of the millinery began to enter her mind, she forcefully cast them aside, already having convinced herself it was God's will for her to work for Kathleen. She also thought about Jonathan and his lofty attitude, and quickly asked God to help this young man see the error of his ways. Julia did not pray aloud, feeling somewhat humbled by her uncle's earlier words. After Levi closed the session with a lengthy prayer, Julia quickly asked to be excused to go to her room.

Though Julia's homework had been done Friday evening when she returned from school, she wanted to work on her recitations for religion class. She was determined to show her professor she could indeed do the work assigned. Though many Friends thought doing any kind of work on First Day was breaking the Sabbath, Julia personally felt a little time with the books helped one get a start on the new week. Somehow she did not think Uncle Levi would understand, thus the request to return to her room.

"I hope thee awakens refreshed and ready for the new week tomorrow." Uncle Levi said as Julia rose to leave.

I will be ready, Julia thought determinedly. No teacher will ever make me the example of the class again. Julia crawled into bed, silently repeating the verses she had learned. Tomorrow she would confront Jonathan with his behavior. Perhaps he would be wanting to seek her forgiveness for his rudeness and condescending manner.

Tomorrow..tomorrow...she whispered quietly, finally drifting off to sleep.

CHAPTER 15

EVANGELISTIC MEETING

The 'tomorrow' Julia fell asleep thinking about never happened because three feet of drifting snow prompted Levi to declare a holiday from school. "I would not think of sending my horse into weather like that!" he said when returning from the barn where he had gone to hitch up the sleigh.

The one day holiday turned into three as the snow seemed like it would never quit. By the time classes resumed, Julia was so glad to be out of the cabin that she chatted with everyone— Suzannah, Jonathan, Peter, Harriet, Sarah, and even Joseph. She quickly forgot her anger with Jonathan's attitude and her quest to find the 'sinner' of the group.

The rest of the winter session began to fly by like the trains passing through Pleasant Plain on their way to Ottumwa. Modeling for Kathleen at the millinery had taken very little of Julia's time—even less than she would have liked. Fortunately, there were no more encounters with any of her friends outside the millinery, and as far as she knew no one other than Jonathan was aware of her secret employment.

Julia was startled to look out the window of the cabin one morning and see a robin pecking the now barren path to their cabin where just a few weeks earlier snow had stood several feet deep. It was already the beginning of the fourth month, and the winter school session would be dismissed in a few weeks.

"I do not know what I will do when you return to Salem," Anna said one morning a few days later as Julia came to join the family for the first meal of the day. "Thee has been such a wonderful help with Timothy and Andrew. They are going to miss thee nearly as much as I!"

Julia looked down at her plate, struggling to keep the rush of emotion she was feeling from spoiling the meal.

"I will miss thee all a great deal," she finally said when she felt in control again. "Thee has been like—no thee *has* been a family to me, and I am looking forward to another year with thee."

Julia thought she caught a strange look pass from Levi to Anna, but when neither one said anything, she decided it must have been her imagination. Just then the twins entered the room, quickly running to give Julia a squeeze, one on either side. She had long ago established the rule that there was enough of her to go around and one boy could not have her all to himself. It had saved many arguments between the two lively characters who felt more like brothers than cousins.

"Juwea?" Timothy queried. "Will dee lib wif us forever?"

Julia laughed. "I wish I could, Timothy, but when school is over I have to return to Salem. But I promise to come back in the fall."

"Oh boy!" Andrew chimed in. "We wike da 'tories dee tells!"

"Eat your oatmeal, boys," Anna admonished, "before it gets cold."

Giving each of the boys a hug, Julia rose to leave and get ready for the walk to school with Levi. They had to leave early to avoid the treacherous mud that now covered most of the familiar path to town. Julia disliked the spring thaws immensely, and she couldn't wait for the earth to dry out.

"Julia," Levi began as soon as they were on their way, "Anna and I have been going to share with thee a most difficult decision we have recently had to make, but neither of us has had the courage to do so."

Immediately Julia's mind was in a whirl, sensing the next words were going to be ones she would not want to hear. She braced herself, keeping her eyes on the muddy path before them.

"Julia, thee knows how much we have enjoyed having thee live with us these past months. Thee has become a member of the family."

"I feel the same way about thee and thy family, Uncle Levi," Julia said warmly, feeling a bit better about the conversation.

"Thy father has been most generous with the sum he has sent each month for thy room and board. But the boys are getting bigger and our expenses are increasing. I know Chester pays his teachers as generously as possible once the expenses of the academy are taken care of, but some months it is less than five dollars."

Julia was shocked. Five dollars for a month's work? Levi was surely worthy of a higher sum than that! "Levi, thee deserves to be paid a fair wage!" Julia burst out, hoping her uncle knew she was speaking for the other students as well as herself.

Levi smiled, knowing Julia would respond in such a manner. "The problem is," he said quietly, "I can not figure out how we will survive with three young ones to care for."

For a moment Julia was silent, not certain she had heard correctly.

"What does thee mean by *three* young ones?" she finally asked.

"Anna is expecting a child the ninth month," he said simply.

Julia was silent, thinking not only of Anna but also of her mother who had to be quite large with child by now. She had not seen her parents since the eleventh month, for the one time Levi had planned to take her to Salem to see her family, a terrible snow had prevented their journey.

"Julia? Is thee all right?" Levi finally asked after there had been no reply from his niece following his announcement.

"Yes, I was just thinking about Mother." Then she added quickly, "I am happy for thee and Anna. Perhaps thee will have a girl for the boys to play with."

"Just so the child is healthy. That is all Anna and I really care about. Except for the money, of course. We have prayed diligently for God's leading in this difficult situation, and we finally believe our prayers have been answered."

Julia was instantly alert.

"I have received word that I have been accepted as a professor at William Penn College in Oskaloosa."

"I do not understand...how could they even know about thee? Is Chester trying to be rid of thee? Because I have a lot of friends who will speak to him on your behalf!" Just the thought of the principal trying to get rid of her uncle made Julia's blood boil.

"No, no," Levi laughed. "When we were in Oskaloosa last ninth month for Yearly Meeting, I had a chance to meet with the president of the college. When I told him I taught at the academy, he asked if I had ever thought about teaching college students. He said they were beginning to see more and more students enroll in their school, and they had a need for good instructors. He also convinced me that the school was not likely to be closed any time in the near future since they were already in their sixth year. As we finished our conversation, he encouraged me to think about the possibility of joining their faculty.

"I quickly forgot his words until Anna became fairly certain she was with child. I decided it would not hurt to at least write to the college, expressing my interest in a teaching position. Remember when I took the train to Oskaloosa last month?"

"Yes..."

"Well, the reason for the trip was to meet with the faculty and sign a contract for next year."

"I am really happy for thee," Julia said brightly, then realized what the decision was going to mean for her. "When will thee move?" She asked quietly.

"Probably some time during the eighth month. The college will pay for the train fare to search for a home, just as they paid for my journey last month. I hope thee and thy family will help us move unless thee is too busy with thy new brother or sister!"

"I am sure Father and I can help, even if Mother can not leave the baby," Julia said firmly.

"I have made arrangements for thee to board with the Mendenhalls next year, if thee would like. All of their children have left home, and they have plenty of extra space for thee."

The Mendenhalls? Surely Levi was joking. How could she and Jonathan both stay at the Mendenhalls? Julia could hardly bear to visit with her one time friend these days. How would they ever live under the same roof?

"As I said before, Julia, it was a very difficult decision for us to make. We are excited about the city, though. Oskaloosa is several times larger than Pleasant Plain, and we hope to be able to secure a nice home close to the college."

Julia was no longer hearing Levi's words as her mind was still dwelling on living in the same home as Jonathan. She would simply decline the offer and search for a boarding home herself.

"I am sorry, Levi, what did thee say?"

"I said, I am sorry we will not have thy company next year."

"Well, maybe I will apply to William Penn myself!"

Levi laughed, hoping he didn't embarrass his niece. "I do not believe thee has enough schooling yet to be accepted, though thee might certainly take the entrance exam if thee would like."

Realizing her uncle was probably right, Julia laughed too. "Thee need not worry, Levi; I *will* finish my schooling at the academy. But some day I just might be in one of your college classes!"

"I just believe you might!" he said with admiration. Levi appreciated the tenacity with which Julia attacked life, and he knew she would accomplish whatever she set her mind to do!

News of Levi's departure soon spread among the students, and it was the topic of conversation during the noon hour.

"Your uncle is the best teacher I have ever had!" Suzannah said emphatically. "I wonder who will replace him?"

"Probably some young teacher who does not have half the knowledge Levi has!" Sarah added.

"Not to change the subject," Harriet chimed in, having joined the group at the last minute, "but have any of you heard about the evangelist that will be in Richland next week?"

"Who is it? A Friend?"

One by one the group of friends began to ask Harriet about the traveling evangelist.

"All I know," Harriet replied, "is that several families are going to make the trip next sixth day, and they are going to gather at the meeting house here in Pleasant Plain at four o'clock in the afternoon. I suppose there will be room for a few extras if any of thee wish to attend."

"I have never been to an evangelistic meeting," Joseph said, then added with a laugh, "of course, until a few months ago I had never been in a Friends meeting, either."

"Have any of you ever attended a revival service?" Julia asked, wondering if she should try to go or try to *avoid* going!

"I have been to a few," Jonathan admitted. "There was an evangelist at West Branch a few years ago."

"What was it like?" Sarah wanted to know.

"It was so different from the silence that I sat in amazement most of the night," Jonathan admitted. "There was a lot of singing together, a few testimonies, and then the evangelist started preaching like nothing I have ever heard before. He was a powerful speaker and there were many members who came forward to the kneeling bench to pray for forgiveness of their sins when he finished the altar call!"

"I am not certain whether that sounds like fun or torture!" Julia said lightly. "I think confessing one's sins is a private matter. I do not believe I care to have anyone looking at me kneeling with sinners!"

"Julia!" Joseph laughed. "We are all sinners—even you!"

"I do not believe *you*, of all people, should be accusing *me* of sinning!"

"All right, you two, quit arguing!" Jonathan quickly intervened. "So how many of you would like to go to the service? It might be fun to go as a group. I could probably get the Mendenhall's large carriage and we could travel together in it to Richland."

Thoughts of the last group gathering silently flashed through Julia's mind. As if reading her thoughts, Joseph quickly spoke. "I promise to be on my best behavior, and I will even leave the corn whiskey at home!"

Julia refused to join in the group's laughter. "I, for one, think perhaps you should stay home with the whiskey!"

"Julia, why must thee always be critical where Joseph is concerned?" Jonathan quickly reprimanded his friend. "Thee, of all people, should have noticed the change in him these past few months."

"I am sorry, Joseph. You will have to forgive me if I am not quite as quick to forget as your friend Jonathan here."

"I am sorry too, Julia. I really have tried to seek the Light within, and live my life in such a way as to please God."

Knowing she had opened her mouth one too many times, Julia sought to bury the hatchet. "All right, Joseph, I admit you have been nicer the past few months."

"Was that an apology?" Suzannah asked teasingly.

Julia quickly picked up her books and started to class. Let them carry on themselves. She had tried to be nice to Joseph and they thought she was trying to apologize!

Levi announced to the family a few days later that he believed they would try to go to the evangelistic services in Richland on sixth day. Julia was glad the decision was made for her, having struggled with whether or not she wanted to attend.

"I hear a group of young people are going to travel together in the Mendenhall's carriage," Levi added. "I suppose Julia will want to travel with her friends."

"Well, I would just as soon travel with thee," Julia said.

"Nonsense!" Anna spoke up. "Thee should be with thy friends since school will soon be finished and thee will not see each other for a long time."

And so plans were arranged for the group to attend. She only hoped they would at least have a better time than they had had at the Snow Fest.

The carriage of laughing young people stopped in front of Levi's cabin the evening of the service, Jonathan having earlier offered to stop for Julia since Levi's cabin was on the road to Richland. Everyone was sitting on the back seats leaving only the space up front beside Jonathan.

"Greetings!" everyone called, and their lightheartedness soon eased Julia's apprehensions. She quickly took Jonathan's offered hand and climbed up beside him, not unaware of the firm way he gripped her hand, seeming to hold it a bit longer than necessary.

As soon as they were on their way, Julia turned to look back at the others. Suzannah and Joseph were sitting in the back, Peter, Sarah and Harriet were in the middle. Julia felt a warmth inside as she thought about these friends she had made this school year. All of them had their faults, yet she could not imagine what she was going to do all summer without them. Even her disappointment in Jonathan seemed unimportant now.

"What thoughts are going through thy pretty head?" Jonathan teased, noticing the half-smile that seemed to have come from nowhere.

"I was just thinking about how I am going to miss all of you when I go back to Salem."

"It will be difficult, but most of us will be back for at least part of next year."

"Hey Julia!" Joseph called from the back. "Want a swig o' whiskey?"

Julia whirled around just in time to see the five young people behind her doubling over with laughter. "Just teasing!" Joseph laughed, holding both empty hands over his head to prove his point.

Julia laughed, realizing they had planned this little encounter before stopping for her. "All right, you win! I promise to never again mention the jug of whiskey!"

From that point on the trip went quickly, sometimes the whole group talking together, sometimes conversations occurring between those sitting next to each other. Julia was happy to be sitting beside Jonathan, realizing perhaps she had judged him a bit too harshly after their encounter in front of the millinery.

Julia hated to admit it, but she was sorry when they saw the town of Richland up ahead. The days were getting longer and it was just now beginning to get dark. The sunset had been beautiful as they headed westward, everything seemingly perfect for their outing.

Jonathan stopped the carriage in front of the meeting house so his passengers would not have to walk through the streets that were still a bit muddy. "Let's wait outside for Jonathan," Julia suggested, as he drove the carriage down the street looking for a safe place to tie the rig. Men and women would be sitting together tonight, the partition having been removed so the evangelist would not have to give the same message twice.

The meeting house was nearly full when Jonathan returned from taking care of the carriage, and it seemed strange to Julia to be sitting in a meeting house with men. She recognized many Friends from Quarterly Meeting sessions, though there were a number of people of other faiths present. And while Julia and her friends were used to silence when entering for worship, on this night there were a number of quiet conversations being conducted, though the crowd became still when the evangelist entered. At least Julia assumed he was the evangelist. The man was stopping to shake hands and give an occasional hug to those waiting to hear him. At last he reached the front of the crowd and the service began. Julia could almost feel an excitement in the air as the evangelist began to lead them in an upbeat tune she had never heard before.

It was only the beginning of a night Julia would never forget!

CHAPTER 16

HOLINESS

Julia could never in all her sixteen and a half years have imagined the happenings that were about to transpire in the Richland Friends Meeting House where she sat with her friends. She felt more than just a little apprehensive, wondering if perhaps this 'evangelistic service' was too far a departure from the traditions of Friends.

The Richland Meeting's clerk of Ministry and Counsel rose to introduce the evangelist. "Friends," he began earnestly, "I pray none of thee will leave this meeting tonight without having experienced the power of God. Our Friend and evangelist, Lawrie Tatum, is filled with the Holy Spirit, having been sanctified in '73 and called to evangelize the nation. Open your hearts to the message he has and to the leading of the Holy Spirit."

Julia noticed the look of admiration on the face of the clerk as he sat down and waited for the events of the evening to unfold. She wondered how this Lawrie Tatum had managed to have such a powerful influence in such a short time. Her thoughts were quickly interrupted when the evangelist jumped to his feet and began walking between the rows of benches now filled with anxious worshipers.

"Friends, you are going to witness a miracle tonight—no, you are going to witness MANY miracles before this night is over! The Spirit of God is upon this place and God wants to do a mighty work among us." No sooner had the last word been spoken than Lawrie began to sing a song that Julia, belonging to a silent meeting, had never heard. To her astonishment, many of those present began to sing with him, a few even standing and clapping their hands. Julia felt a slight embarrassment, not certain whether she should be appalled at the forwardness of these Friends, or allow the excitement of the song to move her. The words spoke of the "blood of Jesus cleansing all our sins." In spite of the stillness of her body, Julia felt her heart beating just a bit faster as she became caught up in the quick and lively rhythm of the song.

One song followed another until nearly everyone in the room was involved with the music. Some clapping, many singing, a few waving their hands in the air. Julia quickly glanced down the row of Friends she had come with. Somehow she was not surprised to see Joseph singing some of the words while his hands clapped to the rhythm. What did surprise her was Suzannah, who was nearly as active as Joseph. Harriet, too, seemed to be enjoying the music, her hands clapping and her body swaying to the beat. Only Peter and Jonathan remained seated like herself. The three of them were probably the only true Friends in the gathering, she thought with a bit of disgust. How could these true believers of George Fox engage in such behavior?

After a number of hymns and choruses had been sung, Lawrie returned to the front of the room, head bowed. He began to pray in a loud and somewhat strange sounding voice, pleading for God to anoint him with the power of the Holy Spirit. Julia continued to wrestle with the issues at hand. Would God possibly do what this man asked? Could one be filled with the Holy Spirit simply by requesting such an anointment? Surely not! This man had to be a fraud. Julia had been taught by her parents to avoid all appearances of evil. And while Lawrie Tatum was not exactly what she would call evil, this type of worship was a far cry from sitting in the silence.

Almost as quickly as Lawrie had begun praying he finished, though his head remained bowed. Finally, after what seemed like an eternity of suspense, he raised his head and began to speak, first quietly and calmly; gradually increasing the volume until Julia was certain he must be shouting at the top of his lungs.

"Ah, Friends, God wants to save you. He wants to give you new birth. Ah, my brothers and sisters...have you been born again? That is the first step. But brothers and sisters, ah, my sweet brothers and sisters in the Lord, it is not enough to be born again. God wants to do a second work of grace in your lives. I myself struggled with grievous temptations even after the Lord saved me from my sins. Ah yes, I suffered in my ignorance, but you do not have to go through what I did for I am here to tell you that God wants to sanctify you and make you holy.

"Now Friends, I must speak truth with you tonight. You might have noticed I do not use the plain language of Friends, nor do I dress in the common attire of most of you here. But Friends, there is a reason. Ah, my brothers and sisters in Christ Jesus, have you become complacent? Has the plainness of Friends become a form of false security for you? Are you hiding behind your bonnets and broad rimmed hats and plain speech? Consider this...even the Hicksites, who we know do not follow the teachings of the scripture—even they wear the plain clothing. But it is a false cloak. Now lest you think I scorn the plain clothing, I do not. I believe George Fox had a reason for wanting to step apart from the frivolity of his day. But we are living in a new time and a new country. I will say it again, dear Friends, our peculiarities are nothing more than a false security. Break free from the past and see what great things God wants to accomplish!

"God is calling Friends to rise up from the ashes of silence and become new and alive in him. Is it a sin for people to praise the Lord? Our good friend and brother Amos Kenworthy says it is a sin for people NOT to praise the Lord! Silence can be a sign of spiritual deadness! Are you dead tonight? How long has it been since you felt the freedom you feel in this meeting tonight? How long since you felt like singing till your lungs burst?" Pausing to let his words sink in, Lawrie wiped his sweating brow before continuing. "Here is another matter for your to consider. How many of you have been taught that only through discipline, peculiarity and endless silent meetings can one experience holiness? I see those nodding heads. Ah, my beloved Friends, I am living breathing proof that the Baptism of the Holy Spirit can happen here and now in an instantaneous act of faith. This is the second work of grace. And, dear friends, this gift of holiness will bring joy, not suffering. Peace, not peculiarity. Ah Friends— will you continue in your sin or will you seek the face of God this very night?"

The evangelist's voice continued on but Julia's mind was in a whirl, trying to sort out the various exhortations she had just heard. What did Friends believe? She knew she had experienced salvation, having asked God to forgive her of her sins at an early age as she knelt by the side of her bed. But what about this 'second act' Lawrie kept insisting believers should experience? Could one really be holy without years of good works and seeking God's face in the quiet? Julia had no idea. She tried to think how her parents would respond to this man's words, but her mind just seemed to be in a jumble. She was only slightly aware of the men and women that were slowly making their way forward to kneel at the facing bench in the front of the meeting house. Lawrie's voice continued to plead with his audience, admonishing them to come forward and let God do a work of grace in their lives. He promised great peace and joy to those who came.

When the room became suddenly quiet, Julia quickly looked up to see what was happening. She was shocked to see the finger of the evangelist pointed directly at her and her friends. "I say it again, young people. Is He speaking to you? What will you say to God this night? Paul told Timothy to let no one think less of him because he was young. Are you willing to set the example for your elders? You can become the true Light within your meetings. Many of the elders will want to remain with the teachings of the past...are you willing to speak for the truth? It takes courage and commitment. I am not asking you to do an easy thing, but the rewards are great, dear young people. Will you come forward and kneel and pray?"

Julia felt the warmth rise in her face as she quickly looked down at her feet. She tried not to look up as Joseph and Suzannah quietly rose and made their way to the front, quickly followed by Harriet, Peter, and...surely not...could it be? Quickly glancing upward, Julia's eyes met Jonathan's as he rose and slowly walked past her to join the others. How could he? Feeling deeply embarrassed, yet determined not to be coerced by this smooth talking man, Julia dropped her eyes and pretended not to hear anything else that was being said. She could not deny the tugging of the Holy Spirit on her heart. It was similar to the feelings she had experienced at Yearly Meeting. And yet, something kept her rooted to the bench, unable to make the commitment Lawrie was urging every Friend in the room to make.

By the time the service had ended nearly everyone had moved to the front of the meeting house to pray. Julia's concealed glance took in several elderly and a few mothers with children still seated. And herself. Why had she been unable to move to the front to seek the 'second act of grace,' as Lawrie had put it? Why did she feel so 'sinful' for being the only one of her friends still sitting on the now hard bench? She could hear a mixture of soft crying and the prayers of the elders and Lawrie. She fervently wished she had never set foot in the Richland Meeting House!

After what seemed like hours, first Jonathan and then Joseph, Harriet, Peter and Suzannah returned to the bench, gathering their belongings and preparing to leave. No one said a word, though Julia was certain they were wondering why she had not joined them in their treks to receive something more from God. One by one they quietly exited the building, though once they reached the crisp spring air, everyone seemed to burst into conversation at the same time.

"That was the most awesome experience I have ever had!" Harriet began. "I had chills running up and down my spine when Lawrie pointed his finger at us!"

"I had never heard of a second act of grace," Peter confided, then added with a shy smile, "but it sure feels great!"

"You all know how I received a new birth in the barn at the Mendenhalls," Joseph added, "but it seemed like there was more I needed to do. Now I know it was sanctification I lacked. I want you all to know I received a second act of grace tonight and I finally feel at peace with myself."

Suzannah added a similar testimony, leaving only Jonathan and Julia to speak. "I do not know if God performed the same act for me that he did for each of thee," Jonathan began, "but I know I was obedient to His calling, and I did feel at peace like the rest of thee. Julia," he said quietly, wishing to draw her into the conversation, yet not wanting to embarrass her, "what did thee think of the meeting?"

Julia quickly forgot the urging of the Holy Spirit she herself had felt as she quickly began to defend the principles Friends had sought to maintain for decades. "I think Lawrie Tatum is an entertainer. I also believe Friends have a good reason for spending time in the silence. God speaks to individuals when the time is right. I do not believe an evangelist has the right to stand up in front of a group of people and point his finger at them, expecting them to respond to his pressures! How can this one man negate the teachings of hundreds of Friends in England and America?"

It was Jonathan who finally spoke for the friends who seemed shocked by Julia's negative response to the meeting. "Julia, I agree with thee in many ways. I do not wish to cast aside beliefs we have been taught. But I have to admit that a number of the things Lawrie said tonight made sense to me. I believe many in our meetings do use the plainness of dress and speech as a source of false security. And I know I have set in the silence many times when my mind was totally distracted. Please do not misunderstand...I am not saying thee is wrong, only that we have been given much to think about tonight."

The conversation continued on the way home with Joseph asking many questions about the history of Friends. "Who were those 'Hicksites' Lawrie was speaking of?" was his first question.

Jonathan seemed to be the designated historian as he tried to briefly explain a bit of church history. "Elias Hicks was an elderly farmer-preacher from Long Island who believed American Friends had drifted from the principles set forth by George Fox. He believed the Light of God would eventually reveal all things to a person if they sat in the silence long enough. Probably the most troublesome of Hicks's teachings had to do with his thoughts on Jesus Christ. Hicks believed that Christ was the son of God, but only in the same sense that all people are sons of God, and that it was Christ's example of achieving divinity through perfect obedience to the Light that made Him important."

"Did this man have many followers?" Peter asked. "Those teachings sound a bit heretical to me!"

"Surprisingly," Jonathan continued, "Hicks did have a number of supporters which led to a separation among Friends."

"Was there not also a problem with the scriptures?" Julia added, "It seems I remember Mother telling Father how Grandfather Wilson was adamantly opposed to the teachings of Hicks regarding the Word of God, and warned his East Grove Meeting to stand firm in opposition to this man."

"Thee is right, Julia," Jonathan said warmly, pleased that she also knew about this man of controversy. "Elias thought the scripture was the Word of God, but that it was far inferior to the Light as revealed to man through the Holy Spirit."

"Then I suppose Pleasant Plain Friends is not one of the 'Hicksite' group?" Joseph asked.

"No, we are commonly referred to as 'Gurneyite Friends'," Jonathan said, laughing at the words he knew must be totally confusing to a convinced Friend like Joseph.

"Joseph John Gurney was an English evangelist whose view of the Bible gained him many supporters," Julia spoke up, having often heard her Mother speak of this man. "He believed the Bible was the infallible word of God and that Bible studies and First Day Schools were needed to help Friends know what the Word said and how to apply it to their lives."

"But Gurney also believed that sanctification—that 'second act of grace' Lawrie was talking about—was a gradual, protracted process, not a single act like Lawrie claims," Jonathan added.

"And what does thee believe?" Suzannah asked from the back of the carriage.

"I am not certain," Jonathan said quietly. "I know one thing, though. It has certainly given me much to think about the next time my mind wanders during worship service!" The others laughed, relieved to hear Jonathan add a bit of lightness to the otherwise solemn conversation.

"Now Suzannah, here," Joseph spoke up, "she prays with her eyes open!"

"JOSEPH!" Suzannah exclaimed, obviously embarrassed by his revelation.

"And how would thee know?!" Peter shot back, knowing Joseph had been seen in the company of Suzannah a number of times the past few weeks.

"Suzannah tells me everything!" Joseph said smugly, though everyone knew he was joking. Everyone except Julia, that is.

"Suzannah knows better than to tell thee everything!" Julia exclaimed, irritated at the presumptuousness of Joseph.

"Oh, Julia, Joseph is just teasing!" Suzannah interrupted. "Thee knows I tell thee everything about my life *and* more!"

Except where Joseph is concerned, Julia thought, realizing the two of them must be spending more time together than she had noticed.

"Here we are," Jonathan exclaimed as he stopped the carriage in front of Levi's cabin, his voice just a bit too cheerful to suit Julia.

Quickly climbing down to help his friend, Jonathan was surprised when Julia jumped down of her own accord, ignoring his outstretched hand.

"I will walk thee to the door," Jonathan offered.

"I can find the way, thank you," Julia said, already several steps from the carriage.

"Farewell to all of you," she called back, hoping no one realized how disturbed she had been by the events of the evening.

Fortunately, Levi and his family were spending the night with friends in Richland, so she had the cabin all to herself. Not even bothering to light a lamp, Julia undressed by the light of the full moon which streamed in through the generous window in her room. Kneeling beside her bed, Julia began to weep, somehow feeling she had been a disappointment to her friends *and* to God. Though she still was not certain this Lawrie Tatum could be trusted, the testimony of her friends was a strong endorsement of his message. Her mind numb, Julia eventually climbed into bed, hoping that sleep would mercifully end her turmoil. Next Meeting, she vowed, she would seek God in the silence, and hope He provided the answers.

CHAPTER 17

NEW BIRTH

Though Julia had no answers to her questions the next morning, or the next time she met with Friends for worship, the flurry of activities revolving around the end of the winter session at the academy helped take her mind off the revival meeting and the questions she had. The Mendenhalls had planned a get-together for Jonathan and his friends the last week of school, and Julia was both excited and dismayed. Excited at the prospect of spending time with her friends, yet dismayed because she knew they would soon be parting. She had grown especially close to Suzannah, Peter, Harriet, Jonathan, and even Joseph during the months they had shared so much of their lives with each other.

On the eve of the gathering, Levi told Julia to take the horse and carriage to meet her friends since it was but two miles to the Mendenhalls and the roads had finally dried out from the spring thaws and rains. Julia felt especially pleased that her uncle would trust her with the carriage, and she sat tall as she passed the now familiar landscape into Pleasant Plain and on south to the

Mendenhalls. The special smell of spring was everywhere, and Julia's heart felt lighter than it had for months.

Most of the others were already there when she arrived, sitting on the wide front porch of the Mendenhalls' modest frame home. Waving as she approached, Julia was certain she had never seen a happier group of young friends.

"It is about time thee arrived!" Suzannah exclaimed as Julia tied the horse to the railing. "We were about to come looking for thee!"

"I suppose I must have dawdled on the way over. The weather was perfect, and the air smelled so fresh and clean, and the birds were singing..."

"We know, we know...thee just preferred the company of your uncle's horse to your dear friends who were breathlessly awaiting thy arrival!" At Peter's words everyone broke into laughter, and Julia knew the evening was off to a great start. Quickly scanning the group on the porch, Julia noticed Peter and Harriet sitting on the top step while Suzannah and Joseph were sitting on a wooden bench along the wall of the house. Only Jonathan was standing, though Julia was not certain whether he had been sitting earlier and rose when he saw her coming, or if he had been standing all the while. Julia quickly went to a second bench, this one smaller than Suzannah and Joseph's, yet large enough for two if they were sitting close together. She made sure Jonathan did not get any wrong ideas when she sat in the middle of the seat and spread her skirt to cover the entire bench. Jonathan seemed not to mind as he excused himself to get some refreshments that Martha had made for the students.

"It is hard to believe this is the last week of classes," Peter said a bit wistfully. "I hate to admit this, but I was so scared that first week at the academy that I had made up my mind to go home on that first seventh day."

"What kept thee in school?" Harriet asked.

"Joseph."

"Oh really!" Julia said, still not willing to give Joseph credit for doing anything except annoying her and anyone else who got in his way.

"Yes, really!" Peter said defensively. "Joseph was the only one in my English class who knew how to write poetry, and he helped me with that first awful assignment. Remember? The one where we had to write a sonnet?"

"How could I forget!" Harriet agreed. "I had a great deal of trouble with that assignment! I even asked the teacher why he gave us such a difficult beginning poem!"

"You always have been a forward one!" Peter said admiringly, looking fondly at Harriet.

"She is forward, all right!" Julia added, turning to Harriet. "Remember when I brought my brother to the wedding shower and you tried especially hard to get to know him?" Julia had waited a long time to tell Harriet what she had thought of her behavior that night. To Julia's surprise, Harriet's face turned bright pink as she did indeed remember her actions at the shower.

"I hope I did not embarrass thy brother too much. I know my behavior was not very Christ-like, but I hope I have changed at least a little since then!"

"You have changed a great deal," Jonathan confirmed as he returned with a platter of pastries, giving Julia a glance that spoke of his displeasure with her remark.

"Remember the shivaree we gave the newlyweds when they returned?" Peter asked, anxious to avoid any confrontations. "They were so surprised when we all showed up after they were in bed and banged on our pans and made all that racket!"

"That was a great night," Joseph agreed. "I had never heard of a 'shivaree' until you all told me how much fun they were."

The friends continued to reminisce about the happenings of the school year, many times laughing at their own past concerns which seemed so trivial to them now.

"Will thee remain at the Mendenhalls this summer, Jonathan?" Suzannah asked when the conversation became more serious.

"Yes, working at Mealey's Drug Store is the only way I can save enough money to go to law school next year when I finish at the academy."

"Are you going to work at the millinery next year?" Joseph asked, looking at Julia.

"I...I...I do not know what you mean!"

"The millinery, you know, that women's hat place. You DO work there, do you not?" Joseph seemed to be intent on exposing Julia's secret.

"What ever makes you think I would work at the millinery? Friends do not even wear fancy hats, for goodness sake!" Julia tried to keep her voice light, though from the looks on the faces that surrounded her, she knew her secret was anything but a secret!

"Julia," Jonathan said slowly. "Everyone knows of thy work in the millinery, though I am not the one who revealed thy secret. In fact, everyone in Pleasant Plain knows thee works for Kathleen O'Donnell. And besides...why would thee feel the need to keep it a secret?"

"Well...I...it just seemed like something thee might not approve of," she said honestly. Then a rather disturbing thought occurred to her. "When you say everyone knows of my work, do you mean everyone as in Uncle Levi?"

"Everyone, I am afraid," Suzannah said gently, then hastily added, "Though no one thinks thee is evil or anything!"

"Wonderful!" Julia said sarcastically. "I suppose thee had a prayer meeting in my behalf!"

"Well, we thought about it!" Jonathan teased, "but we decided we would let thee handle thy own problems!"

"Seriously, Julia," Joseph added, "As Christians I believe we need to be less concerned about the sins of our brothers and sisters and more concerned about our own weaknesses. We know you must have prayed over the matter, and if you feel the affirmation of the Light, then why should we judge your actions?"

For the first time since Julia had met Joseph she felt a strange sense of gratitude. "Thank you for your support, Joseph. It might interest all of you to know I told Kathleen last week that I would not be working for her next year. Even though I do not feel there is anything sinful about the millinery, I never felt quite at peace when I was there. If there are others who think I am sinning by being there, then it would not be right for me to earn a wage from such an activity."

"Thee has really changed since thee first came, Julia!" Jonathan said warmly.

"And just what do you mean by that?"

"I remember when thee told Joseph thee thought tuition should be raised! Thee was always saying the first thing that came into thy head!"

"And now?" she asked.

"And now thee seems to be more considerate of others...well, most of the time, anyway!" Jonathan laughed as Julia took a playful swing at him.

The darkness was beginning to overtake the gathering, and Jonathan suggested they go inside for a while.

"Before we go inside," Joseph spoke again, "Suzannah and I have something we would like to tell all of you."

Instantly all eyes were on the couple, realizing the seriousness in his tone of voice. Looking at Suzannah before continuing, Joseph finally told them the good news. "Suzannah and I are going to ask the Meeting for permission to marry when we both are finished with school."

"Congratulations!" Jonathan was the first to speak. "Thee are both special friends, and I have no doubt the Meeting will approve of thy union."

"Yes," Peter and Harriet agreed, "congratulations!"

"Will you two be next?" Suzannah asked slyly, looking at Peter and Harriet as they sat close to one another. "It seems to me that the two of you have been spending a great deal of time with one another these past few weeks!"

"Not me!" Harriet said firmly. "Not that I do not care for thee," she said quickly, looking apologetically at Peter. "I simply do not want to be committed to another person right now, especially since I would like to go to William Penn College when I finish at the academy."

If Peter was embarrassed by Harriet's revelation, he didn't let on. "We are just good friends," he said warmly.

Julia had remained silent, still shocked by Suzannah and Joseph's announcement. She knew the two of them had been seeing a great deal of each other, but she had no idea it was that serious. She wished she had told Kathleen long ago that she would no longer be working for her. It seemed like she was spending two or three afternoons a week modeling at the millinery which meant she had had little time to spend with Suzannah. No wonder she had not known the seriousness of her friend's feelings for Joseph.

The friends gradually moved inside the warm home, their talk centering on future plans. Everyone seemed reluctant to leave, knowing it would be several months before they would have the opportunity to visit with each other again. Finally Julia rose, knowing Levi would be worried if she did not return with the carriage soon. "Thank you for the refreshments, Martha," Julia said, turning to their hostess. "It was lovely of thee to allow us to use your home."

Martha's gentle laugh spoke of her tender spirit. "We love having you young people around. It helps us stay young ourselves!"

The others rose to leave as well, exiting the cabin in a solemn line. "As soon as we return," Joseph said, "we will have to have another gathering. I will make the plans over the summer."

"Can we trust thee with the planning? What if thee decides we need a bit of corn whiskey to loosen our tongues?!" This time Julia's words were accompanied with laughter, and everyone knew Joseph was finally forgiven for disrupting the Snow Fest.

As Joseph and Suzannah and Harriet and Peter climbed in their respective carriages, Jonathan walked with Julia to Levi's rig. "I will ride to Levi's with thee," he said firmly.

"Now why would thee want to do that?! Ride with me to Levi's and then what? Walk home? That is ridiculous! I will be fine!"

"I am riding with thee," Jonathan reiterated. "I will tie my horse on the back of the carriage and ride back when thee is safely at Levi's. Besides, thee never knows where wild animals might be lurking!"

Julia laughed, knowing this time Jonathan would not be dissuaded. "All right, oh mighty protector! Climb aboard!"

They rode in silence for a bit, enjoying the mild temperatures of the end of the fourth month. Finally Jonathan spoke what had obviously been on his mind for some time.

"Julia," he began, then paused as if trying to think of exactly the right words.

"Yes, Jonathan?" Julia asked in a teasing tone.

"Julia, thee knows.. I think thee.. is a very special girl," he stammered. "And I...and I...I wonder if thee has any feelings for me...special feelings, that is."

Julia was surprised at his question, thinking he had long ago dismissed her as a spur-of-the-moment person, a 'fiery one' that needed to be eldered every once in a while.

"Julia?" Jonathan asked anxiously. "I hope I did not offend thee?"

"Jonathan, if thee were any more perfect they would make thee a saint! Thee did not offend me, though I must admit I am a bit surprised at thy question."

"But thee did not answer me!"

"That is because in all honesty my answer is probably not what you want to hear. I like being with you—and the others. But I have too many faults for you—I mean thee—to be interested in me. You see? I can not even discipline myself to use the plain language all the time. And remember when we went to the evangelistic meeting and all of you went to the front to pray? I was the only one who could not make myself go forward. Surely thee can find someone more spiritual to spend thy time with."

"Julia, THAT is the very reason I like thee so much! Thee is not easily persuaded to follow what everyone else is doing. Thee has the courage to be true to thyself. I even admired thee for having the courage to work in the millinery when it is fairly obvious that many Friends think hats are frivolous."

"Really?" Julia asked, totally surprised by this revelation. "Thee really feels that way?"

"Really, Julia, really!"

As the lamplight of Levi's cabin came into view, Jonathan quickly reworded his original question.

"I am not asking thee for a commitment, Julia, I know thee is young and the future holds great things for thee. But I would be grateful if thee thought thee might like to spend some time with me when thee returns for the new school year next tenth month."

Julia thought for a moment before replying. "Oh Jonathan, I do enjoy thy company. There are other times, however, when I feel like thee is too...too... perfect is the only word I can think of."

"Then that alone is reason enough to spend time with me! Thee needs to see my faults. And believe me, I have many!"

Julia knew she must tell Jonathan exactly how she felt. "Jonathan, I am not interested in finding a mate just yet. I do not know exactly how to explain it, but I just feel God has something special for me to do. I have no idea what that might be, I just know I have to prepare myself and be ready when the call comes." Julia went on to share with Jonathan how she had felt the Holy Spirit speaking to her at yearly meeting, and again during the revival service. Though Jonathan remained silent, admiration shone in his eyes as yet another facet of this amazing girl was revealed.

Just then Levi opened the cabin door to make sure Julia was all right.

"Julia!" he called. "Is that thee?"

"Yes, Uncle Levi. Jonathan accompanied me to the cabin. He was afraid a wild animal would attack me!"

"Of course," Levi said wryly, having a good idea of Jonathan's motive. "Just be sure to take care of the horse when thee finishes thy business."

Jonathan and Julia laughed once the cabin door was shut, knowing Levi had known they were not watching for wild animals!

"Very well, then, Julia. I will respect thy wishes. But please consider my words. I would never push thee or demand thee take a special interest in me. If God is truly calling thee, then I will pray that the Light will lead thee. But please do not close all the doors where I am concerned until thee knows for certain just what God's calling is."

The full moon reflecting from Jonathan's face revealed the earnestness of his words. Not wanting to completely disappoint this young man who had been a good friend, Julia said simply, "All right, Jonathan. I will not close any doors just yet. But I intend to spend the next few months seeking God's plan for my life."

"That is all I can ask of thee. Perhaps my horse will wander down to Salem some time this summer—with me on his back!" Jonathan finished as he gathered the reins to lead Levi's horse to the barn.

"That would be nice," Julia called back, knowing a visit from Jonathan would always be welcome.

Levi and Anna were both sitting at the table when Julia entered the cabin. "What time is it?" she asked curiously, surprised to see them still up.

"It is nearly the eleventh hour," Anna answered.

"We thought perhaps we had best have a talk," Levi said seriously.

The solemn looks on their faces quickly caught Julia's attention.

"We have been blessed to have thee in our home—thee knows that," Anna began. "If there was any way we could have stayed here at Pleasant Plain we would have done so. We just feel like we have let thee down by not being here for thee next year."

"I will be fine!" Julia reassured them. "There are several boarding families that will have vacancies next year. I am certain it will not be difficult to find a good home for the school session."

"We know thee can find a place to live, Julia, but we are concerned about thy spiritual development." Levi was looking intently at Julia, as if trying to think how to phrase his next words. "Julia, we know thee has been working at the millinery in town."

So that was it! Her aunt and uncle were worried about her job! "Thee will be happy to know I have told my employer that I will not be working for her next year."

"That is a relief!" Anna exclaimed. "We have been so concerned..."

"I am sorry. I had no idea all of you knew I was working!"

Levi laughed. "Julia, thee is talking about a town of a few hundred people, many of them Friends. Did thee not realize someone would think it their 'Christian duty' to inform us of thy activities?"

Embarrassed, Julia admitted that it had never occurred to her. She had been convinced that if no one saw her enter the store, her secret would be safe.

"Thee need not worry about my spiritual progress," Julia added, "Jonathan has promised to keep me on the straight and narrow next year!"

"Yes, well that in itself might be a concern!" Levi said with a knowing smile.

"Levi!" Anna reprimanded her husband. "Jonathan is a special young man, and we know he can be trusted."

"I am going to miss thee, though," Julia said seriously, knowing that in a few days she would be forever leaving this home where she had so enjoyed herself.

"Then thee will just have to take the train to Oskaloosa and visit us!" Anna said firmly.

"That sounds like fun!" Julia said enthusiastically. She had never ridden on a train and was always anxious to try new things.

"Then it is a promise! We will see thee next year—possibly over the Christmas break. Maybe Jonathan will want to accompany thee."

"Maybe, but I would not count on anything transpiring any time soon between Jonathan and me," Julia said candidly, though the memory of his kiss still gave her a tingly feeling. "Now if you will excuse me, I think I will retire before falling asleep on my chair!"

"Surely!"

"Of course. Sleep well, Julia."

"I will. Good night."

And farewell, Julia thought sadly as she retired to her room.

CHAPTER 18

UPHOLDING ONE ANOTHER

"Julia, it is high time thee arose and helped thy mother," came Charles's firm command, irritated at his daughter's oblivion to her mother's condition.

Julia slowly became aware of her old familiar surroundings and a pang of disappointment threatened to once again shadow her thoughts and feelings. It had not been easy to return to her home in Salem after classes finished at the academy. Julia missed her friends more than she could have imagined, hardly a day passing without poignant memories filling her mind. She wondered how Suzannah and Joseph were doing, realizing that she had been wrong about Joseph's conversion. Joseph had indeed become a new person in Christ and his behavior reflected that change.

Julia also wondered about Peter and Harriet, though she knew they were wise to pursue their own interests and education before considering a commitment to one another. And then there was Jonathan...Jonathan was every girl's dream...not only was he handsome, but also responsible and intelligent and hard-working and concerned with spiritual matters and...interested in her! Then why did I not jump at his invitation to get to know one another in a special way? Julia asked herself. An intelligent woman would have snatched this man as quickly as possible!

"Julia!" This time Charles's voice was less than patient and Julia knew she would have to put her thoughts aside for now and see what her father wanted. It seemed like ever since she had arrived back home he was always upset with her, expecting her to know what was on his mind before he even spoke.

"Yes, Father," Julia called, now fully awake. "I will be there in a short while."

"Make it a *very* short while!" came Charles's muffled response.

Julia dressed quickly, thinking how modern this room looked compared to the one at Levi's, yet missing the simple furnishings of her aunt and uncle's cabin. She also missed the high-pitched voices of her cousins as they had run through the cabin early in the mornings before she left for school. It was surely going to be different next year when she would have to board with another family.

Rebecca was sitting at the kitchen table when Julia entered the room, obviously feeling a bit of discomfort from the look on her face. "Good morning, dear," Rebecca greeted her rapidly maturing daughter. "Would thee like a cup of tea?"

"No thank you, mother. I never have liked putting hot liquids into my stomach first thing in the morning. "

Rebecca smiled, realizing just how much she had missed this free spirited child. It had been hard for her when David had gone to Chicago to study medicine, though it was something she had wanted him to do for a long time. With both of her older children gone, the winter months had seemed to pass more slowly than ever. Charles had been gone much of the time taking care of patients, though as the time for the baby began to draw closer he had been arriving home before darkness set in, just in case Rebecca needed him.

"Rebecca," Charles called as he picked up his medicine bag in preparation for leaving, "thee needs to spend most of the day resting in bed. Thy blood pressure has been too high to suit me, and we do not want anything to happen to thee or our baby. Now that Julia is home, I expect thee to let her do the work."

Great! thought Julia. I am on sabbatical from school and have to keep house! It was difficult for her to talk with her mother, not to mention look at the bulge of her abdomen. For some reason Julia still felt repulsed at the idea that her mother was going to have a baby. She had shuddered when she had stepped through the door when arriving home that first day and seen her mother looking like she was carrying a watermelon under her skirt.

Seeing the look of disgust on Julia's face, Charles immediately asked her to walk to the carriage with him. Knowing better than to voice her discontent, Julia slowly rose to follow her father through the door. Once they were out of earshot Charles began his admonition. "Julia, if thee knew what thy mother had gone through these past few months, thee might be more anxious to be of assistance."

"I am sorry, Father, I suppose I still find it hard to believe she would allow herself to be in this position." As soon as the words were out of her mouth, Julia knew she was going to regret her impulsive response.

"Julia, I find it extremely difficult to have you speaking such disrespectful thoughts, especially about thy mother. One does not always choose the paths God leads him or her on, but once the journey has begun there are joys to be found if one is not constantly looking to the past and what might have been. Can thee understand what I am saying?"

"Yes, I suppose. It is just difficult for me to imagine having a baby brother or sister. Mother should be...should be...doing *anything* other than knitting baby blankets!"

"I know it has been hard for thee to accept thy mother's pregnancy. I am not asking thee to be excited about the changes that will occur in just a few weeks, but I do ask thee to be respectful of thy mother. Did thee know that at one time thy mother thought she would never have a child?"

When Julia was silent, Charles continued.

"When thy mother and Joshua were married, they had no children. It was a time of great stress in Rebecca's life, and she felt like a failure when the months passed and she was unable to produce a child for her husband. Eventually she became my assistant and that helped take her mind off her barrenness, though it always seemed to haunt her. Once we were married and she discovered she was with child, it was the happiest day of her life." Pausing a moment, Charles added with a twinkle in his eye, "After her marriage to me, of course."

Julia laughed, recognizing her father's attempt at humor, then asked the question that she had pondered ever since receiving news of the impending birth. "I still do not understand why thee had no children for sixteen years after I was born, and then all of a sudden mother is expecting a child!"

"Some things even we doctors have no answers for, Julia. Rebecca and I firmly believe we have committed our lives to God and in whatever way he chooses to bless us we will be happy. But we would like for thee and thy brother to share our joy in this newest member of our family. And I would like to see thee at least try to anticipate the needs of thy mother and offer to help in any way thee can. It has not been easy for her to keep from overexerting herself, and I know she was looking forward to having thee home to help."

"I will try to do a better job from now on. Now that thee has explained it to me, I do understand the situation a bit better. When does thee think the baby will arrive?"

"I am not certain," Charles said slowly, "but I imagine thee will have a new sibling within a week or two. Now...I must be on my way. I know thee will do thy best to help thy mother." And with those remarks Charles climbed into the carriage and swiftly departed.

Julia walked slowly back to the house, hoping she would be able to do what she had promised her father. Just as she was about to enter the kitchen she heard a shout from across the field behind their home. Turning sharply on her heel and walking to the edge of the porch, Julia could just make out the figure of a man on horseback coming over the rise. The shouting continued as Julia stood rooted to the porch planks, not knowing whether to run and meet the rider or wait until he reached the house. Not recognizing the man, Julia kept to the security of the porch. In a few minutes he reached the railing, jumping quickly from the laboring horse.

"Where is the doctor?" he demanded. "I have to see Dr. Jones!"

"I am sorry, but he just left a moment ago. Thee just missed him."

"Then don't just stand there, tell me where he went!"

"Perhaps if thee were not so rude, I would!" Julia was rapidly becoming annoyed with this presumptuous young man. A quick look told her he was near her age and while not exactly handsome, she sensed a strength emanating from him in spite of his agitation.

"Can thee not see this is an urgent matter? Thee females can be so impossible! Will thee please just tell me where I can reach Dr. Jones?"

"Just follow the path." She pointed to where her father had disappeared from view a few minutes earlier.

Turning without a word of thanks, the stranger remounted his still sweating horse and quickly turning down the path.

"Who was thee speaking with?" Rebecca asked when Julia returned to the kitchen. Julia proceeded to tell her mother of the rather disturbing conversation she had had with the agitated young man.

"What did he look like?" Rebecca asked curiously.

Julia described the rider as best she could after their brief encounter, noticing her mother's nodding head when she finished.

"That must be Will Clark," Rebecca said when Julia had finished her description. "His family just moved into the Hoover place a few miles south of here. From what I understand, they belong to the group of Hicksites that have relocated in this area from Virginia. I wonder what has happened...did he say what was the nature of the problem?"

"No, he was rather short with me and I did not think it prudent to query him about his mission! Now, I think it is time thee went to bed for a bit. I will take care of the house keeping this morning and prepare a bit of dinner for us." Once Julia had made the decision to accept her mother's condition, she actually felt a bit sorry for the difficult time Rebecca was having.

"All right, Julia. I know thy father will be happy to know I have obeyed his orders!" Rebecca laughed softly as she rose to go into the bedroom. Turning back to Julia she added, "I know this has not been easy for thee, but I hope things will get back to normal once the baby is born." Julia could only nod, uncertain whether things could ever *get back to normal*.

When Charles returned at noon, he seemed pleased to find Julia stirring a pot of stew she had prepared for their dinner. "I see thee has had a busy morning!" he said warmly, patting Julia on the back, obviously having forgiven her for her earlier lack of enthusiasm for the work he thought she should be doing.

As they sat enjoying the meal together, Julia remembered to ask about the stranger she had spoken with earlier that day. "Did thee have a patient early this morning by the name of Will Clark?"

"Yes, I am afraid I did. Such a tragedy." Charles looked off toward the direction from which young Clark had ridden that morning.

"What happened?" Julia asked impatiently.

"Will's father was attacked by a cow this morning when he

attempted to help her baby calf get its head out of the fence. The cow, being protective of her offspring, got John pinned in a corner of the cow shed and eventually gored him with her horn. When Will heard his father yell, he ran and saw the cow repeatedly butting John with her head. Will was successful in distracting the cow so his father could crawl from the pen, but by the time Will could ride for me and get back, John Clark had bled to death."

Julia's face was ashen. "How horrible!" She remembered with guilt how she had responded to Will's question as to the where abouts of her father. "Had his father been gone long when thee arrived?" she asked cautiously, almost afraid to ask.

"No, only a few minutes. His body was still warm and I did my best to revive him, but it was no use. It is times like these that being a physician is the most difficult."

Julia could not finish her dinner, her stomach seeming to turn over as she thought again and again of how she had detained Will Clark rather than telling him immediately where to find her father. Noticing his daughter's withdrawal, Charles sought to console her. "Julia, these things happen. Working with livestock always presents a risk, and I am certain John Clark would try to save the calf again if he were in the same situation."

Julia remained silent, not wanting her father to know she might have been partially responsible for the death of this man.

"I plan to travel to the Clark farm this afternoon to see how they are holding up. Would thee like to join me?" Charles asked. "Perhaps Will might appreciate thy presence."

"NO!" said Julia forcefully, knowing she could not possibly face the grieving young man nor his family.

"All right," Charles said reassuringly. "I did not mean to imply thee should go; I only meant thee might go if thee wished."

Julia quickly cleared the dishes from the table and went to her room. Her thoughts chased each other around in her mind as she felt first guilty and then innocent of any wrong doing. Surely the few minutes Will was detained could not have made a difference in his father's life...or could they? Finally Julia knelt by her bed and poured out the anguish of her heart, asking God for forgiveness. As she remained on her knees seeking the peace of the Holy Spirit, she suddenly knew she was to go to Will and seek *his* forgiveness as well. Rising from her knees, Julia quickly went in search of her father. Hearing voices from her parents' bedroom, she waited until Charles came into the kitchen.

"I believe I will travel to the Clarks with thee after all," she said quietly.

Obviously pleased by his daughter's change of heart, Charles reached over and squeezed her hand. "I am certain Will could use thy comfort."

Probably not, Julia thought to herself as they left the house and made their way to the carriage. In fact, Will would most likely refuse to speak with her, though she would try her best to apologize for her actions.

As Charles and Julia approached the farm stead, they could see a number of horses, carriages and wagons gathered around the cabin. Some friends were standing outside near the carriages, while others could be seen inside the open door of the cabin. Stopping the carriage a distance from the Clark home, Julia and her father slowly climbed down and began walking toward the cabin door. Julia quickly scanned the men and boys gathered outside, but the face of Will Clark was no where to be found. As she and Charles entered the cabin, again there was no sign of Will. She did notice the clothing of those present and realized her mother had been right about them being Friends of some persuasion. Whether or not they were Hicksites was difficult to discern as their dress was similar to that of many of the Friends at Salem. Charles went directly to John's wife and offered his condolences. When he finished, Julia spoke up. "Would thee please tell thy son how sorry I am about his father? I was outside when he came in search of a doctor." She was not about to add, 'and thy husband might still be alive if I had realized the seriousness of thy son's mission."

"I thank both of thee," she said simply, "but I wish thee would try and speak with Will...he is out back, convinced he is responsible for his father's death."

"I will have a word with him," Charles said firmly. "The cow's horn managed to find a major artery in your husband's side, and I probably could not have saved him even if I had been there when it happened! Julia, let's see if we can find Will and explain it all to him."

Julia was so relieved at her father's words that she gladly joined him as he left the cabin. Sure enough, Will was out behind the cow shed as if being at the scene of the accident could somehow bring his father back.

Determined to ask forgiveness while she still had the courage, Julia spoke quickly before her father had a chance to speak with Will about the accident.

"Will," she began, though his back was to them and he made no effort to turn around, "I am sorry I did not tell thee immediately where my father was when thee rode to our home this morning. I had no idea the situation was so grave. I would like to ask thy forgiveness."

When there was no response, Charles tried to comfort the distraught young man by sharing the same words he had spoken to Will's mother.

"Just leave me alone!" Will said angrily, kicking the side of the shed and walking away from the doctor and daughter who stood looking helplessly at his slouched figure.

"Will... wait..." Julia called, starting to follow him until she felt her father restraining her with his hand.

"Let him go, Julia. He needs a chance to grieve for his father. He will be all right when he has time to realize it was not his fault. I will make it a point to visit him and his mother after the funeral service and make certain they are handling John's death."

Slowly Julia and Charles walked back to their carriage, speaking to a number of the men and boys Charles knew through his practice. Julia refrained from looking at anyone by keeping her eyes fastened to the carriage. I will just have to visit Will on my own and make him understand it was not his fault, she thought to herself. Feeling genuine pain for this young man who had just lost his father, Julia felt the tears sliding down her face as they traveled back home. Letting the rushing wind slowly dry them, Julia fervently wished she were back in Pleasant Plain with her friends. The days and months she would have to remain at home seemed insurmountable to her at that moment.

Julia realized her vow to find God's will for her life had been forgotten in the trauma of their neighbors' tragedy and the anticipation of the new child. She would make it a point to spend at least an hour each day in prayer and scripture reading until it was time to return to the academy. Surely God would reveal His will if she were diligent.

CHAPTER 19

WHERE THERE'S A WILL

Julia continued to be of assistance to her mother who was now forced to spend most of each day in bed. Loneliness was Julia's most frequent companion, and she often escaped the cabin for long walks across her family's land. She sometimes headed in the direction of Will Clark's cabin, though she had never had the courage to seek him out. What do you say to someone who has just lost his father? Julia could not imagine life without her own father, and just the thought was enough to pity Will even more.

It had been two weeks since John Clark's death and Julia was feeling especially low. When she had heard her mother's moans the night before, she was certain she would awaken to the squalls of a new sibling. When she had cautiously entered her parent's room the next morning, however, her mother was asleep and obviously still carrying her child. Julia wondered where her father was until she found a note on the table when she reached the kitchen.

Julia-

I have been called to the McCracken farm. Henry had some sort of attack in the night and may not pull through. If it were anyone but Henry I would have refused to go, knowing thy mother may go into labor at any time. Henry has helped me so many times in the past that I feel compelled to attend to his need. Please watch thy mother and ride for me at once if she calls out.

Thy loving father,
Charles

Julia read the note a second time, fervently hoping her mother remained asleep until Charles returned. She quickly tidied the kitchen, realizing from the clutter that her father had indeed been called away in a hurry. She then decided to make an apple pie for dinner, knowing it was one of her father's favorites. Just as she began to peel the apples she heard a sharp cry from mother's room. Ignoring the water that splashed over herself and the table as she dropped the apple and knife into the bowl of water, Julia's heart began to pound as she rushed to her mother's side.

"What is it?" the words came rushing from Julia's mouth.

"Julia..." Rebecca's face was ashen and her body curled on its side. Her breathing was labored as she fought the pain. "Please ride to the Clarks and get Will to bring his mother. She has helped several women in the area birth children and I need her NOW!"

"But mother," Julia began to protest, "Father is at the McCrackens and said for me to ride for him if thee..."

"Julia!" Rebecca said through clenched teeth, "Henry McCracken needs thy father more than I...now go for the Clarks at once! There isn't much time..." her words stopped as another severe contraction contorted her face. Julia quickly rose, trying to know what to do. She knew her father would be furious if she did not fetch him, yet she sensed there might not be enough time to ride the five miles to the McCracken's and back. Hearing yet another cry from her mother, Julia's decision was quickly made. Not bothering to put a saddle on the horse, she quickly rode to the Clarks, both hands clutching the horses's mane as tightly as possible.

Fortunately, Will was chopping wood near the road when Julia arrived. After listening to Julia's anxious request, Will was immediately in control of the situation.

"I will get the carriage, thee must get mother. She is out in the garden." And with those brief words Will was gone. Julia stood for a moment, then quickly went in search of Sarah Clark.

The three were back at the Jones's home within a matter of minutes and they could hear the moaning of Rebecca before opening the front door.

"You two heat some water and get some clean sheets," Sarah said crisply as she headed for the bedroom, obviously having been in similar situations in the past. Will looked at Julia and she stared in return, neither of them happy to be in the other's company. After a few moments, Julia began to obey Sarah's orders, hoping Will might decide to go home instead of stay with her.

"I believe I can handle these few chores," Julia said, trying to force a lightness to her voice. "If thee would like to return to thy home, I am certain my father will drive thy mother home after the baby arrives."

Will just stood by the stove, staring at the furnishings in this modern home. Though the various items were simple, one could sense they were well constructed and of the finest materials. Will's home was the cabin of his grandparents, and much of it had remained untouched since its creation. Compared to his home, this doctor's house was a mansion!

"Will, did thee hear what I said? Thee may go home now," Julia insisted, this time trying to sound more forceful.

"What about thy father? Should thee not try to find him?"

"That was my intention, but Mother asked me to ride for thy mother because she did not want Father to be taken away from Henry McCracken's bedside. Henry has done a lot for our family in the past and mother felt he should not be left unattended."

"That does present a problem..." Will conceded. "If I were in thy father's place, I believe I would want to know if my wife were in labor."

Just then the water began to boil and Will quickly called out to his mother. "What would thee like for me to do with the water, mother?"

"Just leave it on the stove," Sarah called from the bedroom. "Tear the sheet into strips and dip them in the water and then put them in the wash pan and bring it to the door."

Will did as his mother asked while Julia stood and watched, wishing there were something she could do. When Will had completed the task, he asked Julia if she would like to go outside and sit on the porch. "That way," he said, "If Mother calls for my help I will hear her. It is so hot in this kitchen that I am sweating like a stuck pig!"

Julia shuddered at the analogy, but followed Will outside where they warily sat down on the edge of the porch, feet dangling off the edge. Julia thought perhaps Will's eagerness to be out of the cabin had more to do with the loud cries of her mother than from the heat in the kitchen. They sat for a while in silence before Will finally spoke. "I am sorry I was short with thee the day thee came to offer thy condolences after my father's death. I was so upset with thee when I came in search of the doctor that I blamed thee for father's death. I knew Dr. Jones was right when he said father's artery had been ruptured, because I had seen the blood spurting from his side. I suppose I just needed someone to blame and I took it out on thee. I hope thee will forgive me."

Julia hoped her embarrassment was not evident as she tried to think of something to say. For once in her life she remained silent.

"Is thee upset?" Will asked anxiously. "I did not mean to upset thee...perhaps I should see if mother needs me." Will rose quickly and left Julia to her own thoughts.

Before long he returned. "Mother says things are progressing nicely and there are no problems. Thy brother or sister should arrive shortly."

Julia turned to get a better look at this new neighbor. In some ways he reminded her of Jonathan, though she sensed a deep strength within him that had come through adversity and from assuming the role of 'man of the house'. But Jonathan's life had been similar, she told herself, having lost his father at an even earlier age than Will. She did not know why Will possessed this strength of character, but she found herself admiring him for it.

"Julia, did I say something to offend thee?" Will finally asked when there was no response from this beautiful girl who sat beside him. Her face had come back to him time and again in the two weeks since he had first seen her, and he knew that in spite of his anger with her she was indeed a fine looking young woman.

"I am sorry, Will. I suppose my mind is on my mother right now. I hate to hear her in so much pain."

"I know what thee means...I was there when my little brother was born two years ago, and it was hard to see mother in so much agony. I really pity women having to suffer so much in order to bring a new life into the world."

Julia was amazed at Will's compassion and his ability to put her thoughts into words. Feeling somewhat better, she decided to try and find out a bit more about this interesting young man.

"So tell me...when did thee move to thy farm stead?"

"My grandparents both went to be with the Lord two years ago," Will began.

"Were they in an accident?" Julia interrupted.

"No, it just seemed that when Grandmother went to be with the Lord, Grandfather lost a great part of himself, and life was no longer meaningful for him. It was no surprise to our family when he too passed on a few months after Grandmother."

"That kind of love is admirable, I suppose," Julia found herself saying, "though I would hope I would be strong enough to look for fulfillment in other ways if my husband were to leave me."

Will was taken back, never expecting to hear such a profession from a girl. He thought all girls wanted to find a man who would love them in a special way and always be there for them.

"Where was thy family living when thy grandparents were still alive?" Julia asked, wanting to hear the rest of the story.

"We were in Virginia, trying to raise a few cattle and a bit of grain. Our soil was rocky, and there were many years when we had little to spare. We used the cattle hides for some of our clothing and we ate a good deal of beef. When father heard that Grandfather had died, he eagerly made the decision to come to Iowa. Prairie Grove Monthly Meeting was another reason Father was anxious to move to Iowa. Grandfather was one of the founding members of that Meeting, and Father wanted to make certain that it remained strong."

"I have heard of Prairie Grove," Julia admitted.

"I am certain thee has not heard many good things since thee is a member of the Salem Friends—an orthodox meeting!" Though Will's voice was not angry, Julia thought he sounded a bit annoyed.

"I have heard Father speak of Prairie Grove, though the only thing he said was that it was a Hicksite Meeting."

"I am certain thy father has definite feelings about Hicksite Friends—he would not be normal if he did not. I just find it difficult to understand why we are shunned by the orthodox group."

Julia sat pensively, wondering if she dared ask what was on her mind. Hoping Will would not be offended, she finally asked him the question. "Will, do Hicksites really believe the conscience is the source of the Light within? And do you really believe Jesus was just another man?"

Will laughed. "I have been asked those same questions several times before. And the answer is simple: *some* Hicksites believe the Light of God and the conscience are the same, while others believe the Light is the Holy Spirit. And the same is true with Jesus...*some* think he was just as we are—sons of God. Most of us, however, realize he was more than just *one of us*. Jesus died for our sins, making him far greater than you or me. And I personally believe the Light within is the Spirit of Christ drawing us into communion with him."

"Thee should be an evangelist!" Julia said admiringly. "Thy words make a great deal of sense—and I am certain our beliefs are quite similar."

Will laughed. "I am afraid most Hicksites look with disdain on the evangelical Friends. They would no sooner listen to an evangelist—a mere 'man'—speak, than they would quit wearing the plain clothing. Though in all honesty I believe many of them are too rigid in their beliefs."

"Has thee ever been to an evangelistic meeting?" Julia asked.

"No, I really wanted to go to Richland when Lawrie Tatum was there speaking, but Father would not even listen to my reasons. He said I was to remain true to the teachings of George Fox and not become like the other Friends who had betrayed their heritage. Has thee attended one?"

"I was at the meeting with Lawrie Tatum," Julie said quietly.

"Really?" Will asked excitedly. "Tell me what went on."

Julia proceeded to tell Will everything that had happened that evening—except for the fact that she was the only one of her friends not going forward to the alter to pray.

"Some day I am going to attend a revival service," Will said determinedly. "I just feel there is something missing in my life and I need more than sitting in the silence to discover what it is."

Just then Sarah came to the door, smiling broadly. "Julia, would thee like to see thy new sister?"

A sister. There had been many times in her life when Julia had wished for a sister...someone to play with, someone to confide in, someone with whom she could lay awake at night and make plans for the future. But a sister now? This baby would be more like a niece than a sister.

"Julia?" Will's voice brought her back to the present. "Would thee not like to see thy new sister?"

Quickly Julia got to her feet, ignoring the outstretched hand of Will, and ran in to the bedroom.

Rebecca lay in the bed sleeping, obviously worn out from not only the last few hours but also the past weeks. Nestled in her arms was a tiny being whose most notable characteristic was the thick, dark hair covering her head. Sarah gently lifted the baby from her mother's arms and placed her in Julia's. Julia instantly felt a bond with this tiny creature who shared the same ancestry. Talking softly to the baby, Julia began to rock back and forth, gently swaying with the baby in her arms. Suddenly she knew everything was going to be all right with this new sibling, and she began to look forward to helping take care of her until school started again.

As Julia returned the baby to her mother's arms, she heard her father's anxious voice calling from the kitchen. Hurrying to meet him, Julia tried to explain why they had not ridden for him. When there was no immediate response, Julia knew her father was not pleased with her decision.

Finally Charles spoke. "Why did thee not come for me, Julia? Did thee not read my note? I specifically asked thee to come to the McCrackens and get me if thy mother went into labor!"

"I asked her to go for Sarah, Charles," Rebecca said faintly from the bed. "Do not blame Julia. I just felt thee needed to spend thy time with Henry. I made sure there were no problems before I decided to send Julia to fetch Sarah. How is Henry?"

"Henry had a stroke and is paralyzed on the right side. I have no idea if he will regain any use of that part of his body. It was not a life-threatening situation, however. I could certainly have come when thee needed me!"

"Thee trained me well, Charles," Rebecca said with a weak smile. "I would have sent for thee if there had been a problem."

Finally looking at his new daughter, Charles began to smile, the sight of this tiny beauty nearly moving him to tears. "She is beautiful!" he said softly, then added, "Just like her mother and sister!"

Sensing her father and mother needed some time alone together, Julia quietly left the room and joined Will and Sarah as they prepared to leave. "I am so grateful to thee," she began, hoping they did indeed know how much their presence had meant to her that day. "I would like for thee to come to supper on seventh day," she heard herself saying, trying to think of some way to show her gratitude to this woman of the Hicksite faith. Sarah's smile was bittersweet. "Why not wait a while before asking thy mother to entertain guests."

"Nonsense!" Julia retorted, "I am the one doing all the cooking and cleaning anyway, and I think mother would be happy to have some company in a few days."

That strange look crossed Sarah's face again. "Please wait a while and see how thy mother gets along. When she is better, talk to both of thy parents, and if they agree, then we will be happy to come."

Julia stood on the porch long after Will and Sarah had vanished over the horizon. She finally felt free of the guilt she had carried since Will's father's death. Will seemed to be pleasant enough, and Julia was curious to know more of the Hicksite faith. Will was surely just the type of man she should be looking for in a husband, but Julia was somewhat dismayed to realize she had absolutely no desire to even think of finding a marriage partner. Not Will, not even perfect Jonathan. What was wrong with her? Was she truly following the leading of the spirit or was it her own ego that gave her the desire to do something more than just be a wife and mother? And if she dismissed these boys from her life would she be missing out on a normal future?

Julia slowly moved inside the house and up to her room, her mind trouble with these new thoughts.

CHAPTER 20

A LIGHT AT THE END OF THE TUNNEL

Rebecca made a remarkable recovery after the baby's birth, somehow gaining strength from the new creature with whom she had been entrusted. Rachel was nearly a perfect baby, seldom crying, often smiling—especially at her big sister. Julia loved to take her outside and walk among the leaves which would soon be turning colors. Occasionally Will Clark would 'happen' to be riding by and would stop and visit with Julia. Each time Will was there Julia tried to think of him as a suitor, but there was simply no attraction for her. She liked him as a person, as a friend and neighbor, but nothing more.

When Julia had asked her parents about inviting the Clarks to supper some night, thinking they owed the Clarks a gesture of thanks for helping with the birth of Rachel. Julia was somewhat puzzled by their reluctance to extend the invitation.

"I am certain the Clarks are not expecting any type of payment for the service they performed for our family," Charles had replied. "Our thanks to them at the time certainly seems enough to me."

"If it were not for Sarah Clark," Julia reminded her parents, "Rachel might not be the healthy child she is today. Why can we not invite Sarah and her family to supper some evening? Surely we owe them a debt of gratitude!"

Charles looked at Rebecca, wondering how to put the thoughts they were both thinking into words. "Julia," he began slowly, "thee knows the Clarks are followers of Elias Hicks?"

"Yes, but..."

"And thee knows that orthodox Friends such as our family do not share the same ideas with regard to the Inner Light and Scripture reading as the Hicksites?"

"Yes, but..."

"And thee knows that we are called to be a separate people, not touching the unclean things of this world?"

Julia was disgusted. Here was her father, obviously an intelligent man, refusing to associate with another group of Friends because of some long held prejudice. Did she dare offer an argument in support of the Hicksite family she had come to know? Did her father not need to be enlightened on the difference in Hicksites? "Father, does thee know what Will and his family believe regarding the Inner Light and Scriptures?"

"I know that the Hicksites believe..."

"Please forgive me for interrupting, Father, but does thee know what *Will and his family* believe? There is a difference."

Charles looked curiously at Julia, having no idea she had given any thought to the beliefs of their neighbors. "I suppose I do not know specifically what the Clarks believe, though I have read enough about the Hicksites in *Friends Review* to know their beliefs are a good deal different than ours."

"Actually," Julia contradicted, "their beliefs are amazingly similar to ours." She then proceeded to tell them what Will had shared with her the day Rachel was born.

"That is interesting," Charles had to admit.

"Perhaps this family is not as far from the truth as we suspected," Rebecca said quietly.

"One must still be careful to uphold the truth as we know it," Charles cautioned.

"But Father," Julia said, exasperation coloring her voice, "can it be right to condemn a man because of something his Meeting supposedly believes?"

Charles began to smile, pleased that his daughter had the ability to argue a point with such tenacity. "I suppose we might invite them for one evening if thee would like. Thee does have a point about not passing judgment too quickly."

Julia felt a sense of accomplishment, like she had been defending the underdog and been triumphant. "I thank thee, Father. Could we invite them tomorrow?"

Rebecca laughed. "Unless thee has more ambition than I, I suggest we give ourselves a a few days to become prepared. How would next sixth day be?"

"I will ride to the Clark's tomorrow," Julia said firmly. "I think thee will see that thy prejudices have been unfounded."

Will's mother had been nearly as reluctant to accept the invitation as Julia's parents had been to extend it.

"It is not necessary to repay me for anything," Sarah had said kindly. "I was simply using the gifts God has given me to help a neighbor in need." Julia had continued to press Sarah to accept the invitation and finally it was Will who helped persuade his mother.

"Mother," he said gently, "Thee needs to be with people. Thee has not been out of the house since Father..."

"Since thy father went to be with the Lord," Sarah finished the sentence for her son. "It is proper, William, for a woman to grieve for the man who provided for her and fathered her children."

"Yes, but it has been four weeks since thee left the house except when thee assisted Rebecca in the birth of Rachel—and I am certain thee would feel better if thee would begin this first step toward becoming a member of the community once again."

Sarah turned once again to look at Julia, deciding to get at the heart of the matter. "Is thee certain thy parents wish to break bread with a member of the Hicksite persuasion?"

"We had a long talk about the beliefs of thee and thy family, and they realized our beliefs are quite similar."

"And just how did thee know what my family believes?" Sarah asked pointedly.

"Will and I had a good deal of time to discuss a number of subjects while thee assisted Mother," Julia replied.

"I suppose if thee is certain thy family is in favor of this, we should not be so rude as to decline their invitation," Sarah said reluctantly.

As the grins spread across the faces of the two young people, Sarah began to wonder if there were something more than just an acquaintance between her son and this pretty young girl. Though she was still reluctant to risk scorn at the hands of an orthodox family, the Joneses had seemed like honest, caring Friends, not ones given to that sort of judgment.

Julia and her mother spent the next several days preparing for their invited guests. As there were four other children besides Will and his mother to provide for, even deciding how to seat everyone at the table was a concern. Finally nearly all the preparations had been made and Julia was anxiously awaiting the evening. As she swept the front porch a few hours before the expected arrival of their neighbors, Julia was surprised to see someone riding up the lane on horseback. The rider was slowly approaching, leading Julia to believe this was not an emergency requiring her father. As the figure grew closer, Julia recognized the form of the visitor. But surely she must be mistaken. It could not possibly be...could it?

"Greetings, Julia," came the familiar voice. "I know this is a surprise, but I did say my horse might find his way to your home some time this summer!"

"Greetings, Jonathan! This is indeed a surprise!" Julia thought of all the times she had wished for a visit from one of her academy friends, yet now that Jonathan was standing before her she was torn between wanting to see him and wanting him to leave before Will and his family arrived.

"Well, is thee going to invite a thirsty traveler in for a cool drink of water?" Jonathan teased, thinking Julia's speechlessness was solely due to his unexpected arrival.

"I am sorry, Jonathan. Please. Come and meet my mother and new sister."

"I did not know thy mother was expecting a child!" Jonathan said curiously. "Thee never mentioned thee would be returning to school with a new member in thy family."

"I was not very excited about the prospect, I am afraid," Julia confessed. "I did not even tell Suzannah the news, hoping if I did not think about it, it would not happen." She laughed. "That was rather childish, I must admit! But Rachel is a beautiful baby, and I have enjoyed her more than I could ever have imagined."

"She can not be as beautiful as her older sister," Jonathan said with a smile.

Julia laughed, thinking how Jonathan had always managed to say just the right things to make a person feel special, and she was glad he had made the effort to find her home and stop for a visit.

As they entered the kitchen, Jonathan immediately noticed the table set with far more places than would be necessary for Julia's family.

"I am sorry, Julia. I can see thee is planning to entertain guests this evening. I will greet thy mother and sister and be on my way."

"But thee has traveled all this way..."

"Actually, I have been in Salem the past two days visiting my aunt and uncle. When I told them I knew thee from school, they suggested I at least greet thee while I was here."

"Julia, is someone there?" came Rebecca's voice from the bedroom where she had been nursing Rachel.

"It is a friend from the academy," Julia called.

Soon Rebecca emerged with a sleeping Rachel in her arms. Jonathan quickly moved to view the baby, a gentle smile forming as he touched Rachel's tiny hand. "She is so precious! I love children and some day I hope to have a whole house full!"

Julia saw the wistful look on Jonathan's face and felt a pang of guilt that she did not share those same feelings. "Thee will make a wonder father some day," Julia said sincerely, hoping Jonathan would not read more into her words than were there.

But Jonathan simply smiled and began to tell her what had been happening in the lives of the friends she had left behind in Pleasant Plain.

"I must be going," Jonathan said when all the news had been shared.

"We would be happy for thee to stay and join us in the evening meal," Rebecca offered. "Thee has traveled all this way to see my daughter, and it would be a shame if thee did not have a chance to spend some time together. The meal is planned and it is a simple matter to add another plate to our table."

MOTHER! Julia thought! Please do not encourage Jonathan to stay! What would Will think if he arrived for supper and found Jonathan there? Julia did not feel like trying to explain Jonathan to Will or Will to Jonathan when she considered both to be good friends and nothing more.

"I really would not want to interrupt thy plans," Jonathan said.

"Nonsense! The Clarks have a son nearly thy age, and I am certain the three of thee would have a nice time together."

"Well..." Jonathan hesitated.

"Perhaps his aunt and uncle are expecting him for supper," Julia suggested, hoping that might be the case. Julia looked imploringly at her mother, desperately wishing she would get the message that this was not a good idea.

"No, actually I told them not to wait for me as I was not certain what my plans would be," Jonathan turned and smiled at Julia.

"Good," Rebecca said firmly. "Then it is settled. Thee will break bread with us tonight."

Wonderful! Julia thought. This was not going to be an enjoyable evening at all. Perhaps she should pretend to be ill and retire to her room. No, she thought, that will not solve anything, and she knew she would just have to make the best of it.

The Clarks arrived at the appointed hour, and the introductions went as well as Julia could have expected. Will looked curiously at Jonathan, though he extended his hand in greeting with a smile. Jonathan, too, seemed to be sizing up this neighbor, though his manner was congenial.

The conversation around the supper table was light: the weather, the prospects for the upcoming harvest, and Charles's current patients being the main topics. When they had finished eating, Rebecca insisted Jonathan, Julia and Will move to the porch were it was cooler. Charles volunteered to help Rebecca and Sarah clear the table, and Will's siblings were content to try and get Rachel to smile at them.

Once they were seated on the porch, none of the three young people knew quite what to say. Finally it was Will who broke the silence.

"Tell me about the academy. Are there many students attending?"

Jonathan spoke first. "I believe they are expecting around fifty to enroll this fall. It seems like a lot when everyone is together in the assembly hall."

"We both have a lot of friends," Julia added, hoping Will would think Jonathan was just one of many friends she had made while at Pleasant Plain.

"Does one have to be of any religious persuasion to attend?" Will asked.

"No, we have students from a variety of backgrounds," Jonathan said.

"They even accept Hicksites!" Julia teased.

Will laughed, then said wistfully, "I wish I had the opportunity to attend."

"Why not come and enroll?" Jonathan suggested. "They are always looking for new students. Our principal even suggested last spring that we make sure we let those in our home towns know of the academy."

Julia knew Will would never feel he could leave his family now that his father was gone. Her heart went out to him as he shared the tragedy his family had experience just a few weeks ago.

"I truly am sorry," Jonathan said empathetically. "Perhaps when thy brother is older he can assume some of the responsibilities of the home so thee can attend."

Will looked sharply at Jonathan, not believing he could even suggest such a thing. "I am the head of the home now, and I will remain in that position until I am old or my mother finds another man to be a helpmate."

Julia sought to ease the mounting tension between the two boys. "Jonathan lost *his* father a few years ago as well," she said.

"But I have felt that going to school and getting a good education was the only way I could assure my family would be provided for in the future," Jonathan added.

"We each must do what we feel best," Will said with a trace of bitterness. "I, for one, know my place is with my family."

"Perhaps some day they will not need thee as much as they do now," Jonathan said quietly.

Will looked away, obviously disagreeing with Jonathan.

"Would thee like some lemonade?" Julia was determined to get the conversation on a lighter note.

"None for me, thank you," Will said.

"Nor I. I am about ready to burst from all the supper I ate!" Jonathan concurred. "In fact, I probably should be returning to my aunt and uncle's before dark. I am not very familiar with this area, and it would be a pity if I were to wander around lost for a day or two!"

Both Will and Julia laughed, sensing Jonathan was not the type to ever get lost. Julia excused herself, walking with Jonathan as he went to get his horse from the barn.

"I am glad thee came tonight," Julia began, realizing that she truly had been glad to see him, in spite of the terrible timing of his arrival.

"Is that right?" Jonathan asked with a wry smile. "I do not believe thy friend Will was quite as happy as thee to have an intruder present!"

"Thee is not an intruder!" Julia said emphatically.

"Is thee seeing Will?"

Julia was taken back by the question. Not one word had been spoken by either herself or Will to indicate they were anything more than neighbors and friends.

"No," she said carefully, "I am not seeing Will. Why would thee think that?"

"I saw the way he kept looking at thee, Julia. He is obviously more interested in thee than thee thinks!"

Julia tried to be diplomatic. "Will is a nice neighbor, and his family has been through a terrible ordeal with the death of his father."

"As I said, Julia, I saw the way he looks at thee. My only question is, how does thee feel about him? Is there any hope for me?"

"Oh Jonathan," Julia said quietly, "I tried to share my feelings with thee that night thee rode with me back to Levi's. Thee knows I am seeking God's call for my life and I do not believe it involves marriage and family."

"And has thee heard the call this summer as thee had hoped?"

"No," Julia said sadly. "I pray and read the scriptures every single day, but there is no Light to show me the way. Perhaps God wants me to develop patience!" she finished, trying to lighten the mood.

"Will thee be at Yearly Meeting this year? If thee received the Light at last year's gathering, perhaps God will speak to thee again this year."

"I had nearly forgotten about it," Julia admitted. "I have no idea if Mother will feel like attending or not, nor if Father can leave his practice right now. Will thee be attending?"

"I would not miss it! I have heard that Elizabeth Comstock intends to be present for at least part of the sessions. I have heard so much about her from the Mendenhalls that I am anxious to meet her. She has been a powerful voice in the Friends' movement."

"Did she write an article recently for the *Friends Review*?" Julia asked, excitement evident in her voice.

"Yes, did thee read it?"

"I occasionally read articles that look interesting, and I did take time to read what she had written. I am always interested in reading what other *women* have to say, and everything she wrote was almost exactly what I believe!"

"Then maybe thee can persuade thy family to attend this year. It would be great to see thee again and have a chance for a *real* visit."

Julia knew Jonathan was referring to their less than personal evening. "I will see if I can persuade my parents," she replied, though her desire to attend was to meet Elizabeth Comstock, not to spend more time with Jonathan.

"Thee can always stay with the Mendenhalls if thy parents can not attend."

Julia knew her father would never allow her to attend on her own, but she simply nodded her head, realizing she had left Will alone for too long and should be getting back.

"I thank thee for coming," she said again, turning to go.

"I still care about thee a great deal," Jonathan said as he turned to climb on his horse. "Please do not totally dismiss a future with me. I still believe that could be God's plan for thee."

Julia had no reply, realizing there was nothing she could say that would change Jonathan's feelings toward her. Only time would help him accept the truth.

As soon as Jonathan was on his way, Julia quickly ran back to the porch. Just as she climbed the steps she could hear Sarah's voice as she began gathering her family to leave.

She had to talk to Will and salvage what she could of the evening. When Will came out the door Julia motioned for him to follow her out of earshot of their families.

"I am sorry Jonathan came today of all days!" she said apologetically. "I had no idea he would be here!"

Will looked curiously at this girl he so admired, wondering just what kind of relationship she had had in the past with Jonathan. "Is thee seeing him?" he finally asked.

"That is exactly what Jonathan asked about thee and me!"

"And what did thee tell him?"

"I told him nothing."

"That is what I supposed," Will said sadly. "I had hoped we could become better acquainted and one day I could ask to come calling in thy home. I should have known thee would have a suitor at school."

"Jonathan and I are just good friends, which is what I thought you and I were."

"But I am certain that will change when thee is back at school. I saw the look on Jonathan's face when he spoke of thee returning to school together."

Where had she been, Julia wondered, when all these looks had been going on?! Trying to keep the conversation on safe ground, she thought. The last thing she wanted to do was hurt Will, or Jonathan for that matter. Now it seemed they both had been hurt.

"I am sorry, Will. There is much I need to tell thee."

Julia began to repeat what she had shared with Jonathan, including the call of God on her life. "I am sorry if I said or did anything to mislead you," she finally said, feeling miserable for having disappointed two fine young men in one evening. "Will thee still ride over for a visit now and then?" Julia asked hopefully.

"I will probably be too busy with the harvesting, though I shall try to see thee again before thee leaves for school."

"That would be nice," Julia said warmly, hoping he knew her words were sincere.

Will, too, found a smile and said, "I really like thee, Julia, and if thy plans do not work out, I would be happy to see thee as more than a friend." Will took the horse and carriage he had been in the process of hitching and left the barn.

The farewells were genuine, and Julia was happy to see their two families had managed to look beyond their prejudices and realize they had much in common. As Julia and her father stood on the porch watching the Clarks drive away, Julia knew she was tense from the pressures of the evening. It gave her a warm feeling to have her father's arm around her shoulder.

"Those are certainly two nice young men, Julia."

"Yes, they are," she said simply.

"Just remember thee is not yet seventeen and there will be many others interested in thee. Thee is smart and beautiful and I am proud of thee."

Julia smiled at her father. Maybe he was finally realizing she was not a child any more. She would try and make wise decisions about her future. *God's* future for her. She had to get to yearly meeting and seek the wise counsel of Elizabeth Comstock, if that were possible. Perhaps another woman—a woman of God, could help her solve the puzzle of her future—her life!

CHAPTER 21

A POWERFUL WITNESS

As the time for Yearly Meeting drew closer, Julia's anxiety rose as she tried to figure out a way she could attend. Her mother had said quite emphatically that she had no intention of taking a six-week-old baby all the way to Oskaloosa, and her father had said he was as busy as he had been in a long time and did not see how he could be gone a week. Julia thought of asking for permission to go with another family from Salem, but she knew her parents would object, not wanting to burden someone else with what they considered to be their responsibility.

Not only did Julia feel disheartened over Yearly Meeting, but there was also the fact that Will had not ridden past their homestead since the night he and Jonathan had both come to supper. She wanted to ride over and see how he and his family were doing, but her pride prevented such action. If Will were angry because of what she had told him, it was probably for the best that they not see one another.

As Julia worked around the house the day Yearly Meeting was scheduled to begin, she had trouble holding back the tears. It simply was unfair that she must stay home when such a wonderful woman as Elizabeth Comstock was to be at this year's sessions. There were a number of things she wished she could talk to this woman about...like the plain clothing and language, not to mention revival meetings and holiness doctrine and, most importantly of all, her future. But could she attend? No, she had to remain at home with her mother and baby sister. Feeling wholly consumed by her unhappiness, Julia did not even hear the horse and rider approach the house the morning she should have been preparing to go to Yearly Meeting. Rebecca was sitting in the rocker her mother and father had brought in the covered wagon from Indiana, trying to get Rachel to fall asleep. She motioned for Julia to answer the knock at the door.

"Will!" Julia gasped in surprise when she saw her neighbor standing on the porch, nervously twisting the brim of his hat.

"Hello, Julia, I hope this is not an inconvenience for thee."

"Actually, I would welcome a bright spot in my otherwise dismal day," Julia said with a bitter laugh. After telling her mother it was Will and that they would be on the porch, she closed the door behind her and was surprised to see Will smiling as if nothing had ever transpired between the two of them. He looked more relaxed than she had seen him since his father's death, especially once he quit playing with the brim of his hat. "It is good to see thee again," he finally said with a smile.

"I thought perhaps thee had decided to speak with me again after our last evening together."

"For a good many days that is exactly how I felt!" he began. "Then one day I said 'Will, you fool, you are just handing this girl to Jonathan White on a silver platter! If this girl is worth fighting for, then fight! Don't lie down and cry about it. So here I am! I know thee said thee was seeking God's will for thy life, but if His will might include me, I do not want to miss out because of my pride!" He looked at Julia for the first time since he had begun speaking, almost afraid to see if there was laughter on her face.

Julia, however, was so embarrassed by Will's proclamation that she simply stood looking at him, not knowing what to say.

"I am sorry, Julia. I did not mean to offend thee by my words. I realize I am too forward at times, but I have always thought it better to say what was on one's mind. I have never spoken much to a girl, or should I say *a woman*." Will paused as if uncertain whether to continue or remain silent.

"I am glad thee decided to return," Julia finally said, "though I must tell thee nothing has changed in my thinking where marriage is concerned. I have to know what God wants of me."

"I respect thy wishes, Julia, but surely thee plans to marry *some* day!"

"Whether or not I marry some day remains to be seen. It is difficult to explain, but at this moment I have no desire to marry, and certainly no desire to begin a family! Since I know that is what thee wants, it would not be honest of me to encourage thee in any way. It simply would not be fair to thee."

"All right, Julia, I will not discuss this with thee again."

"I would like to be friends, Will. Does thee think that is possible?"

Will took a long time to answer, but finally he was able to speak. "If I can not have thee for a wife, I would still like to be thy friend."

As Julia and Will began to walk down the path that led to the grove of locust trees, the words seemed to flow freely between the two friends, as if the dam of silence had been broken and a flood of words unleashed. Will spoke of his family and his plans for the harvest. Even though he knew what harvest involved, he had never before had the total responsibility on his shoulders. He shared of the sleepless nights he had spent trying to plan for the unexpected as well as the expected. Julia felt compassion for this young man who had been thrust into the role of 'head of the home' at such a young age.

Julia, in turn, shared with Will the frustration she had felt at not being allowed to attend Yearly Meeting, though Will did not quite understand why she would want to gather with a group that had been so negative towards the Hicksite Friends.

"It is the friendships I have made with various Friends over the years that makes the time so special—that and the opportunity to meet with Elizabeth Comstock," she said sadly. "I just know if I had a chance to speak with her she would help me discover God's plan for my life."

As they turned back toward Julia's home, Will reached over and took her hand, a gesture that disturbed Julia—though she did not pull away from him. She was surprised at the roughness of his skin, never having felt a working man's hand before. Will's grip was firm, just as she would expect. Afraid of what her father might say, Julia quickly let go of Will's hand as they neared the porch. Sensing her discomfort, Will stopped before they were within hearing distance of the cabin.

"I hope thee has a good school year," he said smiling.

"And I hope thee finds the girl of thy dreams," Julia said sincerely, for this fine young man deserved a lot more than she could ever have offered him.

Will leaned forward and kissed Julia on the cheek, a gesture quite similar to Jonathan's that night in Pleasant Plain. "Farewell, Julia. I hope to see thee before thee returns home next spring."

"I would like that too, Will," she said simply.

Will continued to look at Julia for a few more minutes, then quickly remounted his horse and headed back toward his home. When Julia entered the cabin, her father looked carefully to see if Julia's expression would reveal what had transpired during her time with Will.

Seeing the solemn look on her face Charles quickly asked the question he was quite certain would bring back her smile.

"Julia, I was wondering if thee might be up to a bit of traveling?"

"What does thee mean?" Julia was instantly alert, hoping against hope that he might be speaking of yearly meeting.

"What I mean is, if someone were to travel to Oskaloosa for a day or two, does thee think thee could tear thyself away from thy friend Will and thy new sister in order to make the journey?"

Julia moved closer to her father, wondering if she dared believe what she thought he might be saying. "Is there a possibility...might thee mean...could we possibly..."

"Yes, Julia," Charles was now openly laughing, deciding it was time to tell Julia his plan. "Would thee have any interest in attending Yearly Meeting for a few days?"

"How can thee even ask such a question?!" Julia exclaimed. "Thee knows I have a great longing for just such an opportunity. But I thought thee could not leave thy practice."

"I have delivered two babies this week which were not scheduled to arrive for several days, and my most severely ill patient went to be with the Lord. It is as if God were arranging my schedule to allow us to attend a part of this year's gathering of Friends. But only for a few days," he added, not wanting her to become too optimistic.

Julia impulsively wrapped her arms around her father, letting him know just how much this announcement meant to her. "When do we leave?" she asked impatiently.

"How soon can thee be ready?"

"I could be ready in a few minutes!" she said eagerly.

"Then I suggest thee get thy belongings together because if we leave within the half hour we should arrive in Pleasant Plain in time to catch the 7:15 train to Oskaloosa."

Julia flew to her room and began to pack her belongings. Since they would be there for only two or three days, it did not take her long to gather the things she would need when they got to Oskaloosa. Soon she was impatiently sitting in the kitchen waiting for her mother to finish saying farewell to her father. Finally they both emerged from the bedroom, Charles with a small carpet bag in his hand, Rebecca with tears in her eyes. After a few words of admonition for his wife about avoiding strangers who might come to the cabin, and not taking the baby out too long in the damp fall air, father and daughter were ready to travel.

"I hope thee has a wonderful time!" Rebecca said warmly, though Julia knew her mother's smile was masking her true feelings.

"I wish thee could come with us," Julia whispered in her ear as she hugged her good-bye.

"We will go together next year, that is a promise!"

Though Julia nodded in agreement, she somehow knew that this might indeed be the last time she attended yearly meeting with her parents. The thought frightened her, while at the same time bringing a feeling of exhilaration. What *would* she be doing a year from now? She hoped to have the answer, soon.

After Charles gave Rebecca one last hug and kiss, he joined Julia in the carriage and quickly urged the horse toward their destination.

They rode in silence for a time before Charles finally decided to ask the question that had been on his mind for a while. "Julia...it is hard for me to believe thee is nearly seventeen and going into thy second year at the academy."

"I should think thee would be happy to have me learning at an institution that teaches its students to be aware of their abilities. And one that is so far from home," she teased.

Charles laughed. "Julia, thee has never been an *easy* child to nurture, but thee has *always* been a delight!"

Julia felt the warmth of her father's words, wishing they had had more opportunities to share with each other the way they were doing right then.

"I am concerned, however, about thy future..." he paused, waiting for her response. When there was none, he continued. "I have seen the way Will Clark looks at thee, and when Jonathan White was in our home, he, too, seemed to be quite smitten with thee. Now either of these fine young men would be suitable candidates for marriage—IF thee were a few years older. But

Julia, thee is so young, and there are so many opportunities for thee. I believe God has a special plan for thy life, and I would hate to see thee settle for a husband and family at a young age and miss what God might have for thee."

Julia was touched by her father's concern, and quickly assured him she was not planning a future with either Jonathan or Will.

"Please keep me in thy prayers, Father. I want to do what God wants me to do, and right now I am not certain just what that calling might be. I do enjoy being with both Will and Jonathan, but we are just friends for now."

The look Charles gave Julia spoke of his doubts where the two boys were concerned, but he did not say what was on his mind. Instead, he turned the conversation to the happenings at Yearly Meeting.

"I understand Elizabeth Comstock is quite an evangelist!" he said.

"What can thee tell me about her?" Julia asked eagerly, wanting to know more about this highly regarded woman.

"Thee has heard of Elizabeth Fry, has thee not?"

"Of course! Every Friend who has listened at all in Meeting knows of Elizabeth Fry's work in the prisons."

"Well, Elizabeth Comstock has tried to emulate Elizabeth Fry. It has been said that as a young girl in England, Comstock was drawn to Fry and her work, often seeking the older woman's counsel. When Comstock moved to America, she began to feel a burden for the women locked away in our prisons. Some say she has visited more prisons in America than Fry ever entered. She has also taken an interest in both the Orthodox and Hicksite Yearly Meetings, encouraging Friends to reconcile their differences. I heard one man say she was the most powerful messenger of the Lord he had ever heard!"

"She must really be filled with the Holy Spirit if *men* are speaking that highly of a *woman*!"

"Julia!" Charles laughed. "We men are not all of the persuasion that the male is superior to the female!"

"I have met a few in my life who believed they were superior, especially at school. Joseph Bell, for example, was nearly intolerable!"

"When you say 'was', am I to presume you no longer have that opinion of him?"

"Well," Julia said slowly, "Joseph became a believer around the first month and he has become more bearable since then."

Charles smiled again, loving this daughter whose strong feelings would guide her when making important decisions. "As far as I am concerned," he said quietly, "God will work in whatever human vessel is open to Him, be it male or female."

Julia was proud of her father, knowing he had a great deal more wisdom than she possessed. The two continued to visit about school and the boarding situation for the coming year. Charles surprised Julia by telling her he had been in contact with Suzannah Johnson's family and had arranged for her to board with them for the coming year.

"That will be wonderful!" Julia said excitedly. "Suzannah is engaged to marry Joseph Bell, though. Will my staying there interfere with her plans?"

"Not at all. Suzannah and Joseph have decided to wait until next summer to marry so I am certain Suzannah will be happy to have thee there to help her make all the plans."

Julia and Charles continued to speak of school and the classes she would be taking during the next session. Before either father or daughter knew it, they were in Pleasant Plain and secured the services of the livery stable for the horse and carriage. The train was only a few minutes late, assuring them arrival in Oskaloosa before the tenth hour.

Though the train ride was a great adventure, Julia's mind was on the future, namely the opportunity to meet Elizabeth Comstock. Would it not be wonderful if she could actually speak with the divine woman? Just the thought was exciting. What had begun as a totally dismal week was now becoming the highlight of her summer—maybe even her life! She could hardly wait until they were actually seated among Friends, listening to the words of the Holy Spirit spoken by Elizabeth Comstock. She just had to find a way to speak to the woman who might hold the key that would open the door to her future!

CHAPTER 22

A HIGHER CALLING

As soon as Julia and Charles arrived in Oskaloosa, they walked the few blocks to their hotel and secured a room. As the hour was late, Charles insisted they retire immediately in order to be ready for a full day's business when they awoke. Julia was anxious to look for some of the others from the academy who might be attending, but she resigned herself to doing as her father suggested.

When Julia awoke the next morning to find her father fully dressed and reading a paper he had acquired in the hotel lobby, she realized she had slept longer than she intended. "Why did thee not wake me?" she asked, quickly moving to change clothes behind the dressing screen in their room.

"I thought thee needed thy sleep...and besides, I was enjoying this time of quiet. It is a rare occasion when I have the opportunity to enjoy a cup of coffee and the newspaper in the morning. Did thee sleep well?"

"This is the most comfortable bed I have ever slept in!" Julia exclaimed.

"It was a bit better than the hard mattresses I used to sleep on as a young boy!" Charles admitted. "If we hurry, I believe we can catch the horse-drawn carriage out to the meeting house before morning worship begins."

Julia quickly finished dressing, and after she and Charles had straightened their belongings they were on their way out of the hotel.

"Would thee like to stop for something to eat?" Charles asked as they approached the hotel dining room.

"No, I am not the least bit hungry," Julia said, anxious to travel to the Meeting House and see if she could catch a glimpse of Elizabeth Comstock.

When Charles and Julia arrived, a number of Friends were entering the place of worship. Julia was surprised to look over and see Jonathan and Joseph walking together. But as the moments before worship were to be a time of solemn reflection, she did not feel free to call to the boys. She tried to wave to them in a way that would not attract a lot of attention. Unfortunately, she could not get *anyone's* attention! I will be sure to find them after the service, she thought to herself as she and her father entered the building for the joint worship service, sitting in one of the last rows of benches.

The service began in the silence with a number of Friends sharing how God had moved in their lives. After a long period of silence, a woman rose and walked to the front of the room, turning to address the meeting. Julia instantly knew this Friend must surely be Elizabeth Comstock. She wore a full black dress, but she also wore a light colored outer cape which seemed to flow after her as she walked. Her dark brown hair was parted in the middle and pulled to the back of her head. Rather than the wide-brimmed scuttle bonnet of most of the women present, this woman had a small, white nearly transparent covering which fit tightly to her head. It was not her physical appearance, however, that intrigued Julia, it was her countenance. She seemed to exude compassion; to be the kind of person with whom you could bare your soul. As Elizabeth began to speak her voice was clear and confident and Julia knew this was a woman who could indeed give her the answers to her questions.

Elizabeth began by telling the gathering of her experiences with both the Baltimore and Indiana Yearly Meetings. She also spoke of the time she met with those of the Christian Church in Washington D.C., and of her friendship with Dwight Moody while living in Chicago. She told them of the splendor and extravagance she had observed in the nation's capitol while thousands were suffering from want.

"Friends," she continued, "we are living in a time of great change both within our meetings and in this country where we live. Our prisons are overflowing with suffering men, women, and children. We allow strong drink to be served to the weak who then commit crimes against themselves and their families. And what do we do?" Elizabeth's voice was growing stronger, her passion for these injustices evident as she began to move from one side of the room to the other.

"What do we do? My Friends, we spend our time arguing among ourselves as to how holiness is obtained, or whether or not one should speak the plain language or wear the plain clothing. We waste our time, we waste our lives, we waste our opportunity to make a difference in this world because we are only looking inward.

"Now some of you are no doubt saying to yourselves, well, she is a woman—what does she know? And I am here to tell you that whether I am woman or man, Friend or Episcopalian, black or white, I am a messenger of the Lord, put on this earth to do His work. I must feed the hungry, heal the sick, visit the lost souls in prison, and speak to gatherings such as this. One of the peculiarities of Friends I have long embraced is the belief that every child of God is a minister, regardless of their circumstances in this life.

"Friends, I am pleading with you today to quit quibbling over such unimportant matters as whether holiness is an instant act or something that takes place over time. At this very hour there are men and women rotting in our prisons without hope. There are black men, women and children who have been freed from slavery but are now suffering because they have no place to live, no way to make a living. They are fleeing to Kansas even as I speak to you this morning, hoping to find a better life. But they need your help...they need money, food, clothing and a chance for an education.

"Friends, I beseech you...how can we sit here with our false pride while humanity suffers? Salvation must include the soul, mind and body. We are so inwardly focused we miss the greater calling! We have become narrow and ingrown."

Elizabeth stopped speaking and Julia thought she was finished. When she did not sit down, however, Julia wondered what else the evangelist might say. Julia knew in her heart that everything that had been spoken up to this point was truth. She had never been as moved as she felt at that moment. This was a powerful feeling, totally different from how she had felt after hearing Lawrie Tatum at the revival.

"Friends," Elizabeth finally spoke, this time in a quiet voice, "I believe there are some of you here this day who are feeling the prodding of the Holy Spirit. I have felt the presence of the Spirit in this place, and I believe God wants to call some of you into His service. Perhaps you are thinking you could never go into a prison, or be an evangelist, or aid a freed man or join the fight to abolish strong liquor. But remember this: if God calls you, He will also equip you to do His work. I am not going to stand here and beg you to offer yourselves to God. But I am inviting you to come and pray with other Friends as we seek to know God's will for our lives in this terrible time we are living."

And with those words, Elizabeth simply sat back down. It was so still in the room Julia was certain everyone could hear the pounding of her heart and her rapid breathing. She knew she wanted to go forward and pray with this woman, but she was afraid to be the first to go, and also afraid of what her father would say. Unlike at the revival meeting in Richland, Julia found she could no longer sit still and she quickly rose and began moving to the front. Others, too, were walking forward, and Julia joined them as they knelt together.

Julia was not certain what she was expected to do, so she simply bowed her head and quietly asked God to reveal to her what He wanted her to do with her life. After several minutes had passed, she felt an arm around her shoulder. Without looking up, Julia sensed it was Elizabeth, though she did not want to turn her head and look.

"Just pour thy heart out in prayer," Elizabeth said softly, "and then listen for the speaking of the Holy Spirit."

"But how will I know it is the Spirit?" Julia asked softly, wanting to be certain she was not just listening to the thoughts of her own mind.

"When the Spirit speaks," Elizabeth said, "you will know in your mind, and in your body, and in your soul. If you have doubts, it is most likely your own thoughts. Would you like for me to pray with you?"

"Please." Julia said simply.

Elizabeth reached over and took Julia's hand in hers and then began to pray. It was a simple prayer, asking God to reveal His will to this young woman through the ministering of the Holy Spirit. As Elizabeth prayed, Julia felt a calmness in her soul as she suddenly knew her calling. But could she do as God seemed to be asking?

There had been several times during the past year when Julia felt the urging of the Spirit into some type of evangelistic ministry, though she had tried to ignore her feelings. She knew her friends at the academy thought she was the top debater at their school, but could a debater be the type of evangelist that Elizabeth Comstock was? Could she help Friends see the narrowness of their thinking and show them the causes for which they *should* be concentrating their energies? Julia did not know the answers to all her questions, but she did know the answer to the most important one. Yes, she would answer God's call.

Finally Julia rose from her knees and joined the other Friends slowly leaving the meeting house. When she realized she was walking next to Elizabeth, she finally allowed herself to study this woman she suddenly felt very close to.

"Would thee like to share the noon meal with me?" Elizabeth asked, sensing Julia needed someone to talk to.

"I would like that," Julia said simply, "though I will need to tell my father."

"Thee may invite him as well if thee would like."

"No, I would rather talk with thee alone, if thee does not mind. There are several questions I would like to ask." Julia then left to find her father, returning shortly to Elizabeth's side.

Elizabeth was everything in person that she had been as a speaker: warm, compassionate, and sincerely interested in Julia's questions. When Julia told her she had felt God calling her into the ministry, Elizabeth's face shone. "That is wonderful!" she said warmly. "There are not enough women who believe God can use them in this way. I sense thee is a strong-willed young woman, which is just what thee will need to be to overcome the prejudices against women that exist even among Friends. It is not an easy calling, that of evangelism. Though I have been blessed with a husband who encourages me to travel in my ministry, many men would not be so understanding. In fact, it takes a strong man to accept a wife who may receive more accolades than he does."

Julia thought of both Will and Jonathan and suddenly knew why neither of them were to be in her future. Will would want a woman who could help him on the farm, while Jonathan would probably settle in a large city where he could work with the poor and downtrodden. Neither would want a traveling evangelist for a wife! So that was why God had not given her feelings for either of these fine young men.

And suddenly Julia realized that she did not need a husband in order to follow God's leading, though she certainly did not want to rule out the possibility at some time later in her life. For now, it was enough to know she had heard the call and answered, and that she would prepare her life to serve God wherever He sent her.

Julia asked for Elizabeth's opinion on a number of issues as they broke bread together, and Elizabeth always gave careful consideration to her answers. The passing of time seemed unimportant as they shared their thoughts with one another. Several hours passed as if only a few minutes, and Julia felt as though she had known this great woman all her life.

When Julia and Elizabeth finally left the dining area to search for Charles, Julia heard the voice of Jonathan as he and Joseph called to her from across the street. Elizabeth gave Julia's arm a squeeze, promising to pray for her. "I know I will hear thy name in the future," she said confidently. "God is going to use thee in a mighty way." She then paused as if considering whether or not to continue.

"What is it, Elizabeth?" Julia asked, realizing there was something on the mind of this great woman.

"Oh, Julia, the Spirit has been nudging me nearly the entire time we have been conversing."

"Oh, please tell me!" Julia implored. "What is the Spirit saying? Does it involve me? Is it about my future? Is God telling thee what I should do with my life?"

Elizabeth's laugh was gentle as she studied the eager young woman before her. Her fiery hair matched her strong will and Elizabeth felt good about the conversation they had had. But she was so young...not even eighteen, she would guess. Would caring parents allow a girl to do what she was feeling led to ask Julia to do? Would she, as a parent, allow her own child such freedom? But if this were really God's will, should she stand in the way?

"Elizabeth, you must tell me what is on thy mind!"

"All right, I will share with thee what the Spirit seems to be saying, and then we can pray together for the confirmation of the Inner Light. First, however, tell me a bit about thyself."

Though Julia thought this was a strange request, she quickly told Elizabeth of her family and of her previous year at the academy.

"And thee plans to return to the academy this fall?"

Julia was slow to answer, not wanting to interfere with what Elizabeth felt the Spirit might be leading her to do. "Yes, I *had* planned to return to the academy this fall...but I could certainly change my plans."

Elizabeth pondered what Julia had told her. "And thee will not be eighteen until the end of this year, is that correct?"

"Yes...but..."

"Then that is what we must do!"

Julia was completely baffled by Elizabeth's words. "Please! Tell me what thee is thinking!"

"Well, as thee knows from my message this morning, I have been working in Kansas these past few months with the black men and women from the south. There is a great need for an evangelist to speak at the morning worship services when I am away soliciting food and clothing for this work. Actually, it would be a great help to me to have another person to preach the messages every day so I could devote my time to other matters.

"When thee spoke of thy calling to evangelism it seemed as if the Spirit had led us to be together on this day. But now that thee has told me about thyself, it seems quite clear that thee must return to the academy for another year and the passing of thy eighteenth birthday. Then, when thee finishes the term thee can see if thee has an interest in the work I have begun in Kansas."

Julia was speechless, but excited. "Why not take me with thee now?" she asked. "I am certain I have enough head knowledge to be a good speaker, and if the Holy Spirit is giving me the messages, what more do I need?"

But Elizabeth was firm. "No, I do not believe this is the time for thee. If God is indeed calling thee into evangelism, then the call will still be there a year from now, and hopefully it will be even stronger. Thee must want to do this work more than thee wants to eat and drink!"

Sensing there was no point in arguing, Julia promised Elizabeth to return to the academy and prepare for her work in Kansas. The two women then prayed together and wept together—tears of joy that they were both doing what God was asking of them. Both promised to write one another, and Elizabeth assured Julia she would make the arrangements for her to come to Kansas if she still felt this was where God wanted her to be.

When Elizabeth had gone, Julia sought to find Jonathan and Joseph and tell them all that had transpired. She was not certain they would believe her, but she had never felt so right about her life. It would not be easy, but her determination had seen her through in the past, and she would let nothing get in her way of answering God's call. The hope of the future burned brightly as she thought of all she must do to prepare for it.

CHAPTER 23

FUTURE CHOICES

Each day of the new school year seemed to drag by as Julia prepared herself for her work with Elizabeth. As she had predicted, neither Jonathan nor Joseph had taken her seriously when she had told them of her call and her plans to travel to Kansas to work with Elizabeth when the school year was finished. Only Suzannah, her best friend, truly believed Julia would follow through with her plans. It had been such a blessing to live with Suzannah's family during the term as they had treated her as one of their own. The two girls had also spent many hours in the kitchen of Martha Mendenhall as the Mendenhalls lived only a short distance down the road from the Johnsons.

Martha was as solid a Christian woman as Julia thought she would ever meet, and she valued her judgment. In fact, Martha was the only other person with whom Julia felt she could share God's call on her life and how she was preparing to go to work with Elizabeth when the school year was finished. Martha had offered to pray with Julia on a regular basis to make certain the call was from God, and both women felt the confirmation of the Inner Light that this was indeed God's plan.

When the school year finished and there was no word from Elizabeth as to how or when Julia was to join her in Kansas, Julia anxiously said good-bye to her friends at the academy, wishing she could tell them of her plans, but beginning to wonder if Elizabeth had actually said she would send for her or if Julia had just imagined it.

Then, after she had been home only a few weeks, it was announced in Meeting that Elizabeth Comstock would be speaking at the Pleasant Plain Meeting the first week of the sixth month if Friends wished to hear of her work in Kansas. Julia was certain this was an answer to her prayers. She immediately sent word to Martha Mendenhall that she must speak with Elizabeth and could Martha possibly try and arrange a meeting for Julia with the evangelist.

And now here she was in the Pleasant Plain Meeting House, the rough hewn wooden floor boards creaking ominously as she paced back and forth, back and forth. Her hands, too, were in continuous motion as she twisted the handkerchief first one way, then another. What would she say? What would Elizabeth think of her if she knew how nervous she felt? Fortunately, the door to the Pleasant Plain Meeting House soon opened and Julia stood, at last, in front of the woman she had so admired since first hearing her speak almost a year ago.

Sensing the young woman's nervousness, Elizabeth quickly sought to put her at ease .

"Julia!" she exclaimed warmly. "It is so good to see thee again."

"I...I...I believe, I mean, I am pleased thee could take time from thy travels to speak with me. I know thy work is so important, and I am so anxious to know of thy accomplishments this past year with the freed men."

"Julia..." Elizabeth began quietly, "I believe we are here to discuss *thy* future, not my work. I can think of nothing more important than a person's call from God! My train does not arrive until tomorrow morning, so we have all afternoon to catch up on the past year and make plans for the future. Now...I believe it is too beautiful a day to sit inside a stuffy meeting house. Let us walk out past the cemetery to that lovely grove of trees I noticed when the train was approaching the depot. We can sit in God's quiet and speak with Him and one another."

Anxious to please, Julia quickly jumped to her feet and led the way outside. Neither woman spoke until they were comfortably seated beneath an old oak tree. Julia quickly stole a glance at the woman sitting next to her, wondering if she might have changed her mind about having Julia join her in her work. As Elizabeth sat leaning against the wide trunk of the tree, eyes closed as if she were in perfect harmony with God's creation, Julia thought again about their first encounter at Yearly Meeting.

Elizabeth had been supportive of Julia's call to the ministry at that time, but did she still feel the same? And would Elizabeth want someone who had not even had the courage to tell her own parents of her call and her plans? Julia had wanted to tell her mother and father of her calling, but each time she thought of trying to convince them that she thought the Lord wanted her to embark upon a life of uncertainty and possibly danger, her courage failed. All during the recently completed term at the academy Julia had rehearsed over and over again just what she would say to her parents. She had been certain there would somehow be a perfect time to discuss her future plans. She began to feel guilty as she thought of the times she could have broached the subject but had kept silent. Perhaps it was for the best, however, since she did not know if Elizabeth still believed she would be an asset to her work.

With eyes still closed, Elizabeth quietly interrupted Julia's thoughts.

"What is the Spirit leading thee to do, Julia? Has the past year at the academy been fruitful, and has it confirmed thy call?"

"Oh yes," Julia said fervently. "I have had a prayer partner and she and I have prayed regularly and we both feel the confirmation of the Inner Light."

"And thy friends—have they been supportive?" Julia laughed. "At first my best friend Suzannah was too amazed to even speak! Once she realized I was seeking confirmation of my calling, however, she was very supportive of my decision."

"And what about thy parents? Are they in support of this mission?"

Julia's face fell as she knew she must speak the truth. "I have not yet found the courage to tell them, and I wanted to be certain thee really wanted me to work with thee."

"Is thee afraid they will not be in favor of thee following God's call?"

"It is just that my father is so protective of me...I had to talk many hours to persuade him to allow me to attend the academy. I have no idea how to convince him that this is what I should do with my life."

"Julia," Elizabeth said gently, "If thee does not have the courage to speak with thy parents, how does thee think thee will deal with the adversities that will be present when thee arrives in Kansas? The Negro race has been downtrodden and mistreated for decades and thy ministry to them will not be easy."

"I know thee will have to teach me a great deal, but I am a quick learner and I will work hard. And I will find a way to tell my parents—at least I will if thee still wants me. I suppose my thoughts this past year have mostly centered on answering God's call...on speaking in such a manner so as to compel sinners to seek repentance and forgiveness."

Elizabeth's gentle smile took some of the sting from her words. "Julia, being an evangelist is one of the most difficult callings Friends may receive. It is not for the weak of heart, nor is it for the doubter—the believer with little faith."

Julia's heart sank. Perhaps she had been deluding herself. How could God possibly call a young woman into the ministry?

More importantly, how could she, a not particularly brave eighteen year old, have ever thought God was calling her into the ministry of traveling evangelism, especially that of working with the Negroes?

"It is, however, one of the most rewarding paths one may embark upon," Elizabeth continued. "If God is truly calling thee to be a minister of the gospel, He will clear the path and provide the protection necessary for thee to carry out His calling."

In spite of her resolve not to cry, Julia felt the hot tears forming. Angrily she brushed them away. She had always been a strong person, and she would continue to keep her emotions in check. Once she felt back in control she asked the one question she had been asking herself every day since she first felt the calling. "But how can one be absolutely certain the call is of God, and not something a person just feels she should do?"

"I can see thou hast given the matter a good deal of thought and prayer. Perhaps if I share the circumstances of my own calling it will benefit thee.

"I, too, wondered how I was to know what God would have me do with my life. I found the confirmation for my calling in three distinct ways. First of all I sought the confirmation of the scriptures. When I read the words of James, chapter one, verse five, where he said, 'If any of you lack wisdom let him ask of God that giveth to all men liberally, and upbraideth not; and it shall be given him.' I knew that I had to ask and then accept the answer I believed He was giving me.

"I also sought the confirmation of other Friends. Each time I sought the wise counsel of other dedicated members of our faith, they confirmed God's call on my life."

"And what was the third way thee sought to know God's leading?" Julia asked.

"The third way was from the circumstances God placed in my life. When I was asked to speak for an evangelist who became ill at the last moment, I felt God working in my life and the lives of those present at that service. As I was open to His leading, He began to direct my paths and I have never looked back. If thou would have told me five years ago I would be working with the freed men in Kansas right now, I would probably not have believed thee. But that is the door God opened, and I chose to walk through it."

"Has thou experienced any of those three confirmations of thy call, Julia?"

Julia thought for several minutes before answering. "I have not had a revelation from the scriptures, but I have had several Friends speak to me about my ministry. It seems that when there is a controversy I am the one to whom everyone turns for my thoughts on the matter—and of course I continued to be one of the top debaters at the academy this past year. Several times I have spoken in Meeting and had women—many of them much older than I—tell me how much my words spoke to their hearts.

"But I really have had no circumstances to help me know God's leading. What does thee think?" Julia looked imploringly at the older woman who sat smiling at the intense young girl who was pouring her heart out to her.

"While I can not say with all certainty what thee should do with thy life, it would appear that God is indeed calling thee into the ministry. Most of my time has been spent in Kansas, primarily in Wichita, providing relief for the great suffering of the Negro slaves who have been freed but can no longer remain with their former masters. I have worked many hours to see that the most elementary needs of these refugees are met: food, clothing, and even providing them with educational opportunities.

"But there is more that must be done. In fact, the reason I happened to be in this area today, speaking to Friends in this Meeting and any others whom I can interest, is to seek collections for these suffering brothers and sisters. We need clothing, bedding quilts, food, and money. If I do not seek these supplies, many will not survive the next winter."

"Would I also be expected to travel and solicit items for thy work?" Julia asked.

"No, but while I am away seeking additional support for the work in Kansas, there is no one there to speak at the daily meetings we hold for the refugees. As I told thee last summer, I believe thee could be the one to minister while I am away, and possibly on a full time basis."

Julia thought of the possibility—and responsibility.

"Julia? Does thou understand I would still like for thee to travel back to Kansas with me and become a part of my ministry there? Thee would be speaking daily to the Negroes seeking to begin a new life there. Thee might live with me in my boarding house, though thee would not have many material possessions."

"I...but...what would I say to the Negroes? Who would want to listen to me, a white girl just eighteen years of age?"

"The Holy Spirit will speak through thee, Julia."

Again Julia had no words.

"Thee need not give me thy answer this moment. I am on my way to the East Coast to seek the support of Friends there for our work. I could return through this area and seek thy final decision at that time—after thee has had an opportunity to speak with thy parents."

"When would that be?" Julia asked.

"In thirty or forty days, I imagine."

"I do feel God is asking me to join thee in thy work in Kansas. But my parents..."

"That is why I believe thee would be wise to spend the next few weeks in earnest prayer, as well as seeking the wise counsel of other Friends. And of course thee must speak with thy parents. I will wire thy home in Salem when I know the day I will pass through Pleasant Plain. If thee is not present at the train station when I arrive, I will continue on to Kansas knowing thee did not feel this was God's leading for thy life at this time."

Elizabeth's words seemed to make sense, but Julia's mind was in a turmoil. As Elizabeth rose to leave, obviously satisfied with her suggestion, Julia quickly grabbed her hand. "Please, Elizabeth. Would thee please pray for me before thee leaves?"

"Of course, my dear child. I would be happy to offer a word of prayer before returning to the hotel."

Gathering Julia's hands in her own, Elizabeth offered a prayer for this young seeker. "Our Father God, whose son Jesus Christ gave His life for the sins of the world, I would ask thee this day to be with thy child Julia. Would thou send thy Holy Spirit to speak to her mind that she might know with all certainty thy will for her life. I ask thee to reveal to her in a clear manner the path she is to take. If it be thy will for her to accompany me to Kansas when I return, help her to know in her heart and mind and soul that this is thy will. In Jesus name, Amen."

Elizabeth then warmly embraced Julia, already feeling an attachment to this young woman. "Would thee like to accompany me to my hotel room?" she asked lightly, obviously putting the seriousness of their discussion behind them. "I could tell thee more about my work with the freedmen."

"I should return to the Mendenhalls," Julia said regretfully, realizing it would soon be time for the evening meal. "But I do hope to hear more about thy work."

"Perhaps in a few weeks?" Elizabeth asked slyly.

"Perhaps," was all Julia would say.

"Then God bless thee until we meet again," Elizabeth said quietly.

"God bless thee, too. And I hope thy trip East goes well."

"It will. This is God's work, not mine. He will provide."

Julia continued to stare at the back of the tall, stout woman as she walked past the meeting house and on toward the hotel. As Julia climbed into the carriage and turned the horse south toward the Mendenhalls, her mind was a whirl of questions and possibilities. She was glad she had planned to spend the night with these fine Friends. Perhaps they could help her decide what to do.

Before she knew it, the Mendenhall's familiar wood frame home was in sight and ...could it be? Was it possible? The familiar sight of Jonathan caused her to slap the horse with the reins. When he saw her approaching, Jonathan quickly got up from the front porch bench where he had been waiting and flashed that warm grin Julia had grown so fond of. Jonathan...perhaps he could help her know what to do. They had been so close the last few months before he had finished at the academy and gone on to St. Louis to study law.

Not only would I probably never see Jonathan again if I were to go to Kansas, Julia lamented as she pulled the carriage to the front of the house, but I would also be giving up my comfortable home and family and friends. How could I possibly sacrifice everything that is important to me to work in less than pleasant conditions? And my parents...Julia shuddered at the thought of telling them of her possible future plans. And baby Rachel, her sister who would soon be a year old...she would miss watching each new discovery this precious child would make. Could she sacrifice everything that was important in her life? And for what? To speak to a few Negro men and women who would probably never listen to what she had to say?

Julia shook her head. Why had she not told Elizabeth to keep going once she got on the train to Kansas? She must be losing her mind! "Julia!" Jonathan exclaimed as he grabbed the reins of the horse and tied them to the front porch. "What world was thee in?" Jonathan asked with a laugh. "The look on thy face was one I have never seen before!"

"I am sorry, Jonathan," Julia said as she gave him a quick hug. "I suppose I was thinking of all the times we shared at the academy and how we will never have those times again."

"I know I *should* believe thee, but I sense there is something more on thy mind."

"Perhaps a few other things," Julia conceded, "but tell me about thy studies in St. Louis. Is it difficult to learn the law? Are the professors helpful? And most importantly, are there any beautiful women there?"

By this time Jonathan was chuckling to himself. "Oh, Julia...thee has not changed one bit! Still full of questions, and still talking as fast as the wind! Now, to answer thy questions...the law is difficult, but it is mainly a matter of memorizing the various cases where the laws have been upheld by the courts. And yes, the professors are generally helpful, though they would like for students to discover the answers on their own. And no, there are no beautiful women there, at least none as beautiful as thee."

"Oh Jonathan," Julia exclaimed as she gave him a playful shove. "I do not believe there are no women in St. Louis!"

"I did not say there were no women, only no women as beautiful as thee!"

"Jonathan, remember the Friends' practice of honesty in all things?"

"Perhaps thee has a point. Let me see...well, there is one beautiful fair-skinned woman who helps me with my laundry."

"I knew it! What is her name? Does she like thee? I mean, as a special friend?"

"I thought *we* were special friends," Jonathan said seriously.

"We were-uh, are-oh, you know what I mean!"

"I thought I did! But to ease your mind, this woman might be a special friend, but she is as old as my grandmother!"

"Jonathan, thee is teasing me again! So tell me...what brings thee back to the Mendenhalls?"

"The university has a four week break before the summer sessions begin, and I wanted to go back to visit family and friends in West Branch. I stopped by the Mendenhalls to say hello and they gave me the good news that I might also see thee if I could wait. Now my question for thee is similar...what brings thee back to Pleasant Plain? The school session has been finished for several weeks now."

"Yes, I did indeed finish my year at the academy. And with perfect marks, I might add!"

"That does not surprise me!" Jonathan said warmly. "Thee always could debate the socks off us other poor students! So what does thee plan to do now? And thee still did not answer my question...why did thee return to Pleasant Plain—alone, I mean?"

"Well... I had an appointment here," Julia said vaguely.

"An appointment for WHAT?" Jonathan's voice was laced with both curiosity and annoyance.

"An appointment with Elizabeth Comstock," was all Julia would say.

"Elizabeth Comstock, now *there* is an amazing woman!"

"How...who....how does thee know about Elizabeth?"

"She is going to be in West Branch tomorrow night to speak about her work. I am hoping to attend. The West Branch meeting has been very supportive of her work. Why did thee have an appointment with her?"

"Remember at yearly meeting when I had a chance to break bread with her following the service when she spoke to the combined body?"

"Oh yes, I do remember. Thee had a glow on thy face after being with her, and I believe thee told Joseph and me that thee had felt a call into the ministry. Is that what this meeting was about? Has thee actually decided to become involved in this ministry?" Julia sensed a bit of disbelief—and disappointment in Jonathan's voice.

"Oh Jonathan, I do not know what I should do!" There was such a forlorn sound in her voice that Jonathan guessed Julia's time with Mrs. Comstock had left her with more questions than answers.

"Can thee talk with me about it?" Jonathan asked quietly. "I am a good listener."

"I know, Jonathan. It is just that I thought this was what God wanted me to do, but when Elizabeth explained exactly what the work would involve, I began to question whether or not I should be making plans to go to a far off place like Kansas!"

"Come and tell me about it," Jonathan requested, guiding her to the porch swing.

"There is not a lot to tell, Julia said as she sat on the newly painted swing. "I did feel God calling me to some type of evangelistic ministry that day at yearly meeting. Elizabeth felt I should complete another year at the academy which would give me time to think and pray about my life. Since that time I have had no 'signs', if you will, that this is *really* what God wants me to do. When I met with Elizabeth this afternoon, she asked me again to consider traveling with her to Kansas to speak at the daily services they have for the Negroes."

"That sounds wonderful, Julia! Just the type of service thee would be good at. All those times thee beat the rest of us at debating, and every time someone had a problem to solve who did they turn to? Julia Jones, of course! I think thee would be a perfect assistant to Elizabeth. Thee should feel honored that she asked thee!"

"I do feel honored, but what about my family? And marriage? Does this mean I will never have a family or home? A year ago I thought it did not matter, but now..."

"Julia, I truly believe that when God calls one of his children into service, it will be the only way they can find true happiness. Marriage and family may follow, but the call must be answered with no strings attached."

"But I am not certain I can give everything up to go to a far off state like Kansas to work with people I know nothing of!"

"Of course it must be thy decision," Jonathan said, "but if thee has prayed about it and at one time felt this was God's will for thee, how can thee now say 'no'?"

"And what of thee? Does thee feel the law is where God wants thee?"

"Yes, I believe this is what God has been preparing me to do. Remember when we first met and I told thee of my desire to help the poor, those who could not afford legal aid?"

"Yes, I remember thee saying something like that."

"I believe that is my calling, and everything I have done to prepare for that career has worked perfectly—from my having the opportunity to work to pay my way through the academy, to the scholarship I received that is allowing me to attend law school.

God has provided for me every step of the way...as He will for thee, Julia."

Julia suddenly realized that she had now received two of the three signs Elizabeth had spoken of. The circumstances were in place with the offer from Elizabeth, and now a good Christian Friend had confirmed the call. She would have to make a point of studying the scriptures before retiring to see if she might also receive the third confirmation.

"I thank thee for thy words, Jonathan. Dost thou think God might have arranged our being here on the same day?"

"I believe God has perfect timing, Julia."

"Julia, Jonathan..." it was Martha Mendenhall. "If you two can afford to pause for a time, the evening meal is ready."

"Coming, Martha," they said in unison. Jonathan rose and offered his hand to Julia. Once again they settled into their familiar roles, friends who cared a great deal for one another, who would support and pray for each other. Friends whose futures might soon be traveling in opposite directions.

CHAPTER 24

THE ANSWER

The evening with the Mendenhalls—and Jonathan—was very pleasant, though nothing more occurred to convince Julia of her calling. As Jonathan prepared to leave the following morning, he asked Julia to walk with him to the end of the farm lane. The Mendenhalls hastily bid Jonathan a safe trip and disappeared through the front door.

"Julia," Jonathan spoke as the two slowly began to saunter down the tree shaded lane, "I have thought a great deal about what thee told me last evening."

Not wanting to know what Jonathan was thinking, Julia quickly interrupted him. "I am sorry I burdened thee with my quandary, Jonathan. I know thee must have many concerns of thy own."

Jonathan quickly moved to the other side of his horse where Julia was walking. Grabbing her arm, he stopped her and stood so close she could almost hear his heart pounding. "Please, Julia, listen to what I need to say to thee."

When there was no response, Jonathan continued. "As I said, I could think of nothing all night but thy words of yesterday. I tried to hide my concerns when thee spoke of traveling to Kansas to work with the freedmen. But now that I must leave thee, I need to at least share my thoughts with thee. A single woman wandering alone in the Midwest...possibly speaking to black men and women who might not appreciate her efforts...it just seems too dangerous. Surely God would not call thee into an area where thy life might be in danger."

When there was only silence from Julia, Jonathan continued.

"And there is another thing...after we went to our separate rooms last night, I realized once again how very much I care for thee...

"Julia? Did thee hear me? I believe I love thee. And if I love thee, how can I allow thee to enter into a work that poses such risks?"

Julia began to feel the anger rising as she considered Jonathan's words. Taking a few steps back, she tried to sound as calm as possible.

"Jonathan, need I remind *you* of your words last evening? Let me see...does 'that sounds wonderful, Julia, thee would be a really good evangelist' sound familiar?

"You also said that following a person's calling was the only way to true happiness, did you not? Or did you mean a *man's* calling was the only way to happiness? Are you telling me something different today?"

When Jonathan finally looked up at Julia, she saw a look of dismay on his face. "I had that coming, Julia. I am sorry if my words sounded unkind."

"Unjust is a better word."

"All right. Unjust. I *do* want thee to follow the Lord's leading in thy life. But..."

"But what, Jonathan? What is really bothering you? Are you afraid I will be hurt? You, yourself, said God would protect me if I were following his leading."

"It is not only that I am a bit afraid for thee..."

"Then WHAT?"

Jonathan looked so forlorn that Julia almost laughed. "Please, Jonathan, tell me what is on your mind."

"When we were sitting around the table last evening I realized how very much I had missed thee these past months since I finished at the academy. I suppose I began to wish I could have a home and family of my own. And then when I looked at thee—thy beautiful red hair, thy fiery disposition—I felt I was losing my opportunity to have thee for my wife."

Jonathan was looking at the ground, obviously embarrassed by his admission.

"Jonathan," Julia said quietly, "I care a great deal for thee, but thee knows my feelings have never gone beyond friendship. If I were to agree to marry thee without knowing for certain what God wanted me to do, I would be doing us both a grave injustice. And besides, you deserve a wife who will love you unconditionally, not one who would always wonder what might have been."

"Does this mean thee will not ever consider marrying me...it does not have to be right now...thee could go to Kansas and work for a year or two while I finish my law degree and start a practice, and then we could be married and have our own home and family."

Julia took a long time to reply. Looking closely at the intense young man with the imploring eyes, Julia was once again reminded that Jonathan would be everything a woman could want in a husband...kind, caring considerate. Would she be making a grave mistake in turning her back on this opportunity?

But when she thought of the calling, she knew what her answer must be. If only she could make Jonathan understand. She had no desire to hurt the one person she had felt closest to the past two years.

"Jonathan, please look at me," Julia requested. "You are the most wonderful man I have ever met—aside from my father, that is! I know you will be the perfect husband and father some day.

I could not ask you to wait until I return from Kansas—if I go, that is—because that would not be fair to either of us. Can we not just do as you suggested yesterday? Let God plan our lives and if He desires for us to some day be together, let Him take care of the details?"

"Then thee will consider marriage at some time in the future?"

"Jonathan, you are listening but not hearing what I am saying. Let me try again. I want to be free to go wherever God leads me, to do whatever He asks of me. I do not want to worry about whether you have found a wife or are still waiting for me. I can not make a commitment right now—for this moment or for the future—except for my commitment to God."

"All right, Julia. Thee knows what thee must do. But will thee promise to write and tell me of thy work? I would feel more at peace if thee would at least write so I would know of thy whereabouts. Whether or not thee realizes it, I think thee has already decided to accept Elizabeth's offer to work in Kansas."

Though Julia was somewhat startled by Jonathan's words, she realized that what he had just said was true. She had already begun to think of the work in Kansas, to see herself in the role of minister and evangelist to the Negroes. And suddenly, as though God himself had spoken to her, Julia knew she must go to Kansas. God was calling her, and she was answering His call.

"Yes, Jonathan, I am going to Kansas—though I just now felt the confirmation from God. I thank you for being a part of the answer—for speaking truth. And yes, I will try to write to you when I get to Kansas. Will you be staying at the same residence in St. Louis?"

"Yes, Mrs. Dalrumple said I was welcome to stay in her home until I finished my degree. Actually, I believe she would like for me to stay there permanently! She really does appreciate the help I can offer her with the house. My years as custodian at the academy taught me a great deal about repairing and fixing what gets broken!"

"You must be a great help to her."

"Julia," Jonathan said teasingly, "if thee hopes to be a great Friends' evangelist, thee had best practice using the plain language at all times!"

Julia laughed, and they were once again on familiar terms...friends, good friends.

By this time the two young people were walking once again and nearing the end of the lane. Jonathan put his foot in the stirrup to climb on the horse's back, but suddenly changed his mind. He quickly turned back to Julia and tightly embraced her, never wanting to let her go. He could not stand to leave without one last try as he pressed his lips against hers, gently at first, then with more urgency.

"Jonathan..." Julia gasped, pushing him away, "please! My leaving will be hard enough without this!"

"I am sorry. I thought perhaps...oh, never mind. I must be going now." Jonathan quickly climbed on his horse and headed toward the road, looking back only once. Though Julia did not know what the future would hold, she knew her life had been blessed because Jonathan had been a part of it.

The walk back up the lane was a time of reflection for Julia, as well as excitement as she thought of working with Elizabeth. Although the final decision had been made only minutes earlier, it seemed to Julia as though she had been preparing for this work the entire two years since she had first felt God's call at yearly meeting. She had such a feeling of peace as she entered the Mendenhall home.

The Mendenhalls had been more than just friends during her time at the academy. As elders in the Pleasant Plain Meeting, they had provided spiritual guidance and Julia was anxious to tell them of her decision.

"That is wonderful, Julia!" Martha exclaimed when Julia told them her news. "Thee will be a marvelous evangelist. I have seen the fire in thy eyes when thee spoke in Meeting, and I know thy walk with the Lord has become something very special! And we both felt the confirmation of the Inner Light during our times of prayer together."

Julia smiled. Unlike Jonathan, Martha had not mentioned the adversities she might encounter, and Julia was certain Martha would remember to pray for her each day. John, Martha's husband, was always a bit more reserved, but he, too, had only words of encouragement for her. "I wish thee well, Julia. God will go with thee and direct thy paths. Thee knows Martha and I will remember thee each evening when we have our time of prayer and scripture reading."

"Thank you both for all you have done for me these past two years. You have shared your home with me and treated me as a daughter. I have learned many lessons from thee that were not taught at the academy!"

"The pleasure was ours, Julia," Martha reassured her. "John and I would grow old and crotchety without the exuberance of the young people who share our home!"

"I suppose I had best be on my way," Julia said reluctantly, knowing she must return home to face her parents and tell them of her decision.

"Could we have a time of prayer before thee leaves?" Martha asked.

"I would like that very much," Julia said, a lump forming in her throat as she thought of not seeing these two wonderful Friends again.

The three rose and gathered each others hands, each gripping tightly as if trying to hold on to what they knew they must let go of. John offered a prayer of blessing on Julia's life, and the tears that slid down Martha's weather-worn cheeks spoke of the depth of her feelings for the young woman she had grown to love.

"Please write and let us know of thy work," Martha called as Julia climbed into the carriage. "Have a safe journey back to Salem, and greet thy parents for us."

"I will. Thank you again for everything. Farewell!"

"Farewell, Julia," John and Martha said in unison.

• • •

Every mile of the journey home found Julia rehearsing what she would say to her parents when she reached their home. But each time she repeated the words, she knew all the rehearsing in the world would not adequately prepare her parents for the announcement she was about to make.

Dr. Charles Jones was very protective of his children—especially his two daughters. David was still in Chicago preparing to be a physician, following in his father's footsteps—a choice that had pleased her father immensely. She, on the other hand, had had to use all her powers of persuasion just to get her father to allow her to attend the academy!

As Julia approached their modern, yet modest frame home on a hill overlooking the community of Salem, she realized how fortunate she was to have parents who were well thought of in their city and meeting; parents who had been able to provide for her every need. She almost felt guilty for thinking they would be unreasonable when she told them of her plans. Charles and Rebecca were both intelligent...surely they would understand how she must accept a call from God.

But Julia knew deep in her heart that she would have the battle of her life if she were to be successful in persuading her parents to approve of her work in Kansas. No, there would be no easy time ahead when Rebecca learned her eldest daughter was about to leave the community for a life of uncertainty!

"Juwea!" Rachel squealed with delight as Julia approached the grassy area in front of their home and climbed from the carriage.

Julia smiled. Rachel's pronunciation of her name reminded her of her two nephews whom she had not seen in almost a year. Julia felt a twinge of sadness as she wondered what the two boys looked like now. She wondered how Levi was doing at William Penn College and if he had any regrets about leaving the academy.

"Juwea! Up!" Rachel implored with outstretched arms. Julia was amazed that Rachel was beginning to talk at such a young age. Picking her up, the two sisters proceeded into the house.

"I am home," Julia called out as they entered the front door and went into the kitchen.

"Julia!" Rebecca said warmly as she came from the front room where she had been mending one of Charles's shirts. "How was thy trip? How are the Mendenhalls?"

"The Mendenhalls are wonderful, as always. You know, Mother, I do not know of a finer couple than John and Martha."

"I know that, Julia. It was one of the reasons your father and I allowed thee to return to the academy after Levi moved to Oskaloosa. We knew the Mendenhalls would keep a watchful eye on thee! How about thy business...that urgent matter thee said thee must attend to. Did thee get it taken care of ?"

"Yes, as a matter of fact there is something I need to discuss with..."

"Mommy," Rachel interrupted, "canny!"

"Rachel, thee may not have candy. Thy father is spoiling thee with new dresses and candy every time he comes home." There was a touch of irritation in Rebecca's voice.

"I wan' canny!" "I wan' canny!"

"Rachel, if thee does not stop thy whining I will have to take thee to thy room."

Rachel looked first at Rebecca, then Julia as if trying to decide which might give her what she wanted.

"Sorry, Rachel," Julia said with a smile. "I have no candy for you."

"Thee, Julia," Rebecca reproved. "I see thee has not broken thy bad habit of using *you* instead of *thee*."

"I am sorry, mother. You are—thee is right. I will try to remember next time."

The look Rebecca gave Julia was a mixture of curiosity and disbelief. In the past Julia would have argued with her—told her this plain speech of Friends was an antiquated practice that was no longer meaningful in modern times. Had something happened to this once rebellious daughter?

"What was thee going to tell me before Rachel interrupted us?" Rebecca's curiosity had definitely been aroused.

Suddenly feeling scared again, Julia hesitated. "Oh, it was nothing. I know thee must have to get the evening meal started. I will help thee."

"Yes, thee is right. I had not realized how late it was. Charles said he would try to return in time to eat with us since thee might be home. He seemed anxious to speak with thee."

Julia's face paled. "About what?"

"That is something thee will have to ask thy father."

"Did he say anything that would help me know what to expect?"

"Julia, is something bothering thee? Thee seems...anxious, I suppose is the best term."

"No!" Julia said too quickly. "Nothing is wrong. I am fine. I just get a bit nervous when Father wants to speak to me."

"Julia! Thy father loves thee very much! He would never do anything to upset thee!"

But I might do something that is going to upset *him*! Julia thought with dismay. How will I ever tell him? He still sees me as his little girl! Perhaps tomorrow would be a better time to give him my news. Yes, tomorrow. If mother starts reproving him about spoiling Rachel it will most likely make him angry. Not a good time to hear startling news like I have to tell!

Yes, tomorrow would be a much better day. And besides, it would give her a few more hours to rehearse her speech.

"I will help thee prepare the meal," Julia said again, forcing her voice to be light and cheerful.

"Thank thee, Julia. It is so good to have thee home again! I have so many plans for thee this summer!"

Julia turned away. This was going to be worse than she imagined. Much worse!

CHAPTER 25

HONOR THY FATHER AND THY MOTHER

As it turned out, Julia need not have worried about telling her father of her plans. With a particularly heavy work load, Charles did not return home until late each night, long after Julia had retired. He had come to her door the first night she had returned, but they had merely exchanged greetings and a few perfunctory questions. It was obvious to Julia that her father was weary from his day's work and not at all in a position to listen to a discussion of her future.

When the First Day finally arrived, Rebecca cornered Charles as he prepared to leave around the sixth hour. Though Julia was still in bed, she could hear the heated conversation between her parents.

"Charles, thee has been gone until all hours of the night for days now. The children have not even had an opportunity to talk with thee. I am particularly concerned about Julia. She has not been herself since she returned from Pleasant Plain. Surely thee can take some time for thyself on the Sabbath!"

Julia could almost see her father's frown as he pondered his wife's words. She knew Charles had been a good father in spite of the long hours he spent caring for the medical needs of the Salem community.

"Rebecca," he finally said, "I know I have been working more than usual this past week..."

"Past month, past year!" Rebecca interrupted. "We never see thee!"

"That is not true, Rebecca. I have tried to spend at least one evening with you and the children each week. Thee knows how Salem has been growing and expanding which means more and more patients must be cared for."

"Then perhaps it is time thee hired an assistant!"

A wistful smile crossed Charles's face. "I used to have a wonderful assistant! She was bright, and beautiful and could sew a perfect suture. All the patients wanted her to stitch their wounds."

Rebecca smiled at the memory. "I *was* a good assistant, wasn't I?!"

"The best. I have had several others since thee left to raise our children, but no one that compares to thee."

"Flattery will not make me forget my concerns, Charles Jones. Thee must find a way to get some assistance. Thy health is a concern as well. There is a reason the Sabbath is to be a day of rest, Charles. The human body can only work so long before it must have rest and renewal."

"Yes, *Dr*. Jones!" Charles teased. "And if it will ease thy mind, I spoke with Professor Smith from the Chicago School of Medicine a few days ago, and he believes David will be able to complete his training in one or two months."

"When did thee see Dr. Smith?"

"He stopped by the office on his way to see his brother in northern Missouri. It seems David was anxious for me to know of his progress, and Andrew offered to deliver the message."

"Thee never told me," Rebecca said stiffly. "This is the problem we have...never time to even talk with one another."

"I know thee is right, Rebecca, but what would thee have me do? Let my patients suffer while I wait for the Sabbath to pass?"

"No, of course not. It just does not seem fair to Rachel or Julia to have their father absent from their lives."

"What is your concern for Julia?" Charles suddenly remembered Rebecca's earlier comment.

"I can not say for certain, but something happened when she went to the Mendenhalls. She seems ill at ease a great deal of the time, and I have noticed an absence of that old rebellious nature she so often exhibits."

Rising to leave, Charles sought to reassure Rebecca. "I will return early today, that is a promise. I have only two patients I must see this morning, and in fact, I hope to finish in time to attend at least part of the worship service. This afternoon I promise to have a long visit with Julia and see if there is something bothering her. Perhaps it is just the uncertainty of her life right now. As far as I know there are no young men asking for her hand in marriage! It is difficult for a woman to know what to do with her life when marriage and a family are not in the picture."

Julia lay in her bed trying not to jump up and immediately confront her father with her plans. Her father was so out of touch with the times. Thinking a girl had to have a marriage prospect in order to have a future! Today was going to be the day, that was certain! Julia would tell her father of her plans and make him see how important it was for her to follow God's call. When she had heard her father mention the years when her mother had been his able assistant, she knew this would be a point in her favor. If her mother thought it important to have meaningful work, surely she would support her daughter's desire for the same.

Julia enjoyed the worship service with the Salem Friends women. Many of them had been childhood friends who were now married, or at least thinking of marriage. Although Julia felt comfortable visiting with these friends, she did not feel the least bit envious. In fact, when she thought of the work she would soon be doing with the freedmen, she was somewhat sorry these young women would be confined to the roles of wives and mothers.

True to his word, Charles finished his rounds in time to attend the worship service. It was the first time in many weeks that they had all been present for the service, in spite of the fact that the men and women still worshipped in separate rooms. Julia thought this was definitely one practice of Friends that needed revising. She knew that the reasons given for separate worship satisfied many, but she for one felt that if men and women were truly to be considered equal in God's eyes, they should be sharing their times of worship. To think that women would be too distracted by the men sitting next to them was really an archaic idea.

The silence of Friend's worship had not always been easy for Julia. It had taken many years of sitting in the quiet before she had been able to keep her mind on the things of the Spirit during the sometimes lengthy period of worship. Julia knew there were some Friends' meetings who were now hiring pastors to bring messages to the congregation rather than having silent meetings where members spoke as the Holy Spirit led them. Julia was not certain how she felt about hiring a pastor, especially considering her call into evangelism. Somehow she felt there was a difference between an evangelist who went to various meetings preaching the word of God and calling people to repentance, and a pastor who spoke week after week to the same congregation.

Though Julia did not feel the leading of the Spirit to speak in worship on this particular day, she definitely felt the nudging to speak to her parents regarding her future plans.

When the services were over it was nearly an hour before Friends finished speaking with one another outside the meeting house. The warmth of the summer sun was such a welcome change from the bone-chilling winter Sabbath days that Friends seemed to linger even longer than usual.

When they were finally home and her family had finished with the noon meal, Julia knew the time had come to finally speak with her parents. As soon as Rachel was down for her nap and everyone was in the sitting room for a time of reading, Julia began.

"There is something I would like to say to you both."

Quickly both parents looked up from what they were reading. "What is it Julia?" Charles began. "Is there some man thee is interested in? Someone thee has neglected to tell us about?"

"No there is no man—please! This is serious."

"Does that mean thee is not still seeing Jonathan?" Rebecca asked. "He seemed like such a nice boy when he visited here last summer."

"Jonathan and I are very good friends, but nothing more."

"Oh, I am sorry to hear that," Charles said. "I also thought he was a fine young man. I must tell thee, Julia, a young woman needs to keep her eyes open for suitable young men. I had hoped that by the time thee finished at the academy next year thee might be ready for marriage and a family."

It was all Julia could do to keep from shouting, 'I am sick and tired of hearing about marriage and family!' When she felt her anger begin to pass, she answered.

"Father, Mother, I am not getting married, nor am I looking for a 'suitable young man' as you put it. What I have to tell thee does concern my future, however."

After pausing to gather her courage, Julia began to tell of the events that led to her decision to travel to Kansas. She told of her experience at yearly meeting where she had felt God calling her into an evangelistic ministry, and then of the recent meeting with Elizabeth Comstock at Pleasant Plain where Elizabeth had once again offered Julia the opportunity to return to Kansas with her. She also told them how she had felt God confirming her call through her prayers with Martha Mendenhall as well as her conversation with Jonathan.

If Julia wondered what her father thought of her announcement, the look on his face said it all. "Julia, thee cannot be serious. If thee believes thy mother and I would allow our daughter—a young girl of eighteen years of age—to go hundreds of miles into undeveloped lands where savages still shoot their arrows at white folk, then I am sorry we paid for two years of education for thee because thee has obviously learned nothing of the world! Not to mention the fact that thee has another year left of thy studies at the academy."

Julia looked to see her mother's reaction only to find her staring into space. Charles, on the other hand, continued to state his opposition.

"Where is this Comstock woman now? I would like to give her a piece of my mind! Imagine putting such an idea in the mind of a young woman!"

"Father," Julia knew she was raising her voice, but somehow she felt that was the only way her father was going to listen to her. "Elizabeth Comstock is the most Godly woman I have ever met. She did not 'put ideas in my head' as you seem to believe. She speaks from her heart and from the leading of the Holy Spirit. GOD is the one who spoke to my heart, not Elizabeth Comstock! She was merely the messenger."

"She was more than a messenger. She was the one who offered thee the 'opportunity' to go to Kansas. She was the one who suggested thee leave thy family and friends and even the chance to marry Jonathan!"

"Father, I respect thy opinion on nearly every matter, but thee is wrong where Elizabeth is concerned." When Julia realized she had just talked back to her father—something she had been careful to avoid in the past—she fell silent.

"Go to thy room, Julia," Charles said with a controlled tone. "Thy mother and I need to discuss this matter."

"Mother, please!" Julia implored. "Can thee not understand? Did thee not feel a calling to help treat thy neighbors' medical problems when thee was a young woman?"

"Julia, I will not speak to thee again!" Charles said angrily. "Go to thy room!"

Julia knew from the tone of her father's voice that she had best obey. She couldn't help but add one more declaration. "I have been called of God and I intend to go to Kansas with or without your permission."

Rebecca felt a smile form in the corners of her mouth as she heard the fire and determination in Julia's voice. That was the Julia she knew and loved!

"What could she be thinking of?!" Charles exclaimed when he heard Julia shut the door to her room. "Imagine believing we would approve of such a venture! I still would like to find that Comstock woman and give her a piece of my mind!"

"Charles," Rebecca began gently. "If Julia feels that God is calling her to this work, is it right for us to interfere? I know she is young, but if God is truly asking her to do this work, will He not care for her?"

"Rebecca, I do believe thee has also lost thy mind! I am the head of this household, and I will hear no more talk of traveling evangelists or missions in Kansas! Julia will remain in Salem until she finds a suitable husband. I happen to know young Will Clark is still living at home. At one time I believe Julia was quite interested in him. I will make a point of visiting him soon and suggesting he consider courting our daughter once again."

Not intimidated by her husband's tirade, Rebecca spoke again. "If Will Clark is interested in Julia, he will not need thee to grant permission to like her! Will knows Julia is home from school, and if he has an interest, I am certain he will come calling. This is the eighteenth century, Charles. Fathers are no longer arranging marriages for their daughters!"

Looking a bit sheepish, Charles seemed to calm a bit. "Thee is right, of course. But what am I to do? I have a responsibility to protect my children. Does thee believe this is a good choice for our daughter?"

Knowing how she answered would be extremely important to Julia's future, Rebecca took a long time before speaking.

"I understand thy need to protect Julia, Charles. I, too, have reservations about allowing her to travel to Kansas and other states as God may call her. But just as I could never have planned my future except to allow God to have His way, so do I believe we must trust Julia to know when God has spoken to her. I have read many wonderful things about Elizabeth Comstock's work. The *Friends Review* has carried several articles explaining her mission work. I can not believe she would ask an eighteen year old to travel and work with her if she thought there were any danger involved."

"But what if something happens to her? Can thee forgive thyself if she is injured, or even killed?"

"Do we need to make a decision right now? Julia said she was to leave in four or more weeks. Surely we can pray about the matter before saying yes or no."

"Thee has not convinced me, Rebecca. I will not consent to this folly unless something happens to change my mind. Now. I have patients to see. I had hoped to have a relaxing afternoon with my family, but I can see that is not to be."

Charles rose quickly and gathered his bag. Without looking back he was out the door.

Rebecca sat for a long time thinking about the afternoon's developments. She could never have guessed what had been on Julia's mind. She had to admit she was just a bit proud of her daughter. She knew how much courage it had taken for Julia to tell her father, let alone feel brave enough to leave everything behind to accept God's call.

Julia, too, spent the rest of the afternoon thinking about her father's words. She knew he would have a hard time accepting her plan, but she had not been prepared for his total rejection. If he loved God, as he professed in Meeting and in those times when he was able to share in Bible reading and prayer with the family, then how could he forbid her from doing the same? For it was her love for God that compelled her to share the message with others.

Walking over to her beloved book case, Julia lovingly ran her fingers over the well-worn spines of the volumes she had loved to read. Some books had been read over and over, each time offering something new. This time she picked up her Bible, remembering the day she received it. Her twelfth birthday. Since that time she had read it from cover to cover a number of times, often amazed at how the passages spoke to her specific situation.

This time Julia decided to read from wherever the Bible happened to fall open. The passage where the book opened was Matthew, the fifteenth chapter. She read, *For God commanded, saying, Honour thy father and mother; and, He that curseth father or mother, let him die the death.* Julia paused to consider her parents. Surely she had honoured them. She had never cursed them, as she had heard some students do, nor had she raised her voice to them—well, not often, anyway.

Julia continued reading in Matthew until she came to the twenty-second chapter. When a lawyer had tried to trap Jesus by asking him which of the ten commandments of Moses was the most important, Jesus had replied in verse 37, *Thou shalt love the Lord thy God with all thy heart, and with all thy soul, and with all thy mind. This is the first and great commandment. The second is like unto it, Thou shalt love thy neighbour as thyself.*

Yes, Julia knew the fifth commandment of Moses was to love her mother and father. But she also knew that the most important commandment she was to obey was to love the Lord with all her heart and mind and soul. She hoped that she would not have to choose between loving her parents and loving God. But if she did, she knew now that she must obey God's call rather than her parents commands.

And suddenly Julia knew she had received the third confirmation—the truth in the scriptures. God had directed her eyes to the passages in Matthew, and they confirmed what she must do. She must put God above everything and everyone. No matter what the future held, she, Julia Jones, would follow God's leading. Unfortunately, that might mean her father would never speak to her again! That was something she would deal with if and when the time came.

Once again Julia felt the peace of God and knew that she had made the right decision.

CHAPTER 26

BY ANY MEANS AVAILABLE TO MAN

As the days passed with no more discussion of Julia's announcement, she began to hope that at last her father was going to treat her as an adult—as someone capable of making good decisions regarding her future. Just to be certain, though, Julia made sure she remained in her room until her father had left each morning, and tried to be busy in the evenings when he happened to arrive home early. She was delighted when he spent most of his time with Rachel, happy there was a diversion to help take his mind off his elder daughter.

Charles, on the other hand, had done anything *but* forget about Julia's ridiculous announcement. As he ate the morning meal a few days after his confrontation with Julia, he told Rebecca of his plans.

"Rebecca, I feel thee should know what I intend to do to prevent our daughter from making a mistake she may regret for the rest of her life."

Knowing that nothing she could say was going to dissuade her husband, Rebecca remained silent.

"The first thing I intend to do after seeing my critical patients this morning is to call on Sadie Pickard and Wilma Rogers. As elders of the Salem Friends women's meeting, it is their responsibility to guide the young women of the meeting toward making wise choices about their futures.

"And if that does not put some sense in Julia's foolish young head," he continued, "I also plan to speak with our neighbor, Will Clark. He took quite a fancy to Julia last summer, and I happen to know he has not yet married. If Julia were to become attached to this young man, if could certainly make a difference in her future."

"Charles," Rebecca said indulgently, "if Will Clark were truly interested in our daughter, would he not have asked to call in our home last summer? He has not even visited this summer."

"It occurred to me that perhaps young Clark believes we would not permit him to see our daughter because of his association with the Hicksites. I thought that if I were to assure him we would welcome him in our home, it might be just what he needs make the first move."

"But we invited Will and his mother into our home for a meal after Sarah assisted in Rachel's birth. Surely both Sarah and Will know that we do not think less of them because of their affiliation with the Hicksites."

"That was a year ago and there has been some increased friction between the orthodox meetings and the Hicksites. It will certainly do no harm to make certain Will knows we would enjoy his presence in our home."

"Whatever thee thinks, Charles."

"I have one other plan, also. I believe Hannah Johnson would be just the person to help Julia think more clearly. Hannah is a quiet, thoughtful young woman, and she *will* be a member of the family as soon as David finishes his medical education."

"I am certain thee believes thee is doing what is best for Julia," Rebecca finally said. "But I must tell thee Julia and Hannah were never very close. As much as her mother, Betty, and I wanted our daughters to be good friends as we were, Julia and Hannah were never very comfortable with one another. Julia has such a flamboyant personality, and Hannah is so...so...well, plain, I suppose is the best word. I do not want you to misunderstand. I love Hannah like a daughter, and David loves her very deeply. It is just that I doubt this girl will have much effect on our daughter."

"And I suppose thee supports Julia in this foolishness?" a note of disgust was evident in his voice.

Careful of her answer, Rebecca spoke quietly. "I, too, have reservations where Julia's future is concerned. But I also know she is a strong young woman who feels a call on her life. There comes a time when we must let our children make their own choices."

"I will never agree to allow Julia to traipse half-way across the country to do who knows what with the Negroes. It is my responsibility as head of the house to do what is best for my children. And I say it is never 'best' to allow a girl to make terrible choices about her life."

Charles picked up his medical bag and prepared to leave. "Please do not mention any of our conversation to Julia. I will speak with the elders and Will and Hannah very soon and we will see what happens."

"I will not say anything, Charles, but I believe it would be wise for thee to speak with Julia in the near future. She may feel thee has accepted her decision since thee has not spoken of it again."

"I will indeed visit with Julia, but I want to wait until after these others have a chance to speak with her. Now. I must be on my way. Give Rachel a kiss from her daddy and tell her I will be home to read to her this evening."

"I will, Charles. I will also tell Julia how much her father loves *her* and cares about her."

Charles had a strange look on his face as the door closed behind him. Of course Julia knew he loved her. If he did not care about her he would let her go to Kansas without a second thought. His mind quickly turned to speaking with the two elders. If he hurried, he would have an opportunity to meet with them between checking on his critical patients and going to the office.

As Julia was walking to the Jones's carriage after worship services on first day, she was surprised to hear someone calling her name. Turning around she saw Wilma Rogers and Sadie Pickard walking quickly toward her.

"Oh Julia, dear," Sadie called to the tall, slender red-haired beauty ahead of her.

As Julia stopped and turned toward the women, Wilma continued. "Oh, uh, Julia, Sadie and I were wondering if we might call on thee tomorrow afternoon."

At first Julia was a bit suspicious of this sudden desire for these two women to come calling in their home. Then she remembered that they were both elders in the women's meeting, and as elders one of their jobs was to speak with any young woman who had matured spiritually and inquire as to whether she was ready to become an active member of the Salem Friends Meeting.

"I believe tomorrow would be satisfactory," Julia said easily "but perhaps I should speak with Mother to be certain she has no other plans."

"Oh, thy father has already told us tomorrow will be satisfactory."

Again Julia sensed there might be something more to this request.

"We spoke with thy father as he was entering the meeting house before worship," Sadie added.

"Oh, I see. Well, then of course you may visit in our home. Thee may want to wait until after two, however, to be certain Rachel is down for her nap. It can be hard to hear oneself think when Rachel is making her demands on everyone!"

"Oh, she is such a delightful child," Wilma said warmly.

"Delightful, yes. But annoying as well. So we will expect thee at two?"

"Yes, of course," the two women said in unison, seemingly anxious to be on their way.

When Julia mentioned the request of the two women to her mother on the way home, Rebecca seemed not surprised at all. "I had thought perhaps thee would be having callers," was all she said.

Now that is quite strange, Julia thought. Wilma and Sadie had said they had spoken with her father, but not her mother. Julia was beginning to feel uneasy about the entire situation, though she kept her thoughts to herself.

When the two elderly women arrived promptly at two the next afternoon, Julia answered the door. "Please come in," she said, holding the door open. "Mother is in with Rachel so we will go to the sitting room." Julia led the women to the neatly furnished room. Since her father was a physician, there were occasions when he needed to meet with the family of a severely ill patient. He had added the sitting room to their home in order to be prepared for such times.

Each of the women chose a straight-backed chair, and both sat on the edge of the finely stitched needle point seats. Julia chose one of the softer chairs, and they all sat down in an uneasy silence.

Julia looked from one woman to the other, hoping to soon know their mission.

"Well...uh...oh my but this is a lovely room," Sadie began, looking at the various pictures on the wall.

"Yes!" Wilma quickly joined in. "It must be wonderful for thee to live in such a fine home."

"We enjoy our home, but it is quite simple compared to some of the fancy homes in Salem," Julia said.

"Oh, of course we did not mean to say thy family was indulging in the ways of the world," Wilma said quickly.

Unable to stand the suspense any longer, Julia looked from one woman to the other. "What exactly did thee wish to speak with me about?"

"Well, dear," Sadie began, "it occurred to us that thee had become a mature young woman..."

"And..." Julia was quickly losing her patience.

"And of course as elders of the meeting it is our responsibility to see that young women make wise choices where their future is concerned," Sadie continued.

"And?"

"And we were wondering if there was a marriage we might help thee prepare for?"

"No, there is no marriage."

Sadie looked nervously to Wilma before continuing. "But of course thee does plan to marry and have a family, does thee not?"

"Some day, perhaps." Julia was not about to discuss her marriage plans, or lack thereof, with these women until she knew exactly why they were there.

"Salem Friends will be needing young men and women and their families to keep the meeting strong," Wilma added.

Beginning to sense where this discussion was headed, Julia decided it was time to disclose her plans.

"I am surprised my father did not tell you of my plans," Julia said, looking from woman to woman. "I will be going with Elizabeth Comstock in a few weeks to work with the freed men in Kansas."

"Oh, my!" Wilma exclaimed. "Dost thou know of the dangers that that type of work might involve?"

"Elizabeth has assured me that although the work will be challenging, it is also very rewarding. I do not expect it to be dangerous at all. I also believe that because God has called me into this work, He will watch over me."

"But what about the scriptures that say we are to honour our fathers and mothers? Surely thy parents do not support thy leaving Salem to go to Kansas," Sadie said rather piously.

"If thee continues to read in Matthew, after the place where Jesus talks about honouring one's parents, thee would also know that He says the most important commandment is to love the

Lord thy God with all thy heart and mind and soul, and to love thy neighbor as thyself. If answering God's call takes me to Kansas, then I must go because that is the greater commandment. Would thee not agree?"

"Well, yes, I suppose thee has a point," Wilma said. Then leaning closer to Julia, she asked a question that completely took Julia by surprise.

"Is Elizabeth Comstock really a giant woman?"

Both elders were intently waiting for Julia's reply. "No," she said, trying not to laugh. "Elizabeth is not a giant woman. She is quite large, though, and when she speaks, everyone listens. She wears long flowing black dresses and capes and she has a booming voice. So I suppose in that way she *is* a giant. Did either of thee hear her at yearly meeting last year?"

"No, we neither one were able to attend," Sadie answered. "I was not feeling well at the time. Wilma, why was it thee did not attend? We seldom *both* miss yearly meeting."

"You remember, Sadie, that was when my dear Elmer was down in the back and I had to care for all the livestock."

"I remember, now," Sadie nodded. "But tell me, Julia, dost thou really believe the Negro race can be helped? I have doubts that they can be educated, as this woman seems to believe."

"The Negro race has been kept in slavery for so long that of course it seems to some that they have lesser abilities than white men. But Elizabeth believes—and so do I—that when Negroes are treated as equals and given the opportunity to learn, they will do very well. But we must begin by supplying such basic needs as food and clothing. That is what Elizabeth is attending to right now—seeking support for her work from Friends in the East."

"I have sometimes wished I had been able to have an opportunity to serve the Lord in a way like thee plans to do," Wilma said wistfully.

Julia was quick to answer. "Thee has been a wonderful influence in my life, Wilma. Many times when thee spoke in worship I felt the Spirit speaking through thee. God calls each of us in different ways, and thee has had just as important work to do as I will be doing."

The wistful look on Wilma's face was replaced by one of pleasure as she listened to Julia's words.

"Well, Wilma, I believe we must be going," Sadie said as she rose from her chair. "I am sorry thy mother could not join us, Julia, but I am glad we had this opportunity to visit with thee."

"Yes, Julia, it was a pleasure to speak with thee. Thee must write and let us know of thy work. In fact, we could even meet as a women's group to raise support for Elizabeth and thy work!" Wilma said excitedly.

Julia smiled. "That would be wonderful. I know Elizabeth and I would appreciate any food, bedding, clothing or money thee could secure."

"Then we will do it!" Sadie declared. "Come, Wilma, if we work quickly we may be able to speak with several ladies in our group before the afternoon is over."

"Farewell, Julia," they called as they quickly left though the kitchen. "And remember, thee promised to write!"

"I will, thee can depend on me!"

As Julia closed the door behind the women, she couldn't help but smile at the interesting turn of events. It was quite clear that her father had been behind the elders' visit, and that he had no doubt asked them to try and discourage her from going to Kansas.

"Julia," Rebecca said quietly as she closed the door to Rachel's room, "did thee have a good visit with Sadie and Wilma?"

"Thee knew the purpose of their visit, did thee not?"

With a look of guilt on her face, Rebecca admitted she had been aware of her husband's plan. "But thee must know, Julia, that thy father has thy best interests at heart. He truly believes it would be foolish for thee to leave Salem for a life of uncertainty."

"And thee, Mother? How does thee feel about my leaving?"

"Oh, Julia, I was afraid thee would ask me that question."

"And what is the answer?"

"Thee knows I believe a woman must respect her husband. But thee also knows that I believe a woman should be free to answer a call from God in the same way that it is acceptable for a man to do so. If thee truly believes this is God's will for thee, then I hope thee will follow His leading."

Julia hugged her mother. "Thank you...thank you for believing in me."

"*Thee*, Julia, *thee!*"

Mother and daughter both burst into laughter, the seriousness of the moment forgotten.

"I still believe Friends are guilty of clinging to the old ways—and using thee and thou are old ways, Mother."

"But it can still be a powerful message to those around us. We take our faith seriously, and we treat all men as equal."

"But Mother, NO one says 'thee' and 'thou' except Friends! Are we not setting ourselves above the rest of the world? Acting superior, if you will?"

"I am glad thee will have Elizabeth to discuss these issues with rather than me! In all her travels she has spoken with Friends of the Hicksite persuasion, the conservative persuasion as well as those of the orthodox group. I am certain she can give thee a good reason to continue with the plain language."

The afternoon passed quickly as Julia and Rebecca discussed other matters of concerns to Friends. The revival services were still an issue to many, as was the hiring of pastors that some meetings were doing. Before they knew it, Rachel had awakened from her nap, and it was time to begin preparing for the evening meal.

Charles was home early for a change, and he and Rachel were romping together on the kitchen floor.

"Oh, by the way, Julia," Charles said rather nonchalantly. "I saw young Will Smith at the hotel today when I went to treat a patient. It seems he is learning the business and may even purchase the hotel."

"Really?" Julia was quite surprised by the news. "I knew Will did not want to farm after watching his father die, but I had no idea he was interested in the hotel business."

"The current owners are both elderly and not well. In fact, it was the owner's wife that I went to care for. When Will came to them for a job last winter, they were so taken with him that they worked out an arrangement whereby he will eventually assume management of the hotel. As part of the agreement, they will continue to live there the rest of their lives."

"I have not seen Will for such a long time. I wondered how he was doing."

"Well, uh," Charles stammered, which was very uncharacteristic for him, "I did mention that perhaps he might stop and see thee some time."

"That would be nice," Julia said, as she really did want to see her old friend again.

Conversation around the table at the evening meal centered on Rachel, as usual, as she took great delight in mixing her food together. When she threw a fresh garden pea across the table at Julia, Charles quickly picked her up and began to wash her face and hands.

"Thee is a mess!" he exclaimed. "We will get thee clean and then Daddy will read thee a story."

Rachel clapped her hands in anticipation. Julia and Rebecca cleared the table and were just about to join the others when there was a knock on the door.

"Three callers in one day?" Julia said with amusement as she went to answer the knock.

"Will! What is thee doing here?" she asked incredulously.

"I came as soon as I could!" he said breathlessly. "When thy father was in the hotel today he said thee was having an emergency and I should come and see thee as soon as possible."

Julia looked toward the living room where she could hear her father's booming voice.

"Come in, Will. I do believe there is something we indeed need to discuss. But it is not an emergency, let me assure thee."

A look of relief crossed the young man's face.

"Actually," Julia continued, "there *may* be an emergency if my father continues to try to run my life!

"Sit down, Will. This may take a while."

CHAPTER 27

OVERCOMING OBSTACLES

"Would thee like a piece of cherry pie, Will? We have two pieces left from the evening meal and I would hate to think thee came all the way over here for nothing!" Julia said as she proceeded to get the pie.

"Cherry pie is my favorite, and I am a bit hungry since I did not want to take time to eat before coming to see thee...what with thee having an emergency and all."

"As I said, Will, there is no emergency. I will explain everything to thee after thee finishes thy pie."

"I believe you two young people can have a good visit without me," Rebecca said quietly as she quickly exited the kitchen to join Charles and Rachel.

"Tell me, Will, what has been happening in thy life? I thought I might see thee before now, but father said thee is working in the hotel. Tell me about it."

"Last winter when there was not much work to be done on the farm, I decided I needed to find a job to help support the family."

"How is your mother doing?" Julia interrupted.

"Mother is doing quite well. It has taken her nearly all of this past year to recover from my father's death, but she seems happier now than she has for some time."

"And thy brothers and sisters?"

"Everyone pitches in to help with the farm work, and I am hopping to make enough money working at the hotel to help them go to school this fall."

"What about thee? Thee did not get to finish thy schooling after thy father died."

"Being the oldest child, it is now my responsibility to provide for the family. The two boys will go to high school this fall, and the two girls are still in the primary school led by our Meeting."

Julia suddenly felt a sadness for this special friend who had already suffered a great deal in his short life. She thought back to the times they had spent together the past summer and how much they had enjoyed talking about all that was important in their lives.

"I wish thee could have gone on to school, too, Will. But tell me about the hotel."

"As I said, I knew I had to find work to provide food for our family. I went to every business in Salem asking if anyone needed help, but every store I entered already had all the help they needed. The hotel was the last place I went because I did not think I would be very good at working in the dining area, or making beds and cleaning. But after I talked to the owner, Mr. Simpson, I decided I would give the hotel business a try. As it turned out, Mr. Simpson and his wife had been looking for someone who might be interested in taking over the business. They do not have any children, and they want to continue living at the hotel after they turn the business over to someone else. That is why they did not want to sell the hotel to some outsider for fear they might not have a place to live."

"So they just offered to let thee buy the hotel?" Julia asked incredulously.

"Well, not at first!" Will said with a laugh. "When I first began to work I was washing dishes in the kitchen, sweeping floors, making beds, carrying wood and just about anything else they asked me to do. Father taught all of us the importance of hard work. I was so grateful to have a job that I put in extra hours at the hotel. When I would find repairs that needed done, I would simply take care of them, and sometimes when it was late the Simpsons would ask me to dine with them. Eventually I told them about my family and how I was trying to earn enough money to help my brothers and sisters continue their education."

"And you became an invaluable friend and employee," Julia said admiringly. "You have always been a strong person. I sensed that the first time we had a chance to get to know one another. But how will you manage to buy a hotel?"

Will smiled at Julia's use of *you* instead of the preferred *thee*. He had always admired her independent spirit and ability to quietly follow her conscience. "That is the incredible part of the story," he continued. "The Simpsons are such kind people...they are going to leave the hotel to me in their will. I will continue to work for them, eventually taking over the management duties. They will pay me from the profits, and then at the time of Mr. Simpson's death, the hotel will be mine. Can thee believe how God is providing for me and my family?"

"Yes, it seems God is rewarding you for your faithfulness. And I am very happy for you." Julia smiled warmly at her friend.

"Enough about me, Julia," Will suddenly remembered why he was there. "Please tell me about this emergency *which* is not an emergency!"

Julia laughed. "Oh, Will...where shall I begin?!"

"From the beginning, of course!"

Julia proceeded to tell Will about the happenings of the past few weeks. She had shared her calling with him right after she returned from yearly meeting the summer before, but they had not spoken of it since.

"So thy father has not taken thy call seriously?"

"Not only does he believe it would be a terrible mistake for me to go to Kansas, but he has been doing everything in his power to keep me here in Salem. Just this afternoon, in fact, two elders from the women's meeting came calling to try and persuade me to find a husband and settle here in Salem."

"Thy father asked them to speak to thee?"

"Yes, mother admitted that she knew he was going to speak to them."

"And were they successful?"

Julia laughed again, this time finding it hard to stop as she thought of the women's offer to begin a support group for her future work.

"Actually," she finally said when the laughter subsided, "when these dear women learned of the work Elizabeth is doing in Kansas, they offered to gather the women of the Salem meeting together to raise money and supplies to send out there."

"That is what happens when we are following God's leading," Will said thoughtfully. "What else has thy father tried to do to keep thee here?"

Julia felt herself blushing. "Thee, Will. I am certain Father thought that if he could get thee here, and thee heard that I was planning to leave the area, thee might fight to keep me here."

"I am afraid I do not understand..."

"Will, Father would like for thee to see me as a good marriage prospect."

"Oh, I see..." now it was Will's turn to blush. "I do like thee, Julia, and if I had ever thought I had a chance against Jonathan White, I might have asked to court thee. But I knew thee and Jonathan were together the entire year at school, and I could not fathom thee choosing me, a poor farmer, over an educated lawyer!"

"Will, please do not speak so poorly of thyself! You have many fine qualities any woman would find admirable. I am simply not interested in anything but answering God's call on my life right now."

"I thank thee, Julia, for being so honest with me. Now I want to be honest with thee. I am engaged to be married to a woman of our meeting. She is not as interesting as thee, but she will make a wonderful wife and mother."

Now it was Julia's turn to be embarrassed. "I guess Father has lost again!" she finally said. "I am happy for thee, Will. It seems like everything is really falling in place for thee and thy family. When is the wedding?"

"We have not yet set a date yet, though I imagine it will be some time before winter. I would like for thee to attend if thee is still here. When will thee go to Kansas?"

"I am not certain. Elizabeth is in the East raising support for her work, and she will wire me when she knows the day she will be coming back through Pleasant Plain. She said it would be four to six weeks, and it has already been four. I am expecting to hear from her any day."

"Thee is a strong woman, Julia Jones! I have no doubt thee will be a great asset to Mrs. Comstock's work."

"Thank you, Will. I am just hoping Father will have a change of heart before I must leave."

"I will pray for thee, Julia. And if I happen to see thy father at the hotel in the near future, I will make a point of telling him I believe thee is following God's call."

The two spent another hour catching up on the events of the past year. At last Will rose to leave. "I am surely glad we had this time together," he said, "I would have been unhappy if thee had left for Kansas without telling me of thy plans."

"So perhaps it was an emergency after all," Julia said teasingly.

"Take care of thyself, Julia. I will pray for thee and thy work."

"That would be wonderful. And best wishes for thy marriage. I hope to meet the lucky woman someday."

"I am certain thee will. I know we will see thee when thee returns to Salem to visit thy family."

"I will make a point to come and see *thee* at the *CLARK* hotel!"

"That does have a nice sound, but I could never change the name—not after all the kindnesses the Simpson's have shown me."

"I suppose not."

As they went through the front door and onto the front porch, Will turned to Julia one last time. "Does thee think an old friend might give a farewell embrace to another old friend who is leaving the state?"

"I think that would be most appropriate," Julia said simply.

Will took Julia in his arms and held her for a long time. "May God bless thee and go with thee, Julia," he whispered as he finally let her go.

"Farewell, Will, and thanks for coming to rescue me!!"

Will's laughter could be heard as he walked slowly to his horse.

As Julia reentered the kitchen, Rebecca greeted her.

"Did thee have a nice visit with Will?"

"Yes, it was quite nice, in fact. Will was full of news"

"Oh? What sort of news?" Rebecca asked carefully.

"Well, for one thing, Will is going to own the Simpson Hotel one day."

"How in the world will he do that? I doubt if Will has a dime to his name!"

"Sometimes things cannot be bought with money, Mother." Julia went on to tell her mother how Will had so impressed the Simpsons that they were leaving the hotel to him after they passed on.

"What other news did he have?" Rebecca wanted to know. "Thee said Will was 'full of news.'"

"His other news was quite amazing, actually. Will is engaged to be married. I am certain Father did not bother to find out if Will might be interested in someone before he urged him to call on me."

"Oh, dear. Yes, well that does make a difference! Is it someone thee knows?"

"Actually, no. It is some young woman from their meeting, the one we are not supposed to approve of."

"Julia, thee knows we do not agree with the Hicksites on several matters, but your father and I have certainly come to accept them as good neighbors."

"But how can thee disapprove of people if they are sincere and truly believe that their views of worship and the Bible are correct?"

"I am tired, Julia, and I do not wish to have a great theological debate with thee this evening. I am happy Will has found someone within his faith to share his life. That is one of the most important things one should consider when seeking a mate."

"Mother, I am not seeking a mate. I am seeking to follow the Lord."

"I know, Julia, I know. Shall I tell thy father about Will's upcoming marriage, or would thee like to give him the good news?"

"Thee may tell him, Mother. I have no desire to speak with Father right now. But tell me one thing...has Father planned any other 'surprises' to dissuade me from going with Elizabeth?"

"Oh, Julia, I wish thee had not asked me that question."

"Then there is more! At least tell me enough so that I might prepare myself."

"I can only say that it has to do with someone thy father considers to be thy good friend. Now, good night. And I hope thee will not waste sleep trying to out guess thy father."

"All right. The way things turned out today were certainly in my favor. I just hope Father realizes that no matter how many schemes he plans he will never convince me I am wrong to follow God's leading."

"Good night, Julia," Rebecca said wearily as she rose to leave. She felt as if she were being pulled between her husband and daughter, and being in the middle was becoming quite uncomfortable.

A few days later Julia awoke to the sound of laughter from downstairs in the kitchen. The voices sounded familiar, though she could not tell who they belonged to at first. She dressed quickly and hurried down stairs to find her mother talking animatedly with her oldest and dearest friend Betty. Hannah was also seated at the table, politely listening to the two women. Julia knew her mother had always hoped that she and Hannah would become good friends, but they simply had nothing in common, except for her brother, David, of course.

"Good morning, Julia," Betty said warmly. "I am sorry if we woke thee. Thy mother was telling us about some of Rachel's antics, and it reminded me of the humorous things my own children used to do."

"It was high time Julia was rising anyway, Betty." Rebecca said reprovingly. "Thee need not apologize for enjoying thyself!"

"Hello, Julia," Hannah said shyly. "Did thee sleep well?"

"Actually, I have not slept well for several nights now. Thanks to my Father."

Hannah looked puzzled, but did not ask Julia to elaborate.

"Please tell us about this past year at the academy, Julia," Betty said, quickly changing the subject.

Julia proceeded to tell the guests about her past year at school while she ate breakfast. She did not mention her meeting with Elizabeth or her future plans. Let her mother tell them if she wanted them to know.

The women visited for nearly an hour before Rachel began to call for her mother. As Rebecca rose, she asked Betty if she wanted to go with her to get the little live wire up and dressed. Having always loved babies, Betty jumped at the chance.

When Julia and Hannah were left in the kitchen, Julia tried to carry on a conversation with her soon to be sister-in-law. "Have you heard anything from David lately?"

Quite uncharacteristically, Hannah laughed. "Julia, if thee thinks thee is going to be a Friends' evangelist, thee had best practice thy 'thees' and 'thous'! Will thee always seek to rebel against authority?"

For once in her life, Julia was at a loss for words. How had Hannah known about her plan to be an evangelist? Had Charles said something to David who had in turn spoken to Hannah? No, there had not been enough time for that to have happened. Perhaps her mother had said something to Betty and she had told Hannah. But when had her mother seen Betty? She had not left the house for days.

"How did thee know I planned to be an evangelist, Hannah?"

Realizing what she had said, Hannah began to fidget. "Uh, well, I thought most Friends knew of thy plans."

"No, there are only a few who know, and none that you would have spoken to. Please...be honest with me. Did my father speak to thee?"

Never having purposely told a lie in her life, Hannah spoke the truth. "Thy father did stop by our home the other day."

"Let me guess...he just happened to mention that I had some wild idea in my head about being an evangelist in Kansas, and perhaps if thee happened to be visiting in our home would thee consider speaking with me about the folly of such a mission. Right?"

"Yes, he did mention something to that effect. But I can tell thee right now that I did not promise him I would try to persuade thee not to go. In fact," Hannah paused, and then leaned closer to Julia and spoke in nearly a whisper. "I admire thee for having the courage to embark on such a journey. I have always admired thee, Julia. I know thee thinks I am a dull sort, but I can appreciate the qualities thee possesses that I do not. My greatest desire in life is to be a good wife to thy brother, and someday a good mother to his children. But that does not mean I do not admire thy desire to do something special, something thee believes God is calling thee to do."

Julia sat in amazement. Hannah had just spoken more in the last two minutes than she had in all the times they had been together their entire lives!

"David is a lucky man, Hannah. And I mean that. You will be everything he could want in a wife. If I tried to get married and settle down my poor husband would be the one who would suffer!"

"Tell me about the work thee will be doing," Hannah said excitedly.

Julia and Hannah chatted about the work with the freedmen as two old friends. Julia was actually beginning to appreciate the fine qualities of this young woman when their mothers returned with Rachel.

"It sounds like the two of you have been enjoying each other's company," Rebecca said as she prepared to feed Rachel.

"Oh, we were," Julia said warmly. "In fact, Hannah wishes she could go with me to Kansas."

"JULIA!" Hannah said emphatically, "thee knows I want nothing more than to marry thy brother when he finishes his medical training." Then, noticing the grin on Julia's face, she knew Julia had gotten the best of her.

Just then there was a loud knock on the door. "Now who could that be?" Rebecca asked. "I thought we had had all the visitors we deserved for one week!"

"I'll see who it is," Julia said, rising to answer the door.

"Telegram for a Miss Julia Jones," came the voice from outside.

"Thank you—I mean thee. Is there a charge?"

"I could use a drink of water, if it would not be too much trouble."

Julia quickly got the messenger a drink and returned to the anxious friends around the table.

"What does it say?" Hannah asked impatiently when Julia seemed to take forever to read the message.

"This is almost like a foreign language! But let me try to read it aloud.

"Will be in Pleasant Plain seventh month, twentieth day. Stop. Meet at station eighth hour. Stop. E. Comstock."

Rebecca's face had paled with the finality of the date. How would she tell Charles? What if he refused to let Julia leave? And could he stop her if he tried? One look at Julia's face and she knew the answer. Julia was beaming and Rebecca knew it would take an act of God to keep this daughter from going to Kansas.

"That only gives me two days to prepare!" Julia suddenly realized. "I must go and begin to pack my things." Turning back to Hannah, she added, "Hannah, would thee like to help?"

"Surely, Julia."

And with that the two girls hastily left to help Julia prepare for whatever lie ahead.

CHAPTER 28

THROUGH THE OPEN DOOR

Julia knew she must speak with her father when he returned home that evening, but she had no idea how she was going to break the news that in two days she would be leaving her home of the past eighteen years.

When the family had finished the evening meal and the kitchen was in order once again, Julia sat at the table, trying to summon the courage needed for what seemed a nearly impossible task. When she could put it off no longer, she finally went into the living room where her father was reading the newly arrived *Friends Review*.

"Good evening, Father. Are there any interesting items in the new *Review*?"

"Oh, there are two articles on the pastoral system, one in favor, one opposed. There is also an editorial on Friends taking the sacraments. It seems to be quite an issue in some meetings."

"How does thee feel about breaking bread and drinking wine during worship?" Julia asked, still anxious to avoid the real matter at hand.

"As thee knows, Julia, I have not always been a member of the Society of Friends. In fact, there was a time after I lost my first wife that I had no use for God. It was thy mother who lived her faith in such a way that I saw that of God within her. When I began to attend the Salem Meeting, I was not always comfortable with their ways. I thought one needed to be baptized in water and take the physical elements of communion to enter heaven."

"What changed thy mind?"

"When I began to experience communion in the Spirit, I realized how much greater that communion was than simply eating a bit of bread and drinking the wine. I became convinced that Friends had discovered the true meaning of communion."

"And baptism?"

"When I reread the scriptures where Jesus was baptized by John the Baptist, I began to understand the verses where Jesus said John baptized with water, but a time was coming when believers would be baptized with the Holy Spirit. Jesus himself refused to baptize anyone with water. It just made a great deal of sense to want the baptism of the Spirit. Why all this sudden interest in the controversies of Friends?"

"I have always been interested in spiritual things—at least since I have been at the academy."

"Yes, well, I believe it takes many years for a person to fully understand the scriptures and apply them to their life."

Julia knew Charles was speaking of her. She also knew she must convince him that she *did* understand the scriptures, and she *did* know what they meant in her life.

"I know thee believes I am too young to truly understand the scriptures and what they mean, but I can assure thee that the Holy Spirit can speak to all ages, and the Holy Spirit has spoken to me. I would not be planning to work with the Negroes if I had not received confirmation of my calling."

"Humph!" Charles muttered. "Thee thinks thee has heard the Holy Spirit, but it seems to me thee has only been listening to thy own mind. This entire notion of traipsing across the country to speak to black men and women may seem glorious to thee now, but thee is not there. It is only a dream in thy mind. Thee has never experienced any type of hardship in thy life! Thee is simply not prepared for the task thee *thinks* God is asking of thee."

Julia was beginning to realize the futility of their conversation and decided to plunge ahead with the news. "Father, I received a telegram from Elizabeth this morning. She is to arrive in Pleasant Plain in two days, and I plan to be there to meet the train and join her. I know thee does not approve. I also know thee asked the elders, and Will, and Hannah to speak to me with the hopes they would persuade me to abandon my plans. But each time thee sent someone, God used it to confirm my call."

A look of surprise crossed Charles's face. "What does thee mean?"

"After I explained the work I would be doing with the freed men, Sadie and Wilma offered to organize the women in the Salem Meeting to gather supplies and funds for our work. And when Will came rushing over because thee told him I was having an emergency, he told me he was engaged and that he would pray for my well-being. Hannah, as well, offered her prayer support for my mission. Even Mother believes my call is from God. Father, *Thee*, is the only one who is opposed!"

"I am the one with whom the responsibility for thy safety lies, Julia. And I am doing what I think best. I think it quite presumptuous of that Comstock woman to expect thee to run and meet her just because she sends thee a telegram. She does not even have the decency to come to thy home and speak with thy parents. I will tell thee right now, Julia, that thee will simply not be there when the train arrives. When Mrs. Comstock does not find thee at the station, I am certain she will assume thee has decided not to join her."

"But Father!" Julia began to protest.

"I do not wish to hear anything more from thee, Julia. The matter is finished. Thee will not go to Kansas." Charles immediately returned to his reading.

By this time Julia was fighting tears and decided to leave the room rather than allow her father to say he was right about her not being ready to leave Salem.

Julia returned to her own room and threw herself across her bed. Sobs wracked her body as all the tensions of the past weeks came pouring from her soul. Why was her father so unreasonable? Why did he refuse to see her point of view? And what would she do now? Surely Charles would not lock her in the house, or stay with her every minute of the day. He probably thinks no child of his would dare disobey him, Julia thought bitterly.

But I am a child of God's, first, she told herself. *He* is the one I must obey! As certainly as the sun would rise in the morning, Julia knew she would go to Pleasant Plain the twentieth. The only question was—who would take her? She thought of the possibilities. There was her mother, but she would not ask her mother to come between her husband and daughter. There were members of the Friends Meeting that she was fairly certain would help her, but none she really felt comfortable asking. That left friends, and right now she had Will and Hannah. Neither prospect looked promising. Will had said he was working extra hours at the hotel, and Hannah would never want to go against the wishes of an adult, especially a male adult.

Julia continued to think of the hopelessness of the situation until she fell asleep, not even bothering to make the usual bedtime preparations.

Julia's heart was heavy the next morning as she woke from a restless night's sleep. All the problems of the previous day came flooding into her mind. Then she stopped. If God had cleared the way up to this point, would He not continue to provide for her? Suddenly she felt as if a great burden had been lifted. If she professed to trust in God, why was she worrying? Trust meant believing without doubt. She would trust in God no matter how scared she felt or how hopeless the situation might appear.

Julia continued to prepare her things for the journey, even though she had no idea how it would work out. When the day arrived for her to leave, she was up early to finish packing. Her father had been fetched to help deliver a baby before dawn, and he had not returned to the house. Just as Julia and her mother sat at the table to share in the morning meal, the door burst open and it was none other than Betty Johnson.

"Betty, thee scared me!!" Rebecca laughed. "What brings thee this way so early?"

"I am sorry for interrupting thee like this," Betty began, "but time is of the essence. Luke and I were preparing to go to visit his brother and family in Pleasant Plain when Hannah remembered this was the day Julia was to meet Elizabeth Comstock in Pleasant Plain. At first I thought thee and Charles would want to take her, but later I realized how unlikely it was that Charles would be able to leave for the entire day, and thee would have a struggle taking Rachel on such a trip. So I rode over as fast as I could make that carriage fly to see if Julia might like to travel with us today. If thee has other plans, I will simply ride back and we will leave. It just seemed a shame to make two trips if one would suffice." Betty stopped and took a deep breath.

Rebecca looked at Julia, and Julia could not help the smile that escaped and lit up her face. "It is an answer to prayer, Mother. I have trusted God to provide the way, and He has answered my prayers."

"But thy father..." Rebecca began to protest.

"Mother, please. I know thee believes in my calling, and thee can see that God is opening all the doors which will allow me to fulfill that call. Please speak with Father in my absence and help him understand why I must go." Turning to Betty, she continued. "I will get my things and come with thee immediately."

"I had best help thee," Rebecca started to rise, "as it will take thee some time to get thy things together."

"Mother," Julia said quietly. "I am already prepared to go. I will only be a minute, Betty."

Rebecca sat back down, feeling numb. Julia had already gathered her possessions...she had always believed she would go...how had she, mother of this child for eighteen years, not realized the strength, and *faith* this daughter possessed?!

Betty put her hands on Rebecca's shoulders. "I know what thee must be feeling, Rebecca. If Julia were my child I would be just as concerned. When all three of my older children left home it was a time of uncertainty for me...I wondered if I had done an adequate job of preparing them for the challenges life would present."

"But thy children were all married when they left," Rebecca protested. "Julia will be all alone!"

"Not alone, Rebecca. God will be with her, as will Mrs. Comstock."

"How can I let her leave when Charles has forbidden her to go? How can I go against his wishes?"

"Julia is a woman, Rebecca. It is time thee and Charles let her make her own decisions, no matter how the outcome. I have heard wonderful things about Mrs. Comstock and I am certain she will keep Julia in her watchful care."

Just then Julia dragged the last of her belongings into the kitchen. "I hope there will be room on the train for three bags," she said nervously.

"I am certain there will be enough space," Betty said. "When I have taken the train to Oskaloosa to see our oldest son, James, there was always plenty of space for baggage. Many travelers had only one bag for a short journey."

After the bags were loaded into the carriage, Julia turned to her mother. "Thank you, mother, for all you have done for me. I will write to you and father. Please pray for me—and Elizabeth."

Rebecca could not speak for the lump in her throat and the tears that flowed. She simply held Julia in her arms for several minutes, then smiled. "God bless thee, Julia. And please remember thy manners and to say 'thee' instead of you!"

Both women laughed and Julia knew things were right between herself and her mother. "Farewell, mother. I love *thee*, and tell Father I love him as well. Please give Rachel a kiss for me and tell her I will see her soon."

Rebecca sighed, knowing 'soon' might be months or years.

"We must go, Julia," Betty said heading toward the door. "I have been gone longer now than I had hoped. Thee has a train to catch!"

The women continued to wave to each other as the carriage rolled down the steep path to the road below. Once they were on the road, Betty was the first to speak.

"It is a brave thing thee is planning to do...Hannah could talk of nothing else the evening we returned from our visit. She has always admired thee, Julia."

Julia looked up, surprised by Betty's praise. "I am sorry to say that I have not always treated Hannah in a way that would be pleasing to the Lord. I thought we had nothing in common...Hannah always looked at life differently than I. She wanted to be a wife and mother...I wanted to do something more with my life. Of course," she added quickly, "I believe Hannah will be a wonderful mate for my brother."

Betty smiled. "I had hoped Hannah might like to be a teacher, like your mother and I were when we were her age, but she simply has no interest in working with young children. I still pray that perhaps God will use her and David in a special way after they are married."

Julia and Betty continued to visit until they reached the Johnson's homestead. After picking up Luke and their baggage they were on their way.

The trip to Pleasant Plain was uneventful. The roads were smooth from the span of dry weather they had had during the sixth month. The dust was bothersome, but Julia was so excited she hardly noticed. Luke asked her a number of questions about her future work.

Julia kept looking at the position of the sun in the western sky, hoping they would not miss the train. She did not know exactly where they were in their journey, but she hoped they would soon be at their destination.

As they approached the town of Pleasant Plain, the blast of the train whistle shattered the late afternoon air. "The train is coming!" Julia said worriedly. "Will we make it in time?"

"Be patient, Julia," Luke said calmly. "We are only a mile from the station. I believe the train is a bit early, which seldom happens. If that is the case, it will be there at least until it is scheduled to depart. They will need to take on water and coal which also takes time. And if I know Elizabeth Comstock, she will not let that train leave the station until thee arrives!"

"But she does not know for certain if I am coming," Julia lamented.

"Yes, she does," Betty said confidently. "Thee said Elizabeth knew of thy calling which led to her ask thee to help in her work. I am certain she knows thee will accept."

"I hope thee is right, Betty," Julia said, still worried she might miss the opportunity she was so anxious to pursue.

"There is the station up ahead," Luke called a few minutes later. "I can see the train, and there are several people standing on the platform. I am certain we have plenty of time."

As Luke pulled the carriage in front of the tracks, Julia quickly scanned the faces for the strong features of Elizabeth Comstock. She did not know anyone there. What if Elizabeth got detained? What if she had to travel on an earlier train?

The Johnsons and Julia climbed from the carriage, leaving Julia's bags. Julia's heart beat rapidly as she continued to search for Elizabeth's familiar face. What would she do if Elizabeth were not there? How would she face her family, especially her father, if she had to return to Salem? More importantly, what would she do with her life if she did not go to Kansas?

Just then she heard someone call her name. "Julia, dear, over here."

Elizabeth had rounded the corner of the station and headed for Julia and the couple with her. "I am so sorry I was not here when thee arrived. When the train was early, I thought it wise to find the latrine." By this time she had reached Julia and she quickly embraced the frightened looking young girl.

Had she made a mistake in asking such a young woman to join her in the sometimes grueling work with the Negro? No, Julia was young, but she had such a strong will. That was why Elizabeth knew Julia would be here today. She knew Julia wanted to follow God and was going to let nothing stand in her way.

"Would thee please introduce me to thy parents, Julia?" Elizabeth said with a smile.

"uh, well, uh..."

"We are not Julia's parents, Mrs. Comstock," Luke said quickly. "I am Luke Johnson, and this is my wife Betty. Since Betty and I were coming to Pleasant Plain to visit my brother and his family, we offered to bring Julia to the train."

"I see," Elizabeth said, though the look she gave Julia said, 'I think there is more to this story than thee is telling me.' "And thy family, Julia, did they support thee in this mission?"

"Yes and no," Julia said reluctantly. "My mother supports my desire to follow God's leading, but Father did everything known to man to prevent me from coming."

"Then how did thee finally persuade him to allow thee to join me?" Elizabeth asked.

Julia shifted from foot to foot and tried not to look at Luke and Betty. "I did not receive my father's approval...but I have received a great deal of support from nearly everyone else in the town of Salem, and I truly believe I must obey God even if it means disobeying my father."

"I am sorry," Elizabeth said. "I had just assumed thee had made all the necessary arrangements."

"I did," Julia said firmly. "I am going on the train with thee to Kansas. This is what God has called me to do, and I am going to do what He asks."

"Thee is a determined one, Julia," Elizabeth said with a laugh. "Thee will work beautifully with the Negro men and women.

Now...we had best get thy bags checked and secure thy ticket." And with that Elizabeth quickly took Julia's arm and steered her toward the ticket master. Luke retrieved Julia's bags from their carriage and brought them in to be checked.

Soon the two women were ready to board the train. After a fond farewell and a promise to write on Julia's part, the two women boarded the train.

Luke and Betty waived as the train slowly began to pull out of the station. "Farewell, Julia," Betty said to herself. "God bless thee and keep thee."

CHAPTER 29

NEW TRAILS TO TRAVEL

Julia still could not believe she was actually on the train sitting beside the woman she had admired for nearly two years. Away from the academy where she had spent the past two years; away from every friend she had ever made; away from the family she loved dearly.

But Julia was so excited over the prospects of the future that she had little time to reflect on the past. The countryside they were passing looked quite similar to that around Salem, so Julia turned her attention to the interior of the train. The seats each held two persons, and there were two rows of seats, one on each side of the car. Made of wood, Julia thought they would have been more comfortable had they had a bit of cushioning.

The train was nearly full of passengers, most of them men. From the looks of some their attire, Julia guessed they were men down on their luck who had spent their last dime to escape life as they knew it for something better down the rail line. There was one group of five that Julia presumed to be a family, and she suddenly felt a knife twist in her stomach as she thought of her own family. The children were all young and well dressed. Julia could not decide if they were simply traveling to visit another part of the country, or perhaps moving to another city. As their journey would take several days, Julia decided she would try to find the answer to her question before one of them departed.

"Tell me about thy family," Elizabeth said, interrupting Julia's thoughts. Turning to look at the woman who sat beside her, Julia was warmed by the genuine smile she saw on her round face.

"Well, there is my father. I suppose I should start with him."

"Thee would be surprised at the number of Negroes who have no father in their family..." Elizabeth was suddenly transported back to her mission field. "I am sorry, Julia. It seems I have left my heart in Kansas. Now, tell me about thy father."

"My father is a physician in the town of Salem. He works many long hours treating patients from miles around our home. He is well thought of by everyone in our community and Meeting."

"And how does *thee* feel about him?" Elizabeth asked kindly.

"I respect the work he does. I know he loves his family. He and my mother had both lost their marriage partners and found that as they worked together they were quite fond on one another."

"Thy mother is also a physician?" Elizabeth asked curiously.

"No, she worked for my father. She had always had an interest in medicine and when my father offered to teach her the fundamentals of medicine so she could help treat the members of the East Grove community, she accepted the opportunity."

"But she was married at the time?"

"Yes, she was married to Joshua Frazier, but they had no children. Since they were unable to have children, Mother was happy to have the work to take her mind off her barren state."

Elizabeth looked with curiosity at this young girl who spoke so forthrightly. "How did thy father come to marry thy mother?"

"Joshua had a tumor that my father removed, but it was malignant and he eventually passed on. My father's wife had died during the birth of their first child. Once my mother recovered from the loss of Joshua, she began to realize she had feelings for my father that went much deeper than simply work mates.

"They were eventually married and had their first child a year later. That would be David, my brother. He is in Chicago studying to become a doctor."

"And then thee came along," Elizabeth surmised. "Are there any other children in thy family?"

"Yes, I have a one-year-old sister. She was rather a surprise to my parents and me. I must admit I was not too happy with the prospect of my mother having a baby at her age." Julia paused, realizing she had been talking nonstop about her family, about feelings she was did not normally share with near strangers!

"That must have been difficult for thee," Elizabeth said sympathetically. "I imagine thee will miss thy young sister now that she has become a part of thy life."

"Yes, I will miss her, but at times she was quite annoying. My father has spoiled her rather badly, I am afraid, and she is good at demanding what she wants!"

"Demanding what one wants is not always a bad thing," Elizabeth said with a laugh. "I have found that there are times when one must demand the things one truly sees as a need."

"Tell me about thy trip East," Julia said, anxious to know more about the work with which she soon would be involved.

"I had the most remarkable time!" Elizabeth said, her eyes sparkling as she began her tale. "It does not yet seem a reality that I was honored to speak with some important people."

"Did you speak to anyone I might know?" Julia asked curiously.

"I imagine thee has heard of President Garfield!"

"President Garfield? The president of the United States? Thee actually spoke with our president?" Julia asked incredulously.

"Yes, I was granted a visit with President Garfield in the presidential library. I had written to him expressing my concerns for the Negroes, and he invited me to the White House so that he might become better informed on the issue."

"What did thee say to him?"

"Fortunately, I had plenty of time while on the train to prepare what I would say. I narrowed my list of concerns to four major areas."

"Which were?"

"First of all, I wanted him to know how important it was that the Negro be protected in the South. The refugees that are pouring into Kansas are telling horror stories of white folks—sometimes their former masters—beating them, sending their bloodhounds after them, and sometimes even killing them. There need to be laws that will protect the Negro, and those laws need to be enforced.

"I then suggested that a tract of land be set apart for those now in Kansas, and that they be given a fair and speedy chance to become American citizens. These poor refugees have always been someone's property. Many of them have no idea what it means to be respected as a member of society. I am fearful that some states will make it difficult, if not impossible, for them to become citizens."

Julia sat in awe—not only because Elizabeth had spoken with President Garfield, but because she had such a compassion for a race of people Julia had never even had contact with.

Elizabeth continued, her voice becoming more and more animated as she spoke. "It will also be important that some of the older states form a national organization which will receive Negroes and from which they can more easily be scattered to other states where they can find employment."

"That sounds like a good idea, but will the states be willing to work together to form such an organization?" Julia asked.

"I must admit I have reservations, but if the president were to get behind the formation of such a group, it would certainly have a better chance of succeeding."

"What was the fourth thing thee told the president?"

"I asked him to reenact the law which would allow English donations for the freedmen to enter the country duty free. There are many Friends in England who want to help our cause by sending supplies, but the duty attached makes it nearly impossible for us to accept them in the states."

"Was the president supportive of that idea?"

"He seemed be in favor, but whether or not he can convince congress to pass such a law remains to be seen."

"What else did thee speak of?"

"We visited for nearly an hour of our work at the Agricultural and Industrial Institution and Training School that we have built near Columbus, Kansas. We are trying to aid, teach, and elevate the Negro as fast as possible. I must say that the president was very pleased with our work and he heartily approved of our efforts."

Julia looked admiringly at the woman next to her. She knew Elizabeth was well known in Friends' circles, but she had no idea the woman was recognized by the government of the United States! She began to wonder about Elizabeth's personal life. "What about thy family? They must be very proud of thee."

"I have the most wonderful husband in the world. I have long felt that women must be on an equal footing with men since we Friends profess to be the only pure democracy in the world, men and women being equal in the Lord Jesus. If my husband did not adhere to this belief, we would have parted ways long ago. Fortunately for me, he has supported me in my work and understands the importance of what we are trying to do in Kansas. We are apart more than we are together. But the times we spend together are special because of the wonderful bond we have in the Lord."

Julia just sat in awe. Would she ever find a man who would share her views and treat her as an equal? Her thoughts quickly shifted to Jonathan. She did not really know whether he thought men and women were equal in the Lord. She had a feeling that Jonathan might believe his law work was more important than her evangelistic work. But why am I even thinking such thoughts, she wondered. When I return from Kansas, Jonathan will no doubt have found a woman who accepts his love. He will probably do what Will has done...become engaged!

Elizabeth lapsed into silence, obviously remembering her husband and the time they had been apart. Julia respectfully waited for a bit, then asked, "Did thee have children?"

"Our children are grown and have families of their own," she said simply.

"And does thee have family still in England?" Julia asked.

"There are a few aunts and uncles and cousins...my parents have been with the Lord for many years now."

"Does thee have occasion to visit them?"

"I have made several trips back to England, the latest being to secure support for the work in Kansas. Each time I return I am reminded of how much I miss the constant climate of that area. I do so despise the extreme cold of winter and heat of summer here in the Midwest."

"I suppose we are so accustomed to this climate that we accept it because it is all we have ever known," Julia admitted. "I personally do not mind the summer months, but the bone-chilling cold and snow of winter are often hard to enjoy!"

The two women continued to share bits and pieces of their lives with one other, soon feeling as if they had known each other for years in spite of the difference in their ages.

As the days on the train passed, Elizabeth acquainted Julia with every aspect of the work she was doing. Julia was surprised to learn that in the two previous years over sixty thousand Negroes had fled their homes in the south to move to Kansas. Elizabeth spoke of the need to travel around the state of Kansas where various Negroes had settled, seeing that their needs were met.

Julia also noticed that Elizabeth, in spite of her enthusiasm for her work, seemed to be weary a good share of the time. She wondered if someone who worked for such an important cause could forget to take care of her own body! She did not feel that she and Elizabeth knew one another well enough for her to suggest that the older woman might be pushing herself too hard!

Julia managed to meet several of the passengers who remained on the train. The family she had wondered about when they first boarded the train were traveling to Topeka to visit the mother's sister. The father was an investor who owned part of the railroad, so they were able to travel anywhere the rail line went. Julia talked with the children and told them stories from her imagination. It helped the days pass quickly, especially since Elizabeth spent a great deal of her time resting.

At last the train pulled into the station at Topeka and the two women gathered their luggage and began to walk toward the home where Elizabeth had lived since beginning her work two years earlier. The home was owned by an elderly widow woman who rented out rooms to support herself. Julia was relieved to learn that there was an extra room available for her. The only question was—where would she get the money to pay her share of the rent? The morning Julia had left for the train her mother had given her a small sum she had been saving at home. It would hardly buy food for a week, let alone pay for her room.

Once she had unpacked the few belongings she had brought with her, Julia went and timidly knocked on Elizabeth's door. In spite of the days they had spent together on the train, Julia still felt a bit shy around the older woman.

"Please enter," came a faint call.

When Julia opened the door, she was surprised to see Elizabeth lying in bed, under the covers. "I...I am sorry to bother thee..." Julia stammered.

"Come in, dear. I am just weary from the long journeys of the past weeks. When I saw the bed had been turned down by Mrs. Hollingsworth, I simply could not deny myself the pleasure of indulging in some peaceful rest. Now...what is on thy mind?"

"I am embarrassed to admit this to thee, but I am afraid I was unable to bring much in the way of currency with me—since my father did not approve of my departure. I am not even certain how I will pay my share of the rent for my room."

"That will not be a problem," Elizabeth said softly. "Anna has provided me with the room for two years now and has never expected me to pay a cent. She is in full support of my work, and since she has nothing else to give to the cause, she donates the room as her contribution. I am certain she will do the same for thee."

Julia was relieved, but somehow concerned for the figure which lay so still under the hand-sewn quilt. "I will leave thee now. I hope thee will feel better after thee has a chance to rest."

"Um..." was all Julia heard. As quietly as she could, she tiptoed out of the room and gently closed the door. She hoped Elizabeth was not going to be ill. Elizabeth was her lifeline...her only link to this new land and culture.

Feeling somewhat let down after the weeks of anticipation, Julia decided to go for a walk. Quietly moving down the squeaky steps, she found herself in the living room where Anna sat at the quilt frame which took nearly half the space in the small room.

"Sit down, young woman," Anna Hollingsworth commanded.

Julia did as she was told and chose a straight backed chair by the large window which overlooked the street.

"Now..." Anna continued, "I understand you're gonna work with Lizzy, that right?"

Julia tried to stifle a giggle as she considered 'Lizzy' as a moniker for the woman she had come to know fairly well. "Yes, I am going to be speaking at the daily services that Elizabeth conducts for the Negroes."

Anna raised her eyes from her work and lowered her eye glasses. "You say you is gonna speak at the daily services?" Her voice contained a disturbing note of disbelief.

"Yes," Julia said slowly, not certain what the sprightly woman's tone of voice meant.

"Well, well...Lizzy is full of surprises. I would have thought she'd a found somebody besides a girl barely out of grammar school!"

Julia felt the sting of Anna's words, but was determined not to be intimidated by the frail looking, hunched back woman with sharp features. "I am seeking to follow the leading of the Lord in my life," she said simply. "When Elizabeth asked me to come with her, I prayed about it and I believe this is what God wants me to do."

"I don't suppose Lizzy told you anything about these services? Or about the last three preachers who got so discouraged that each of 'em quit after only a few weeks?"

"We did not discuss the previous evangelists," Julia said defensively, trying to ignore the knot forming in the pit of her stomach.

"Well, that Lizzy is a miracle worker, and them black folks think she's about as perfect as a human can get. But they has their own ways of worship, and they don't take much to white folk—other than Lizzy, course."

"Of course."

"Where'd you say you was from?"

"Iowa. Salem, Iowa."

"Eye-0-way, ya say. Never been there. My husband and I came out here by covered wagon in '55 from Tennessee. Howard always loved trains, and he signed on to help lay the tracks. It took us three years to get here, him workin' on the tracks, and all. I camped with the wagon along the way. Once we got this far Howard decided to use the money he'd earned to buy this house so we could settle down. He never did like stayin' in one place, though. When he heard there was new work out in Utah, and they was needin' workers real bad, he decided to go for just a month or two. 'Course that was the last I heard of him. I been livin' here by myself ever since, rentin' out the rooms upstairs to support myself. Don't get me wrong—it ain't a bad way to live. I been lucky to have Lizzy here...she tells me what's goin' on out there with them Negroes, and I think she's doin' a good work. But you, Missy, I think you got your work cut out if you think them Negroes is gonna to listen to you!"

Julia squirmed nervously. "I will trust the Lord to supply the thoughts and words He would have me to say. Surely the Negroes will respect someone who is preaching the Word of God."

"Well, we will jist have ta see, Missy. All I know is, I sure ain't wantin' to be in your shoes!"

Deciding she had had about all of Mrs. Hollingsworth that she could take for the moment, Julia rose to leave.

"I thank thee for allowing me to live here, rent free. I will do my best to minister to the black man."

"Free? Who said you was stayin' for free? How am I gonna make a livin' if I give you a room for free?" Anna's asked.

"Oh, well, I thought, I mean," Julia stammered, "Liz-Elizabeth said my room would be free."

"It ain't free, child. Lizzy's payin' for your room."

Now Julia was really puzzled. Why would Elizabeth say the room was free if in fact she were paying for it?

"I am going for a walk," Julia said quickly, rising and passing by Mrs. Hollingsworth before the little woman with the sharp tongue had a chance to further disturb her thoughts.

"Be careful, Missy," Anna called. "There's bound to be lots of surprises for a young thing like yourself."

Julia tried to swallow the lump in her throat. Had she made a mistake in coming? First Elizabeth gets sick, and then a nosy landlady gives her all sorts of ominous warnings. No, she would not give in to her fears. God *had* called her to this work, and he *would* take care of her.

As Julia walked along the earth packed streets of Topeka she thought of all that had transpired in the past two years. She had asked God to reveal His plan for her life to her and He had done so, though at times she had doubted her call. She had left everything she had ever loved back in Iowa to come to a cattle town that was teaming with thousands of Negro men, women and children. She had defied her father and she hoped he would some day forgive her. Mother must have done a mighty job of convincing him to let me go, Julia chuckled, because he had not sent someone to stop the train!

Jonathan and Will had both stated their interest in having her for a marriage partner and she had turned them down. She was now living with a crotchety old woman and a weary evangelist and she had no idea what she was to say to the gathering that would be expecting a message in the morning.

Yet in spite of everything, Julia felt at peace. A warmth spread through her soul as she offered thanks to God for giving her an opportunity to make a difference in the world. As she turned to head back to the boarding house, the sun broke through the dark clouds in the western sky with the most beautiful sunset Julia had ever seen. Yes, God was with her, and she would do His work as long as He needed her.

AUTHOR'S NOTE

Though Julia Jones is a fictitious character, Elizabeth Comstock was one of the most remarkable women in Friends' history. Beginning in the spring of 1879 she ministered to many of the 60,000 Negroes who fled to Kansas from the reconstruction South. She raised $60,000 for this work by traveling across the United States and England. She also organized sewing circles and aid societies with the help of Laura Haviland, a young woman much like Julia.

Elizabeth's visit to Iowa Yearly Meeting left her troubled, and she penned the following words after talking with many Friends:

"There has been great discussion and controversy in our Friends' papers recently—how I wish they would leave off disputing about non-essentials, and unite all our forces, our energy and strength, to aid poor suffering humanity. The time and talent and money would be better spent caring for the refugees."

In January of 1882 Elizabeth's health failed and she spent the rest of her days in a sanitarium in New York. Her work was carried on by Laura Haviland.

Kansas governor St. John paid great tribute to these two women when he said, "God never made two nobler, grander women than Elizabeth Comstock and Laura Haviland."

May we strive to share their compassion for the suffering as we seek to put our faith into action.